DeathQuest

Book 1 of

The VIKINGS! Trilogy

Jay Palmer

ISBN-13: 978-0991112708

ISBN-10: 0991112709
Version 2

All Books by Jay Palmer

The VIKINGS! Trilogy:
- DeathQuest
- The Mourning Trail
- Quest for Valhalla

The EGYPTIANS! Trilogy:
- SoulQuest
- Song of the Sphinx
- Quest for Osiris

The Magic of Play

The Heart of Play

The Grotesquerie Games

The Grotesquerie Gambit

Souls of Steam

The Seneschal

Jeremy Wrecker – Pirate of Land and Sea

Viking Son

Viking Daughter

Dracula – Deathless Desire

Website: **JayPalmerBooks.com**

Cover Artist: **Brooke Gillette**

DEDICATION

With eternal love and devotion,
to my beloved Karen Truong,
for inspiration beyond imagination.

Chapter 1

The Invasion

ERIC

Eric leaned on the tiller as he sailed across the breakwater to see armed peasants guarding the creaking docks of Demril. Glints off harpoons and pitchforks shone across the harbor; Eric's callused hand ached for his broadsword, yet he forced himself to remain calm and stroked his long gray beard; although nearing sunset, it was too early for the real sailors, the tough fishermen of Demril, to have returned from their day's labors. Eric didn't need to kill these village fools; their deaths would ruin his plan.

Eric grinned wickedly and steered his dragonship closer. Spray showered the deck as his sturdy oaken vessel cut through the swelling surf. The evening breeze was blowing inland, his square, striped sail billowed taut, its colorful canvas catching the wind's invisible speed. Timbers groaned and flexed as his dragonship rose upon the last wave and rode it into Demril's sheltered harbor.

Eric could hardly blame the Saxons for bearing weapons; even one dragonship justified Saxon fear. Soon those fears would be realized: King Svenson Two-Sword was halfway across the North Sea and sailing fast, his whole army hungry for vengeance. All of Demril would be slaughtered when Svenson's horde arrived.

Hoping the Gods were watching him, Eric sailed closer to the armed peasants guarding Demril. If he killed them while they held weapons then they should thank him because, according to Norse lore, the only purpose for living was to die a warrior, but Saxons were strange. For more than four decades, Eric had marched, sailed, and ridden past thousands of fools like them, farmers and fishermen who lived only because men like Eric, warriors of steel destined for the glories of Valhalla, saw no profit in killing them. Saxons were short-sighted: what good was a century of peace in this world compared to an eternity of regret in the next? All men die. Few truly live.

Silently Eric scolded himself; this was no time for philosophy. Svenson Two-Sword was hunting ... and Eric was his prey.

Eric looped a line over the tiller to hold it steady and hurried across the loose deck planks to the tall, polished mast. Carefully gauging his speed, he grabbed the main spar line, waited until just the right moment, and then pulled the knot loose and jumped back. The freed line flew upwards, the rigging spun in its pulley, and the great square sail crashed down across the deck in a tumble of puffed sailcloth, heavy spar, and loosed lines.

The huge dragonship slowed abruptly as the wind lost its canvas catcher, though its momentum pushed it onward. Eric ran aft as the deck surged and rocked beneath his clomping boots. He pulled off the line and threw his full weight against the tiller. The massive ship, built for two hundred men, dangerously neared the old, waterlogged posts. Eric leaned hard against the tiller, then reversed it twice, hearing complaining roars of seawater slosh against its wooden rudder. The vast dragonship slowed to a steady drift, and Eric wielded the tiller like a mighty oar, slowing as the alarmed villagers stepped back, worried the great dragonship might ram their tiny, aged dock.

Eric grinned at their nervousness; they had to see by now that he was alone on his ship.

Smoothly Eric steered his great warship beside their dock. Eric dropped the tiller, vaulted over the fallen spar and sail, and snatched up a rope. Leaping up onto their worn, weather-beaten dock with an agility his age belied, Eric looped his rope twice around one of the tall posts. When the rope went taut, the weather-beaten dock groaned and creaked as it lurched underneath both him and the startled townsmen, and then the dragonship settled quietly in its berth. The villagers glanced at each other nervously and stared at Eric; few could dock such a vessel alone.

Eric flashed a toothy, reassuring grin. He knew how he must look; they'd expected a savage raiding party to pour off his boat and instead received only one aged Viking. Eric stepped back down into his ship and strapped on his swordbelt, upon which hung his heavy broadsword.

The villagers eyed his deadly blade and tightened their grips on their weapons, of which several were leveled to point at Eric. Eric ignored them; he hadn't come to fight. Eric lifted up his rough burlap sack, swung it over his shoulder, and then jumped back up onto the dock and faced the villagers calmly.

"I need a horse," Eric said, eyeing the few mounts tied to a nearby rail. "Any kind, as long as it's saddled and ready to ride. Have any of you a horse I can purchase?"

The villagers stared at Eric, confused, holding their weapons like farmers hold hoes. Disgraceful: weapons are the measure of the warrior, and the respect men hold toward their weapons shows their respect for the life the Gods gave them. Most of these villagers were old men in ragged tunics, the rest were red-faced drunks; the lay-a-bouts of Demril, probably roused from sleeping in their only tavern by shouts of their hard-working wives and daughters. Their trembling fingers and worried expressions revealed a degree of cowardice rare even among Viking women; Eric's arrival in an otherwise empty ship, prowed by a red-painted dragon's head with fangs of walrus tusks, baffled them. Eric tried not to smile, yet his request to purchase a horse had bewildered them entirely.

Slowly, one old man, a thin graybeard with an oval brass broach which pinned a thin, stained quilt around his shoulders, and weakly holding a rusty short sword as if his grip hadn't the strength to lift it, stepped forward.

"H-how much money do you have?" the old man asked, his voice heady with nervousness.

"None," Eric grinned widely. "An even trade, my ship for your horse."

The gathered townsfolk gasped; a dragonship was worth thirty good horses even without its valuable sail. Eric laughed, walked toward the stunned villagers, and gently took the old man who'd spoken by his thin, unmuscled arm. The befuddled townsfolk lowered their weapons and stepped aside to allow them to pass.

"She leans a little to port," Eric said, laughing heartily to reassure the old man. "Always put your weakest oarsmen on the starboard side."

Eric untied the reins of the biggest horse and climbed up onto its saddle; he didn't know or care whose horse it was. Waving farewell, Eric rode away, leaving the armed villagers standing speechless on the dock. Eric had no use for thirty horses, and besides, he'd stolen the dragonship, and its owner was on his way.

With great reluctance, Eric rode past Demril's rustic tavern. After days alone at sea, the weathered old sign, of which only traces of a painted foaming beer mug remained, shined to Eric like a beacon-fire in a storm. Eric could use a stiff drink to steel his nerves for what he was about to do, yet he doubted if even a full keg would be enough.

The rest of Demril was barely worth noting; old wattle and daub houses in disrepair, one narrow muddy street, and a few dirty children clutching rag dolls and stick ponies who stared in disbelief as the old Norseman rode past. What a horrible place, Eric mused silently; not a good place for dying, let alone living.

Demril Harbor sheltered in the shadow of the white cliffs of Othar, a nearly vertical wall of stone. High atop the majestic bluff stood the tall marble towers and thick, high walls of Castle Bristlen. It'd been eight years since Eric had visited there. He hoped no one recognized him; they might want revenge.

Pressed for time, Eric cantered his horse past the last decrepit building toward the base of the cliff. A rough trail looped around the cliffs and snaked up the backside to the gate of Castle Bristlen. It would be a long, arduous ride, but delay was unthinkable.

Like Eric, his horse was an old, worn beast, a bit round and sagging in the middle, with a lot of gray mane. Eric nursed it along, never pressing too hard. Old horses could be ornery when provoked, and steep cliff-side trails were no place to test their deference. Eric let it amble along, occasionally stopped to let it rest and chew some weeds growing out of the weathered rocks, and nudged it only when it needed encouragement.

The red sun touched the ocean's horizon as Eric summited the white cliff. From his high perch, Eric spied several distant fishing ships sailing toward Demril; the sailors were returning. He grinned slightly, imagining their faces when they spied his mighty dragonship resting beside their dock.

Castle Bristlen was an imposing structure towering over the wide Atlantic atop the white cliffs of England. Two formidable towers flanked its heavily-protected gate, and a taller watch-tower faced the shining sea. Its great hall's wooden roof peaked over the top of the high wall, and its towers and walls were slashed with many arrow-slits. The wall near its gate was rough stone blocks stacked twenty feet high, crenellated to provide even more protection to those defending Bristlen, with murder-holes visible for those with eyes to see them.

Eric chuckled to himself; even with a hundred of his kinsmen and all the weapons they could carry, Eric could never force his way into Castle Bristlen. Fortunately, he was alone.

The thick portcullis was closed, and two dozen guards with long spears stood on the parapets above the gate. Eric wasn't surprised; they must've been frantic, seeing a Norse dragonship sail into their harbor. Frowning deeply, Eric raised his hand in peaceful greeting and rode onward.

"Halt!" cried a large, black-bearded man with a voice like a snarling bear, standing the wall above the gate. "What business have you here, Viking?"

Eric reined in and glared up at the black-bearded man. Eric was vastly outnumbered and far from home. Several Saxon guards wielded strung bows and Eric had no shield; they could kill him at will.

"By what business dares any Saxon question me?" Eric shouted. "I am Eric Bjornson, Ambassador of His Majesty Svenson Two-Sword, King of Southern Norway! I've been sent here with a gift for your lord, or whatever form of scoundrel you Saxons deem fit to rule this stone-pile. Send him out to me at once!"

"Baron du Harmonn waits on no man, much less a Viking," the black-bearded man shouted. "I'm Captain Sir Gunderson. Convince me of your reason to see our baron or be off!"

"So be it!" Eric shouted back. "I'll take my gold back to Svenson and tell him your baron didn't want it!"

Eric scowled and started to turn his aged horse around.

"Wait!" Captain Sir Gunderson shouted from above. "Prove to me you carry gold and I'll let you see the baron."

Eric clenched his teeth to keep from smiling; these Saxon fools were playing right into his hands.

Eric reached into the burlap sack he'd carried from his ship, lifted out a large gleaming object, and held it up for all to see. Polished yellow metal shined brightly in the setting sun's light, reflecting its rays in all directions. Aloft Eric held a golden mead-horn: a musk-ox horn banded and decorated with over a pound of the precious metal and many sparking jewels.

"Open the gate!" Captain Sir Gunderson shouted.

With much clanking and creaking, the huge portcullis raised. Eric admired the gate; the portcullis was built of sturdy mountain ash beams, a handspan thick on all sides, and braced with riveted iron fastenings. Svenson would require fifty warriors with a stout battering ram just to penetrate it.

Alone, Eric had gotten through with just a few lies and a stolen drinking horn.

By the time the portcullis was raised enough for Eric to ride beneath it, Sir Gunderson had descended the steps and was waiting in the courtyard with a score of soldiers. Captain Sir Gunderson was a tall bear of a man wearing a blackened-steel breastplate engraved with a mighty falcon. Eric stashed his priceless horn back inside his burlap sack and dismounted before him.

"Surrender your weapon," the knight ordered.

"Those who worship Odin never go weaponless," Eric snarled. "I'm no assassin; I'm an ambassador, and not by choice. Let me present this gift, deliver my message, and I'll gladly ride out of here."

Captain Sir Gunderson nodded at his men and several drew bows and pointed them right at Eric.

"Keep them on me, if you wish," Eric said absently, "but I can't surrender my sword. You have my word: I intend no harm to your baron. My message is one of ..." Eric paused, frowned, and then spat on the ground. "... friendship."

"I see," Sir Gunderson said. "Very well, ambassador, but if your hand touches your hilt then you'll be dead before your sword clears its scabbard."

Eric shrugged as if expecting nothing less. "Let's get this over with."

"I'll inform the baron you're here," Sir Gunderson said. "Guards, keep him here until I send message."

"Be quick about it," Eric snarled.

Offended, Sir Gunderson turned and stomped away. The remaining guards glared at Eric but kept their distance. Eric said nothing yet his thoughts were racing. While Castle Bristlen could easily repel a hundred invaders, Svenson's thousands would swarm over this backwater-castle like hungry red ants on a rotten apple. Eric didn't know exactly when Svenson Two-Sword would arrive, but Svenson had sworn Eric would be tortured to death if he captured him alive.

Eric noticed one of the guards watching him intently; a tall youth, well-muscled, just sprouting his first whiskers. He was standing perfectly balanced, evenly distributing his weight, almost poised, not resting or leaning on his long spear; with training, he could be a great fighter. The boy stared at Eric as if he'd never seen a Viking before; probably a farm-boy from the interior who dreamed of being a knight and got suckered into guarding this worthless pile of stones. He had thick brown hair, smooth skin, and steady gray eyes; doubtless the wenches favored him.

"Come here, boy!" Eric commanded.

The youth's eyes flew open.

"Now!" Eric shouted. "Or do you mean to insult King Svenson Two-Sword's ambassador?"

Hesitantly the tall youth glanced at the other guards yet they wisely turned away, unwilling to get involved. The boy took one small step forward, but no more.

"What's your name, boy?" Eric asked.

"Karl."

"Have you never seen a Norseman before, Karl?"

"Only heard stories."

"What stories?"

"Saxon stories," Karl smiled. "I'd gladly repeat them, but I wouldn't want to insult King Svenson Two-Sword's ambassador."

Eric tried not to smile and failed; this youth was quick-witted, intelligent as well as big. His face was too handsome; some men scarred themselves so they would look fiercer on battlefields. Eric grinned; he needed a Saxon to travel with through England.

"How long have you been guarding this stone-pile?"

"Nine days," Karl answered, and every guard listening burst out laughing.

"I fought at the Battle of Ferny Creek!" Karl protested, brandishing his spear.

The older guards kept laughing yet Eric ignored them.

"Have you no sword?"

Karl glanced down, subdued. "All they gave me was this spear."

"Good warriors should wield a sword," Eric said. "Fetch me a tankard of ale and I'll get you one before I leave."

Karl's eyes opened wide, and then he nodded and ran off. The rest of the guards laughed louder.

When Karl returned with a full tankard, Eric greedily took it and drank deeply. It was warm and pathetically weak but it tasted sweet on his thirsty tongue.

Sir Gunderson returned and escorted Eric, surrounded by the guards, through the wide doors of the great hall. The hall was one vast, dark room, half the size of the castle keep. Thick, colorful tapestries hung upon each wall, yet in the sparse torchlight their depictions were shadowy. Long wooden tables and benches lined the walls, the central area clear. Overhead, wooden beams upheld a mighty roof which was mostly lost in thick, dark cobwebs. At the far end of the hall, in front of a huge black and blue banner, stood a tall, polished throne; upon the throne sat a fat old man.

Eric set down his burlap sack and drew from it the jeweled, golden drinking horn and a large earthenware jug. Leaving the sack, he raised the priceless horn and jug for all to see, and then walked straight toward the throne. Baron du Harmonn nervously leaned back as the Viking approached; Eric pretended not to notice.

"Behold!" Eric shouted, turning so all could see and hear him. "I am Eric Bjornson, Ambassador of His Majesty Svenson Two-Sword, King of Southern Norway! I hold here the Horn of Friendship, a great gift of gold for the lord of Castle Bristlen. This very horn did I witness as King Svenson Two-Sword drained it in one great gulp. Now I pass it on to your baron with these words from my king; 'Drink, and forever friends we shall be!'"

Eric raised the heavy jug to his lips and pulled out its cork with his teeth, then poured its contents into the golden horn. The thin yellow mead poured quickly, releasing the sweet scent of honey. Eric filled the horn all the way to the top until it spilled over its edges and splashed onto the floor. Then he stuck the cork back into the jug and raised high the golden horn.

"Behold!" Eric cried, his voice booming distressingly. "This is the Horn of Friendship, from King Svenson Two-Sword to Baron du Harmonn of Castle Bristlen. To empty this horn is to agree to a pact of peace between the peoples of Bristlen and Norway. Let now this truce be sealed!"

Eric stepped forward and held out the overflowing, dripping horn. Baron du Harmonn took it gingerly and feigned a smile. The fat baron eyed the mead suspiciously and glanced at his guards, especially Sir Gunderson. The black-bearded knight only shrugged and the rest just looked frightened. Hesitantly Baron du Harmonn raised the overflowing horn to his lips and sipped. Instantly he gagged and coughed; the horn shook, spilling mead upon his robes.

"Have more!" Eric said sternly. "It's only mead, and I must witness you drain the horn entirely before I return to my king." Eric pulled out the cork with his free hand and leaned forward, overfilled the horn once again, and spilled more mead upon the baron.

Sir Gunderson seized the earthen jug from Eric's grasp. Cautiously he sniffed it, and then he tasted it.

"By my sword!" Sir Gunderson swore. "Mead it is, but I've never tasted the like! It kicks like my horse, and is stronger than Irish whiskey!"

"It was brewed by Gunthar the Ale-Master, the finest there is," Eric said. "But perhaps it's too strong for womanly Saxon throats. If need be, you can prop it in a corner for a while; its bite wears away when left open to the air. By morning it'll taste like mother's milk; a sad waste of good mead. I'll suffer the night here and witness you drink it tomorrow, if there's no other way. But I must leave tomorrow morning, and take the Horn of Friendship with me, if I don't see you drink it."

"Of course," Baron du Harmonn said, although his sneer belied his disgust. "Captain Sir Gunderson will see you have a place to rest tonight. Tomorrow you'll see this horn emptied, We promise, and you may return to Our noble cousin King Svenson Our most glad greetings."

"If it would be no trouble," Eric said, "I'd like a guard to attend me, who can bring me food and ale while I stay. Karl has already served me in this manner; I'd welcome his service again."

Karl, who'd obviously heard every word, startled. The baron glanced questioningly at Sir Gunderson.

"One of our new recruits from the Ferny Creek affair," the old knight explained.

"Of course," Baron du Harmonn said. "Lad, run to the kitchen and fetch a plate for Our guest. And now, We retire for the evening. We thank you for your service to Us and your king, good Eric, and We shall meet again at dawn to complete your mission."

Eric bowed deeply, and then he walked back to where he'd left his empty burlap sack. Sir Gunderson followed him, but the baron took the brimming, dripping, priceless horn and exited the hall through a door behind the throne; Eric noted his passage intently while pretending to pluck something from his beard.

Captain Sir Gunderson showed Eric to a small room in the castle to one side of the great hall. Karl arrived with a huge platter of food and a pitcher of beer; Eric took both and sat down before a small table. Sir Gunderson gave Karl orders to keep the Viking in the room and allow no disturbances during the night. With stern glares at both of them, Sir Gunderson closed the door behind him.

Eric doubted if he'd ever see brave Sir Gunderson again. Outside, night had fallen. Svenson Two-Sword would soon sail into Demril Harbor with thousands of young Viking warriors led by hundreds of fierce berserkers. By dawn, not a single Saxon would be alive in Castle Bristlen.

"Dine with me, Karl," Eric smiled at the youth. "There's much about this castle I wish to ask, and if you answer well, I'll get you that sword."

Obviously nervous, Karl pulled up a chair and sat down opposite the old Viking. Eric grinned; this youth would serve him well ... whether he wanted to or not.

"This is a mighty castle," Eric said. "Is it the first you've ever seen?"

"Yes," Karl tore off a chicken leg and began to eat.

"How many warriors do you think this castle could repel?"

"Only fools would attack a fortress like Bristlen," Karl chuckled.

"Really?" Eric laughed. "So, you think that if a hundred warriors, say, Scottish clansmen, attacked this castle, they'd never make it inside your walls?"

"Three times that," Karl said seriously. "The guards here are well-trained."

"Ah, yes," Eric smiled. "The Battle of Ferny Creek. But what of a thousand warriors?"

"If a thousand Scottish clansmen were marching here we'd know about it."

"No doubt, but if they were here, a thousand warriors, you'd be outnumbered ten to one."

"Bristlen would endure," Karl said, "or few would be left to boast of its conquest."

"I've seen greater castles fall to fewer men," Eric said. "But what if even more attacked? How many would be required for Bristlen to fall?"

"More than a thousand, I guess, and there'd be no hope. Why?"

"I'm just curious. My people don't pile stones and hide inside them as Saxons do. I just wondered what you'd do if enough warriors attacked that you had no hope. Would you stay to defend Bristlen ... and throw your life away?"

"I'd do my duty."

"Of course you would. You have honor: I see it in your eyes. But no pile of stones is worth my life, and no Norseman would willingly die for rocks. Are Saxons so different?"

"I never asked to become a guard."

"How did you ...?"

"Sir Gunderson watched me fight at Ferny Creek," Karl said. "I guess ... he was impressed."

"Doubtless," the older warrior smiled, even though Karl hadn't fully answered his question. "Do you enjoy your job here at Bristlen?"

"They feed me; slop, but edible," Karl said, "and I have a place to sleep."

"How exciting ..."

"Better than begging."

"Warriors don't beg!"

Karl sipped his beer and said nothing.

"Food and beds can be bought anywhere," Eric said. "If you had enormous wealth, would you stay ... or leave?"

"Why do you ask?"

"I must depart soon. I'd welcome your company on my journey. We could go wherever we pleased, eat the best foods, and sleep in beds that come with wenches."

"I'm not sailing to Norway," Karl said.

"Nor am I. I must leave by morning; that's true, but I intend to depart on horseback and see as much of England as I can before the Valkyrie take me."

"Valkyrie ...?"

"The Handmaids of Odin," Eric said. "Choosers of the Slain, from Yggdrasil, the Immortal Lands where the Norse Gods live: beautiful women warriors who ride over all battlefields. Know you not of the Valkyrie? They're the last sight every true warrior hopes to see! The Valkyrie choose, from the fallen, those of skill and daring enough to serve Odin in Valhalla, the afterlife of dead warriors."

Karl threw back his head and laughed, almost tipping his chair over backwards.

"Believe what you will," Eric said, "but I've seen them myself, their tall forms outlined in swirls of dust over battle. I've seen them swoop where heroes fall in wars forgotten before you were born. You're a soldier now, trained to kill; what reward has your Christian God for such deeds?"

"I worry more about this life than the next," Karl said, still chuckling.

"That's a foolish choice," Eric said. "Many elders I once respected thought the same. Now they're old and withered, unworthy of the attention of the Valkyrie. They await their deaths joyless, objects of pity and scorn. I'm forty-five years old, just beginning to feel their pain. My skills have earned me great acclaim, yet they betray me; my sword arm would keep me alive, if I let it, beyond the measure of my fighting prime. No man lives forever in this world; I'll have my immortality in the next.

"Yet I'm not ready to die this instant. My offer stands: I wish to see England one last time, and a Saxon to travel with would prevent many troubles."

"I saw you give your golden horn to the baron. Your bag looked awfully empty after that. Where's your 'enormous wealth'?"

"Only fools tell others where their wealth is hidden."

"Only bigger fools believe in wealth they haven't seen. There are only three places where you could have gold: on your ship, on your person, or buried somewhere between the dock and Bristlen."

"There's one other place, but you'll never guess it."

"Then you'll be traveling alone."

"I think not. Before this night's over, I'll wager you'll beg me to take you."

"I've no money to wager ..."

"You will," Eric smiled. "When all in this castle are asleep, I'll tell you where it is."

Karl shook his head, stretched out, and closed his eyes, a knowing grin plastered on his face.

He thinks I'm mad, Eric mused. *No matter: his fate is decided.*

Eric scooted his chair around to face the small fireplace and used one of the sconces to light a fistful of straw. The kindling ignited the piled, half-charred logs, and Eric pulled out a bench to prop his feet upon, sat back, and tried to relax. His plan was working, but Svenson was coming, and Eric had to be gone before his vengeful king arrived.

Chapter 2

Svenson's Siege

KARL

"Hey, I was sleeping ...!" Karl complained, eager to remain undisturbed as the old Viking prodded him; Karl's cot in the guard's shack wasn't as comfortable these wide, cushioned chairs.

"Shhhhh!" Eric shushed him. "I'm ready to tell you where my gold is."

Karl groaned, but the word 'gold' rung in his ears.

"Where?" Karl yawned, blinking his eyes open.

"In your baron's treasury," Eric grinned, "just waiting for us."

Karl smiled and closed his eyes, but then they flew open.

"Where ...?!?"

"That golden horn wasn't given to me by Svenson Two-Sword," Eric whispered conspiratorially. "I stole it. Svenson Two-Sword is sailing here from Norway, as we speak, with seven thousand Viking warriors. He knows I'm here. He'll see his stolen dragonship in Demril Harbor. We can't wait any longer; by morning, Castle Bristlen, and all within it, will be dead."

"Wha...?" Karl started to shout, but Eric's thick hand clamped over his mouth.

"Seven thousand warriors!" Eric stressed, hissing between clenched teeth. "Think of it, Karl! How long will Bristlen endure against such odds? Bristlen's doomed, and anything we take now we're stealing from Svenson. I plan to take as much booty as I can carry, and half of it will be yours, but we must go now! Once Svenson arrives, no man, woman, or child will escape Bristlen alive."

Slowly Eric removed his hand and stood back. Karl glanced at Eric's other hand, which held his naked broadsword, then to the rest of the room, which had every drawer and wardrobe open, and lastly to the bag tied to Eric's belt, which was no longer completely empty.

"What have you stolen?"

"Nothing compared to what I'm about to steal. You owe these people nothing, Karl. Join me ... and live!"

"And if I choose otherwise?"

Eric lifted his heavy broadsword warningly. "Die."

Karl hesitated; Eric's deadly sword-point hovered between them, yet he was an old man.

"Think about it, Karl! Even if you kill me and raise the alarm, what good'll that do? Sir Gunderson'll send you to defend the walls, although he knows you'll die. If he's wise, he'll leave you to face my kinsmen while he escapes. You'll die, Karl! This castle can't survive Svenson's horde! I'm offering you life!"

Karl stood up, his gaze locked on Eric's sword.

"Why should I believe you?" Karl asked.

"I'm offering you life and wealth," Eric said. "What do you get by staying here?"

"What if you're wrong?"

"Then you'll confess I forced you."

"I'm no traitor," Karl took in a deep breath, threatening to shout despite Eric's deadly sword, which slowly rose, ready to cleave him in two.

Suddenly Eric's rock-hard left fist lashed out and blindsided the young guard. Karl crumpled and staggered.

"I've no time for games," Eric said, and his hand clamped onto Karl's arm with a steely grip. "Come, boy. Stay quiet. Reveal me and die."

Karl groaned as Eric yanked him to his feet, and then he heard their door creak open. The great hall was dark, despite several tiny candles glowing in the corners where the servants snored. Stumbling blindly, Karl was drug into its empty center, toward the baron's throne.

Though buried in darkness, the flashes in Karl's head glared like the midday sun; only Eric's firm grip kept him from falling. Karl staggered, scarcely aware of where he was.

Pulled to the thick door behind the throne, wincing all the way, Karl blinked as Eric opened the door and light met their eyes. Candle sconces upon the walls lighted a long, narrow corridor. Quickly Eric drew Karl inside, and then he closed the door behind them.

"Which is the baron's room?" Eric whispered. "Speak softly! I can't afford to be gentle!"

"I ... no idea," Karl gasped. "Never ... been ... here ..."

"Then we find the trail," Eric said, and he pulled Karl down the narrow hall.

Trail ...? Karl couldn't guess what Eric was talking about, but when they came to a pair of doors, Eric dropped to one knee, half-dragging Karl with him. It was utterly quiet, save for muted snores coming from behind the doors. Karl shook his head; his senses had started to clear, although the hammering-pain remained. Karl could shout, but Eric still held his heavy broadsword in his strong right hand. Karl had badly underestimated Eric as old and weak; he wouldn't make that mistake twice.

Eric pulled Karl along to the next pair of doors. There he knelt again, and Karl distinctly heard Eric sniffing, like a dog. Then Eric extended his little finger, without letting go of his sword, dragged it across the wooden floor, and lifted it to his lips.

"Mead!" Eric whispered. "This is the room we want!"

Eric pressed against the door but it was locked. Quietly he tucked his sword under his arm and reached into his heavy fur vest. From a hidden inside pocket, Eric quietly drew a collection of large keys looped on a leather thong. Careful not to clink them together, he selected one after another, trying each until the lock spun and clicked open.

Gently the door opened. The room inside was black as a cave.

Eric motioned to Karl to bring one of the hall lights, and Karl reached up and lifted the tiny clay jar, its candle still burning, from its sconce on the wall. Then they crept into the dark room.

A woman's face looked up at them. She was trembling, sitting on a chair by the door, naked, wrapped in a quilt. Eric jumped inside and propped his deadly blade warningly against her throat, pulling Karl so hard he spilled hot wax onto his fingers. She started to scream but froze silently as Eric's sword stopped only an inch from killing her.

Baron du Harmonn snorted in his sleep and rolled fitfully under a thin blanket on a huge bed. Beside the frightened woman and the sleeping baron, the rest of the room was just as Karl would've expected, richly decorated, filled with wardrobes and tables pushed against tapestry-covered walls. Karl turned and looked at the strange woman.

Radiant candlelight illuminated her beautiful face. No woman will ever know, nor man control, the reaction of men to beauty such as hers. Karl stopped short, stunned, as if he'd stepped through a doorway from this world into another, where angelic exquisiteness beyond his comprehension existed. Karl softly gasped, unaware of where he was or what he was doing.

His hesitation faltered; the moment passed. She was still staring at Karl, Eric's sword at her throat, but she looked more confused than frightened. Karl suddenly realized streaks of tears trailed down her cheeks.

"Please, help me," she whispered.

Karl and Eric exchanged glances.

"Where's the treasure?" Eric whispered to her.

"Will you let me go?"

"Tell us or ...!"

"Let her go!" Karl whispered urgently, and he carefully pinched Eric's sharp blade with two fingers and drew it away from her throat.

The sleeping baron muttered something incomprehensible, then rolled over again. Karl smiled up at Eric; if the Viking forced the issue then they'd awaken the baron.

The woman pointed across the room.

"The treasury door's behind that tapestry. The baron has the key; I don't know where."

Eric lowered his sword, seized Karl's empty hand, and wrapped it around her bicep.

"Hold her!" Eric whispered.

Karl lightly held her arm through her thick quilt, and Eric grabbed Karl's other arm and pulled both of them over to the baron's bed; she shuffled with them, clutching her quilt tightly about her. Then Eric let go of Karl and held his empty hand over the Baron's sleeping, chubby face.

Despite its throbbing, Karl franticly shook his head: *he could be executed for this!* Yet Eric, with a warning glare, whipped his broadsword around to stab lightly into the youth's stomach.

Karl paused: his chance to stop Eric might come, but this wasn't it. He couldn't let the Viking push him around much longer, but Eric's sword could kill him in an instant; he'd have to choose his betrayal carefully. No other weapons were in sight, nothing he could defend himself with. If Eric killed the baron before help arrived then Sir Gunderson would have Karl beheaded.

Yet ... *would stopping Eric save Karl's life?* If Eric was telling the truth then an entire horde of Norsemen could arrive at any minute, and dead on the battlements was no better than dead in the baron's bedroom.

Eric gave Karl no time to decide; Eric roughly cupped his palm over the sleeping baron's mouth. Unexpectedly awoken, the startled baron jumped, flailed under his thin covers, and would've leapt from his bed had Eric's strong, smothering grip not pinned his head against his pillow.

The baron didn't struggle at all; only childishly trembled and whimpered; Karl couldn't believe any nobleman could act so cowardly. When Eric leaned over and demanded the key to the treasury, the baron reached up without hesitation and opened a tiny, secret drawer disguised as ornamentation on his massive bed's headboard. Eric lifted out the tiny key, smiled, and suddenly smashed the pommel of his heavy broadsword down upon the fat baron's head.

The baron collapsed and laid still. The woman in the quilt bit back a scream.

"Quiet!" Karl hissed at her.

"Put her out!" Eric ordered, and both Karl's and the woman's eyes flared.

"I can't do that!"

"Sure you can; heads crack easily."

"I mean ... I can't hit a woman!"

"Svenson's dragonships will be here any second, and Bristlen's walls won't even slow Svenson's thousands. If she screams then we'll never get out of here, and if we wait ..."

"Don't hurt me!" she interjected.

"Sorry," Eric said, and he balled up his fist.

"No!" Karl said firmly, and he stepped between them. "We don't have to hurt her. We can ... take her with us."

"A hostage? They just get in the way."

"No argument," Karl said flatly. "Choose, Viking, or we debate until your kinsmen arrive."

Eric scowled and gave Karl a warning glare.

"She's your baggage," Eric said gruffly. "Now let's try this key!"

Slowly the woman glanced at the shaggy, aged Viking wielding the sword, and then turned back to Karl. Finally she looked down at the unconscious Baron du Harmonn.

"Are dragonships really sailing toward Bristlen?" she asked.

"Svenson Two-Sword's whole fleet," Eric said as he pulled the tapestry aside. "Twenty-seven dragonships: seven thousand men."

"We have to get out of here!" she said.

Eric looked at her appraisingly.

"You're no scullery maid," Eric sneered. "Who are you?"

"Roselyn," she replied curtly. "Can you get me out of Bristlen?"

Roselyn glanced at Karl, and both of them looked at Eric. The old Viking paused, then laughed softly, holding up the tiny key.

"Not without my treasure!"

"They'll think that I'm dead ...," Roselyn muttered softly, and suddenly she balled up her fist and punched the unconscious baron as hard as she could.

"Hand me my dressing gown," Roselyn pointed at a pale nightshift draped across a chair.

After a few awkward moments fumbling on her nightgown under her quilt, Roselyn pushed past Karl and approached the treasury door. Eric inserted the key, twisted it, and the door opened.

Gold and silver reflections gleamed in the candlelight. The treasury was a huge closet, walled with stone, and everything of value in Castle Bristlen lay inside it. On a square table sat two small chests of coins, one piled with silver, one half-full of gold. Stacked, folded scarves of precious silk and bottles of rare, expensive oils lay beside them. Several suits of polished, decorated parade armor were stacked on the floor alongside matching weapons and shields. Many silver platters and cups lay arranged on shelves, and beside them, propped in a corner, was Svenson Two-Sword's golden, jewel-encrusted drinking horn.

Eric grabbed the horn, raised it to his lips, and slowly drained every drop.

"Take everything, but quietly!" Eric handed his bag to Roselyn. "Hurry, before the alarm's raised."

Roselyn took the sack and pushed Eric aside to get into the treasury. She grabbed all of the scarves first and lined the sack with them. Then she poured the chest of gold coins atop them. Clinking coins rang out in the silent castle, and all three cursed at the noise. Roselyn closed the lid on the silver coins and stuffed the small chest into the bag, and then she opened a larger chest full of jewelry.

"Will I get any part of this?" Roselyn whispered, motioning toward the sack of treasure.

"What about your baron?" Eric asked.

Roselyn scowled. "Filthy French bastard! His crimes against me merit death."

"Help us get out and a share is yours," Eric said.

Eric reached deep inside the treasury and pulled out a fantastic, ornate longsword in a gleaming silver scabbard on a wide leather belt. Eric handed the sword to Karl.

"I promised you a sword, boy," Eric smiled. "Here, with armor to match: true warriors always keep their word."

As the woman moved deeper into the closet, Eric rummaged through the parade armor she stepped over. Karl stood there, holding the beautiful sword, just looking at it. It was perfect, its crossguard and pommel encrusted with tiny rubies: a weapon of kings and emperors such as Karl had never hoped to see, let alone hold.

Roselyn's hand reached out and took from Karl's other hand the tiny candle, drawing the light inside the treasury. As his hand was emptied, Eric lifted up to him a heavy bundle. Karl staggered under the weight of it; a full coat of mail, riveted rings, silvered, with full sleeves. Like the sword it was worth many times more than Karl could earn in a lifetime.

Guilt welled; Karl should draw the sword and cut the Viking's head off. He should shout and summon Sir Gunderson. He should do something, but Karl couldn't; the greatest treasures he'd ever dreamed of lay in his hands, and Eric had promised him half of everything.

"Throw that mail on!" Eric hissed. "Put a heavy coat on underneath it; get one from one of those wardrobes. Hurry! I'd hoped to be away from Bristlen by now."

"My dresses are there, too!" Roselyn added. "I'll need them!"

Karl stared at the treasures in his hand. He should kill the Viking, but ...

Karl went to the closest wardrobe and rummaged through it. He pulled on a thick, quilted coat, better than he'd ever worn, and slipped his new, heavy mail shirt over his head; its weight felt great.

Suddenly a cry rang out in the night.

"Vikings ...! Vikings in the harbor! To arms! To arms ...!"

"Time to go!" Eric said.

As Karl buckled his new swordbelt over his coat of mail, Eric handed him a silver-plated helmet and a large steel shield, and then Eric snatched up an even larger bronze helm and shield for himself. Roselyn ran out of the treasure room, yanked open another wardrobe, and madly pulled out dresses and stuffed them into the bulging sack. Karl and Eric exchanged worried glances; over her shoulder Roselyn bore a stout longbow and two quivers of arrows.

"Enough," Eric said. "If we don't flee now we'll never escape. Can we get to the stables without going outside?"

"I've never been in here before," Karl said.

"I've only been here five days," Roselyn said.

"We find it or die," Eric said, "Got everything? Let's go!"

Eric flung the door open and suddenly froze. The door across the hall opened at the same instant, and Sir Gunderson, half-dressed and carrying his boots in his hands, ran out into the narrow hall. Unarmed, half-dressed, Sir Gunderson stopped short, his shocked eyes wide. Without hesitation, Eric plunged his broadsword clean through the black-bearded knight's thick chest. Sir Gunderson gasped, dropped his armor and boots, and fell back against the doorframe.

A young girl screamed from the room behind him. Eloise, the baron's only daughter, whom Karl had only seen once before, was kneeling naked on her bed, holding up her covers to shield herself.

"Which way?" Eric shouted to Roselyn over the screaming girl.

"She knows the way!" Roselyn said, pointing at Eloise.

Eric jumped over Sir Gunderson's fallen body and charged into Eloise's room. Eloise screamed shrilly as the murderous Viking charged her, and she jumped off her bed to the far side.

"Eloise ...!" Roselyn shouted. "Come! I'll get you to safety!"

Roselyn clutched the heavy bag of stolen treasure tightly and stepped over the dead Sir Gunderson, and then ran toward the younger girl. Eloise embraced her, fearfully sobbing.

"Eloise, there's no time to explain. Grab a dress and come with me. You have to lead us to the stables!"

Flickering candlelight from Eloise's nightstand illuminated a face not listening. Eloise's eyes were wide with horror, locked on the corpse of her fallen lover. Roselyn spun her around so Eloise couldn't see him and shouted for her to listen, but the young girl showed no sign she heard.

"This way!" Karl shouted, but Eric turned to Roselyn.

"That sack's coming with us!" Eric warned.

"We're right behind you," Roselyn said. "Lead the way!"

"Come now!" Eric shouted as he stepped back into the hallway. Karl stood waiting for him, as frantic as a deer hearing wolves howl.

"We know it isn't that way," Karl pointed toward the great hall, and he headed in the other direction.

Roselyn appeared, struggling to keep herself between Eloise and Sir Gunderson, the heavy bag gripped with one hand and Eloise with the other. Naked, eyes shut, still screaming, Eloise clung to Roselyn, who pulled her through the door, almost lifting her to keep her from tripping over her lover's corpse.

Three doors Karl shouldered or kicked open, once frightening a pair of castle guests who'd locked themselves inside. Then Karl pushed open a fourth door and heard the whinny of horses.

Karl and Eric ran into the back of the stables, Roselyn pulling Eloise behind them.

The stable was a madhouse. Rafe, whom Karl knew as Bristlen's stable-master, was yelling orders at three busy guards while shouts echoed from the towers:

'Vikings in the harbor! Demril aflame! Torches coming up the road ...!'

"Horses!" Eric shouted loudly. "Four! The baron wants these women taken to the hills!"

Rafe shouted for his men to saddle four horses just as a loud cry burst from inside the castle.

"Sir Gunderson is dead! The baron is dead!"

"Wolf-pits!" Eric cursed.

Rafe's eyes opened wide; he was old and fat but keen.

"Traitors!" Rafe cried, and he pointed at Karl and Eric. "Kill them!"

At once, two of the stablehands pulled swords from scabbards hanging by the door. The third had no weapon; Rafe shoved him toward the door with orders to bring help.

Both stablehands attacked the Viking. To Karl's amazement, Eric swung his sword with a mastery Karl had only heard of in tales; Eric struck down both stablehands with flashing single-blows.

Almost too late, Karl spied Rafe charging him with a deadly pitchfork. Karl raised his shield just in time; Rafe's sharp points slammed and stuck into Karl's defense. Karl stabbed forward with his sword, but stopped short: *Karl didn't want to kill ...*

"Traitor!" Rafe cried at him.

"Look down from the battlements!" Karl shouted back. "That's seven-thousand Vikings! Bristlen's dead ... and those guards are barricading us inside!"

Rafe's expression suddenly paled.

"Take me with you!" Rafe begged. "Please! I'm no sailor to sink with his ship!"

"We need horses!" Karl demanded. "Five, including yours!"

"Fool Saxon!" Eric shouted. "We can't take everyone!"

Four guards, weapons in hand, suddenly charged into the stables.

"Saddle those horses!" Rafe shouted at the guards.

"We heard ...!" one started.

"You heard wrong!" Rafe shouted. "Do as I say: saddle those horses!"

Rafe set aside his pitchfork and gave curt orders. Intimidated, the confused guards obeyed, and Rafe gave them no chance to argue. Quickly Rafe selected mounts and gear, ordered the guards to hurry, and threatened death upon any that dared open his mouth.

Five horses were quickly saddled and bridled. As even more guards arrived, Rafe snatched up his pitchfork and shouted for them all to clear out of his stables and hurry back to the battlements. All stopped and stared at Karl, Eric, and Roselyn, who were standing shoulder to shoulder, blocking their view of the stablehands Eric had slain, and at Eloise, who was naked and sobbing, still clinging to Roselyn, her young face buried in Roselyn's embrace.

After chasing the guards away, Rafe directed each to mount a specific horse. Eloise had finally realized she was naked when Rafe wrapped a thin horse-blanket around her and set her atop a mare. Karl and

Roselyn mounted brown riding horses. Rafe gave Eric a huge black warhorse and, of course, mounted his own gray-speckled steed.

"Follow me!" Rafe cried. "The guards will open the postern gate for me!"

Karl hesitated one last time. Castle Bristlen and any who stayed behind would die. He'd accepted the position of guard; Karl's duty was to stay. Yet what good would it do? Karl couldn't defeat seventy-to-one odds; he'd be throwing away his life.

With a shout, Rafe led the way, Eric riding close behind. Eloise followed Roselyn as she rode out carrying the bulging burlap sack. With a final curse, Karl kicked his heels into his horse's flanks and cantered directly behind the women. Rafe led them towards the back wall of Castle Bristlen and shouted for the guards to open the postern gate. One guard argued only to hear a furious string of curses and find the sharp prongs of Rafe's pitchfork threatening him; the distressed guard relented and opened the heavy wooden door. They rode their mounts slowly, in single file, through the narrow doorway in the thick stone wall, and then they were outside of Bristlen.

Angry shouts from the guards on the wall tormented Karl; he hung his head in silent disgrace. He'd saved his life but his fellows were going to die. Karl had let fear and a moment's greed blind him, although his own life would've ended on those battlements.

He'd never shirked his duty before. *Where was his honor now?*

Chapter 3

Wolven Forest

RAFE

Hours later, weary from riding blindly into unseen branches, Rafe led the strangers to an old hunting cabin on top of a silent, moonlit hill. The cabin wasn't much to look at; a modest sod-roofed house nestled amid dark sheltering trees, with a covered pen for the horses. The few windows were heavily shuttered, but otherwise it looked quite serene. When he saw the cabin, Rafe smiled as if it were an old friend. Silently Rafe wondered if he could settle down here and make a new life for himself, but he knew better; Rafe was no farmer or trapper, and he was no longer young or strong enough to learn a new trade. Horses had been his life, and he'd been looking forward to a quiet retirement by the end of the year. Now Bristlen, and his retirement, were gone, and everything Rafe owned, save for the pitchfork in his hand and the horse under his butt, was plunder for some heathen Viking.

Rafe carefully considered his fellow refugees. Eloise, the only one he knew, had wept during most of their journey. He could hardly blame her: her only home had been lost in one terrible hour; her world lay in ruins. The same was true for all of them but Eloise was the youngest. Rafe had led them here as a reward for saving him from the Viking invasion; it was the Christian thing to do, but he had no idea what their intentions were.

"This is it," Rafe said, dismounting. "Baron du Harmonn's hunting lodge. I used to come here often when I was young. Soldier, there're flints on the mantle. Take the women inside and start a fire. We'll tend the horses."

With professional ease, Rafe grabbed and jerked the saddle strap under his horse, and seconds later he pulled off his worn saddle and sweat-damp blanket and hung them over the rail of the pen. Karl jumped down and accepted the bulging sack from Roselyn, who quickly dismounted, then hurried to assist Eloise. Together they opened the door and entered its dark interior.

As the trio vanished into the gloomy cabin, Rafe picked up his pitchfork and turned to face the Viking. Eric had dismounted and stood facing him, shield raised, his hand on his scabbard, as if expecting the challenge. Undeterred, Rafe pointed his pitchfork at him.

"You knew your brothers were coming ...?" Rafe accused.

Eric frowned deeply.

"They're my kinsmen, not my brothers."

"Did they want gold ... or you?"

Eric hesitated, as if gauging his response. Rafe didn't want to fight him; there wasn't anything to be gained, but he wouldn't feel safe until he knew the foreigner's intentions.

"They wanted me."

Rafe glared at the Viking yet remained still; a threatening move from either would demand a response, and fights started were hard to stop. The Viking could've lied but didn't; Rafe considered that, but he'd feel safer with his pitchfork's prongs poked through the Viking's chest.

"Seven months left until my retirement," Rafe growled. "Now I have nothing ... because of you!"

Rafe had dreamed of retiring for years. Half-pay for doing nothing, with a pallet in the bunkhouse for sleeping, and his worries would've been over.

Eric sighed and lowered his shield.

"I never intended to wrong you, horse-trainer. We never would've escaped Bristlen without you. If I pay you twice what your retirement would've, tonight, in gold, will you forget this feud?"

"I recall the last time your brethren sieged Bristlen ..."

"I was there."

"Why should I trust you?"

"Before we entered your stable, we plundered the treasury of your baron," Eric said. "The wealth of Castle Bristlen escaped with us."

Rafe's eyes widened slightly; a year of half pay wouldn't equal a single gold coin.

"My needs aren't small," Rafe said flatly.

Eric smiled.

"I'm Valhalla-bound," Eric chuckled. "Gold holds little worth; the Valkyrie prize only courage and skill. Befriend me, take your payment now, and claim my entire share when I'm dead."

"Show me this treasure," Rafe said.

Rafe squeezed the grip on his pitchfork, feeling comfort in the solidity of it, but he was willing to wait. He'd believe Eric's story only when gold touched his hands.

Rafe made Eric enter the cabin first, after they tended and penned the horses. Several candles were lit and Karl's crackling fire had started to warm the room. Karl, now unhelmeted, sat at a table before the fireplace, prodding the fire with a well-blackened stick. On the table was the bag Roselyn had carried from Castle Bristlen, missing only the colorful dresses that had been sticking out of its top. Roselyn and Eloise were now both dressed in Roselyn's gowns, looking oddly formal in the rustic setting.

The inside of the cabin looked exactly as Rafe recalled: dry and cozy. Two small beds were against one wall, a large bed against the other. The windows were heavily shuttered and braced.

Eloise and Roselyn were whispering to each other nervously, and Rafe noticed both women now wore jeweled daggers tucked into sturdy belts. Also, Roselyn's bow was now strung and her quivers of arrows were piled beside it in the corner.

Eric stripped off his helm and shield, set them aside, walked over to the table, and grabbed the burlap bag with both hands. Without hesitation, Eric upended the sack. The loud clatter of coins and jewelry, silver plates, and gold-chased daggers deafened them all as the wealth of the barony spilled out.

"We divide evenly," Eric announced loudly in the silence afterwards. "Equal shares to all, and friends we'll be."

"Father's treasure ...!" Eloise gasped. She stared at the piled wealth, then glanced at the smiling faces of the others. *"Thieves!"*

"Not thieves," Eric corrected her. "These treasures belong to the liege of Castle Bristlen, so, in a sense, we saved them from Svenson Two-Sword."

"These belong to my family ...!"

Eloise was right, Rafe thought. Her stepfather was dead now; of that he was certain. Her mother had been carried off by a group of savage Norsemen when Eloise was only a child, part of a wergild the baron had paid to an army that had besieged Castle Bristlen eight years ago. Eloise had no other family: this treasure belonged to her.

Rafe stepped up to the table and grinned widely. He reached out and scooped up a handful of gold and silver coins, which were now mixed together, and felt the unbelievable wealth sift through his fingers. Many of the silver coins were cut in half; hacksilver, very thin and used for small purchases. Eric looked at Rafe questioningly, and when their eyes met, Rafe smiled and set his pitchfork to lean against the wall; no retirement would compensate for his years of service like a handful of this treasure.

"That's my treasure ...!" Eloise shouted.

"Eloise and I would like our full shares now," Roselyn interjected. "Tomorrow we'll ride to the nearest convent or abbey. If you men will escort us there, we'll be very grateful."

"No!" Eloise shouted. *"That's ...!"*

Roselyn's hand clamped onto Eloise's thin shoulder, digging in with her nails.

"Eloise and I need to speak privately." Roselyn said.

Eloise glared at her with youthful stubbornness, but the older woman pulled her forward, toward the cabin's door. Eloise resisted slightly, yet allowed Roselyn to lead her out into the dark. Roselyn closed the door behind them.

"Where are they going?" Karl asked.

"To try to talk some sense into Eloise, I suspect," Rafe said. "We could kill them and keep all the gold."

"I don't kill women," Karl said.

"I wouldn't allow it, either," Rafe said.

Both Saxons glanced questioningly at Eric.

"You could be hanged," Eric warned. "If those women report that we kidnapped them, no soldier would question their claim. I seek the favor of the Valkyrie, so I doubt if I'll live long enough to see a rope, but you two ..."

"Christian Saxons don't kill women," Rafe said.

Eventually Eloise and Roselyn came back inside, Eloise much subdued.

Eric suggested they divide up the treasure. They pulled up benches and sat encircling the table, and each selected one item, in order. Eric insisted on going first, and he selected Svenson's golden horn. He claimed he'd need it to enter Valhalla, and Rafe saw no point in arguing. Also, no one argued about the two jewel-encrusted knives both girls had scavenged while Karl was lighting the fire; there was just too much treasure for anyone to fight over any one piece. The biggest jewels went first, followed by the women taking most of the jewelry and the men taking most of the gold coins, and they divided the hacksilver evenly. Within an hour the center of the table was cleared; each sat before their own pile of treasure, and everyone but Eloise seemed content.

If only they'd had food or drink it would've have been a merry celebration.

Eric dumped his share back into his sack, yet the others had no way to carry theirs. As the cabin stored more than enough blankets, Karl used his sharp new sword to cut one blanket into quarters, and each rolled up their stash inside a section. Eloise and Roselyn selected several pieces of jewelry to wear, bracelets, necklaces, and rings, but nothing too extravagant. Rafe thought they were crazy but said nothing. Being more practical, he sorted out all of his thin hacksilver into his belt-pouch and kept the rest rolled up out of sight.

A sudden whinny of horses startled them. Experienced riders, they all recognized the cries of terrified mounts. Rafe grabbed his pitchfork and dashed outside, with Eric and Karl close behind.

Wolves ...!

From the shadows of the bushes, Rafe glimpsed low shapes, reflections of hungry eyes, and sheens of gray fur. A steady roar of growls filled the darkness. Dozens threatened them, a whole wolf pack, after the horses. Rafe raised his pitchfork and shouted, expecting the wolves to flee, but they didn't.

Roselyn joined them outside, her longbow in one hand and a quiver of arrows in the other.

"Nock an arrow, quick!" Eric whispered.

"What is it?" Roselyn asked.

"Wolves," Rafe said. "It's like the old tales ...!"

"Never seen wolves act like this," Eric said. "They should've run off; wolves hate the scent of men. If these wolves get our horses we'll never get out of this forest alive; we have to be gone before Svenson surrounds us."

"Surrounds us ...?" Karl demanded, pausing to look at the Viking.

"Svenson won't stop just because Bristlen fell," Eric explained quickly. "Kings fight for profit ... and we plundered Bristlen before he got there. All he gained was a small castle, which Svenson has no use for. He'll leave some men to hold Bristlen, but the bulk of his army will come after us."

"What ...?!?" Karl angrily turned to face Eric.

"Enough!" Rafe shouted at them. "We'll be lucky to get out of here alive!"

A brave wolf jumped suddenly into view, its silver coat bright in the yellow light of the full moon. Roselyn shot it with her bow; it yelped and leapt high into the air, then fell thrashing onto the ground. Rafe ran forward and stabbed it with his pitchfork. The wolf screamed.

Eric jumped forward, swung his heavy sword, and ended the wolf's agony. But other wolves charged forward. Rafe stabbed, Eric swung, and Karl ran to help them. Roselyn drew her bow but, in the moonlight, she couldn't shoot without risking hitting the men.

Suddenly the cabin door slammed shut. From inside the cabin, Eloise's terrified scream burst out, startling everyone. Karl, Rafe, Roselyn, and Eric all froze and stared at the closed cabin door, their weapons still raised.

The remaining wolves suddenly fled, vanishing into the brush of the forest as if Eloise's scream had been a signal. In seconds, every wolf had disappeared.

"Dear God in Heaven!" Rafe gasped.

"What in Niflhiem ...?" Eric shouted.

"Eloise ...!" Roselyn screamed.

Roselyn ran to the door and squeezed the latch, but the door had been braced from the inside. Frantically, Roselyn shoved against the door with her shoulder, but to no avail. Rafe couldn't move, disbelieving his senses, while Roselyn pounded on the door and ordered Eloise to open it.

"Around back!" Eric shouted, and he took off running. Karl and Roselyn trailed after him, seeing no other hope. Rafe finally shook himself free and followed.

In the back of the cabin, under long branches, heavy wooden shutters lay in pieces on the weeds.

The oiled sheepskin windowpane was shredded, hanging in tatters. Inside the ruined window the candles and glowing fireplace illuminated their bags of treasure, untouched, on the table. The only thing missing was Eloise.

"T-the Wolflord ...!" Rafe made the sign of the cross.

"What?" Eric demanded. "What was that?"

"N-nothing!" Rafe said, but his face was flushed, his voice strained, and he couldn't stop trembling. "Just a ... children's tale ... about these woods ..."

"Find her!" Roselyn shouted.

"I will," Karl said, and he cried out Eloise's name and ran a short ways down the trail, his sword raised against the threat of wolves. Karl called three times yet Eloise never answered.

"Tell me this tale," Eric demanded.

"It's nothing; the Wolflord is a fireplace-story ..."

"Tell me ...!"

"I don't remember!" Rafe pleaded. "It's a dumb story, one of hundreds told to children in these parts. The Wolflord is a ... demon-wolf. All I can remember is his name: the Wolflord!"

Eric scowled.

"While in these woods, we shouldn't ignore stories about it."

"Fool's tales," Rafe insisted. "Murderous demons and spirits, evil witches as old as the mountains; no one believes them."

"Many have died to things they disbelieved," Eric said.

The dark forest swallowed Karl's shouts. Nothing showed, human or beast, only a distant owl hooting in the moonlight. Eloise was simply gone.

Despite objections, Eric forced them all back inside the cabin. Roselyn was beside herself. The darkness and silence outside of the glaring hole in their ripped-open back window taunted them, evidencing their helplessness.

"It'll be dawn shortly," Eric said. "In daylight we can track her, if a trail exists."

"She's lost!" Rafe insisted. "Let's flee before we're dragged into Hell!"

"Coward!" Eric sneered, glaring angrily. "We have to search, at least; the eyes of the Valkyrie watch us."

"Heathen barbarian!" Rafe glared blackly.

"No fighting!" Karl shouted, imposing himself between the bristling older men. "We don't have to stay together! Some can search, and ..."

"We have to leave our treasure and horses here while we search for Eloise," Eric said. "We have to stay together so no one sneaks back and steals everything."

"Christians don't steal," Rafe snarled.

"No, they just run away," Eric scowled.

"Eloise wasn't the first young girl to vanish in these parts," Rafe warned. "There've been others, all taken after dark, and none were ever seen again.

They're called the Brides of the Wolflord, stolen to be his mates."

"That means Eloise is only a prisoner," Eric said. "If we can find her in time ..."

"No!" Rafe shouted. "Lucifer himself ...!"

"Please!" Roselyn shouted, turning to Rafe. "Please, we have to find her ..."

Rafe stared into Roselyn's desperate, pleading eyes, and then he slowly bowed his head.

"No man can steal from the devil, not if he's a Christian," Rafe said. "Besides, I'd be of no help. Courage ... is a game for the young."

"Wrong, horse-trainer," Eric said, placing his hand upon Rafe's back. "Courage is life. Fear is death. You're not dead; you don't have to fear."

Rafe lowered his head and said nothing. Eloise couldn't be alive, yet Eric had reminded him of his youth; how brave and strong Rafe had once been. He'd once lifted a year-old horse just to prove that he could, and then he arm-wrestled every man in Bristlen. Now even lifting a saddle seemed an immense effort. Rafe had always prided himself on his immense strength; when that faded with age, his pride had failed, and he'd lived in a world of bravado ever since. The cherished strength of his youth was forever lost, and that bit deeper than any wolf's fangs.

"Courage avails little when the devil howls," Rafe warned.

"At dawn, we'll find Eloise and face this Wolflord together," Eric promised.

Chapter 4

Rescue

KARL

Karl saw Roselyn glance at him; he quickly turned away so she wouldn't see him blush. Roselyn was incredibly beautiful; never had Karl believed a woman could mesmerize him so. He was surprised she tolerated his company, considering how they'd met. If wandering around for a few hours shouting for the baron's silly daughter would keep Roselyn beside him then he'd gladly do it. Eloise had probably been frightened by the wolves, busted out of the back window, and fled. By sunup, they'd find Eloise stuck in a thicket of brambles; the usual fate of fools who run though a forest at night. Then Roselyn would be grateful, and that would be reward aplenty. If the old Viking and the stable-master chose to depart then Karl would be alone with Roselyn, and that would be best of all.

Karl had to find Eloise; he couldn't abandon a helpless girl lost in the woods. Perhaps finding her would quell his disquieted soul; Karl still felt he'd tarnished his honor by not staying to defend Bristlen. He certainly didn't believe in Rafe's wild tales; Wolflords only existed because adults liked to frighten children.

Dawn came slowly. When the sky lightened enough to track Eloise, Eric led them around back and pointed out several strange marks, but mostly he complained about Karl's boots spoiling clear signs. Rafe and Roselyn followed Eric as he roamed the paths behind the cabin, but Karl left them behind, walked farther down the path, and shouted Eloise's name, surprised she hadn't responded and worried she might've hurt herself ... or that the wolves had killed her.

Eric cried out and Roselyn screamed. Karl ran to the sound of their voices; Rafe stood white-faced, repeatedly crossing himself. Eric was standing behind the cabin, twigs and leaves in his hair and beard. Between his thick fingers hung a single long strand of yellow hair.

"The tracks are strange," Eric warned. "They go down an animal trail, barely visible. Karl, let's get our helmets and shields."

"Helms and shields to fight wolves?" Karl asked.

"Whatever took Eloise wasn't a wolf."

"Nothing 'took' Eloise; she ran off."

"Eloise was barefoot, and there're no tracks of her anywhere. Unless she flew, she must've been carried. Follow me and I'll show you her assailant's tracks. But first we must hide our treasure, in case someone else comes here before we get back."

"Eloise needs us now!" Roselyn insisted.

"Haste while facing the unknown gets everyone killed," Eric said.

"I'll dig a hole under the bed," Rafe said. "We can bury the treasure and throw the excess dirt in the horses' pen."

"Hurry ...!" Roselyn urged.

Eric and Karl strapped on their helms and shields while Rafe buried their treasure, using his sturdy pitchfork to break up the packed-dirt floor. Then Eric led the way down the narrow animal trail. Karl followed behind Eric, plunging through the thick brush, glad for his helmet despite its discomfort. Thorns and branches poked at them from every angle, but Karl, in his mail coat and helm, and Eric, in his thick leathers, barely noticed them. Together they plowed a path the others could follow.

Karl often off-balanced or struggled to control his shield as it caught on every branch. He was unused to walking in heavy mail and hadn't realized how uncomfortable it was, or how difficult it made traversing rough terrain. Their path wasn't easy; it led down and up sharp ravines which hid swampy mires and dangerous pools of slimy water underneath thin layers of fallen leaves. They walked over downed trees, and twice Karl and Eric laid their shields face-down over deep mud as a bridge they could walk across. The pools were frightening; their depths were a mystery no one wanted to explore.

Eloise's trail sent shudders down Karl's spine; among the countless recent wolf-tracks, little different from any large dog, was one set of prints that were obviously human but which had deep claw-marks instead of toes. These inhuman tracks were deep; Eloise's additional weight would sink any carrier's feet deep into the mud, just like Karl's heavy mail caused deep tracks wherever he stepped. The bizarre path didn't make sense; Karl wondered if they were chasing a madman who lived in the forest like an animal, but madness wouldn't explain the clawed footprints. And Karl worried about Eric's kinsmen; Svenson wouldn't push his troops into deep woods; he'd just order his army to encircle it.

Chasing Eloise might ensure their doom.

Late that afternoon the tracks led to a wide, smooth path under a canopy of elms. They were all exhausted; none had slept well since the morning before Eric had arrived at Bristlen. The ground was drier here, which made tracking difficult, so they just kept going and hoped the worn trail would lead them to Eloise.

Not far from the trail grew a huge, thick wall of blackberry bushes, and they stopped to pick all they could. The early spring berries were hard but plentiful; local deer would've eaten them all, but few deer feed near the home of a wolf pack. Soon their fingers were stained purple-red from berry-picking yet none stopped eating until the gnawing in their stomachs gave way to the bloated feeling of too many under-ripe blackberries.

As Karl finished off the last blackberry he could stand, he turned to see all of the others collapsed on the grass. Karl's coat of mail weighed forty pounds, his helm felt as if it was squeezing his head, his arm tired from carrying his shield, and he was exhausted just from walking in all of it. Rafe was already snoring; Karl couldn't blame him. Eric, lying on his back, had his eyes almost-closed and was dreamily staring at the clouds peeking through the trees; Karl wondered if Eric fancied his Valkyrie watching him from their flying steeds. Roselyn lay stretched out in the tall grass with a mossy rock for a pillow and seemed equally exhausted. Being young and strong, with nothing to carry but her bow and two quivers, she had the easiest trek, but Roselyn was nobility, unused to hardships.

Karl was still standing but only because he was certain that, if he sat down, he wouldn't rise again.

"Eloise ...!" Eric shouted suddenly. "Wake up! I heard Eloise!"

Karl startled at the sound of Eric's voice, although his exact words were lost in the fog of sleep. He awoke chilled and confused, unused to sleeping outdoors. The sun was setting; they must've slept for hours.

"What ...?" Karl asked.

"Eloise!" Eric said as he jumped to his feet. "I heard her! I was just waking up and I heard her scream!"

"Which way?" Roselyn asked.

"I can't tell," Eric said. "Sounds travel strangely though forests. Curse my sleepy eyes! We shouldn't have fallen asleep, certainly not without a guard!"

"What do we do?" Karl asked.

"Wait here," Rafe said. "Maybe we'll hear her again."

"Eloise was screaming for a reason," Eric said. "She may not be able to scream again. We should head into the wind, down the trail a little farther. If we get no more signs, we start circling, expanding our range. But we'll have other troubles soon; there's wolfscent in the wind. Those wolves that attacked the cabin live here. They'll hunt us tonight."

"Wolves can't climb trees," Rafe suggested.

"They could sit under trees and starve us out, even if it took days," Eric said.

"Quit arguing!" Roselyn shouted impatiently, and she headed off down the trail in search of Eloise.

Karl glanced at Eric and Rafe and shrugged; he'd rather follow Roselyn than stand around. Rafe made the sign of the cross, whispered a prayer, and reluctantly picked up his pitchfork. Eric came last.

Karl wondered why he was doing this. Eloise wasn't worth this. He didn't even need the treasure; Karl's gem-encrusted sword, silvered mail, helm and shield were worth a fortune. But any hope of honor would be lost to him forever, and Saxons were an honorable race, according to his father's favorite lecture. Yet, as Karl watched Roselyn lead the way, his eyes focused on her willowy, swaying hips, and Karl knew why he was seeking Eloise; it wasn't his honor that bound him.

A wolf howl startled them, coming from close by. Roselyn nocked an arrow and paused to let Karl catch up. Her clinging dress, damp from lying on the ground, was no protection against a wolf's sharp teeth. There'd been another shirt of mail on the floor in Bristlen's treasury and he wished she'd put it on. With every step their situation grew worse. Lone wolves seldom attacked people but wolf packs were dangerous. They had no hope of outrunning the fleet predators.

Sunset quickly swallowed the forest, leaving only shadowy shapes to guide them. Roselyn stayed only a pace ahead and Karl followed close behind her; her arrows would do little good if she feathered him or Eric when the wolves attacked. He kept his left hand on his scabbard, holding it straight as he walked, in case he had to draw steel in a hurry. Karl knew better than to draw early; walking with a naked blade down a dark trail was just asking for a root or stone to trip you. More than one fool had stabbed himself, or the person before him, by tripping in the dark with a bare blade in his hand.

Karl recalled how the wolves had attacked them in front of the cabin. Never had he heard of wolves acting so strangely! Something was amiss, but he couldn't show cowardice before Roselyn by abandoning Eloise.

"Curse these woods!" Eric scowled. "We need to be in a field where the starlight is unblocked, not under dark trees. We need to be able to see wolves before they attack us."

"Maybe they won't attack ...," Karl suggested.

"'Maybe's a fool's hope," Eric said. "If they don't attack then we waste a little effort, but if they do, then we die; I say we make the effort."

"'Effort' won't guarantee survival," Karl said.

"There are no guarantees," Eric said.

"Quit arguing!" Roselyn hissed. "Which way?"

"Off the trail," Eric said. "It's too dark here and the ground's too open; we need a wall or thorn-patch at our backs, so the wolves can only ..."

"Lead the way!" Roselyn ordered.

Eric stepped off the path, gazing into the dark forest. Karl's instincts told him they should go uphill, where the trees might be thinner, but the wolf's howl had come from there. Deep ravines with sharp sides divided these rolling hills; they had to be careful. The bottoms of those ravines would be black as raven wings, and wolves would tear them apart in darkness.

Eric stumbled over the rough ground yet pushed through the thin underbrush easily.

"When you don't want them you can barely walk ten paces through strange woods without finding thorn bushes," Eric grumbled. "When you need them they're never around."

Ducking under a half-fallen tree, which had been caught in the branches of another as it fell, Eric led them deeper into the woods. Another wolf howl sang out; several voices, their chilling wails echoing through the forest. Eric urged the others to hasten. The ground beneath them was soft save for the numerous fallen tree trunks they stumbled over; they had to find better ground. Ahead, Karl spied a clear patch of starlight.

"Stop!" Eric shouted suddenly, flinging his arms out to halt his companions. They all stumbled into him, complaining.

"Boar's tusks!" Eric cursed aloud.

They'd found their starlight: they were on the edge of a tall cliff, looking up at the stars, and down at a deep ravine lost in shadow; they couldn't go further.

Growls and thrashing leaves sounded in the distance, punctuated by numerous barks and yips; the pack was coming.

"This way!" Eric hissed, heading off to the right. A few thin, scraggily trees grew there, and he stumbled along the edge between their slim trunks and the cliff. The others followed him anxiously. If they could push into thick underbrush then they might have a chance.

The muddy cliff's edge suddenly collapsed under their weight. Abruptly, the young trees tilted toward the cliff and pushed them over; Roselyn and Rafe screamed as Karl and Eric cursed. All resisted, but with their hands tightly clutching weapons they couldn't grab for trees. The soft ground beneath their feet crumbled completely; all four toppled over the brink.

The cliff was steep but not sheer. Roughly they slid on weeds, amid a hail of dirt and pebbles, to hit solid dirt only twenty feet below.

Shaking with fear, they climbed carefully to their feet. They'd landed on a narrow ledge on a cliff, barely wide enough to stand on. The drop off of this ledge was considerably higher; at least thirty feet straight down, starlight reflected off water and wet rocks. If this ledge collapsed then they were doomed.

"Damnit ...!" Eric cursed.

"We're saved!" Rafe said at the same instant.

"We're on an animal trail," Eric explained grimly. "Wolves can come at us from both sides, and there's no time to look for another site. Karl, you're armored; switch places with Rafe."

The pack arrived at the remains of the crumbled ledge above, peeking their heads between the thin trees now tilted above them. Seeing their prey, the wolves howled and quickly ran in both directions; their prey was trapped.

Karl hugged Rafe close as he edged around the heavier stable-master, trying not to let the weight of his mail pull them both off of the ledge. Rafe clung to him and finally pulled him to the far side, probably glad to have someone armored between him and the jaws of the beasts.

Wolves poured down the narrow trail towards them like sands in an hourglass, barking and yipping. Karl crouched low and braced, holding his shield before him, his sword high, point forward. As the first wolf leapt, Karl stabbed and felt his blade penetrate, but the impact of the large wolf, almost a hundred pounds, slammed into his shield and knocked him back against Rafe. Impaled on Karl's sword, the first wolf whined and fell over the edge, but another instantly took his place, locking its jaws onto Karl's boot above the ankle. Karl screamed, but then Rafe leaned over Karl and stabbed the beast with his pitchfork. The wolf shrieked, a shrill, startling whine, as it jumped back. Karl struggled to his feet and braced himself for another attack.

Behind the wounded wolf pushed a dozen of his brothers and sisters, eager for the kill.

Kneeling on the ledge, his shield protecting him, Karl stabbed at the hungry wolves while Rafe jabbed over him with the long prongs of his pitchfork. Several more wolves cried out and fell into the gloom.

Karl risked a quick glance behind; Eric wasn't even trying to fight. Throwing his weight against the cliff wall, Eric had braced himself behind his large wooden shield and was pushing off the wolves as they tried to come around it. The wolves he toppled screamed as they plummeted down to the hard rocks below. Roselyn had drawn her bow but she couldn't shoot because Eric was in her way.

"Stay down!" Roselyn shouted, and Karl heard her bow twang. Another wolf howled and fell, tumbling over the cliff.

A thin shower of dirt rained down upon them. Several dark outlines of wolves moved above them on the crumbled cliff they'd fallen from, dangerously attempting to scale down the steep slope. Karl shouted to Roselyn, who shot an arrow as best she could in the dark. One wolf yelped and jumped as if it was shot, and slipped partway down the cliff at them, but it scrambled back up and fled from sight. The other wolves drew back, yet Karl kept an eye on the summit in case they should try again.

Rafe's shout startled Karl. Rafe taunted the wolves, trying to get them to come closer. The lead beast was holding back; Rafe's prongs had taught him to respect his range. The wolves behind it were pushing forward but it was huge and unlikely to move.

Karl glanced to see Eric in the same stalemate. Having seen their brothers and sisters pushed off the deadly cliff, the wolves were holding back. They weren't stupid; their prey was trapped, and wolf packs could hold out longer than humans. A chill ran down Karl's spine; *eventually the wolves would win.*

Suddenly a small circle of red-yellow light appeared on a distant hill across the ravine. A figure of a man stood eclipsed, and then it vanished, as if a thick curtain had been drawn over the light.

The Wolflord! High on the hill facing them was a cave, its mouth covered by some kind of curtain, a bright fire inside. When closed, it was hidden from view, but when he'd drawn the curtain aside to look out, the firelight had illuminated him like a beacon.

Karl steeled himself. Eloise was probably in that cave, trapped, if she lived at all.

"Karl ...!" Eric shouted. "How many ...?"

"Eight on this side!" Karl shouted. "What now?"

"Make them come to you!" Eric shouted. "We have to kill as many as we can while they're enrapt in the hunt! Do whatever it takes!"

Taunting them closer, Karl and Rafe sent two more over the edge of the cliff to the rocky waters below. Eric, unable to coax his wolf closer, had Roselyn shoot it, and better success came with the rest. Roselyn shot another arrow at some movement atop the cliff above them but her arrow hit nothing but leaves. If wolves were there, darkness hid them.

Karl focused on the wolf biting at his shield and realized how tired he was, shaking, shivering as if frozen, although overheated from his exertions. Never had Karl been so afraid! Fear was exhausting him; he had to control it.

Another shower of dirt rained down. Karl looked to see a growling wolf come sliding down the slope at them. Karl screamed and shouted, but the beast slid like a stone and fell atop Rafe. The stable-master cried out as the snarling wolf slammed into him, and together they toppled over the brink. In one blink, both Rafe and the wolf were gone.

Karl screamed, watching Rafe fall. He'd liked the old horse-trainer, but more important, he needed him ... and his pitchfork.

Suddenly, a moment after Rafe fell, Eric cried out. Karl glanced back to see two wolves had leapt over his shield while another had charged forward, biting at his boots. Eric stumbled backwards into

Roselyn. His boots were thick but wolf-jaws couldn't be stopped by leather. Eric flailed hard, thrashed violently against three attackers, and then tumbled off the ledge.

The wolves charged Roselyn; they wouldn't even taste her thin dress and slippers as they bit into her. Roselyn leapt off the ledge, shooting at one last wolf before she plummeted into darkness.

The wolves slammed into Karl's back and piled atop him, alone on the ledge. Had Karl not been armored they'd have torn him to shreds, but even wolves couldn't bite through steel mail or a helmet. They hurt; one growling wolf held his forearm seized in its teeth, and its crushing pressure caused Karl to buckle in pain. Others were scratching and biting at his steel armor, and digging to get under his mail; eventually they'd succeed. With a final cry, Karl pushed off of the ledge, dragging half-a-dozen wolves with him into the abyss.

Pain enveloped Karl as he struck bottom, but no rocks broke him; Karl landed with a small splash onto a meaty, hairy carpet. Karl shook himself, barely aware of Eric's swinging blade or Rafe's stabbing pitchfork. In the darkness he could feel the strange carpet he'd fallen upon; the bodies of over a dozen dead wolves had cushioned his fall. Eric and Rafe quickly dispatched the wolves Karl had pulled over the edge.

The wolves above barked and yammered, furious that their easy meal had escaped. Seeing their prey alive, the wolves ran off eastward, ready to begin the hunt anew.

"Mother of God!" Rafe cried, watching the wolves dash along the ridge. "They'll be here in moments!"

"They'll be here, but we don't have to!" Eric shouted. "Run!"

Eric took off, but Karl noted that his bulk ran slowly uphill; Eric was incredibly strong but running wasn't his greatest skill, and they were all exhausted. Rafe ran after Eric, even slower. Roselyn helped pull Karl to his feet and then dashed off after them. Despite being sore from the impact of his fall, Karl chased after Roselyn; the ground was damp but solid, deep with leaves and fallen branches, and his mail weighed him down. Unarmored, he could've run faster, but he'd need his mail soon enough. As they ran, Karl recalled that Roselyn had stayed to help him stand, desperate though their situation was; with death closing in, that seemed inexplicably important.

Roselyn quickly caught up with Rafe and then Eric, running with her bow in one hand and a handful of skirt in the other. Behind them, the wolf pack yowled and barked, approaching far faster than their prey could escape.

"There!" Eric shouted to Roselyn. "That open space! It's our best chance!"

Eric ran the short distance. Roselyn followed hesitantly. They'd found a small area, flat but open, exposed.

"Here ...?" Roselyn asked.

"Good footing, no trees ... to block sword-swings," Eric quickly explained, breathing heavily as he unbuckled his shield and tossed it aside. "No time to ... find any place better."

Passing Rafe, Karl ran up and glanced around, but said nothing, deeply gasping for breath. Personally he didn't see why it mattered where they stood as long as it was dry; Karl didn't want to die in the mud.

Chapter 5

The Wolflord

ROSELYN

Roselyn reached for an arrow, surprised to find one quiver entirely empty. She hadn't fired them all; the rest must've spilled as she'd fallen from the ledge. She drew one arrow from her last quiver, wondering how many wolves she'd be able to shoot before they got her. After the opulence of her father's court, and the fussiness of her mother's mindless lectures on etiquette, Roselyn was going to die to mangy wolves in a forgotten forest ... and they'd never know it.

As she watched, Rafe ran up, puffing and huffing, leaning on his pitchfork as if he'd collapse without it.

The forest was dark; Roselyn strained to see between the trees, down into the ravine. The gray wolves surged up towards them like a wave of death splashing upon midnight sands. Roselyn drew and aimed carefully. She shot, hit her first mark, and then Eric stepped in front of her, his sword in both hands. Karl raised his shield one last time and Rafe lowered the prongs of his deadly fork as the wolves charged.

Roselyn should've fainted by now, her mother's voice echoed inside her head. Noble women should always protect themselves by fainting during times of crisis, but then, her mother would've never been sent to Bristlen. She was everything Roselyn wasn't, demure, obedient, and silent in a man's presence. She never could've endured a crisis like this and would've never been here to begin with. Roselyn had been trained to be a perfect lady, but inside she'd always rebelled, and now her rebellious streak was going to cost her life. Roselyn nocked a final arrow, ready to fight to her last.

Wolves raced towards them like a snarling gray avalanche rolling uphill.

"Hello!" squeaked a thin, creaky voice.

The companions startled; Roselyn loosed her arrow into a nearby tree. Behind them, half in shadow, a withered old hag swathed in rags stepped out from behind a tall bush.

Suddenly the wolves yelped in horror and turned on their pads. Some skidded to a halt, falling over in a panic, and others simply turned tail, yipping and whining as if suddenly wounded. As one, the whole wolf pack turned and fled down the slope, darting between trees until they vanished.

Roselyn spun desperately, fearfully turning her empty bow to aim at the old woman. Karl stepped up beside her, keeping his shield facing the direction in which the wolves had vanished, yet he pointed his sword at the old woman; Eric clamped a hand on Karl's shoulder and pulled him back.

Exhausted, seeing the wolves flee, Roselyn collapsed to her knees, uncomprehending. *Why had the wolves fled?* No simple old woman could startle them so; they could've devoured her easily. Yet the wolves were gone; their frightened whines were still clear, though distant.

'Evil witches as old as the mountains' Rafe had said, but Roselyn couldn't believe it.

"Hello, strangers," she creaked as she stepped out into the starlight. "Lost, are ye? What be ye a'doin here? These mountains ain't no place fer strangers at night! Them night-howlers, they play rough. You shouldn't ought to play with 'em at night!"

"Forgive us ....!" Rafe cried suddenly, and he dropped to his knees and made the sign of the cross.

"Forgive ye?" creaked the old hag. "Why, I's don't mind ye here, day or night. What ye come fer? Not much of civ'lized folk around here, just 'ungry beasts and withered old crones like me."

"Withered old crones ...?" Eric shouted so loudly he startled them all. "T'was a beautiful act you

did, saving us, and beautiful deeds a beauty makes!" Eric strode forward, grabbed the old hag's head on both sides, and planted a kiss firmly on her withered lips.

"Well!" she gasped, her aged eyes wide. "Fer such a welcome I would'a come sooner and a'gain! Never have strangers greeted me so!"

"Eric is bold and hasty," Roselyn said softly with a smile, "but we're all in your debt. You saved us from an untimely death."

"The night-howlers? Pfah, them's scared of their shadows. They ne'er bother me. C'me now, tell an old woman what brings the likes of thee here."

"The Wolflord kidnapped our companion," Eric said gravely. "We hope to rescue her."

"Wolf-Lord ...?" she cocked an eye at Eric. "Ain't no one here 'bouts like that. Ye sure ye know what ye's doin?"

"But I saw him!" Karl argued. "In his cave on this hill!"

"Ye means Ol' Garn'n?" she creaked. "Why did't ye say so? 'e's a queer one, 'e is. Ain't respec'able like the rest a us. Took a friend from ye? Aye, I's wondered 'bout 'im. Some'em keeps 'im busy up un his cave. But I'll sees ye up there, if ye likes. 'een a long 'ime sins I looked in on 'im."

"We don't want to put you out," Roselyn said, struggling to stand. "It could be dangerous."

"Ain't nu'tin dangerous un these mount'ans," laughed the hag. "I'd a met it by now ifn there wuz."

"Who are you?" Karl asked.

The hag's eyes flashed.

"Me? I's called 'iz Apple by thems folks around 'ere," she said. "'iz Apple. Ye can 'all me dat."

"Miss Apple," Karl repeated.

"No! No!" she cried. "'iz Apple! 'iz Apple!"

"Elizabeth!" Roselyn guessed. "Liz Apple!"

"Dat's me name!" Liz cried. "Now who be ye, and where from ye come?"

"I'm Karl, from Castle Bristlen," Karl said, "and this is Rafe, and Roselyn, and Eric, who you already met."

"Met well!" Liz laughed, her crackling voice arcing to a peak of wheezy giggles. "Now 'ets go see Ol' Garn'n. We kin goes to me place fer 'upper after dat, if yer 'ungry. It ain't far, jest o'er the hill."

"Wait a minute!" Karl demanded. "What just happened? Why did those wolves run away?"

"Thank you, we shall be honored to dine with you, Liz," Eric said firmly, shouldering Karl aside with an evil glare.

Karl gaped at the old Viking. Roselyn smiled; Karl had committed a terrible social blunder, common for a peasant. Roselyn was surprised Eric had understood the propriety; this wasn't the time for questions.

Eric picked up his shield, and then he grabbed Rafe, who was still mumbling prayers, and dragged him to his feet. Roselyn laid a restraining hand on Karl's arm; Karl glanced at her with an expression of utter bewilderment but she merely pulled him along like an errant child. Until they knew more about Liz Apple they needed to tread carefully.

Liz led them up the hill slowly, walking from tree to tree, bracing herself against each as she went. All the while she laughed and chattered, never seeming to cease.

"These hills jest ain't what they used to be," Liz said. "Strangers comin and goin always. Decent folk, most a 'em, but some 'as strange as ye would't like t' meet. We drove 'em out once an' they aint come back, but they took some awful nice folk wit' 'em when they left."

"O-others live around here?" Rafe asked fearfully.

"Oh, lots o' folk," Liz said. "'sides Ol' Garn'n, theres Aunt 'elly up on the hill, and Gree'zer in Plough'ans Dike, and Dix' and Dee' by the river, oh, and others farther off. I don't see 'any more often, but I gets 'round. Some comes t' sees me!"

"Sounds friendly," Karl grumbled disgustedly.

"Ye 'oung folk ought'nt wait fer me," Liz said. "Moon's coming, and Ol' Garn'n gets ornery with the moon. 'urry on! Y'er child needs ye now, or it'll be too late! Ol' 'iz Apple will be comin soon."

"How do you know our friend is young ...?" Karl demanded.

"If you advise it, Liz, we'll go on ahead," Eric quickly interjected, frowning deeply at Karl. "Hurry, or we'll meet you coming back down."

"I's won't takes all night, I's prom'ses," Liz laughed.

"God save us!" Rafe gasped. "That story of the Wolflord did say something about the moon."

"Then, let's go!" Eric urged, and he edged past Liz Apple and pushed on up the hill.

Roselyn understood why Eric was accepting Liz Apple's word as gospel without a shred of evidence, but what could the moon have to do with it? Yet now wasn't the time to ponder; Roselyn held tight onto Karl's arm and pulled him past the wheezing old woman. If Liz Apple spoke true then Eloise needed them, and they could argue lesser matters later.

"Good-bye, Liz Apple!" Eric shouted. "We'll meet again soon."

"Meetin's with ye can be fun fer me!" Liz laughed. "'urry! Moons on 'er way!"

No more wolves showed, which made Roselyn uneasy. The hill was crisscrossed with innumerable paths, and Eric led them up the steepest, straightest course. The trees thinned out as they climbed higher. The first tip of the full moon peeked brightly behind them, and as they circled around a huge pile of tumbled stones, they saw a large deer-hide tarp staked across the face of the hill with a bright firelight glowing behind it.

They approached the deer-hide with caution. Red light wavered from within, flickering around the edges of the curtain, lighting a small grassy lawn with a shadowy glow. Fear began to ripple up Roselyn's back; she wondered how long her courage would last.

Eloise better appreciate this!

Nervously Roselyn raised her bow, an arrow firmly nocked. The cave's mouth was about Eric's height and as wide as Karl was tall, set in barren rock with thick smoke pouring out of its entrance. As Eric lifted aside the crude curtain with the tip of his sword, a wave of heat and black smoke puffed out. Yet distant, pathetic whines struck them: over the loud crackling of a fire floated the crying whimpers of a young girl's sobs.

Quietly Karl and Eric raised their swords and slipped inside, Roselyn close behind. Rafe peered inside as if staring into the gates of Hell. Repeatedly he crossed himself, yet Rafe didn't enter.

A large fire burned about thirty feet down a shaft that seemed drilled into the hill, as if a mighty spear had crashed down from the sky and plowed into the center of the Earth. Smoke and heat blasted their faces; they were walking down a slanted chimney, yet they pushed on. The shaft was rough and rocky, and Karl had to stoop as he walked down the slope, trying to make as little noise as possible. Both Karl and Eric held their shields before them, and Roselyn followed closely with her bow.

They inched around the roaring fire, feeling a clean draft upon their faces. This cave must tunnel through the whole mountain, Roselyn thought, but she was wrong: hanging moss wafted from thin cracks in the ceiling through which fresh air was pouring.

The bottom of the cave was but an end of the shaft, littered with filth. Amid the filth lay Eloise, curled against one wall, the remains of Roselyn's dress knotted around her wrists and ankles. No magical Wolflord stood revealed, only a filthy, skinny old man dressed in rags squatting before her, leering over his helpless prey.

"Some Wolf-Lord ...!" Karl shouted.

Eloise's kidnapper jerked up his head, surprised.

"Help!" Eloise screamed. *"Help ...!"*

Eloise burst into tears.

The filthy old man jumped up, grabbed a short spear from amid the rubbish on the cave's floor, and brandished it threateningly. Neither Karl nor Eric advanced; the tunnel was too narrow to use swords effectively. Roselyn pushed between them and aimed her bow. The stranger's expression turned to horror as Roselyn let her arrow fly. It stabbed deep into his right breast; the filthy old man screamed as his blood sprayed. He dropped his crude spear and staggered back. Karl charged forward, stabbed clear through the

Wolflord's stomach, and nailed him to the back cave wall.

"Mercy!" he grated between his teeth, but Karl looked again at Eloise, bound and sobbing, and twisted the hilt in his hand.

Roselyn watched without wincing, surprising even herself. The ragged Wolflord was powerfully built, bulging with muscles, but he seemed short and wiry thin. He did earn his name, for his old, lined face was narrow and long, his teeth sharp and pointed; he looked more wolfish than human, but he screamed and bled like any man. Karl pulled out his sword and let him collapse in the throes of death.

Suddenly the wounded man leaped up and shouldered Karl aside. Karl staggered; the weight of his mail off-balanced him, and he stumbled on the uneven floor. Eric had bent to sever Eloise's bonds, and the unexpected move caught him unprepared. The filthy man pushed past and knocked Roselyn down, despite her flailing at him, and he scrambled past her, fleeing up the cave towards his roaring fire.

Eric spun to give chase, cursing as Roselyn unintentionally blocked his way, trying to nock an arrow, when the wounded fiend's strength gave out. The Wolflord fell, mortally wounded, coughing blood and clutching his stomach.

Then a change came over him. He screamed loudly, and as they watched, his whole body started to shake. The dirty hairs on his legs grew long and black.

He rolled onto his back and ripped Roselyn's arrow from his chest, howling in pain. His arms grew fur and his face sprouted curly black hair. The wounds on his torso suddenly closed, and his mouth bent outwards, fangs squeezing out of aged gums. He howled and writhed in agonies greater than any Roselyn had ever imagined, so horrible even Eric winced at the sight.

The full moon had risen.

The Wolflord rose panting, the fire outlining his new form from his pointed ears to his long, sharp claws.

Roselyn screamed; such things just didn't happen, and all of her experiences and beliefs told her she was right. Yet this nightmare belied her truths. Only Eric dared challenge it, and he only with words.

"Evil thing ...!" Eric cried, holding out his sword warningly. "Child of Loki and Hel the damned! Spawn of Niflhiem! Stay back! In Odin's name, I command you, leave us! Return to the troll pits from whence you came, lest Holy Thor in his anger of your vile existence hurl his hammer upon you! Die and be damned!"

The creature snapped its fangs at the air and snarled. Roselyn barely heard Karl's urgent whisper. Obediently she nocked her arrow, drew to her ear, and fired. Her steel-tipped arrow shot through the foul beast's heart, but it only howled and tore the arrow from its flesh. The wound magically closed, pouring black smoke and leaving only a trickle of blood to show it had once been wounded.

Eric stepped forward, sweat pouring down his face, his sword quivering. Truly here was a creature from Rafe's Hell ... *and they were trapped in its lair.*

The man-wolf leaped at Eric, who cried out but swung firm. His mighty wedge of steel sliced into the Wolflord's shoulder and clove through flesh and bone. Yet the Wolflord only slapped Eric back against Karl, screaming in his hellish night-voice. Again, the bleeding, mortal wound grew black and mended itself with its own evil sorceries. Whatever foul magic had spawned the Wolflord still held strength in the world ... or had filled its creation with a power so vast Roselyn's mind trembled to conceive it.

"Its eyes ...!" Eric shouted, seeing Roselyn draw another arrow. *"Blind it! Shoot out its eyes!"*

Roselyn drew a perfect bead and loosed her shaft, piercing the Wolflord's left eye deep through the socket. The Wolflord screamed and fell, and Karl attacked while the beast lay stricken. His sword hacked deep into the shaggy monster's back, to the bone on its arm, and severed its foot clean off. Eric jumped to join him, and they chopped as if mincing a side of beef. The Wolflord writhed and howled between them. They cleaved apart its head and limbs in a splashing flurry of blood and steel.

Suddenly a black mist rose from it with a stench the pits of the dead couldn't match, and forced them back. The mists covered the Wolflord's body, melted it into a pool of liquid black, and the Wolflord rose, wet but whole, from the streaming black puddle, which dripped off him and poured towards them.

The companions fell silent: *their weapons were worthless.*

"Ol' Garn'n!" creaked Liz Apple's wheezing voice. "Leave these folk be! Go run wit' yer howlers an' chase the moonlight 'cross the sea! Ye got no cause t' harm these folk or steal their young a'ay! G'it! Go on! Or I'll 'ave ye tail a'beating!"

Roselyn gasped. From behind the fire, Liz Apple appeared, Rafe with his pitchfork beside her.

"Liz!" Eric cried. "Beware! The Wolflord heeds no mortal tongue! See to thy safety! Run!"

"Shoot, Roselyn!" Karl urged. *"Now, while you can!"*

"I can't!" Roselyn cried. *"I might hit Rafe!"*

"Back!" Rafe shouted, threatening with his long fork. "In God's own name, back! I command you!"

The Wolflord charged Rafe and Liz. Rafe stabbed him clean through the chest; his pitchfork's sharp prongs stuck out of the Wolflord's back while its butt jammed against the stone wall. The Wolflord slammed against the rocky opposite side, wedged in the narrow tunnel by the fork's long shaft, snarling but pinned. Roselyn put another arrow into him, striking his shoulder, as Eric and Karl started to charge up, but

Liz Apple stepped forward, her voice drowned by thunder from nowhere.

"By powers of the moon and night! By evil's plague and famine's blight! Lady and Hunter, I call thee nigh! Catch this demon and make him d..."

Liz stepped too close. The Wolflord snared her, claws hooking into her feeble throat, and her final gurgling scream filled the cave. Eric screamed, hurled himself forward, and stabbed through the beast so hard his sword cut into the rock wall behind it. The Wolflord howled and flung Liz Apple's broken body up the cave, onto the blazing fire.

The flames roared up, baking them with sudden heat, and the claws of the Wolflord snagged deep into Eric's heavy leather hides. Eric threw his hands against the wall, dropping his sword to protect himself. Karl ran up, but they were pinned against the wall so close he couldn't swing without hitting Eric. Karl threw down his sword and grabbed the Wolflord's hairy hands, straining to pull them from Eric's back before their claws sank into Eric's flesh.

The Wolflord pulled, defying Karl and Eric's strength combined. Slowly Eric was drawn forward, ever closer to the Wolflord's slavering fangs.

Suddenly the flames burst up again. Amid their roaring heat stood Liz Apple, her aged face twisted in anger.

"Garn'n ...!" she cried. *"Die ...!"*

Lightning burst from Liz's out-thrust fingers, arcing around them, filling the cave but touching only the Wolflord's pinned form. The Wolflord jerked and screamed as the jagged white lights tore through its body, and Eric, Rafe, and Karl were all thrown back. The pitchfork trapping the Wolflord sprang clattering against them, knocking Rafe's coin-bag from his belt.

The Wolflord leaped into the roaring flames. The fire burned high, hiding what happened save for Liz's screams and the Wolflord's agonized howls. For long moments they could discern nothing. Then the Wolflord stepped from the roaring fire, Roselyn's arrow still imbedded in its shoulder, his shaggy hair burned to its roots; part-charred flesh now revealed the massive scars Eric and Karl had inflicted on it. Neither wolf nor man it resembled now but a demon vomited from the bowels of Hell.

"Silver ...!" Rafe shouted, snatching up his coin-bag. "That was the weapon they used against the Wolflord in the story I heard!"

Rafe jumped to his feet and charged the Wolflord, swinging his tiny bag. It was a brave act, but the Wolflord absently swatted him aside. The precious bag of hacksilver fell from Rafe's hand into the roaring fire that had claimed Liz Apple. Rafe screamed and Karl jumped for his sword, but the Wolflord leaped and its claws slashed for Karl's face.

Weaponless, Karl twisted his head, and the deadly claws swatted against his helm, and the Wolflord shrieked in agony.

"Your helm ...!" Rafe cried. *"It's silver-plated! Attack it with your helm!"*

Karl heard Rafe, but he snatched up his sword and swung, slicing through the creature's throat. Rafe picked up his pitchfork and stabbed it into the fire. Karl swung again, but the Wolflord kicked him back and tore Roselyn's arrow from its shoulder. Karl fell sprawling against Eric, who toppled backwards, and both rolled down the tunnel.

Rafe pulled his pitchfork from the fire where his money-bag had fallen; its prongs were covered with molten silver, glistening in the bright firelight. The melted, shining metal dripped off of its deadly tips. Rafe swung and stabbed at the Wolflord's back, and his fiery, silver-tipped pitchfork pierced the Wolflord clean through.

The Wolflord's howl shook the mountain. Suddenly the black mist returned and covered its body, but instead of healing, it tore the Wolflord apart, burning him with bursting black flames. The Wolflord fell a crisped cinder, evaporating away in a snow of stinking black ash. All it left was the ruined ends of Rafe's pitchfork; its prongs were burned black and bent in every direction, still smoking.

Rafe fell back against the cave wall.

The Wolflord was dead.

In the silence, Eric's voice whispered a familiar name, and Roselyn looked up. The fire had returned to its normal intensity, but amid the flames stood the white phantom of Liz Apple, young again. Her spirit-glance wove past Rafe and Karl and fell upon Eric, and Eric returned her gaze with wonder, for her flesh was full and beautiful, wrinkled no more. She smiled brightly at him, and then Liz slipped softly down, sinking into the fire and rock below her phantom-feet. Liz Apple vanished into the flames and was never seen again.

Eric, rugged Viking of battle and death, hardened by trials uncounted, fell and wept on his knees.

Eloise still lay curled up in a ball on the bottom of the cave, harshly sobbing. Roselyn untied her, helped Eloise to stand, and kept her arms wrapped tightly about her to keep her from falling. Karl sheathed his sword and took Eloise in his arms, lifted and carried her out of the cave. Roselyn and Rafe followed, and on the soft grass they waited for Eric.

While they waited, a family of three wolves padded onto the grass nearby. Roselyn stood, tall in the moonlight, and spoke at them in mortal words.

"The lord of your kind has fallen!" Roselyn said. "Be gone, and forever free!"

The wolves stared at her, their expressions unreadable by humans, and then they quietly padded back into the woods.

Roselyn was little comforted. They'd beaten the Wolflord but their victory had cost her everything, her very universe, her steadfast belief in her senses. Her wound felt as deep and real as any sword-cut, and Roselyn wondered if she'd ever heal.

Eric came out at last, his eyes wet and red, and in silence they walked back to the cabin.

Chapter 6

Respite

RAFE

Smiling, Rafe carefully lifted one end of the burning log, its heat not quite searing his thick fingers. Swiftly but gently he laid the flaming wood on top of the remains of the other logs, which were nothing but flaming cylinders of hot coals. His fire had been burning brightly, the cabin so warm he'd opened the door a crack, but Rafe was too excited to sit still so he kept building up his fire.

Rafe scolded himself; he was a mature, dignified gentleman, too old to feel giddy, yet he felt like he could dance, a silliness Rafe hadn't indulged in for over a decade. Beside him, propped against the mantle, stood the remains of his pitchfork. It was ruined, hardly worth keeping, but it was also his greatest trophy, the weapon with which he'd slain the Wolflord.

Rafe couldn't wipe the childish grin off his face: *he'd forgotten the feeling of pride.*

The others were sound asleep, and Rafe was careful not to wake them. They'd all been exhausted when they got back to the cabin just before dawn. Their horses were fine, still in their pen, although they'd eaten every leaf and blade of grass they could reach. Rafe had given their horses more hay and water while his companions collapsed on the beds, and then he'd slept next to Eric in the large bed, but he'd awoken first.

Their treasure was right where they'd left it, and by early afternoon he'd be riding out of these accursed woods wealthier than he'd ever imagined. He picked up a thin, blackened stick and poked his fire again.

An hour later Rafe could wait no longer. He'd said his morning prayers, groomed and saddled their horses, packed each person's saddle with their treasure-roll, and plodded about anxiously. He was desperately hungry but there was no help for that. They could've dined on all the wolf-meat they wanted but no one seemed interested.

"Up! Up!" Rafe urged gently but loudly, and the others groaned slowly awake. "It's after mid-day; time to ride out."

Everyone except Eloise groaned and yawned. Eloise's eyes opened but she didn't move or speak. Rafe noticed her intently; Eloise's motionlessness stood out among the movements of the others. Outside of the Wolflord's cave, Karl had taken off his tunic for her to wear, which he didn't need under his thick, long coat that padded his mail, but Roselyn had to dress her; Eloise had no thought but misery. She had to be led as if blind.

Rafe was gravely worried: Eloise was still in shock. After he'd kicked apart their fire, Roselyn quickly stripped Karl's dirty tunic off of Eloise and put another of her few dresses on her. It was too big for Eloise and draped past her feet but neither had the time nor needles to hem it.

Rafe suspected he knew what had happened to Eloise; as they'd wandered back, before the night sky grew light, Eloise had sobbed her tale, whispering to Roselyn, who supported her as she walked. While Eloise had sobbed, Rafe and Eric had walked quickly ahead and Karl had purposely fallen behind, giving the women some privacy while keeping them safely surrounded; it was the Christian thing to do.

"It's all right, Eloise," Roselyn soothed repeatedly as she finished dressing her. "It's all over. Best forget it now."

Eloise looked up at Roselyn, then closed her leaking eyes. Rafe felt tears in his own eyes; the horror of her captivity, her tormentor's depraved touch, would haunt Eloise forever. He'd seen such women many times: she'd closed herself off to mentally escape what she couldn't physically, entombing herself in a prison of her own making. *Now she was trapped.*

Gently but firmly Roselyn drew Eloise outside the cabin. The men waited with their horses ready. Having blocked the broken window, Rafe latched the door to the cabin behind them and Eric lifted Eloise onto her saddle. In silence they rode away.

Fortunately, the main path led them through a different part of the forest than they'd already traversed. Their path was narrow; they rode through most of the forest with leaves brushing them on both sides. Their ride was easy, ambling across forested hills as gray clouds rolled in from the coast. The bright sun was hot yet they rode mostly in the shade, cooled by the forest canopy. No one spoke, each lost in their own thoughts.

Rafe was proud of his companions; they could've easily abandoned Eloise or taken advantage of the women themselves. Instead, they'd risked their lives and souls. Eloise's suffering laid heavily on them. Her sadness distressed Rafe, yet he couldn't overcome his elation. Self-doubts had become his way of life, like a dark, rutted tunnel leading endlessly downhill. Rafe also loved riding but, despite caring for horses every day, he'd spent little time in the saddle; Rafe was free and back in his element.

Rafe smiled at Eric, who was riding behind him, but Eric only scowled.

"What ails you, Viking?" Rafe asked.

"Nothing ails me, Horsetrainer: that's my problem," Eric grumbled. "I've survived again, as I always do. I could've died fighting the Wolflord; a glorious death against the devil himself. Even the Valkyrie, who've watched the mightiest warriors fall, might've been impressed. I'm not sure I want to have died to such evil; its taint would stain me forever. Now that creature's dead, and another credit is added to my name ... well, our names. Gladly I'll boast of my deeds in Elvidnir, the golden hall of Valhalla. But again I've missed my chance. To live forever, Vikings must die."

"I might as well have been slain," Karl groused. "All my life I've laughed at stories of ghosts and trolls. Wolflords didn't exist. Now? It was real enough when we were fighting for our lives. Now it seems ... impossible."

Rafe didn't know whether to curse or laugh. If the Wolflord hadn't been a dream, then how many other things prowled the lonely forests and deep caves of the Earth? Should Rafe watch the skies for dragons and Pegasus, and if he did, wouldn't he be one of the fools Karl laughed at?

The Wolflord had existed, Rafe was sure, but part of his daylight mind rallied against it. He'd heard too many fantastic tales to believe all of them. There was no golden fleece or man with the head of a bull.

Yet he felt uncertain. How simple it had been to just deny any such tale, and now he was doomed to listen, even to Eric's heathen beliefs, wondering if any part of it might be true. He'd survived a night in Hell, faced a demon-wolf powerful beyond his imagining, and wrongly thought he hadn't been wounded. The Wolflord had slain his smugness. Rafe was a fool because he didn't know how big of a fool he was ... yet he had to trust to Christ that somehow it would all make sense.

They let their horses rest and drink when they came to a small stream. Each companion wet their lips and Roselyn carried a handful to Eloise, but the water wasn't clear so they didn't quench themselves. While they stretched their legs, Karl walked up to Eric.

"You claimed you've seen Valkyries fly over battle," Karl said to Eric. "Were you telling the truth?"

"What's truth?" Eric asked seriously. "Two men may look at a glade in the forest; one sees a home where sprites and fairies play and dance, and he might even hear their distant singing. The other sees a worthless thicket that needs to be plowed into farmland. Which is right? The first man will waste his life being happy but poor, the second will waste his life being rich but miserable."

"You're avoiding my question."

"Always avoid questions you can't answer."

"What do you believe?"

"I'm a warrior," Eric said proudly. "I deal with whatever I must, whether I like it or not. Only in tales of great deeds do men live forever in this world. I seek the immortality of great tales."

"Just like knights," Roselyn interjected, looking up from Eloise. "They believe God is glory ... and seek glory to be like God."

"It's the way of the warrior," Eric said. "It's not an easy life, but it doesn't dull the mind with boredom as the hermits suffer, or entice it away like city-dwellers, lost amid endless distractions. It's dangerous, but it's honest."

"Have you ever seen things like the Wolflord before?" Karl asked.

"I've never seen such a demon, but I've seen much I couldn't explain, and met many folk like Liz Apple."

"What have you seen?"

"Does it matter? I've seen lost souls wandering dark, moonless nights, and sea-dragons roaring in deep mists. Do my words convince you? Had you stood beside me, would you have seen them? Ask not another what's real in this world: that burden we all share."

"What of the Valkyrie?" Karl asked. "What are they?"

"The Valkyrie are the handmaids of Odin, Choosers of the Slain," Eric said. "They watch all who die, sword in hand, and take the bravest to Valhalla."

"Like the Warrior's Paradise," Rafe said. "That's the reward for those who raise their sword for God and His holy church."

"But what of those without swords?" Karl asked. "At Ferny Creek, I wielded a spear ..."

"The type of weapon doesn't matter!" Eric laughed. "Weapons are the symbol of a warrior; what matters is the bond of flesh between the weapon and the warrior's heart. For that bond look the Valkyrie! But these are fireside tales and we've much riding to do. Lay aside your questions, young friend. When the stars are bright and the beer flows free I'll recite the ancient lays. But first we must escape Svenson and his army. He isn't easily deceived; we can't stay hidden forever."

Before evening, their trail led to the edge of the hills. From their height they could see the main road that ran inland from Demril and Bristlen. No army of Vikings showed yet that didn't mean no spies were about.

Below them in the valley, distant but not far from the main road, lay a large farmstead. The fields around it were wide and furrowed, and in the distance they spied other farms in wide patch-worked sections, shades of gold and green. Beyond the farmstead the road ran the width of the valley and snaked up into hills on the far side.

Smoke was pouring out of one chimney, and though they were too far away to smell it, they knew it was from kitchen fires. They were starving. They turned their horses and rode down the thick grass into the valley.

Rain began to fall, sprinkles at first, but soon it grew to the heavy showers the Danelaw often suffers. None wore cloaks so they hurried their mounts, yet it was a wide valley, and they knew better than to cross a farmer's newly-planted fields on horseback to beg for food. In heavy rain they rode the long trail down to the road and circled around to the front. Drenched, they rode in through the front gate.

"We need coppers," Eric said.

"Sorry," Rafe smiled. "Gold and silver we have. Of coppers we're poor."

No one laughed at his joke.

"Don't mention our treasure!" Eric growled.

"Rafe and I can handle this," Karl said to Eric. "You'd better stay back. With an army of your kinsmen about they may not let a Viking inside their house."

"Whatever you're going to do, just do it!" Roselyn snapped. "Eloise and I are soaked!"

Karl dismounted, unbuckled his shield, and loosened the knots on his treasure-roll. He carefully slid his hand into it and extracted four small pieces of hacksilver. He left his sword and shield leaning against a wooden post and walked up onto the porch. Rafe dismounted, set his ruined pitchfork beside Karl's weapon, and followed.

Karl removed his helmet and knocked hard on the door. It opened instantly but only enough to peer through; the farmers had known they were there, probably since before they'd ridden inside their gate.

"Yes ...?" asked an old, weathered man through the door.

"Forgive us for intruding, sir. I'm Karl, a guard from Castle Bristlen, and this is Rafe, the Baron's stable-master. We've just ridden down from the hills and need food and someplace to dry out. We have money to pay and women who need shelter ..."

"Show me your coins," the farmer said.

Karl opened his hand, showing him the four small bits of silver.

"You can have any one of these," Karl said.

"Any two!" the farmer said abruptly.

"Begging your pardon, sir!" Rafe exclaimed. "On better days, these coins could buy your house!"

"Not today they won't," the farmer said. "Nor would they afford me the discomfort of standing in a cold rain."

"All right; any two," Karl said, and the door opened wide. The farmer's hand reached out and selected the two largest pieces.

"Put your horses and wet gear in the big barn," he said. "Leave your weapons there. Then you can come in."

"Thank you," Karl said, and they turned away.

"Plain robbery," Rafe grumbled as they walked back.

"I expected nothing less," Karl said. "He reminds me of my father; he wouldn't let a single copper escape his grasp."

They led their company into the biggest barn. Minutes later they'd unsaddled, unbridled, and penned their horses in stalls. Karl found a greasy rag and quickly wiped dry both his and Eric's swords and helms before he hid them under some hay; Eric complained yet there was no other way. Rafe left his ruined pitchfork propped against a wall, but only after he'd dried it with Karl's rag; no point in letting it rust. They slipped their treasure-rolls into Eric's bag, which he knotted closed and carried.

Roselyn led the way and pulled Eloise inside the farmhouse. The farmer's wife seemed shocked to see them and unhappy at the water they dripped onto her floor; she ordered her two sons to fetch towels and blankets and dried the women off as best she could before ushering them into a back room. Karl shrugged off his mail and the farmer laid it on the stone hearth of his fireplace while the men dried themselves with what cloths the women hadn't taken. Karl's mail was wet but it was silvered and didn't rust easily; the fire's heat would dry it. Eric set his bag beside Karl's mail, grimacing at the sound of gold coins clinking together.

The farmer made no expression but stared at the bag intently.

The farmer pulled out a bench and let Rafe, Karl, and Eric sit before his fire. It wasn't blazing but it was warm, and the men thanked him. They were still uncomfortable; their wet clothes stuck to their bodies, but a small fire was better than nothing. Two young farm boys stood back and watched, whispering back and forth. The farmer sat in his large chair and silently faced them.

About twenty minutes later, Roselyn and Eloise emerged. Eloise said nothing but she moved to a small chair and sat down by herself. Both were wearing different dresses, worn, faded gowns, farm clothes the farmer's wife had probably closeted away long ago.

"There's a whole chest of old clothes in that room," the farmer said. "Not fancy, but warm and dry. You should each be able to find something to fit. Of course, old clothes can be expensive on wet days."

Karl sighed and handed the farmer one of his last two pieces of hacksilver. The farmer smiled; Rafe knew he'd collect the last piece before long. As they left the main room, Eric caught Roselyn's eye and nodded to his bag sitting on the hearth. She returned Eric's nod; she'd watch it while they changed.

Half an hour later, when the men returned, supper was ready. Roselyn was the only one who didn't hurry to the table; she was as hungry as the others, but the farmer's two-year-old daughter had emerged and they were playing together. Still, Roselyn didn't have to be called twice.

When everybody was seated around a table decorated with steaming plates and bowls, the farmer asked if anyone wanted to say grace. Rafe volunteered and recited words in Latin even he couldn't translate. Then the farmer served himself and the feast began.

A savage, brutal, scrumptious attack; Roselyn apologized to the farmer's wife several times, between compliments on the exquisite flavor of her cooking, begging her pardon for their terrible manners and explaining how they'd eaten nothing but under-ripe blackberries for more than a day. The others muttered agreement every time Roselyn spoke yet concentrated on eating.

Soon the table looked like a battlefield the day after, strewn with scraped-empty bowls and the bones of the devoured. The farmer had his boys fetch wooden tankards filled with his best ale for him and their guests. After his first drink, he leaned back and addressed them all.

"Welcome to my home," he said. "Samuel Tiller is my name, and my wife is Sara. My boys are Nate and Philip, and my daughter is Evelyn."

"We're forever in your debt," Roselyn smiled before anybody else could talk. "I'm Roselyn, and this is my sister, Eloise. These good men were to escort us to the Abbey of Dunstay before Bristlen was attacked. They are Karl and Rafe ... and their servant."

Eric kept gnawing on a chicken-wing and said nothing, yet Karl and Rafe exchanged glances. Rafe was surprised Eric didn't complain about her calling him a servant, but then, Eric was a Viking, accustomed to deception. Rafe wondered why Roselyn was lying; it suddenly struck Rafe that he had no idea who Roselyn really was. He'd never thought to ask; he'd assumed she was nobility yet he knew nothing for certain.

"I see," Farmer Tiller said. "I didn't catch your servant's name ...?"

"Eric," Roselyn quickly answered. "He doesn't speak much."

Eric darted an evil glare at Roselyn, but went back to eating.

"Of course," Farmer Tiller said. "Well, what can you tell me of Castle Bristlen? They say every Viking in Norway fell upon it."

"They ...?" Roselyn asked.

"Demril's refugees," Farmer Tiller said. "There's been a steady stream of peasants fleeing up the road since the Vikings landed. That is, not including their first ship."

"First ship ...?"

"That's what the refugees reported," Farmer Tiller said. "A single Viking sailed into Demril Harbor around sunset, and six hours later the whole Viking army sailed in."

"That's right," Rafe said suddenly. "I wonder what happened to that lone mariner ...?"

"So do I," Farmer Tiller said, eyeing Eric. "Well, there's no sense wondering. You're welcome to spend the night here, but when the army comes up the road, no matter what time of day or night, you have to leave."

"You think the Vikings will march this way?" Rafe asked.

"My family has worked this farm over a hundred years," Farmer Tiller said. "Ever since Lindisfarne, every time the Vikings have landed in Demril Harbor, they've marched this way."

"How have you survived so many razings?"

"Marching soldiers only want gold and jewels: small treasures they can carry," Farmer Tiller said. "They don't want carpets, furniture, or plows. Sometimes they sleep in our barns, their leaders in our house, but after they've left, we always return to find little disturbed. Yesterday we prepared to leave so we could be off in an instant. Mark my words; we won't have time to wait for strangers."

"We wouldn't expect you to," Roselyn said. "You've a wonderful family and they're your chief concern. You needn't worry about us; we will ride out at first warning."

"If the Vikings took shelter from the rain in old Dobb's barns, as I suspect, then they won't arrive until morning, and they'll pass this house with only a cursory inspection. But they'll march before dawn if the rain stops; usually they try to make it to Grusshire before evening. Hard to say what they'll do this time. The largest army to ever march through here was only three thousand, and I hear that twice that attacked Bristlen. We'll hear them coming; Viking kings always send mounted scouts ahead to check the terrain. Isn't that so, Eric?"

Eric opened his mouth to speak but quickly caught himself. He drank from his tankard, then shrugged and looked away. Plainly Farmer Tiller knew or guessed more than he voiced.

"Well, that's what they've always done," Farmer Tiller said.

"They have horses?" Roselyn asked.

"A few," Rafe said. "They'll have more soon enough. They're an army, you see, so they can take whatever they come across: food, horses, or castles. The only thing that can stop them is a bigger army. But our concern is escaping, not confronting. Nor do we want to be overtaken by scouts. We should ride out as soon as the weather permits."

"Master Tiller, we need to rest for the road," Roselyn said. "Could you have one of your sons stay up and wake us when the rain stops?"

"I'll do it!" cried Nate.

"No, me!" cried Phil.

"Quiet!" Farmer Tiller scolded them both. "I could, but I wouldn't trust young eyes to know when rain stops or merely pauses at night. I could do it myself, of course, for a price."

Karl groaned, reached into a pocket in his new trousers, and handed over his last piece of hacksilver. Farmer Tiller smiled and thanked him.

"Just like my father," Karl whispered to Rafe.

"I'll wake you when it stops raining, or at dawn, no later," Farmer Tiller said. "Once the sun's up, Vikings march, rain or no."

"We'd best get some sleep," Rafe said.

Sara Tiller took two candles and showed them to two rooms, one for the men and one for the women. Each group took a candle and thanked her again before they closed their door.

Chapter 7

Dreams

KARL

A barn door slid open and a deep voice cried out. A naked woman screamed, and she frantically pushed the young man off of her as a thick, red-bearded man burst inside, a long, deadly scythe in his hands. He charged the naked couple, the youth and his wife, his scythe raised high. The youth jumped back and leapt over the nailed timbers into the next stall, leaving the wife lying on her back, screaming as her husband attacked. He swung, as if harvesting wheat, and blood sprayed as her limbs fell away. He struck her again and again; her screams failed, and then he turned to see the naked youth fleeing out of his wide barn door.

The young man turned toward his house but he could never explain this to his father. She'd approached him, and seduced him, when he was very young. She'd been demanding his services for years, threatening to reveal him if he didn't obey.

Naked, the youth fled into the night across fields he'd plowed and harvested. The husband chased him all the way to the woods. There the youth cowered, hiding in the brush, listening to the man's angry shouts and curses as his scythe crashed through bushes. Any second, the youth expected his deadly blade to find him.

Karl awoke with a start, shaking; it'd been long since he'd dreamed of that night. He laid in the dark, hearing Rafe and Eric snore, and tried to calm his nerves. He hadn't slept in a farmhouse since then, although that wasn't his last sight of blood and mayhem.

Afterwards, Karl had been starving, having found no work since he'd run away from his father's farm. He'd walked through several strange villages and fruitlessly begged for work before the heavy hand of a warrior seized his shoulder.

Before he knew it Karl was conscripted. They loaded him into a wagon with ten other vagrants and drove them out to a large camp. There, each was given a twelve-foot spear and a loud-mouthed captain came to yell at them. Being the largest of the conscripts, Karl seemed to hold a special interest for the captain, who called him "Pretty-Boy" and offered to give him some character by carving a few scars onto his face. Then he had them circle a tree and practice thrusting at it while he 'attended to more important business'. The captain walked off and they never saw him again.

The boys talked for some time that afternoon about what each had been doing before they'd gotten caught. Then a shout came for dinner and the hungry conscripts got in line for a bowl of soup and a crust of bread. They overheard others talking and realized their predicament; Sir Laksky had crossed the border into the Barony of du Harmonn with two hundred men to settle a long-standing feud. Sir Gunderson had sent out a conscription crew but had seized only twenty-three men, which added to a total of one hundred and thirty-eight to fight against two hundred.

That evening, Sir Gunderson himself stormed out of his pavilion to review the conscripts. Karl stood in a line with the others as the grim-faced, heavy, black-bearded knight passed slowly in front of each man, keenly memorizing their faces. He announced, as he studied them, that being called into military service was a great honor, and he expected to see each one of them on the front line killing every fool who dared follow Sir Laksky. He also mentioned, with great emphasis, that anyone missing from the front line would be hunted down and tortured to death for treason against Baron du Harmonn. Sir Gunderson left them with orders to sleep on the ground and not leave camp.

The next morning, Karl and the others were rushed into some semblance of a formation and hurried off down a narrow forest trail. Sir Gunderson positioned them on a heavily-wooded ridge behind a thick row of bushes. There, crouched on the wet ground against a rotting tree-trunk, Karl waited for two hours in absolute silence while scouts ran ahead. At the bottom of the hill, beyond the trail, was Ferny Creek; Karl was thirsty but none were allowed to even breathe loudly, let alone move about.

A signal came for absolute quiet. Creaking wagons, horse's hooves, and men marching in armor approached. Two men on foot and one on horseback passed, unnoticing the ridge Karl and the others were hiding behind. Then the main group came down the trail.

Suddenly Sir Gunderson shouted, and a real soldier started kicking Karl and the conscripts forward. Uncertainly they charged up over the hillcrest only to find less than eighty men ambushed beneath them. With cries of delight, realizing it was their foe who was outnumbered, the conscripts charged with the rest.

Bows twanged and arrows tore through the green. Some men screamed in pain while others cried out warnings. The thirty yards separating them seemed but a few footsteps, and then Karl was in the midst of men desperate to kill him. Karl drove his spear into the shoulder of one mail-clad knight, who cried out and staggered under the blow. Then the other conscripts drove their spears into him, and the knight died on the trail.

The rest of the enemy fled into the forest, splashing through Ferny Creek. Yet that avenue offered no hope: steep banks and impenetrable overgrowths blocked their escape. Sir Gunderson ordered the conscripts up front and advanced on their foes.

Arrows whizzed through the thick trees and bushes. Two of the conscripts beside Karl screamed and fell. Another simply dropped, a feathered shaft suddenly appearing between his eyes. Karl realized his odds of survival were less than he'd thought; he jumped behind a tree, but the spears and swords of those behind pressed him on, followed by curses and shouts to "hold the line". Then Sir Gunderson commanded a charge. Karl was running again, straight at his enemy.

The forces of Sir Laksky aligned themselves just beyond Ferny Creek. The creek was small and muddy, the ground around it rough, strewn with fallen branches and moss-covered rocks. Karl and the few remaining conscripts hesitated as they glimpsed their foes, armored men barricaded behind large shields stoutly pointing a fence of heavy spears at the unarmored conscripts. Karl could hear their leader shouting orders to his men but his words were drowned by the general clamor of both sides.

The forces met. Karl sank in the mud up to his knees and swung his spear back and forth, batting away any spears pointed at him, but his fellows weren't so lucky. Intent more on killing than staying alive, their speartips slammed repeatedly into the heavy wooden shields of Sir Laksky's armored warriors, but did little save to attract the attention of their desperate foes. Deadly weapons swung and jabbed with practiced accuracy. Then Sir Gunderson's voice drowned out all others. Men charged past Karl and slammed aside the speartips with shields while others attacked on each side. His boots sunk deeper and Karl was bowled over by his own men, aware only of screams and curses and orders echoing from the chaotic tumult. Karl fought to stand, but the crumbled banks of Ferny Creek had been trampled into a mire. Karl finally threw down his spear and crawled out of the mud.

A faint cheer arose from Sir Gunderson's men as the last of their foes yielded up their swords and begged for mercy. Karl said nothing, too stunned to cheer. Many of Sir Gunderson's men were badly wounded. Of the conscripts, Karl was the only one left alive.

On the march back, Sir Gunderson offered Karl a job as a guard at Castle Bristlen. Karl accepted it grudgingly, knowing he was only being asked to replace those guards who'd been lost. Worse, Karl learned Sir Laksky hadn't been among their foes; all that death had accomplished nothing.

The Battle of Ferny Creek was considered a minor skirmish by the rest of the castle guards, but to Karl it was a major education. Karl was taller than most men, with a longer sword-reach. He was a good fighter, but no longer would he fantasize about the glories of war. His one experience had been quite enough.

A soft sound stole Karl's attention; someone knocked lightly on their door, and as it creaked open, an aged hand set a lit candle inside their room.

"Rain's stopped," Farmer Tiller whispered.

His brow wet with sweat, Karl sat up, breathing heavily; he couldn't help thinking his dreams were an omen. Eric sat up and yawned while Rafe laid and groaned. Unlike the women, who got the only spare bed, they'd slept on a pile of ancient quilts under scratchy wool blankets. Karl's neck felt like someone had driven a nail into it.

Their treasure-sack lay beside them, untouched, next to the candle they'd blown out. Eric jumped up and tore the covers off both of them.

"Hurry!" Eric said. "The sooner we ride the safer we'll be. Viking camps break early and we've far to go."

When Karl stumbled into the main room, yawning and blinking, he found the table already set and Sara Tiller carrying hot dishes.

"Come, see!" Nate cried, pointing, and Phil took Karl's hand and pulled him forward. Before the fire, Karl was surprised to find his mail coat strung over the back of a wooden chair.

"Oiled and dried," Farmer Tiller smiled. "That's a good suit, son. Valuable: be a shame to let it rust."

"Th-Thank you," Karl stammered.

"And here are the rest of your things," Farmer Tiller said, pointing to a stack of folded garments which Karl recognized as Roselyn's dresses, with his tunic on the very top. Beside them lay another stack, part of which he recognized as Rafe's trousers. "Sara stayed up all night cleaning them, and my boys polished your swords and helms."

Karl gasped, seeing their valuable weapons and armor that he'd hidden in their barn now set beside Farmer Tiller's big chair, shining like new.

"Karl!" Eric said, pulling on his old leathers overtop his new clothes. "Look at this! They brushed my furs! These skins didn't look this good on their original owners!"

"But why ...?" Karl asked.

"You boy's don't really think you're fooling anyone, do you?" Farmer Tiller laughed. "Crests on your shields, helmets decorated with silver and gold, your women dressed up for a royal feast; a little rainwater can't disguise that! We're a poor family, and children cost so much to raise ..."

Karl and Eric exchanged glances.

"Send your boys away," Eric said.

Farmer Tiller barked a command in his deepest voice and both boys fled, taking their sister with them. Eric untied his sack and drew out a small handful of gold and silver coins.

"We were never here," Eric said.

"You were never here," Farmer Tiller repeated, his eyes as wide as full moons.

Eric handed him the coins, which instantly vanished into Farmer Tiller's pocket. Karl smiled; those coins were a fortune to the farmer, enough to support his family for years. He was quite impressed; he'd thought Eric a worthless thief, not a generous benefactor. Eric had given Farmer Tiller far more than he would've; perhaps the old Viking deserved more credit than Karl had given him.

"You're a good host, Tiller," Eric smiled. "Now let's eat in haste and be gone before trouble arrives."

The delight of the men was nothing compared to the joy the women expressed when they saw their gowns cleaned and folded. Roselyn took off a thin gold bracelet and gave it to Sara with her compliments. Sara gasped; Farmer Tiller was well-off for a peasant but never before had she held a piece of real gold.

Breakfast was rushed but delicious and plentiful. Farmer Tiller informed them he was packing off his family in a cart as soon as they left, so they hurried to finish. They ate everything, since there was no telling when they'd see such food again, so there was little conversation. When they finally went outside into the damp, chill morning, Farmer Tiller had them wait while he vanished into a storage shed. There he dug out three old, rugged, leather backpacks, which he presented to them as farewell gifts. All thanked him profusely. Meanwhile, Sara laid out a generous feast of hot foods on a small table on their porch, a tribute to the Viking scouts and their leaders ... in the hope they'd leave their house intact.

As they mounted to ride off, Farmer Tiller climbed up onto his huge cart and called for his sons. Sara was already there, with her young daughter, several large chests, and five cages of chickens and geese. Two strong draft horses pulled the cart and four cows were roped to the back of it. The boys jumped on and Farmer Tiller shook his reins and drove them all down a wide trail across the center of his fields.

"Where do you suppose he's going?" Roselyn asked.

"Nowhere," Rafe said. "He'll just ride until it's safe to turn back."

"Probably has an old shed hidden in the woods where they can hide," Karl said. "My father has one."

They rode their horses out onto the road. Several expressed compliments of the Tiller family, and then they pressed on. The gray dawn was chill, the sky still dark and laden with heavy, low clouds. It was growing light: the sun as yet unbroken over the hills, yet they had to be gone before Svenson's scouts arrived.

Karl watched Farmer Tiller's cart drive off with strong regrets. Before Ferny Creek, he'd been looking for such a place, a cozy home with a nice family who needed help on their farm. Tiller did need help; the others might not have noticed but it was obvious to a farmer's son that the huge farm was falling into disrepair. He was tempted to turn his horse around and follow the cart.

Karl spied Roselyn looking back at the cart. She smiled briefly at him. When their eyes met, Karl's heart sank; *he was a fool.* Roselyn may offer him friendship, in a limited way, but she was a lady of the court and he was a peasant with no family.

Still, Karl smiled back at her.

As they rode across the valley they soon reached places where Farmer Tiller's fields were thick with weeds choking unplanted rows. Karl groaned; the Tiller's farm needed at least a dozen hands on it, and Nate and Phil were still too young to do the work of a single grown man. He should've offered them more treasure; they'd probably depleted a month's worth of food on their dinner and breakfast. But it was too late; they'd driven off and he couldn't turn back.

Their path began to rise as forested hills replaced the fields alongside the road. The morning sun rose, broke apart the clouds, and basked them in warmth. Their path became more narrow and rutted as it wove up the hillsides, and the comfort of the sun faded as they rode into the shadows of tall trees. Yet they continued as fast as they could, ever mindful of the Viking army chasing them.

Chapter 8

Thieves

ERIC

Eric led them uphill at a good clip, taxing the horses, loath to waste any time. Invading armies marched afoot, but Svenson's mounted scouts were riding hard, searching for him.

Rafe matched Eric's rapid pace with ease. Undoubtedly they had the strongest horses and the most experience. Eloise and Roselyn rode beside each other, when the trail was wide enough. Their horsemanship was far less than his, their horses more docile, mostly trained to follow the horse in front. Karl brought up the rear. Karl rode terribly; Eric doubted if Karl's father had owned any horses.

Eric frowned; he could easily veer aside, let Svenson's whole army pass by, and save all of their lives. In his youth, that was exactly what he'd done whenever foes had pursued him, but safety no longer mattered. Escape from Svenson would mean a woman's deathbed, no Valkyrie to swoop for him, and no eternity in golden Valhalla. Eric couldn't let this chase last forever.

Leading an army was expensive; eventually Svenson would have to turn back to his ships. Then the Valkyrie would follow the army, and Eric would never enter Valhalla. That couldn't happen: Eric Bjornson wouldn't end up like Thorin Stormgard. If nothing else, he'd be standing alone on the docks of Demril, blocking Svenson's path back to his ships, and there earn his ride across the Rainbow Bridge.

'Make them want to kill you!' Thorin had said.

Eric considered those words and found great comfort in them. Those words were his key to paradise. Yet he was starting to like, and even respect, his young companions, and felt uneasy about dragging them into the attention of the Valkyrie.

As long as Eric stayed on the main road he was safe from escape. Svenson would recognize this path: Eric was leading him on the same circular route they'd taken the last time they'd visited Bristlen, when he and Svenson had stolen Elaina, the beautiful baroness.

That afternoon, as they crested the summit of the hill, a youthful voice cried out.

"Halt! Dismount ... and throw down your weapons!"

From behind a thick bush walked a tall, thin knight, fully armored in the new style, with heavy plates of steel linked into his mail. In both hands he carried a claymore, a great sword almost as tall as he. The knight walked out into the middle of the road and stood next to a large rain-puddle, blocking Eric's way.

"Surrender!" the knight ordered.

Eric reined in and laughed loudly.

"There's too much infancy in that voice for such fierceness!" Eric taunted. "Hide you a diaper under that metal? Begone, child, unless you require a spanking!"

Rafe rode up beside Eric and looked down at the knight. The others rode up behind them.

"What is it?" Karl asked from the back.

"Sir Lancelot here has ordered us to surrender," Rafe chuckled.

"Dismount and throw down your weapons!"

The companions laughed, and even Eloise smiled. Eric couldn't see through the closed-faced helm but he knew the young knight's face was flushing scarlet.

"I'll kill you all!" the knight threatened.

"Shall I feather him?" Roselyn asked, reaching for her bow.

"No, I'll deal with him," Karl said, drawing his sword.

"Why?" Eric asked calmly. "What do you gain? This boy's death will add no glory to your name, and a claymore's a dangerous weapon, no matter who wields it. Every time you fight you risk your life, and you're a fool to take risks when there's no need. Just distract him until Roselyn has an arrow nocked; we've no time for this."

Smiling, Karl nodded to Eric, and then glanced at Roselyn. She nodded back and discreetly slid her unstrung bow off of her shoulder, slipped her leg inside the string and hooked her ankle around the bow's lower tip. Using all of her strength, she bent the bow against her knee and slid the loop of the bowstring toward its notch at the top.

Karl dismounted. He paused to adjust the buckle on his helm, giving Roselyn time to get her bow strung, and then tightened the strap on his shield. When he was ready, the impatient young knight turned to face him, and then backed up.

"Enough ...!" cried a deep voice.

A second knight, helmeted and armored as the first, but with his visor open, stormed out from behind tall bushes. He was much older than the first knight, taller, with a thin black beard cut close in the Norman fashion. "Open your eyes, boy! First, you were supposed to skirt around the puddle ... so that they'd have to come through it to get at you. Second, that wench has a bow and is about to kill you without even coming into your range!"

"Father ...!" the first knight cried angrily. *"You said I could ..."*

"Not this time, son," the older knight said, pointing past Rafe. "Unless I'm mistaken, that's Eloise Elizabeth du Harmonn, daughter of Baron Vandislidge. She's worth real ransom, more than all of the coppers we've robbed from fleeing peasants."

Hearing her name, Eloise startled, as did the others. The youthful knight with the huge sword stamped his boots upon the dirt road like a child having a tantrum, but no one paid him any attention. Standing closest, Karl turned to meet the new threat. Eric drew his sword.

The older knight laughed, not even drawing his sword from its scabbard, and called for his men. Thick bushes on both sides of the road shook, and four filthy, ragged men emerged, each with a bow nocked with an arrow. They drew and aimed at the men, two at Karl.

"Wait ...!" Eloise shouted. "Don't hurt them ...!"

"Easy, lads," the older knight said, smiling wickedly. "Let's hear her out."

Roselyn grabbed Eloise, pulled her close, and whispered into her ear; Eric leaned close, listening.

"That's Sir Athelred ...!" Roselyn hissed. "He is not a knight anymore! Earl Sir Guldwin banished him

almost a year ago for showing cowardice in a tournament."

Eloise looked at Roselyn questioningly. "Earl Sir Guldwin? But that's ..."

Roselyn's eyes flared desperately and Eloise broke off, turning to face their captor. Eric wondered what Roselyn had meant to say but had no time to consider it.

"An honor to see you again, Sir Athelred," Eloise nodded formally. "I trust your health is well?"

"Ever the polite little Baroness, eh?" Sir Athelred laughed. "I didn't think you knew my name. What happened to your father, Eloise? Dead in Bristlen ...? Serves him right, the French upstart, for coming across the channel where he didn't belong."

Eric eyed Karl, wondering what the boy would do, and glanced at the archers aiming their arrows at them. Two were close, about three paces away, but they were equally distant from each other. If Karl raised his shield and charged one then the other would have a clear shot at his back. Mail was made to defend against the cutting edges of swords, not the narrow points of arrows; Karl would die if shot by either archer.

"My father died before I ever heard the name of du Harmonn," Eloise seethed, her face twisting with an anger disconsolate with the innocence of her youth. "Neither my mother nor I ever asked for the name du Harmonn, for ourselves or our barony. We're on our way to the Abbey of Dunstay, if you'd kindly get out of our way."

Looking at the knight, Eric knew her words were empty. Eloise was foreign to life outside Castle Bristlen; did she even understand what knights valued? Sir Gunderson had obviously been her secret lover, but she was too young to know his true purposes, if he'd truly loved her or if he just wished to marry her in the hopes he might someday inherit the Barony of du Harmonn. Sir Athelred was, at least, more honest about his treachery; he was a thief and made no pretensions. Eric respected that, but such a man couldn't be trusted.

"I'm afraid you won't get to the abbey today," Sir Athelred grinned, seeming amused by her youthful fury. "Being a knight, it's my sacred duty to take you under my protection."

"My guards protect me," Eloise said.

Eric gritted his teeth in frustration; he'd let the boy-knight distract him. He should've been more wary, instead of riding blindly into an ambush. These thieves could kill them almost effortlessly and his whole life of fighting would've earned him nothing. The archer aiming at him was too far away to jump at, too close to miss. Eric could fall behind his horse, holding his shield low, but then the other archers would have a clear shot at him, and if they shot his horse then he'd have no way to ride on before Svenson arrived.

"Perhaps I should kill your guards, and then you'll be obliged to suffer my protection," Sir Athelred said. "Men ..."

The four peasants steadied their bows.

"No!" Eloise cried, and Roselyn again pulled her close and whispered into her ear.

"Who's this pretty bed-warmer?" Sir Athelred smiled, noticing Roselyn.

"None of your concern!" Eloise snapped. "She's my maid, a servant."

Eric gave no sign but noticed Eloise was concealing Roselyn's identity again. He wondered who she really was, yet he kept silent, his sword tight in his right hand and his eyes upon the archers.

"Perhaps she'll serve me as well," Sir Athelred said, nodding at Roselyn. "And who are these guards who led you into my ambush? A boy in parade armor, a fat old man, and a Viking? What are you doing in the company of a Viking?"

"I need not answer you," Eloise said boldly. "Now step aside, and drag these weasels behind you."

"A Viking," Sir Athelred mused. "How interesting. Your people have done me a great service, Viking. There's been a steady flow of refugees since your people invaded, all of whom have been delighted to leave their valuables with me, and now you bring me the only heir of Baron Vandislidge du Harmonn; I'm quite indebted."

Eric glared momentarily at the knight, then returned his gaze to the archers. Without their bows threatening him he'd gladly skin the metal shells from these English knights. There was one chance, a trick he'd pulled off only once in his life, and then only by accident.

"We've no time for this," Eric said aloud. "An army of my kinsmen marches only hours behind us. If you have no sense, let us pass, and you can ambush their thousands with your puny band."

"Viking tongues shouldn't be held, they should be cut out," Sir Athelred sneered. "Keep your dogs quiet, Baroness."

"Mind your own kennel," Eloise said haughtily, nodding toward the archers. "They have fleas enough. But Eric's right: the Viking army's coming, and they'll answer all of your questions."

"I'll ride out before the barbarians arrive," Sir Athelred continued. "My only question is what to do with you. With your father dead, someone will pay your ransom."

"Earl Sir Guldwin might," Eloise smiled, her eyes like daggers. "Why don't you ask him ...?"

"That swine ...!" Sir Athelred shouted. "He's as unworthy of any title, let alone Earl, as that fat father of yours, who should've never been made baron! The king's a fool, granting lands and titles for money instead of giving them to his knights!"

Sir Athelred smiled suddenly. "Of course! Why waste you on mere ransom? You're a baroness: if we wed, then I'd be baron!"

"You'll be crow-food hanging from a gibbet," Roselyn said coldly. "You know what would happen if you force a royal marriage without troops; Sir Guldwin won't deny your claim, he'll hunt you down and argue over legalities after your blood stains his sword."

"Can't you keep your slaves quiet?" Sir Athelred shouted.

Eloise shuddered and foundered. The idea of marrying this thief and liar must have repulsed her like the touch of the Wolflord; her recent terrors still too fresh. She looked as if she'd collapse.

Sir Athelred frowned.

"Kill the men," he said.

"No ...!" Eloise cried loudly, and then her voice cracked as if she were speaking through intense pain. "Spare them ... and I'll marry you."

Everyone gasped. Eloise sat, bowed in her saddle, her eyes shut, not crying. Eric couldn't believe his ears; few men showed such honor. They'd risked their lives to save Eloise. Now she'd returned the favor.

The jingle of coins broke the sudden silence; Eric tucked his naked sword under his arm and untied his bag from his saddle with a jerk of its cord.

"No," Eric said. "Take all the wealth I have, but leave this poor girl alone. She's already suffered too much."

Eric tossed his treasure bag onto the dirt road at Sir Athelred's feet. It landed with a loud clash, spilling out silver plates, gold coins, and Svenson's priceless horn.

All eyes fell amazed upon the treasure. A long moment they gasped, uncomprehending as greed swallowed all thoughts.

Eric took his sword back in his right hand, laid it over his left shoulder, and then flung it hard at the nearest archer, leaping off of his horse as he did. Intent on the spilled gold, the archer never saw the thick Viking sword flying at him. The heavy wedge of steel caught his chest and pierced him clean through. His nocked arrow released and slammed into Eric's shield, but the archer never knew it; he opened his mouth to scream ... and then fell dead onto the road.

The archer aiming at Rafe turned and fired at Eric, but the experienced Viking was ready, and another arrow thudded into his large shield. Eric hit the ground running toward the archer, who instantly turned and fled; he leapt into the bushes and vanished down a narrow trail. Without an arrow nocked the archer had been helpless.

Karl seized the opportunity and charged one of the archers facing him. His archer didn't waste his shot, but ran backwards, holding his release until he had a clear shot around Karl's shield. Karl chased him down, expecting at any minute to see the arrow released at his eyes.

Rafe saw the other archer aim at Karl's back and stabbed suddenly, jabbing his long-handled pitchfork at the filthy henchman. Rafe leaned too far and toppled from his saddle, but the bent prongs reached and entangled the slender shaft of the bow, tilting it before its arrow was loosed at Karl's back. It twanged harmlessly into bushes.

The archer pulled his bow free of the bent prongs and reached for another arrow, glaring at Rafe, who lay prone on the road. He never nocked it; Roselyn's feathered shaft stabbed deep into his chest.

Karl forced his archer back against some bushes before the archer finally released. The arrow shot straight at Karl's head, but glanced off of his silver-plated helm, leaving only a scraped dent; Karl had survived, and his foe was now weaponless. He swung his sword hard and the archer threw up his weapon to block: the wooden bow snapped in half as the steel sword bit through it, but it saved the archer's life. The archer threw up his hands, fell to his knees, and begged for mercy.

Seeing his archers defeated, Sir Athelred roared in anger and drew his own sword. He charged Eric, who'd thrown his sword through one of the archers and now stood weaponless. Eric turned to run away only to see the youthful knight, Sir Athelred's son, attack him from the other side, his huge claymore held high overhead, swinging down right at him. Eric stood pinned, weaponless, between the attacking father and son.

Desperate, Eric threw himself down, hurling his bulk into the armored legs of the youthful knight. The boy's hard polyens, his steel knee-cops, hammered into Eric's back as the two collided. Eric gritted his teeth and gasped but kept his eyes on the boy's father.

Intent on his helpless foe, Sir Athelred had charged closer, and realized his error too late; Sir Athelred looked up and cried out.

As the boy-knight, in his heavy armor, tripped over Eric, he fell forward, forgetting the long, deadly sword held high over his head. The claymore fell like the blade of a guillotine and caught Sir Athelred directly on his helm. Sir Athelred tried to block it with his sword but, undeflected, the claymore's mass knocked aside the lighter blade and stove in the top of his helmet. Rivulets of blood streamed down Sir Athelred's horrified face.

"Father ....!" the young knight cried.

Sir Athelred toppled to lay sprawled on the dirt.

Quickly the boy scrambled to his father's aid, but too late. With a single glance, Eric saw the empty expression he'd witnessed on countless battlefields; Sir Athelred had died instantly.

Eric rolled to his knees, aching from beard to toenails.

He was too old for this dung!

Slowly he retrieved his blade.

"Is it over ...?" Karl asked.

Eric wiped his sword off on the dead archer's ragged clothes. Again he'd won, despite overwhelming odds, although he couldn't recall the last time he'd felt so battered and bruised. Yet this was no victory to boast of; Eric was a fool to walk into ambush, distracted by the young knight. He'd been lucky: had they slain him weaponless he wouldn't have been counted as a warrior, and to him the Gates of Valhalla would've remained forever closed. His spirit would've been doomed to wander the trackless wastes until it eventually found its way to Niflhiem, Home of the Damned.

The youthful knight pushed his claymore away absently as he clutched his father tightly. The heavy blade had only slightly cut through the helmet's steel but dented it deeply and crushed the skull inside. The boy gripped his father's body and started to cry. If he was still aware of those around him none could tell.

"It's over," Eric said, surveying their foes. Sir Athelred was dead and his son was in shock. The archers were dead, run off, or weaponless.

"Just like Ferny Creek ...," Karl muttered. "What a waste ...!"

"Thank you, Eric," Roselyn said, riding up close to him.

The old Viking looked up at her, smiled, and suddenly he bowed to her. Roselyn laughed, her voice like a happy melody of bells and birdsong, and Eric noted that she seemed accustomed to having men bow at her. He wondered who she was.

A heavy hand clapped Karl across his back, although he scarcely felt it through his mail; Rafe was grinning from ear to ear. Rafe limped up to the cringing archer Karl had disarmed, pointed his still-sharp bent prongs of his pitchfork at him, and motioned for him to flee. The archer didn't wait to question his luck; he ran off down the hill and quickly vanished into the thin woods that lined the road. Then Rafe walked over to Eloise's horse, reached out and petted the beast.

Eloise was sitting frozen in her saddle, her young head bowed, her thin yellow hair blowing in the wind. Her hands still clutched her reins although her horse hadn't moved. Her breathing was labored as if she'd just run a race.

"You honor us with your courage, Princess," Rafe spoke gently. "Your offer of marriage would've saved our lives, though I didn't fight the wolf-beast so I could watch you wed that scoundrel."

Eloise looked down at the old horse-trainer and grinned. Slowly she reached out her hand.

"Princess ...," Rafe took her hand and touched his lips to it, kissing softly.

Eloise smiled.

"We should ride on," Eric said, motioning towards the sobbing boy-knight still holding his father.

Eric and Karl gathered their spilled treasure while Rafe collected three quivers of arrows from the two dead archers; he gave them to Roselyn, who accepted them gratefully. Eric said nothing when Karl dropped several uncut silver coins beside the sobbing boy-knight; he'd lost everything.

Chapter 9

Scouts

ROSELYN

As the boy-knight sadly clutched his dead father, a faint, distant thunder drummed and grew steadily louder. Roselyn glanced behind her and listened intently; a familiar rhythmic beating drifted on the wind.

"Riders approaching," Roselyn said.

"Svenson's scouts ...!" Eric cursed.

"Ride on!" Rafe shouted.

"No, wait," Eric said. "Scouts won't attack unless they must. Mount up, but keep your weapons ready."

Eric retied his treasure bag onto his saddle but tucked Svenson's golden horn into his belt. The men mounted.

The drumming hoof-beats rapidly approached.

Roselyn turned her horse around and fitted arrow to string; she had no idea what to expect but she was determined to be ready. Worried about her companion, Roselyn glanced at Eloise, who sat unmoving on her horse. Eloise had finally spoken up for herself, and spoken well against Sir Athelred; Roselyn had been surprised and humbled by her offer. Despite her foray into the Wolflord's cave, Roselyn wasn't sure she could've offered as much.

Eloise was still a child, just barely old enough to bear children, and far more sheltered than she'd been at that age. Castle Bristlen had been Eloise's life-long prison; as an unwanted stepdaughter, Eloise had seldom been allowed outside its stone walls or given any education, not even to read or write. She'd certainly never learned to use a weapon; probably never been allowed to hold one.

Roselyn had traveled all over England and learned many things her father had forbidden, such as how to shoot a bow. Yet her freedoms came at a terrible price, one Eloise hadn't learned yet ... and hopefully never would.

Roselyn had never known peasants before. Her birthright kept her aloof, and she'd always regarded peasants as dirty, base, and ignoble. Yet how many of the Saxon royal court had ever shown the honor and bravery of these men in the face of enemies so horrible her mind still railed against the memory? Saxon noblemen carried their honor like a holy chalice, fearful someone might notice how empty it is. In politics and feuds they sent others for fear of getting their own hands dirty. Roselyn had never respected them, especially the late Baron Vandislidge du Harmonn.

Dark memories flooded her:

"How dare you!" Baron du Harmonn bellowed as he strode into the chapel. "I told you to await me in my chambers!"

"A child born out of wedlock shall never inherit God's favor," Roselyn said.

"Bear me a son and I'll make you baroness," the baron promised. "That'll make your father happy, at least."

Roselyn turned back to the altar and prayed vehemently. Nothing was worth his flabby, depraved violations, but she feared to disobey; the memory of her father's lash still stung hot across her back.

"Obey me!" the baron shouted.

Baron du Harmon pulled Roselyn up by her arm and dragged her out of the chapel.

That very night, after the baron had fallen asleep, Roselyn had crawled, wretched and trembling, from his unholy bed. He'd locked the door so she couldn't get out, removed all weapons, and his barred windows denied her death's release.

Then two thieves had picked his lock and freed her; no matter what station they were born to, she'd never look down upon them.

But what now? Roselyn had intended to take her share of the treasure and sail to France with Eloise. Perhaps they'd join the French royal court, where their wealth would spare them from marrying any man.

Around the bend rode two Viking soldiers, heavily armed but unarmored, wearing thick wool tunics and furs. The older Viking wore a bright red half-cloak pinned at the shoulder by a huge, ornate broach of gold and bone. Seeing the company, both riders reined in, and the younger angrily drew his sword.

"Bjornson ...!"

"Put that away, Frothgar!" the older Viking commanded. "We're scouts, and we've found our prey. Our job is to report his position to Svenson. Besides, you're no match for Eric Bjornson."

Frothgar turned angrily to face his companion, but the older Viking's glare subdued him.

"Hello, Eric."

"Good to see you well, Hastwulf. How are your children?"

"Halwulf is here with the camp-boys on his first Viking. The girls are at home with their mother."

"Urd's a beautiful woman."

"Yes, but the whole point of raiding's to escape the wife for the summer."

Both the elder Vikings chuckled. Roselyn said nothing, noting every nuance of their manners and the patterns in their speech; few understood the art of parley as one raised in a house of politics.

"Did Hawkin speak to Svenson?"

"Hawkin, Thorin, Gunthar, all of them; Svenson spent the night counseling with them. He agreed to give you an honorable death, but when he found Bristlen plundered ..."

"Is he angry?"

"Like a wounded snow-bear. Bristlen was a mistake, Eric. Men look away when Svenson approaches. He has to regain their respect, and your head is all that'll buy that."

"Tell him I have his treasure safe with me," Eric said, and he patted the golden horn in his belt. "When he catches me he'll have all he wants."

"He wants his son back!" Frothgar shouted.

"Thorland attacked me while we were drunk," Eric said, bowing his head. "Either of us could've died. He chose the risk, he paid the price."

"We've all paid," Hastwulf said to Frothgar. "Eric was made an outlaw, forced to flee, and we to chase him, all because of one drunken swordfight. Thorland was a fool. If he hadn't been the only prince I'd have welcomed his death. But such talk is vain.

We're warriors, not to be concerned with what might have been. What is your plan, Eric?"

"Valhalla," Eric said, "but I'm no fool; a single man who can keep a whole army occupied will earn great attention from Odin's maids, and that's my sole intent. If Svenson wants me then he'll have to catch me. Surely he's guessed my route, since we traveled here before. Tell him I won't hide or evade him, and ask only one favor in return."

"What favor?"

"Pardon for my companions," Eric said. "True friends they've proven to be in the face of dangers like the old tales."

Hastwulf gazed questioningly at the three dead bodies on the road and the youthful knight, who'd removed his helmet and was listening carefully, still clutching his dead father tightly.

"Not this," Eric said. "We were waylaid by a spawn of Fenris in the forests behind Bristlen, which delayed us for over a day. Perhaps someday you'll hear the tale, but I can't speak lightly while Svenson marches closer. These were but trail-thieves who caught us unaware."

"My eyes say otherwise," Hastwulf said. "I'll tell Svenson of your request. Have you any other words for him?"

"We've said all we can," Eric said. "He knows I'm not to blame for Thorland's death, and if he can kill me in a real battle and keep his crown, then we'll both be content."

"So may it be," Hastwulf said. "Now Frothgar and I must complete our mission. Your delay made Svenson think you'd broken your word; this road has been scouted several times, and other scouts now scour the countryside. He'll be pleased to hear you're closer than he thought, but I don't think your road goes much farther. Bristlen delayed Svenson, but he'll come swiftly now."

"Then we must take leave, Hastwulf. You're a good man. May the eyes of the Valkyrie shine always upon you."

"May your journey to Valhalla be joyous. Die well, Eric Bjornson."

Both men raised their swords in salute to each other, and then Hastwulf turned his horse around.

"Traitor ...!" Frothgar shouted, and suddenly the young Viking spurred his horse towards Eric and swung his deadly blade.

Eric blocked Frothgar's swordblow at an awkward angle, keeping his swordpoint facing his charging opponent. The rash, youthful Frothgar rode right into the point of Eric's blade, which caught him in the throat as his horse collided into Eric's. Unable to scream, awash in his own blood, Frothgar collapsed off of his horse only to gasp his last breaths among the dead on the road.

"Another young fool ...," Hastwulf hissed, and he spurred forward, took the reins of Frothgar's horse, and rode off at a gallop back down the hill toward Svenson Two-Sword.

Roselyn didn't know what shocked her the most: Eric and Hastwulf's casual reaction to their dead kinsman or Eric's request that she and the others be spared from Svenson's wrath. Yet now she understood, at least in part, why Eric was being chased, and the bizarre circumstances that had brought her into this odd company.

Strangely, sitting atop her horse, a bow in hand and facing constant perils with her new, trustworthy companions, Roselyn had never felt safer.

By all reports, Eloise's mother, Elaina, had learned of Norse savagery when they'd captured her. Her husband, Eloise's real father, had died in a hunting accident when Eloise was only a child, and her mother had taken over the barony and managed it well for almost a year. Times were prosperous, the peasants happy, and Bristlen's coffers had increased every day.

Then the royal letter came. The king, not believing a woman could manage a barony, had sold her hand in marriage to a widowed French knight named Vandislidge du Harmonn in exchange for foreign lands. Her mother had been furious; she'd wanted to pass her barony on to Eloise, but Vandislidge du Harmonn had other ideas.

Sir Vandislidge was a fat, demanding brute with little concern for those beneath him, especially the young daughter of the husband he'd replaced. He forced her mother to wed him the day he arrived, and she suffered his bed only to keep her daughter from being killed. Roselyn could still remember the ladies of the court snickering about it; it was the gossip of the season.

All Sir Vandislidge wanted of her was a son to assume his coronet. Elaina never once loved him, and everyone in the castle knew it, but Sir Vandislidge didn't care. He renamed the Saxon barony to du Harmonn, a French name, and raised taxes until everyone in the barony felt as raped as Elaina.

Vandislidge du Harmonn hardly ever noticed Eloise except to order her out of his sight. When her mother had been taken away during the last siege of Castle Bristlen, Eloise's young heart had broken forever.

Fortunately, Eloise barely understood Roselyn's desperation. Both were women of nobility born to a world where men ruled. With her stepfather dead, Eloise was now the sole heir to a baronial coronet, a trinket for the king to sell to the highest bidder.

Eloise had been right; the treasures of Bristlen were rightfully hers, but if she'd tried to claim them all she'd have gotten none. Now they each had a fifth share, with no nobleman knowing of it: *a chance to live as something other than a slave.* That thought drove Roselyn more than any other; no matter what, Roselyn wouldn't let herself become a man's possession again.

Chapter 10

Leadership

ELOISE

No ...!

Eloise squeezed her eyes shut, breathed hard, and clutched at her reins. She wanted a bath, a harsh, steaming bath filled with lye so hot it would sear her filthy skin right off, so hot it would boil his disgusting touch out of her. But she didn't want to be clean again; *clean was pretty ... and terrible things happened to pretty girls.*

No, she couldn't do this. It was over, had never even happened. She'd done nothing to deserve this. Surely the Abbey of Dunstay would have a cell deep enough that no one would ever look at her again.

Absently Eloise rode behind Rafe, who was following Eric. Behind her rode Roselyn, with Karl in the rear. Eloise wished she could talk to someone, keep her mind from wandering into darkness, but Eric was setting a harsh pace, and in many places the road thinned to a mere footpath between tall trees; they were forced to ride in single file.

Why had she ever left Castle Bristlen where she'd been safe from thieves and kidnappers?

Sir Athelred's trap had terrified her. Eloise couldn't believe she'd offered to marry Sir Athelred. She'd wanted to save her friends, but she could've never wed a slime like that robber-knight.

Why should she ...?

Where were they while she was being assaulted ...?

Eloise needed a bath.

"A stream ...!" Eric shouted back at them, reining in. "Stop here; the horses need water."

Eloise rode her horse straight to the stream and dismounted while it drank.

She had to stop these wild, insane thoughts from rampaging through her head. These people had saved her, saved her when she couldn't, because she was weak.

No more!

Never again would Eloise be anyone's victim!

Eloise would be strong like Eric, and if anyone ever touched her again she'd kill them.

They all went upstream of their thirsty horses to drink. The stream was small but swift and clear. Eric pulled Svenson's golden horn out of his belt, dipped it, and then passed it around. Everyone drank their fill and then stretched out upon the heather, their backs to narrow tree trunks while thin branches above them waved in the gentle breeze.

"Rafe, how far to Grusshire?" Eric asked.

"A few more miles, maybe less."

"Svenson will be there by nightfall," Eric said. "He won't rest his men now that he knows of me, and there's been no place since Tiller's big enough to camp his thousands. He'll spend tonight in Grusshire and chase me down tomorrow; I must part ways with you before then."

"No ...!" Roselyn objected.

"We can buy food in Grusshire and have one last meal together," Eric said. "Then you must ride up into the hills. I'll ride on; Svenson will follow me, and you'll be able to escape. My advice is to make for Scotland; Svenson won't march his men more than a few days away from his ships, especially not up into mountains."

"Eric ...," Karl began.

"There must be another way ...," Rafe said.

"I'm a warrior," Eric said. "Our delay ... in the woods ... cost too much. Svenson has a man like Hastwulf on every horse he's captured, and they'll all be coming for my head before dawn. I can't hide, and

I don't want you with me when I'm caught. Remember me ... and live long."

"But ... what of your Valkyrie?" Karl asked. "You wanted to die in a huge battle."

"There's little hope of that now," Eric said. "If I could've drawn Svenson towards a big city like Madrone then the Saxons would raise an army to repel them. I would've gotten my battlefield and Svenson would've had a real foe."

"To fight ...?" Roselyn asked. "Wouldn't he just flee before a Saxon army?"

"Not if he can win," Eric said. "It's risky, but wars are vastly profitable. If Svenson could defeat the local Saxon army in one huge battle, then whole cities would be left undefended; Svenson could sack them at will for weeks before another army could be mobilized and marched here. That wealth of plunder would be a tempting prize. Or, Svenson could entrench his men in every castle, claim half of the Danelaw as his own, and crown himself king of two countries. He'd have to send to Norway for more men before the Saxons raised another army, but it'd be worth the risk.

"But that's unlikely to happen. Thorland's death clouded his judgment. He should've never razed and burned Demril. Saxons would've forgiven him sieging Bristlen; peasants have no love for the nobility, but they don't forget when their own have been murdered."

"Why do peasants matter?" Roselyn asked, and then she quickly corrected herself. "Why do peasants matter to Svenson, I mean; only the nobility has the means to raise armies."

"Armies have greater threats than other armies," Eric said. "Wise kings don't invade foreign places; they liberate the peasants from the tyranny of oppressors. That way, grateful peasants reward their saviors with food and news. Invaders find fields of ripe crops burned before they arrive, wells salted or poisoned, and their every movement reported to their enemies."

"You still could have your battlefield," Rafe said. "Just hide from Svenson's scouts and leave no signs they could follow."

"Valkyrie scorn those who hide," Eric said. "I must show my courage or defeat my own quest. I wouldn't ask any of you to abandon your faith; I can't abandon mine."

"Eric ...?"

"Yes, Eloise?"

"Your friend, Hastwulf? Svenson's scout? He said something delayed them. What was left in Bristlen that could have delayed Svenson?"

"Celebrations," Eric explained. "His men won a noble battle, but doubtlessly many Saxons didn't die alone. Besides the victory for those who lived, there were celebrations for those who earned their ride behind Odin's maids. It's customary to mark their entrance to Valhalla with sweet, raucous revelry."

“Of course!” Roselyn smiled. “If Svenson were delayed again, then we could ride on ahead, and you’d get your battlefield.”

“It took a hundred men inside a castle to slow down Svenson,” Karl said. “We don’t have another castle, and we five are too few to man it.”

Eloise brushed the hair away from her face. *Eric was crazy!* Devout as she was, she’d never die for her faith. Not that she had much to live for; her hated stepfather was dead and still she wasn’t free. Roselyn was right; neither of them could go home, even if they had a home to go to. What would become of her? Was she to become a peasant, spending the rest of her life in hiding, alone?

Memories of the Wolflord sent shudders up Eloise’s spine. *Alone:* the thought shivered her whole being. No one to pull her from doomed castles ... or rescue her from demons in the night. These people were the only friends she had, the only friends she trusted.

Where would she be without them?

Eloise needed strong companions ... because she was weak, too weak to save herself ... even when she needed saving the most.

No! She’d be strong from now on.

No one would ever hurt her again!

But Eloise wasn’t ready yet; she needed her friends. More important, she wanted her friends.

"Eric, you understand ... war ... better than the rest of us," Eloise said. "We don't want to part with you. Isn't there some other way ... we could ... delay Svenson?"

"None you could do," Eric said. "I respect each of you; I consider you friends, but you're Christian Saxons. To delay Svenson's whole army, just so I could get back to my original plan, you'd have to think like Vikings."

"How so?" Karl asked.

"Facing mortal danger is easy," Eric said. "Allowing others to face death isn't. Norsemen accept responsibility for their own words and deeds."

"Norsemen aren't alone in that respect," Rafe said.

"You accept your own responsibility, but you deny that respect to those you trust most. I chose my life's path before most of you were born, and I'm on a blade's edge of fulfilling my greatest triumph. How do you honor me? Do you respect my decisions? Do you wish me success and thank me for my friendship? Do you celebrate my life or praise my deeds?

"No; you treat me like a child, like all Saxons treat each other. Who are you to challenge my choices? Long ago I, too, was young and curious. No more. I saw the world much as you see it today, and I chose the life that suited me best, what truths I believed in, and what thoughts and actions I honor. Now, in the final moments of my life, you'd have me change. Why ...? To make my entire life a lie ...? Would you have me end my life thinking that all of my days were wasted? Or do you seek to spare yourselves the pain of losing a friend?"

Eric bowed his head.

"Forgive me, my friends. You're accustomed to speech like pillows; my tongue has little lace."

"You speak your heart," Roselyn said. "We don't blame you."

"No, but you can't deny your feelings," Eric said, looking up at her. "Warriors don't shade truths that illuminate their faults; you don't believe a warrior's death is any better than any other."

"Can you blame us?" Karl asked. "Death is death!"

"You were a farm boy with a spear eager to run to the battlements of Castle Bristlen and throw your life away," Eric faced Karl. "Why? Are you a fool?

"No: you know that death with honor is a grand triumph, far greater than a long life of dishonor. So say not that death is death: you're proof it isn't so.

"The rest of you are no different. Why follow me into the Wolflord's cave? Why did Eloise offer to marry Sir Athelred?"

Eloise glanced away.

"We're sorry, Eric," Roselyn said. "We've no right to question you."

"Some fathers must send their sons to the shieldwall to fight in a war" Eric said. "They have to trust them to do their part, and rightly so. Their sons are responsible for their own choices, and if a son should break formation, it may be the father's duty to order his own son's execution. It'd be sad, but if the father never trusted his boy, what kind of man would he grow up to be?"

Eric looked at each of them, Eloise the longest.

"Life is a single thread, a rope across the river of death," Eric said. "Each of us lives on our own strand, and we walk that cord every day of our lives. Others can't be blamed if we fall off, nor can they claim credit for our balance. Each man, and woman, is responsible to themselves. If you let another pull you off then you've only yourself to blame."

"That's the essence of responsibility," Rafe said.

"But not the end of responsibility," Eric explained. "If those who end your life are blameless, are you not also blameless for the lives you end? How could any warrior blame himself for the deaths of those he must kill to stay alive? He can't, unless he chooses to never become a warrior, which means he's chaff for warriors to harvest at will. None of you are possums who won't fight when cornered, therefore blame not yourselves for those you slay; they chose to let you kill them."

"Then ... all the deaths you caused at Bristlen doesn't bother you?" Karl asked.

"Svenson wasn't going to waste seven thousand warriors. He was planning to invade either Denmark or Ireland. Many were going to die, no matter what I did. You could say I saved countless lives in Denmark and Ireland when I led Svenson to slaughter Bristlen; the world is too great even for kings to control. I'm alive, I haven't betrayed my honor, and I may still seek my final goal. I'm not to blame for fools who chose to cut the threads they balanced on."

"That is a harsh philosophy," Roselyn said.

"Norway's a harsh land," Eric said. "Snowfalls can bury a man in his own fields or freeze him on his doorstep. Saxons call themselves civilized because they're peaceful, and then they commit barbarisms for wealth and power. The truth is all men and women are the same, save we barbarians; Norsemen don't hide their intentions behind falsehoods of gentility."

A silence fell, broken only by the sounds of splashing water, chirps of birds, and horses tearing up the tall grass with their teeth. Eric drained Svenson's horn and then got up and untied his bag from his saddle. Inside it were the three backpacks Farmer Tiller had given them, and all of their treasure. Eric put Eloise's treasure-roll in one pack and gave it to her, and then did the same with Karl's and Roselyn's. All the rest, including his own share, Eric tied up in his bag and handed to Rafe; Eric kept only Svenson's golden horn.

"Here are your shares," Eric said. "It'll be too dangerous to divide this up in town, and I want you each to have your wealth to remember me by. You're worthy friends; I'll sing praises of you all in Elvidnir, Odin's great hall in Valhalla."

Eloise looked down at the grass. This was Eric's good-bye, the last they'd have time for. She didn't want him to depart but was powerless to stop it.

Like in the cave, she was still weak, still a victim …

"No!" Eloise said suddenly, with a firmness in her voice that surprised even her. "We're not going to lose Eric. I won't be weak again!"

"Princess …," Rafe said.

"Silence!" Eloise ordered, and she jumped to her feet. "Obey me! My father was baron, and now that he's dead, I'm Baroness Eloise, the rightful ruler of this land. As you took orders from the Lord of du Harmonn, now take orders from me! Whatever it takes, we're going to get Eric back to his original plan."

Eloise turned to face Karl. "On your feet, soldier!"

Shocked and uncertain, Karl sat staring up at Eloise, his bewilderment apparent in his confused expression. Eloise glared at him, and then turned to stare at the others.

Roselyn stood up and faced Eloise, at attention, as if she was a guard awaiting orders. Rafe watched Roselyn stand, sighed and shrugged, and then he levered himself to his feet. Silently Rafe stood in formation beside Roselyn.

Karl shook his head, sighed resignedly, and pushed himself to attention.

"Good," Eloise said, facing them. "Now, Eric said we have to think like Vikings. We're going to do that. Eric, what else do we have to do?"

"Are you serious?" Eric asked.

"The Baroness of du Harmonn gives you her word."

Eric stood up, chuckling, but his voice became deep and serious. "Very well. You'll have to do very little; simply agree with everything I say, and don't question me in public, even if you don't like what I'm saying. I'll do the rest. But you can't refer to me as your servant, as you did at the farmhouse."

"From this moment, you are Captain of my Guard," Eloise said.

"That'll do," Eric said. "But you all must agree to this. You can't do something like this halfway. One wrong word ... and the men of Grusshire will kill us."

Even the birds seemed to soften their voices in the silence that followed Eric's challenge. Eloise looked up at the tall trees swaying their branches. For a second, she thought she heard a sudden rush of wind, as if great wings had flapped overhead. Then the moment passed, and still no one objected.

"We'd best get going," Eric said. "We'll need time to prepare. But keep your treasure-bags close by. If things go bad, ride fast and don't look back.

Consider it your paramount order from ... Baroness Eloise's Captain of the Guard."

Quickly they mounted and rode off. Svenson was doubtlessly marching fast toward them, and he wouldn't be stopping for rests.

Eloise smiled brightly, her whole face beaming. She'd stood up for herself and gotten what she wanted. Eric wouldn't die, they'd all stay together, and everything would be all right.

Eloise wasn't afraid, and she did need a bath.

Chapter 11

Grusshire

KARL

They galloped into Grusshire as fast as their tired horses could manage. Small fields, terraced into hillsides, surrounded a handful of rustic farmhouses, built together to form a town. Each field was tightly combed with carefully planted rows, recently plowed, some already showing buds in the early spring. The narrow road led between two fields to a single collection of old wooden stables, houses, and shops crowded together. Little grass or weeds were visible; every foot of tillable soil was plowed and seeded.

They galloped around the closest farmhouse and reined in too late. Eric and Rafe halted their exhausted horses masterfully, but the others rode right into the crowded street. Women screamed and fled as three foaming horses drove into their midst. The frantic riders fought to control their mounts as the frightened townsfolk dashed out of harm's way.

Karl clung tight, embarrassed as he fought to control his horse; *they shouldn't have been riding so fast!* Angrily he wrenched his horse's head aside; his horse suddenly turned and bucked him from his saddle; Karl clung tight to his reins as he was dragged through the street, frantically squirming away from crushing hooves.

His armored weight finally drug his horse to a halt.

Eloise and Roselyn were luckier than he. Brave townsmen ran to protect their families, charged Eloise and Roselyn's steeds, and grabbed at their bridles while trying to avoid the deadly hooves. Their horses were quickly halted; the angry shouts of the crowd and the inexperience of the riders more to blame than any panic of the over-worked horses. Yet the townsfolk were furious.

"Baroness …!" Eric cried frantically. *"Baroness Eloise du Harmonn …!"*

Eric leapt from his horse and pushed through the stunned crowd. People parted, allowing him through, shocked by his Viking appearance but more amazed by his shouts.

"Baroness ...!" Eric said desperately, pushing to her side. "Eloise, are you harmed?"

Karl nervously stood, holding tight to his panting horse's reins. He felt ashamed; real men didn't lose control of their mounts. But no one was looking at him. All eyes were fixed upon the young, blonde Eloise. Their dangerous entrance had arrested all attention, and Eric's anxious cries had distracted the entire town.

He's at it again, Karl thought, wondering where it would lead. Despite their questions, Eric had refused to reveal his plans, assuming, in fact, he wasn't making it up as he went.

"I ... I am fine, Eric," Eloise said, seeming confused by Eric's reaction. "Frightened, but that will pass. Um, ... Thank you, Captain."

"We can't stay here," Eric said. "The main Viking army may have turned back, but the traitors will be here shortly after vespers. We may purchase supplies and rest the horses, but then we must press on."

"The Vikings turned back ...?" asked a townsman.

"They had a falling out, apparently," Eric told them. "A feud, perhaps, or a power struggle. We spied them from a distance, in the lowlands, and we heard the clashes of their swords. The bulk of their army and the royal banner of Svenson Two-Sword turned back towards Demril early this afternoon; I suspect they're returning to their ships. They may hold Bristlen for a while, but that's not our immediate concern. Many traitors still march this way at a great pace; pack up your families and flee, if you'd live. Viking warriors approach, and Saxons can't withstand Vikings."

The crowd erupted, a hundred townsfolk shouting and yammering all at once.

They sounded like geese, Karl smiled, and then he caught himself; that was how Eric saw these people: like geese, the same way he'd seen the people of Demril and Bristlen. Most of those people were dead. What was Eric trying to do? The Viking army hadn't split; seven-thousand Viking soldiers were marching this way.

"Liar ...!" shouted a man from the crowd. "That's the Viking what sailed into Demril before the others, all alone on his big ship."

"Aye," Eric said. "I'm Eric Bjornson, whom Baron du Harmonn sent to Norway with a treaty for Svenson Two-Sword. He'd heard Svenson was planning to invade his barony again, and the baron sent gifts to dissuade him. Svenson accepted the gifts and then betrayed his vows; he signed a treaty, promising peace with all of du Harmonn, and still invaded. Baroness Eloise can vouch that my words are true; she's her father's daughter and sole heir."

All eyes turned to the young baroness. Eloise hesitated for a moment, trying to comprehend Eric's lies.

Karl clenched his reins anxiously; Eloise was facing the same decision he'd struggled with in her father's bedroom. Eloise understood; these people would die if she didn't betray Eric, but Eric would die if she did. Would she choose as Karl did ... and doom more Saxons to die?

"Peace!" Eloise shouted as the crowd began to murmur. "Eric is my loyal and trusted retainer, Captain of my Guard. We ride to seek the aid of Earl Sir Guldwin, who alone can slay these invaders. Then will be the time for revenge! Baron du Harmonn should've never trusted the Viking king, and he's paid for his mistake with his life. I'm now your rightful liege, as my mother was before me, and I'll do all that I can to redress the sufferings of these last few days. But for this moment, heed my Captain, I beg you, for he knows much of the matters of war."

After she spoke, the crowd began to mumble, a hundred whispered opinions, with many distrustful glares at Eric. Yet no one spoke openly against Eloise.

Karl shook his head sadly, studying the fear-filled faces around him. Not all in this crowd were townsfolk of Grusshire; many were refugees from Demril and local farmsteads. But they were going to die, just like their fellows did in Bristlen.

"Well, Captain ...?" asked a dirty blacksmith with coal-black hair and eyes wearing an old, scorched leather apron. "What do you say?"

"I say flee," Eric said. "At least two hundred Viking rebels will be here sometime after dark, and that's twice your number of men."

"We can summon more men," the smith said.

"It doesn't matter how many Saxons you summon!" Eric shouted. "They're Vikings!"

The two older men glared at each other, bristling, barely restrained. Karl swallowed hard; this smith was about Eric's size and age, but his thick arms were rippling with muscles; Karl would've feared to antagonize such a stranger. Yet Eric showed neither fear nor common sense, stirring up racial hatreds with no concern for the consequences.

Eric had better know what he's doing!

Already he'd told enough lies to justify getting them all hanged.

"Do as you like, Saxon," Eric said. "My charge is the little baroness. Her father's last order was for me to get her to safety, and I shall. But, speaking as one who's commanded battlefields, I advise you: flee. Even if you out-numbered the Viking troops, you've little hope of victory, and either way the cost will be great."

"On another day I'd tear out your tongue for such words," the smith growled. "There're Saxons here worth any ten Vikings."

"Then defend your tiny town, if you dare," Eric said. "But you'd better work hard and fast, if you'd prepare for a Viking attack."

"Why?" the smith asked. "What will they do?"

"Gladly I'd tell you, but time is short and I've concerns of my own," Eric said. "We've not eaten since before dawn and we need to purchase supplies for several days ... and tend to our horses."

"You'll have all you need if you help us prepare for the Vikings," the smith promised, and many townsmen chorused their agreement.

Karl shook his head in disbelief. Just like inside Bristlen, with a few well-placed lies, Eric was again in command, giving orders and having his slightest request willingly granted. Karl would've laughed if there'd been anything funny about what they were doing to these helpless fools.

Quickly Eric gave orders to barricade the town at both ends, save for a single gap just large enough to ride a horse through at each end, and then the companions were escorted into a large building where food was provided, while village youths were ordered to care for their horses.

The building was a tanner's shop. It reeked of harsh fumes from vats of quicklime and tar, yet it had huge tables, the biggest of which was being cleared by the tanner's apprentices. Chairs were brought for everyone and plates of food set before them. It was common fare, nothing like they'd enjoyed from Sarah

Tiller's kitchen, but filling; a hunk of white cheese beside a thick slice of brown bread large enough to cover most of their plate. A woman came out with a large ladle, and behind her came an apprentice wearing quilted mitts and carrying a big, steaming bowl. She ladled generous amounts of soup, thick with rabbit, chicken, and many vegetables, atop the wide slice of bread. Instantly the fresh bread soaked up the hearty broth and held the rest of the soup like a bowl. Farm fare, Karl smiled, and he thanked her as she served him, yet the farmwife turned her face away and refused to look at him directly. At first Karl was surprised, but then he chided himself; she'd done exactly as his own mother would've, never looking into the eyes of her husband's guests. She'd accepted her servant's status, as his mother had, as most women did. Karl had been traveling with Roselyn and Eloise so long that a normal woman's meekness surprised him.

As they ate, the smith and several other leading townsmen described their resources, the surrounding terrain, and plied Eric with questions. There was an abandoned silver mine nearby and several horse-trails leading up into the hills, but otherwise Grusshire was a narrow stretch of hill-top farmland with a town crowded into it.

"Forget the mine," Eric said. "Unless it drills clean through the mountain, it's a deathtrap. If you have valuables you want to keep safe, then drop them in the mine and seal its entrance. The raiders won't dig it out unless they know something's in there. Send your women and children to the hills at once with all of your horses and plenty of food; they should be safe there until the raiders move on.

"If the Vikings are organized they'll have scouts riding ahead. Shoot them, if you can, before they can ride back. But always assume that word of your barricades have reached your enemy; good leaders never plan anything around a secret."

The townsmen nodded, enrapt by Eric's every word.

"It'll be dark before their main force reaches Grusshire; use their blindness as a weapon. By barricading entrances at both ends, and boarding over all back-facing doors and windows, you'll turn your town into a large wooden fort. The raiders may try to set fires, but that's unlikely; they want to sleep in your town, not burn it, but have water barrels and buckets everywhere. They'll probably just rush your barricade and try to overwhelm your main defenses; they'll be tired from marching all day and in a hurry to finish the battle. Their urgency is your greatest hope.

"While pressed up against your barricade, they'll be hemmed in tight, shoulder to shoulder. Into that press you can toss large flaming bottles of oil, and kill or drive off many without even fighting. But the rest will have to be fought, so the more you draw into attacking early, the better."

"How can we do that?" asked the smith.

"Make them want to kill you," Eric smiled. "The best way to enrage them is to make the first kill. Have every bow ready to fire as soon as they come into range; you can't see arrows against a starry sky. Spears are useful, but every spear will be thrown back. A small catapult would be very helpful; you can build a crude one in only a few hours.

"Strike hard, in one great volley, the instant they come into range, before they're even aware they're being attacked. Then they'll have to flee, with nowhere to go, or charge your barricade. I suspect they'll draw back just long enough to regroup, and then charge. In that press, you should be able to kill or wound a third of their force, maybe half."

"That'd be a great help," the smith admitted reluctantly.

Karl suspected the smith's dislike of Eric was so great he might've wished the Viking's advice would be worthless. Grimacing, Karl stared down at his soup and said nothing. Eric's plan might succeed if only two hundred Vikings were marching up the hills toward Grusshire, but thousands marched, and since it would be dark, these brave men would be dead before they even realized their true odds.

"You'll need long spears, but not for throwing," Eric said to the smith. "When the Vikings charge, they'll try to knock down your barricade, climb over it, or punch a hole through it. Your men'll have to hold them back as long as they can. Your sons can light and fling the bottles of oil."

The smith frowned. "My son left years ago ... to join the priesthood."

"Would that he were here," another townsman said. "Still, our sons will do what they can. Now, what of this catapult? Can you show us how to build it?"

"I promised Baron Vandislidge du Harmonn I'd protect his daughter," Eric said. "This fight isn't mine, and I intend to depart with Eloise before it begins. I'll help you as much as I can until then."

"But who'll teach us to fight Vikings?" another townsperson asked. "My sons are farmers, not soldiers."

"Karl can teach," Eric said. "Don't be fooled by his youth; I've seen him battle foes with skills few warriors ever attain."

Karl almost choked on a mouthful of cheese. *Teach farmers to fight while seven thousand Vikings march towards their puny village?*

"What can we do?" Eloise asked.

"They'll need weapons, Baroness," Eric said. "Anything that can be used to hurt someone must be gathered and stacked near each barricade; all the bottles you can find, and every drop of oil or grease. Oh, and long strips of cloth."

"We'll find them," Eloise promised.

"Rafe, get wagons ready for those who won't be staying behind," Eric said. "All of their horses must be hitched to wagons outside of the back barricade and made ready to depart with their women, babes, and elderly."

Grimly Rafe glanced at Karl with the deepest frown Karl'd ever seen; Rafe had realized what Eric was doing to these people, but he, also, said nothing. *We'd agreed to follow Eric,* Karl thought, *to think like Vikings, but we never asked what that meant.* Eloise and Roselyn were nobility, castle-folk; perhaps the death of hundreds of peasants didn't bother them, but to Rafe and Karl, this was murder.

Yet, what could they do without getting themselves killed? Eric was using this village to buy their escape.

Were their few lives worth the lives of all these people?

Karl had asked himself that question in the baron's bedroom.

Was this situation any different?

After thanking their hosts for the meal, each departed to their own tasks. Eric and the smith marched into a carpenter's workshop down the street and Rafe headed to their stable. Eloise and Roselyn gathered up all the knives at the table and then started collecting tools and other things to complete their makeshift armory. The farmer who'd asked about fighting Vikings eagerly escorted Karl back up the street.

Outside, chaos was rampant. The sun slowly sank toward the treetops as the townspeople ran in every direction. Hammers pounded, driving in nails. Women packed valuables onto already-laden wagons. Older boys carried large, heavy chests, benches, and tables to strengthen the barricade. The village men stacked and lashed it together. Already it was an impressive barricade; six feet tall and thick, spanning the entire road, with only a narrow gap a single horse could squeeze through. More was being hauled atop it as Karl watched. But the high stone walls of Castle Bristlen had failed to thwart these Vikings; this junk pile wouldn't deter them at all.

"There's another group at the east end building the barricade there," the farmer said to Karl. "It's not going to be as big as this one, but it'll hold out if they try to flank us. Do you think this'll keep the Vikings out?"

"No," Karl said.

"No ...?" the shocked farmer asked.

Karl looked at the farmer with pity. He was tall and thin, worn, but hard-muscled from years of tilling fields. He looked like so many men from Karl's home village that Karl felt overwhelmed with guilt. Fear hid behind this farmer's eyes, mixed with doubt and suspicion; farmers were notoriously distrustful of strangers. If Karl told them the truth then he'd be killed before he could warn the others.

"The purpose of the barricade isn't to keep Vikings out," Karl said. "It's to slow them down. If the Vikings charged in here right now then the odds would be against you two-to-one. If they come in slowly, through the doorway and climbing overtop, a dozen at a time, your odds become five-to-one in your favor. Add to that the Vikings you hope to take down with arrows, spears, flaming oil, and this catapult, and you might inflict enough damage to cut their number in half. With that many losses, the Vikings'll break and run. Then they'll be too few to threaten Grusshire; that's what the barricade's for."

The farmer smiled and insisted on shaking Karl's hand. Karl felt relieved; his words had sounded plausible although he knew they were lies. Then the farmer called out to the village youths.

"Boys, come here ... and bring your weapons!" the farmer shouted. "Karl's a soldier from Castle Bristlen, and he's going to teach us to fight."

A bunch of children ran forward, excited village-youths too small to lift a sword. A chorus of laughs and snickers came from the men constructing the barricade; Karl grimaced, feeling foolish as the boys gathered around him, smiling like mama was baking cookies. But the farmer chased the children away and called over half a dozen older boys. The older boys came reluctantly, shuffling their feet in the dirt road, and looked askance at Karl in his shiny mail coat. Karl was only a few years older than them, and they looked hesitant to regard him as superior in any way.

Actually, Karl had nothing to teach them. Ferny Creek had mostly taught him that only fools run willingly into combat, and his nine days of guarding Castle Bristlen had only showed Karl the boredom of walking a post under a hot sun. He'd grown up sword-fighting with his brothers, using carefully-selected hardwood sticks his mother threw in the fireplace whenever they forgot to hide them. Doubtless these boys were no different. What did he have to teach them?

'Make them want to kill you!'

Weighted by his heavy mail, Karl walked up to the tallest boy in the group and suddenly shoved him hard. The surprised boy flew backwards, stumbling five feet before he tumbled heels over head onto his butt. The other boys jumped back, not wanting to be next.

"What's the matter?" Karl shouted at the boys. "Do you think Vikings are going to kill you politely? Are they going to come up and ask if you're ready to fight before they chop off your heads?"

The boys' expressions ranged between fear, anger, and embarrassment, but the approving nods of the men building the barricade told Karl he was doing well.

An hour later the sun set behind the hills. One of the heavier boys stood atop the barricade with Karl's shield and silver-plated helmet, and four boys with long, blunt poles struggled to push him off. Before the Vikings arrived they'd split the blunt ends of the poles and tie on butcher's knives, making them into crude spears. The rest of the boys were practicing with pitchforks, scythes, and the few real spears and swords they had. Many of the younger townsmen had joined them, and every older boy in the village was drilling or watching. Karl's success as a fighting-trainer surprised him more than anyone; he'd assumed he knew little of fighting Vikings, since most of his experience had been trying to escape them. Yet even the oldest townsmen now showed him respect.

Roselyn and Eloise came by about every twenty minutes carrying armloads of farm tools, bottles of oil and grease, and jugs of homemade whisky as flammable as Greek fire. One boy Karl had been instructing stopped to gape at the women as they walked past; Karl bloodied the youth's nose for allowing himself to be distracted during a fight. Yet both women always smiled and waved at Karl as they passed by, and he bowed deeply to them as if at a royal ball.

The last call came for the wagons, and Karl's training session quickly ended. Fathers sent sons to kiss their mothers goodbye and the last of the small children were rounded up. The men also went to say goodbye to their wives, but most stopped to shake Karl's hand and thank him.

Eloise and Roselyn appeared carrying dozens of long strips of cloth.

"Eric's almost finished, and Rafe says our horses are almost ready to ride again," Eloise said. "How did your class fare?"

"Doesn't this bother you?" Karl whispered after glancing about to make certain they weren't overheard. "These men are going to be dead by morning ... and we're responsible!"

Roselyn bowed her head. Eloise stared back at Karl; an expression of subdued horror masked her face. *They knew,* Karl realized.

"Should we tell these people ... and let them kill us?" Roselyn whispered. "Is that what you want?"

"We could tell them from our horses as we ride off," Karl said.

"Then Eric dies tomorrow," Eloise argued. "He'll stand on the road and wait for Svenson's whole army to catch him."

"Eric wants to die," Karl said.

"Then we must keep him alive long enough to change that," Eloise said.

"Does Eric mean that much to you?" Karl asked.

"You all do," Roselyn said. "Karl, why are you asking us? We're only women: do our opinions matter that much?"

Karl hesitated. Roselyn was right; he didn't need their permission. Any of them could've revealed the truth to these townspeople. He'd been alone with them all afternoon and could've spoken a hundred times.

"Your opinions matter," Karl sighed.

"That's why Eric matters," Roselyn said. "And he's not the only one."

Her hand rose so slowly Karl resisted the urge to draw away. Gently Roselyn cupped Karl's chin, playfully brushing his thin wisps of beard, and then she leaned close. Karl froze in horror, but Roselyn's warm lips came at him ... and melted him into an eternal paradise. She kissed him slowly, tenderly, the soft kiss of a passionate lover. Karl barely reciprocated, torn between his burning desire for Roselyn and his fear of their differences; her true station was a mystery but Roselyn was obviously nobility, while he was little more than a serf, a peasant runaway with no home or family. Yet Karl's greatest fear was that he'd wake up to find Roselyn's delicious kiss was only a tantalizing dream.

Roselyn drew away suddenly and blushed self-consciously, as if their kiss had surprised her as much as it had surprised Karl. Roselyn quickly walked away, leaving Karl speechless, and he started to follow, but a pair of youthful hands seized the neck-edge of his mail coat. On the tips of her toes, Eloise pulled Karl's face down and kissed him. Hers was a forceful kiss, more urgent and demanding than Roselyn's, but honest and sincere. Karl kissed her back, more than he had with Roselyn, but twice as confused. Eloise smiled as she drew back, and then she winked at Karl and ran after Roselyn.

Karl stood like a scarecrow in the wind, powerlessly buffeted by feelings he'd never imagined, his mind as uncomprehending as a face-painted bag of straw. He watched Eloise catch up with Roselyn and vanish into some building halfway across town, and still Karl stood unmoving; not since Eric had cold-cocked him in Bristlen had Karl felt this stunned.

"Vikings!" cried a young boy from the top of a building. *"Vikings ...!"*

Karl ran to the barricade and dashed through it. Outside, on the road from Farmer Tiller's, were two riders too distant to make out clearly, but riding fast toward Grusshire.

Karl shouted for archers. Most of the men were watching the carts drive off with their families, and the few men that had heard the warning paled with fright. But one older boy echoed his cry and ran off down the street.

Karl cursed himself. He'd known scouts would eventually arrive and should've posted archers on the rooftops. He glanced at the narrow porch of the nearest house to find the girl's armory, a huge array of tools and weapons, including several strung bows and quivers of arrows. Karl snatched up the largest bow and a quiver and quickly scrambled onto the top of the barricade. The Viking scouts were more than halfway toward the town. Shouts came from behind him, and men with bows raced to join him.

Karl nocked an arrow; he was no archer but he'd shot at crows and squirrels his father's small bow, and scouts were bigger targets. He raised the bow, aimed, and pulled on its string.

Nothing happened. The bowstring resisted Karl with an unexpected tautness; Karl pulled harder, yet only slightly managed to bend the bow. Finally he pulled with all his strength, trying to sight down the shaft of the arrow, but his arms trembled with the strain of holding the bow drawn, and he couldn't aim while his targets rapidly approached. Frustrated, Karl released, the bowstring snapped forward, and his arrow flew ten yards west of the road and thudded into the side of a small wooden barn.

Karl paled, mortified, grateful that only the boy on the roof and the scouts saw his terrible bowmanship. Here he was, teaching villagers to fight, and then unable to use a weapon when it mattered.

Karl's poor marksmanship didn't amuse the Vikings; both scouts reined in short. One raised an open palm to parley just as men of Grusshire scrambled up to join Karl on the barricade or ran out to stand before it.

"Shoot them!" Karl shouted.

"They want to talk ...," an archer argued.

"Shoot ...!"

Bows twanged and arrows flew far more accurately than Karl's failed attempt. Instantly the scouts turned and spurred their horses, but not before an arrow struck one scout in the shoulder. They rode away, but the wounded Viking didn't get far; an arrow pierced his horse's flank and it threw its rider. The other Viking turned back to help his brethren, but the archers of Grusshire knew their business. A dozen arrows flew at the prone Viking figure. He rose to run, then collapsed when half of their arrows hit their mark and sent him to his Valkyrie.

More arrows were loosed. The surviving scout fled, but he had several feathered shafts sticking out from his back before he rode out of range, behind trees and out of sight.

A cheer arose but most of the archers frowned. The escaping scout would warn the Vikings that Grusshire was fortified against them. They'd arrive expecting a fight.

Karl was impressed by the skill of the archers; they'd inflict serious damage before they were slaughtered. The boy on the roof wouldn't live to tell of Karl's pitiful bowmanship.

Suddenly shouts arose. A large group of men carried a huge contraption out of a barn-shaped workshop. Eric helped them carry it, and several men followed pushing wheelbarrows full of rocks. Karl smiled; their catapult was built.

They were almost out of Grusshire.

They set the catapult down just five paces inside the barricade. It was a monstrous machine, made of finished beams and rough tree trunks, each thicker than Karl's arms, nailed and lashed tightly together. Two wide 'A' frames were connected by many stout braces, the thickest of which was stretched across the very top and supported the long throwing-arm. Affixed to the end of the throwing-arm was a small wheelbarrow. Its counter balance was a large, heavy wooden chest; when the counterbalance fell, then the rocks in the small wheelbarrow would be flung far over the barricade.

Eric took a long time positioning the catapult so it aimed straight towards the road, and then they braced the chest on some wooden blocks and filled it with the largest rocks from the wheelbarrows. When the six strongest men in Grusshire could barely lift it, they closed its lid and wrapped long ropes around it many times.

"How many do you think this'll kill?" the smith asked.

"Ten or twenty," Eric replied. "Then they'll spread out and be harder to hit. But it'll frighten; death falling unseen: that'll make them come slower."

They loaded the small wheelbarrow with some rocks, a few arrows, several knives with long strips of cloth tied to the ends of their handles, and one corked bottle of oil with a greasy rag sticking out of its top.

They lit the greasy rag and, at Eric's command, they pulled hard on the rope tied to its brace.

The chest fell like the rocks it contained. It crashed to the ground with a boom like a thunderclap, making everyone jump. The long arm flew forward, heaving the heavy contents of the wheelbarrow high. Long seconds passed, and then they heard the distant rocks crash down. Right beside the road a sudden fire burst up; the flaming bottle of oil showed where the first Vikings would die.

The men of Grusshire cheered, and even the surly smith seemed satisfied. They all thanked Eric many times.

"Take some wood out there in a barrow," Eric said. "Bring back all of the rocks and weapons, but stoke up that fire and keep it burning; that way you'll see when your foes are in range."

Karl spied Roselyn and Eloise walking toward him from the back of the crowd. So much was going on he'd forgotten about their kisses. *What did their kisses mean?*

"Soldier, it's time to leave," Roselyn said impatiently, formally. "Tell Captain Eric that Baroness Eloise wishes to depart."

Karl's eyes flew open; *had his kisses offended them?* Then he noticed several men of Grusshire approaching them; Roselyn wasn't angry with him, just keeping up the charade.

"Yes, Mi'Lady," Karl bowed deeply, and then he ran off to get Eric.

"It's great!" one of the townspeople told the crowd. "The knives with the streamers were stuck blade-first into the ground, just like arrows."

"We first used that trick in Normandy," Eric boasted. "We were trapped in a tall tower, out of arrows, and Normans were hammering our door with a battering ram, holding kite-shields over their heads. First we threw all of the furniture down on them, and let me tell you, a wardrobe falling forty feet ..."

"Captain Eric!" Karl interrupted. "Baroness Eloise wishes to depart."

"Ah, duty calls," Eric laughed. "Forgive me, my friends. Remind me of this tale when I return and I'll finish it then."

"Farewell, Viking," the smith said. "We won't forget what you've done here."

Many thanked Eric and Karl, and both had to shake a dozen hands before they could walk away. Boys ran up to Karl, thanked him, and returned his helmet and shield, and Eric gave a last few orders: light bright fires and torches inside the barricades, post sentries on the roof, and see that every man without some kind of shield stays behind cover when arrows start to fly. Eric also warned that a line of men would try to rush through the opening in a sudden stream. The men of Grusshire promised they'd be ready, nodding and smiling all the time. When they finally walked away, Eric gleefully clapped Karl across the back.

Karl scowled.

"Not yet," Eric whispered through his smiling teeth. "They could still kill us; Roselyn and Eloise, too."

Karl wasn't amused; Eric was toying with him, playing him for a fool, just like he'd done in Bristlen. Eric had named the girls just to force Karl to continue with the charade. Karl recalled all the lies the wily old Viking had told he'd personally witnessed; Karl couldn't believe he'd seen Eric for the first time only a few days before. Eric was a likable old man but Karl was starting to dislike him intensely.

Rafe's anger radiated. When they met outside the stable, Rafe said nothing, just glared, and Roselyn and Eloise stayed close to him, carefully keeping Eric out of Rafe's reach. Their horses were saddled and ready, appearing rested although they'd been exhausted only a few hours before; Rafe was a master of his craft. Each person took their horse's reins and walked in silence toward the smaller barricade at the east end of Grusshire.

As they led their horses through the opening and mounted outside the barricade, the older men and younger boys stationed there cheered them. Eric, Roselyn, and Eloise smiled and waved back. No one seemed to notice Karl and Rafe's grim, clenched jaws.

Outside of the barricade, away from the firelight, it was full night. Stars peeked dimly through low, scattered clouds. A cool breeze was blowing, animating the swaying trees against the night's sky. The companions rode off down the wide dirt trail in single file. Not one of them looked back to see Grusshire in its final hour.

Chapter 12

Wrath

RAFE

I should just ride away, Rafe thought as he rode under the swaying elm branches which filtered the starlight into a pale, barely-visible glow. *I should thank them for their company and depart. I've no business riding with these people any longer.*

Rafe stared at his horse's ears and brooded. Eric was a Viking, a slayer of Saxons. Any debt Rafe owed to Eric for his share of treasure had long since been paid. Karl was a soldier, half his age, and they had nothing in common save that they'd both worked at Bristlen. Besides, Karl obviously wanted to be alone with the girls, who also had little use for Rafe. Eloise was royalty and Roselyn was of the noble estate, at least; neither of them understood or valued the life of a commoner.

Rafe was being a fool; they needed his skills. They were keeping him around for no other reason. They'd never have gotten out of Castle Bristlen without him, and their horses wouldn't have been ready to ride out of Grusshire without careful, experienced tending. They needed him.

What did he need them for?

Rafe shrugged his shoulders. With every sway of his horse, soft clinks of gold and silver jingled. He was rich; his retirement would be swathed in luxuries with servants and women aplenty. The best foods and wines could be his, and all Rafe had to do was say good-bye and ride away.

If the Vikings caught them, they'd take Rafe's treasure and kill him, which would be far better than surviving into old age penniless.

Yes, it was time for Rafe to leave the company and begin his new life.

But ... *life with who ...?*

Bristlen was gone, and even so, he could never retire there; someone might recognize individual pieces of his treasure and wonder how Rafe had acquired the stolen wealth. His few friends had lived in Castle Bristlen; they were doubtlessly as dead as his parents and sister.

Besides, what did Rafe need with servants? What would he do with a big house save wander its empty rooms, lost and bored? Riding with Karl, Roselyn, and Eloise, facing dangers with a pitchfork in his hand, Rafe felt young again, alive, and that treasure was greater than wealth.

But poor Grusshire! Guilt stabbed Rafe like a hundred knives. *He should've told them the truth!* They would've hanged Eric, but the rest of them might've escaped. Yet Rafe had kept his mouth shut and protected himself and his treasure at the cost of two hundred Saxon lives.

It was the most unchristian act of his life.

Eric was to blame, Rafe thought blackly. Rafe wanted to glare at the murderous Viking but he didn't; resolute in his anger, victimized and sanctimonious, Rafe didn't want to break his self-righteous mood with immature posturings, especially since he didn't think Eric would see his hateful glare in the starlight.

An hour before dawn, as the starry sky was just lightening, they rode down the last steep slopes. The waning moon had risen around midnight, no longer full but still very bright, illuminating the world with a pale blue sheen. Their road was even, wide enough for three to ride abreast, yet they rode single file, unspeaking.

Rafe led farther ahead than usual. Eloise trailed close behind, watching him like a hawk. She usually rode next to Roselyn; Rafe suspected the women had separated just to keep watch on them. Karl rode between Eloise and Roselyn, and Eric rode last; *as far from me as possible,* Rafe frowned.

Suddenly their downhill path leveled out and the wooded hills gave way to cultivated fields. They'd crossed the foothills and were again facing vast, rolling expanses of farmland dotted with rustic houses, silos, and barns. No sounds could be heard; even the cocks hadn't crowed. Rafe began looking for a place to take a break, for their horses were ready to collapse.

Soon Rafe noticed the rotting remains of a crude wooden fence peeking through the tall weeds growing alongside the road. A small trail led to the ruin of an old farmhouse which looked deserted but had a chicken sitting atop a coop in front of the house. Rafe hesitated, and then he turned his tired horse off the road and rode down the narrow trail.

Questioningly Eloise paused, and then she turned her horse to follow Rafe. Karl and the others stopped on the road, curious, but didn't follow.

Rafe dismounted in front of the rustic house, noticing the poorly patched shingles and rag-plugged holes in the walls. He walked up to the door and knocked.

"What do you want?" a voice finally demanded from the inside.

"Vikings have taken Bristlen and Grusshire," Rafe said loudly. "They're coming this way. You have to leave."

"How do I know you don't mean to rob us?"

Rafe sighed; he didn't have any proof or time to argue. Anybody who wanted to rob old people in a shack were fools; they had nothing worth stealing, and if they had, these crumbling walls couldn't keep out a horsefly. Rafe set his pitchfork to rest against the wall, grabbed their aged door by its loose handle and broken top hinge, and pulled. Their door broke into two separate halves, the shattered pieces crumbling. Pale in the moonlight, a shocked old man, dressed only in his nightshift, gasped in horror. Rafe gently set the pieces aside and leaned on the useless brace separating them.

"I don't rob my fellow Saxons," Rafe said calmly. "Vikings may be here in an hour, or a day, but they'll come. Take your chickens and a few blankets and hide in the woods until they pass."

"We will," the old man promised.

"Good," Rafe said. "Now, our horses are tired and thirsty ..."

"There's a small well out back, but it runs dry quick. Just up the way, by the crossroads, is a clear running stream; your horses can drink their fill."

"Thanks," Rafe said, and he picked up his pitchfork and walked back to his horse.

Eloise looked down at Rafe from her horse, her face in shadow, the moonlight making a halo of her golden hair.

"You're a good man, Rafe," Eloise said.

"I didn't prove it last night."

"None of us did," Eloise said.

"Those were Saxons, our own people ...," Rafe said, leaning against his horse. "We betrayed them ... our faith ... ourselves."

"We made a promise," Eloise said. "It was a mistake but it saved Eric's life."

"The life of one Viking ...?" Rafe asked. "Is that what we sacrificed a whole Saxon town for ...?"

Eloise's face reddened and she looked away.

"We didn't know what Eric was planning. We'd never have promised to follow him if we'd known, and once things started, it was too late. But that wasn't why Roselyn and I continued the charade; I regret what we did, but not why we did it. We did it for us, for Eric. We'd do it again ... for you."

"I'll never do that again, not even to spare our lives," Rafe said.

"The men of Grusshire chose to stay and fight," Eloise said.

"Because we lied to them."

"They only listened because I'm their baroness. But I was Farmer Tiller's baroness as well; would Farmer Tiller have believed our tale, even for an instant?"

"Probably not," Rafe admitted.

"Eric doesn't understand us anymore than we understand him," Eloise said. "We'll never again let Eric take charge. You concern me most, Rafe. What do you want us to do? Name it ... and we'll do it."

Rafe cocked an eye at Eloise, frowning.

"Are you trying to buy my loyalty, Baroness?"

"If I have to purchase it, I will," Eloise said. "Name your price."

"My price is decency," Rafe said. "My price is honesty and honor, not sacrificing innocents for our own petty purposes. We should be warning our people that Vikings are coming, not leaving them to die."

"I agree," Eloise said, nodding toward the crumbling farmhouse. "We'll warn everyone, every farm and hamlet, from now on. I give you my word."

"Then what ...?" Rafe asked. "What are you planning for next week? Next month? Where do you expect this to lead?"

"I don't know," Eloise said. "I'd hoped I could go back to Bristlen and rule as my mother did, but Roselyn advises me not to try. The king sold my mother to a foreign knight; I'd rule only briefly, and then I'd become a slave to a husband I didn't love, like I became the property of a stepfather who didn't love me.

"Roselyn wants us to buy passage to France or Italy. She hopes Eric'll give up his deathquest and we can buy a villa near Rome or Florence. We'd be a family."

"You're royal," Rafe said slowly, softening his voice. "We're peasants."

"Legally, a woman is property, no matter what class her family is," Eloise said. "Would you seek to be a slave, even in a palace? All Roselyn and I want is freedom, something we'll never have in England."

"You can hire someone to tend your horses."

Suddenly Eloise laughed, breaking the pre-dawn quiet with melodious peals of merriment.

"Is that what you think?" Eloise laughed. "Silly old fool! I don't want you to tend my horses! I want the man who saves my life every day. I want the man who slew the Wolflord and led me out of Bristlen before it burned. I want the man I've learned to trust and respect more than I've ever respected anyone. I want you, Rafe, to be there when I'm happy and hold me when I'm scared. I want the man I know is honest, decent, and more like a father than ...!"

Eloise stopped abruptly, ashamed or afraid that she'd said too much. She sniffed back tears.

Rafe held up his hand and Eloise seized it, pressed it to her cheek, and he felt her trembles.

Rafe bowed his head, moisture welling in his own eyes. He hadn't thought about how Eloise perceived this journey. Rafe had been on many campaigns, riding with the baggage trains, caring for the steeds of noblemen; always on the outskirts of the great events, a spectator, never a participant. Eloise had never seen the world outside of du Harmonn; every place was new and frightening to her, every stranger an unknown threat. Since he'd slain the Wolflord, Rafe had begun to think of himself as brave, but his moment of daring was nothing compared to the courage of this small, helpless child.

"We should keep going," Rafe said.

"Together," Eloise smiled.

Half grinning, Rafe mounted and turned his horse around, facing back towards the road. Eloise waited for him. As he edged his horse past her on the narrow trail, Eloise leaned over and kissed him, not on the cheek but a full, passionate kiss.

Rafe startled; he was no longer young but he wasn't so old he couldn't recall the look she gave him in other women's eyes. Yet he'd seen too much to endure that look from a child her age; Eloise had said she looked at him like a father, and Rafe was more than happy to fulfill that role. Rafe gave Eloise a knowing, fatherly smile, and rode past her without a word.

As Rafe rode towards the others, he masked his face with an angry frown, but their questioning looks almost made him smile. He ignored them, heedless of their obvious confusion, and steered right past them, onward down the road; his actions were Christian and shouldn't need explanations.

Besides, he deserved a little blind trust, and if need be, he'd insist he got it.

An hour later, Rafe dismounted in front of a wide stream which flowed swiftly under a wooden bridge. Dawn had bloomed, and frequent cockcrows came from all around. They'd passed two more farmhouses on the way, both larger and in better condition than the first, and Rafe had ridden up to each, shouting his warnings from the top of his horse. The sturdy farmers at both houses were already awake, being more like Farmer Tiller than the retired residents of the first crumbling ruin. The second farmhouse sent a farmhand on a fresh horse ahead to spread the news faster than the company's tired steeds could go, and Rafe was satisfied that the disaster of Grusshire wouldn't be repeated.

While the horses were drinking, Karl gently clapped Rafe across the back and smiled before walking upstream to get a drink. Roselyn, who was falling asleep, gave Rafe a quick hug, then sat down and yawned. Rafe watched the horses, knowing they'd drink too much if he let them, and that they needed rest as much as he did. None of them had gotten a full night's sleep since Farmer Tiller's; soon they'd have to find some place to rest.

The very next farmhouse they came to welcomed them gladly. The riding farmhand had told them of the strange company warning folks about the approaching Viking army, and they all waved and smiled as they busily packed their belongings. Rafe explained their situation to the head of the household, a crusty old woman who seemed to have nothing to do but shout orders, and she consented to let them rest in their barn.

The barn stank, but it was dry, well-tended, and full of hay. They stripped their saddles and blankets from the horses and tied their mounts just outside the barn where they could see them. Then they spread out the hay and laid their other blankets atop it and used their saddles as pillows, keeping as close to their treasure rolls as possible. Eric insisted they set a guard, but none had slept in more than a day. Despite his arguments, Eric fell asleep with the rest of them.

Rafe's last memory, before he faded to sleep, was the roar of Eric's snore. Rafe fell asleep thinking how foolish he was for staying with the company, and wondered if he'd ever feel at home in it.

Chapter 13

The Trap

ERIC

A sudden, stark, rapid pounding awoke them. Eric jolted awake, snarled loudly and brandished his naked dagger in a suddenly-raised hand as he fought to clear the sleep from his eyes. Sleeping with a drawn dagger was a trick Svenson's father had taught Eric and Svenson when they were children, which Eric had never needed, but had saved Svenson's life twice. Eric still used that trick whenever he slept in the open; a well-practiced snarl made attackers think their prey had been only pretending to sleep, and having the blade already tight in your grip saved precious seconds at a moment that could be your last.

The sudden screams of Roselyn and Eloise awakening beside him startled Eric as his vision coalesced on the tall figure standing beside the barn door. Seconds later, Karl's sword scraped from its scabbard; too late ... had there been any real need. The figure at the door laughed and banged his many large rings on the sturdy wooden doorframe.

"You're getting old, Eric," Hastwulf said. "No one ever caught you unaware before."

"Hast!" Eric gasped, surprised. "You could've killed me!"

"Svenson sent me to find you, not kill you."

Eric glared at his distant kinsman, disbelieving his excuse; few Vikings would pass up such an opportunity.

"I never liked Thorland," Hastwulf grinned.

"I wish more of Svenson's men felt that way," Eric smiled. "You're a good friend."

"You're the generous one, Eric," Hastwulf said. "Those farmers well-earned their paradise."

"How well ...?"

"Over a hundred dead and twice that wounded," Hastwulf smiled. "Svenson thought there were Saxon knights defending that village. You taught them to fight us, didn't you?"

Grusshire had cost Svenson three hundred warriors; better than Eric had hoped. Eric had underestimated the fighting worth of the men of Grusshire; another mistake, one in his favor, but Eric couldn't afford mistakes. His game was nearing its last toss of the dice and one mistake could cost him his eternity in Valhalla.

"The men of Grusshire were strong and valiant," Eric said. "It was a privilege to know them."

"They died as true warriors, even the youths," Hastwulf said. "You should be proud, Eric; they'll honor you in Valhalla."

"They were Christians," Eric said, glancing at his startled companions.

"Have you become a churchman to worry over such things?" Hastwulf scoffed. "They chose their final paths boldly and deserve to be honored, no matter who they prayed to."

"My companions are also Christians," Eric said warningly. "My deeds have disturbed them."

"It's dangerous for different faiths to travel together."

"They've proven their friendship and earned my trust."

"They must be worthy indeed for you to trust them," Hastwulf said. "Yet they've no need to grieve for the valiants of Grusshire; few Saxons die so well. For myself, I believe the Valkyrie proudly ferried them over the Rainbow Bridge. They felled many great names that'll earn them renown."

"Who?"

"Thorin Stormgard was their chief credit," Hastwulf said. "He led a host of elders on the first rush through the wall, and we found him in the place of honor, at the very bottom of a pile of dead, a red sword beneath him."

"Ravens of Odin!" Eric shouted. *"Praised be this day! Thorin Einherjar!"*

Suddenly Eric jumped up and, to everyone's surprise, Eric danced a little jig while cheering joyously. "Drink! I must drink to Thorin's triumph!"

"Triumph ...?" Eloise asked.

Suddenly Eric noticed his companions staring at him as if he'd gone mad.

"Triumph indeed!" Eric shouted gladly. "Thorin died a warrior!"

The Saxons stared uncomprehending.

"You have to consider goals to understand Viking lore," Hastwulf explained to them. "A young farmer may decide he wants to go out into the wild and start his own farm ..."

"Or a shipwright chooses to build a great dragon ...," Eric interjected.

"When those men die, their lives are praised or pitied based upon on what their goals were, and whether they accomplished them or not," Hastwulf finished. "But a warrior's only goal is to always survive and still be able to fight. Since all men die, a dead warrior's goals can't be compared to the goals of a carpenter or a smith; the warrior will always have failed."

"That's why faith is everything to a warrior," Eric said. "Our reward is our payment from Odin."

"Death doesn't end a warrior's battles," Hastwulf said. "Odin didn't make Valhalla for our sake. Odin needs us, and someday he'll call upon us to fight again. When this world ends, Ragnarrok, the final battle, begins. All the forces of Evil shall arise at once, both the living and the dead, and bring war to every corner of existence. On that day, Odin shall raise all the forces of Good against them; men, Gods, all who'll come. Then shall the Einherjar, the Valkyrie-chosen warriors in Valhalla, bitterly earn their paradise."

"Bitterly ...?" Roselyn asked. "Do you mean ... Evil wins?"

"Not even the Norn sisters, whom you Saxons call the Wyrd, or the Fates, know what'll happen at the end of Ragnarrok," Hastwulf said. "The forces of Odin will be vastly outnumbered, and all the worlds of men and Gods shall be broken and cast down into fire. Some say the best that may be hoped for is a stalemate, that both sides will be completely destroyed. For, if Evil wins, then all life ends forever. But if Evil should be vanquished, even though none is left to boast of it, Hope itself may survive, and someday new worlds may rise from the ashes of the old."

"And in those worlds, it's whispered, those who proved their worth in this life will be reborn," Eric said. "A warrior's only goal is to stay alive, and only by a warrior's death can a mortal be chosen by the

Valkyrie to become an Einherjar, to await in Valhalla for Odin's call, and prove his worth in the final battle at the end of all things."

"It's our oldest legend," Hastwulf said. "Passed from our Gods to the fathers of our fathers. It's our people's faith, and it keeps us strong. Our world of the North isn't as generous as your lands. Look around, if you're doubtful; my eyes have seen only a handful of counties in England, yet I've seen richer farmlands here than exists in all of Norway. Our winters, too, are savagely cruel. We have mountains of ice that never melt and snow that buries men alive. Our faith gives us life; we won't abandon it."

Eric carefully examined his companions, judging their reactions. Karl slowly shook his head back and forth. Roselyn and Eloise sat aghast, their jaws open as if both were about to scream. Rafe's face was a mystery, his expression torn between shock and utter dismay.

"No converts today," Hastwulf grinned.

Eric laughed.

"I claim no secret knowledge of the Afterlife," Hastwulf said. "These stories were told to me by my father, and I honor them as I honor him. But you Saxons needn't fear for your brothers in Grusshire. Your Heaven will reward them for killing so many of us heathens." Hastwulf laughed. "Either way, they'll be honored. Such is the way of all religions, is it not? Men mediate, Gods adjudicate."

"If God gave us proofs then faith would have no value," Rafe said.

"Well spoken!" Hastwulf said to Rafe. "But I've dallied overlong. I must hurry back to Svenson and point him this way. Eric, do you travel to Madrone?"

"Yes, and I shan't veer my course. But I have a question for you: how many horses does Svenson have?"

"Nine, when I rode out," Hastwulf said. "All were gotten before Grusshire; every stable there was emptied before we arrived. We scouts were sent to look both for you and more horses. Oh, and Svenson's wise one rides a horse."

"Svenson has a wise one?" Eric gasped.

"Yes, but I know nothing about him, and I've no desire to ask," Hastwulf said. "No one speaks to him, and Svenson hasn't called upon him yet."

Eric shuddered; there were few true wise ones, and when one of them consented to travel with an army, men shunned them like a living plague. None dared cross them; few even looked at them. Fear rippled up Eric's spine like it had in the cave of the Wolflord; *Svenson having someone like Liz Apple was a frightening thought.*

"Well, I must be off," Hastwulf said. "It was a pleasure seeing all of you again, but beware! Eric understands that, when next we meet, it won't be so pleasant. Svenson'll find more horses soon, and those who ride to catch you won't be gentle."

"Thanks for your news of Thorin," Eric said. "He deserves Valhalla."

"He was the first Svenson drank to this morning and he'll be the last drunk to tonight," Hastwulf said. "Farewell, all!"

"Farewell, old friend."

Hastwulf bowed to the ladies as they wished him farewell, and then he vanished outside the door. Moments later, hoof-beats pounded away, yet Eric drew his sword and ran to the barn door; he wasn't going to make any more mistakes. Carefully he peered outside and spied Hastwulf riding out of the gate and back up the road toward Svenson Two-Sword. Only as he watched him ride off into the distance did Eric relax and sheath his sword.

Hastwulf had been right: Eric was getting sloppy, distracted, and making mistakes. He wasn't thinking, or worse, he was thinking like Karl, a teenager with no thoughts beyond the bodice of nearest wench.

"It's past midday," Eric said to the others. "We'd best ride out."

The Saxons groaned, but they were already awake and sitting up, although their blankets still covered them from the waist down. Hair full of straw, Karl complained that he was hungry, and Roselyn threatened them all with a terrible doom if their next hay pile had fleas. Yet they dragged themselves up; this had been their first real sleep since Farmer Tiller's, yet the Vikings wouldn't be delayed again.

Eloise and Roselyn handed out some hard apples and hunks of brown bread from the supplies the women of Grusshire had given them. The farm seemed deserted except for one noisy chicken that had gotten left behind. They whacked their saddle blankets against a post to remove the fleas, saddled their horses, and rode off, eating and yawning.

Eric frowned as Eloise slowed her horse to ride beside him. She was smiling brightly, her happy, youthful face making her look like a young angel in the clear sunshine.

"Will the funerals last all day?" Eloise asked.

"What funerals?" Eric asked.

"In Grusshire," Eloise said. "For your friend. Thorin was his name ...?"

"Vikings don't have funerals like Christians," Eric said. "We've no need for muttering prayers. Thorin died a warrior's death so his paradise is assured. Svenson's men are celebrating his life in this world, retelling all the great tales of his brave deeds. How I wish I could be there! He taught me so much; he deserves the praises I'd sing. All would hear and be humbled by my stories. Thorin would live forever in the memories of those who heard me tell of his greatness."

"That's what they're doing?" Eloise asked. "Toasting and telling stories?"

"What else would you have them do?" Eric asked. "They can't bring his body to life; Thorin would kill them for pulling him out of Valhalla. So they give him life in their memories. Viking warriors seek glory through skill and courage so they might live forever in tales so great bards and scalds cast them into song. Surely you've heard such stories; I've heard the Song of Beowulf recited many times here in the Danelaw, and twice heard the Legend of King Arthur. Those names will never be forgotten, remembered even when wealthy kings are known only in crumbling parchments. That's the gift we give our fallen, and those who hear of champions like Thorin will keep his spirit in their hearts, pass his tales down to their children, and keep his memory alive."

"Is that what you hope for?" Eloise asked.

Eric sneered; Eloise was maneuvering the conversation in an obvious attempt to manipulate him. There was no harm in it, but Eric didn't feel like playing childish games.

"That's not what you want to ask me," Eric said gruffly. "What is it you want?"

Eloise stiffened at his tone. Her face became serious, imperious.

"I want you, Eric," Eloise glared at him. "Alive. Whole. I want you to give up this deathquest and sail to France with us. We're rich, Eric; you can live in any lifestyle you choose ..."

"Except the one I've chosen ..."

"But you want to die ...!"

She'll never understand, Eric thought sadly. *How could she?* Eloise was barely marriage-aged, too soft for thoughts of death. Her whole life had been gentle, growing up behind castle walls, allowed to ride only calm horses; she'd be as helpless in the back alleys of London as she'd be on Eric's spirited warhorse.

Eric had seen death at its worst, scavenging in the moonlight for coins, jewelry, weapons, and armor after battles. About him laid hundreds, sometimes thousands of dead men grasping at wounds that would never heal, with open mouths that would never scream again, and bulging eyes that haunted even after you looked away, dead eyes that stared and followed into your dreams and awakened you drenched in sweat. How many dead had Eric seen? Too many to think he could never lie among them, that those horrible, twisted expressions could never consist of his features.

Eric's thoughts were hard and cold, products of a life of war and murder from a harsh land of snow and famine. His aging body, his memories, and his faith were just as hard. Eric knew death as well as any living man. He'd seen people die well, gloriously, brave and defiant to the last. Others had died pathetically, whining like kicked puppies before the inevitable. Death was the cost for being born. Life was the excess, death the punishment.

"Eloise," Eric said, "you can't understand ..."

"You don't have to do this!" Eloise insisted.

"How long is life?" Eric asked. "Fifty years? Sixty? I'm a warrior, and most of my life has been spent killing other men, sometimes by the hundreds. My faith blesses my life. What would happen if I died and went before your God? Boiled in lakes of fire, isn't it?"

"You could repent ..."

"So, instead of a Christian Hell, you'd have me declare my whole life an error, a mistake, and have me die a fool."

"I don't want you to die at all!"

"Neither do I," Eric said seriously. "I want to live forever, but I won't. All men dream of living forever, but none do. It's a fool's hope; I've seen thousands die and not one of them wanted to be dead. Show me immortality and I'll give up my faith."

Eloise turned her head aside, pouting.

"You're a good girl, Eloise. I care for you more than you know. But I can't turn my back on my faith. It's how I've lived, my whole life, my morals and honor. Without those I'd have nothing, no reason to be alive. None of us can be what we're not. You understand that, don't you?"

"No."

"Roselyn sent you to talk to me, didn't she?"

"No!" Eloise said quickly. "I mean, we talked about it, but she didn't ..."

Eric smiled; Eloise stuck out her lower lip. Eric liked her, but he suspected Roselyn was controlling her. The two of them were always whispering, and Eric suspected even Karl knew they were consorting to manipulate the men. Few women in this world were strong-willed, and most of those were commoners. The nobility seemed to have little use for strong women, and usually beat rebellious daughters or sent them to nunneries. Roselyn was a strong young woman, but Eric could see the scars of her beatings in her posture, and hear them in her voice; no one had ever broken her but someone had tried. Roselyn was courageous and confident, but cautious, more reserved than Eloise. Few of the bravest men would've descended into the Wolflord's cave or kept enough wits to keep shooting arrows at wolves, and yet have the wisdom to manipulate Farmer Tiller. Roselyn was a thinking woman: a quality rare even in men.

"I love you, too, Eloise," Eric said. "All of you. But this is my time. You heard Hastwulf; soon there'll be a dozen Norse warriors riding after me. You'll have to ride away before they arrive, and I'll hold them off as long as I can. Leave the road, if you can, and hide in the woods; Svenson needs your treasure almost as much as he needs my head. He'll send his best warriors, and they'll kill you too, if they catch you. Ride hard and fast; I want to rest in Valhalla comforted that you're all safe and enjoying my treasure."

Eloise pouted, and then kicked her heels in and drove her horse ahead, up to ride beside Roselyn.

Eric grinned; Eloise was too young to understand how easy she was to manipulate.

Now she knew, and could tell the others, his plan for them to escape Svenson's troops. Eric's only fear was that none of them realized the danger they were facing or the cunning of Svenson Two-Sword.

The afternoon passed slowly as they rode past many farms. All were either abandoned or busy scrambling to pack their valuables onto wagons; Rafe's warnings had gone out across the countryside. Peasants were clearing out, taking everything they could. Svenson's supplies would be dwindling fast; he'd love little more than running across a flock of sheep quietly grazing in a field or a few cows he could butcher and cook. Their Saxon owners would be killed if they complained, and their wives and daughters would fare little better than their animals. Svenson needed to buy the loyalty of his men more than he needed the good will of the local peasants. War was a dirty business and Vikings fight for profit; what good was Eric's head to men like Hastwulf? Svenson had to find a prize worthy of days of marching and fighting; sooner or later his men would demand to be paid.

Hours later they topped a small rise. They'd been riding through a rolling countryside of gentle pasturelands, covered in fragrant grasses, cropped close by the animals that grazed there. Eric turned around, facing the road back towards Grusshire.

"Niflhiem!" Eric cursed. "Who has good eyes?"

"I do," Karl said.

"Look behind us," Eric said. "I see something, but my eyes don't work as good as they used to."

"I can't see anything," Karl said hesitantly. "There's a cloud of dust on the road that's blocking my view."

"No wagon kicks up that much dust," Eric said.

"Is it ...?"

"Oh, no ...!" Roselyn said.

"Vikings!" Rafe said.

"Their scouts must've gotten more horses from somewhere," Eric said. "Flee! I'll hold them here as long as I can."

"No!" Eloise shouted.

"Rafe, take them south ...," Eric started.

"How many?" Roselyn asked.

"There's no way to know until it's too late," Eric said. "Go now! Before they see you!"

"We fought together against the Wolflord ...," Roselyn argued.

"Karl, take them away!" Eric shouted. "Those are my peers, Svenson's finest killers ...!"

"Eric's right ...," Karl said to Roselyn.

"We're family ...!" Roselyn argued. "We fight together ...!"

"You won't stand a chance," Eric said. "Rafe ..!"

"We won't leave you behind!" Roselyn shouted.

Eric spurred his horse into hers. With his strong left hand, Eric reached out and grabbed Roselyn by her throat. He made a fist of his right hand and drew it back threateningly.

"I almost hit you in the Baron's bedroom," Eric growled. "Leave now or I'll put you out, and you can escape across Rafe's saddle."

Angrily Roselyn glared at Eric, but Eric glared back without lowering his fist. He tensed, ready to hit her.

Tears leaked from her eyes. Roselyn bowed her head.

"Ride fast," Eric told Rafe and Karl. "Get off the road as quickly as possible. They'll start hunting for you as soon as I'm dead."

Eloise choked and started to cry. Rafe reached out, tugged on Roselyn's horse's bridle, and pulled her down the road.

"Karl, keep them safe," Eric said.

Karl looked at the old Viking.

"Die well, Eric Bjornson," Karl said.

Eric watched for a moment as Karl took Eloise's reins and pulled her away. Her horse yielded to him despite her complaints.

"Faster!" Eric shouted, and then he turned away. He'd no more time to waste; his day had come. Finally: *the Valkyrie were watching and it was Eric's time to die.*

Eric glanced at the approaching dust cloud. He held his sword-hand up and looked at it; hard, steady, and anxious for his leather-bound grip. He wasn't trembling, not even slightly scared of his approaching doom. If anything, Eric felt exhilarated.

How proud his father would be ...!

The sound of rapid hoof-beats made Eric smile. His companions were riding away fast, driving their horses towards Madrone; no longer his concern. He wished them well. They didn't understand him, but he hoped they'd remember him fondly.

Eric spurred his horse, cantering towards the approaching cloud of death. All the while he kept scanning with his eyes, looking at the few low clouds dotting the perfect blue sky, the rolling green hills, the distant barns and fences of men who worked the land. He wondered if he'd ever see such sights again, and wanted to remember them, in case he didn't. At least it wasn't raining; Eric would've hated to die in the rain.

Slowly Eric lifted his sword-hand and flexed it. He'd killed hundreds with this hand, but against those coming for him, Eric would fail at last. Svenson wouldn't waste his few horses if there was a chance Eric could prevail. Against four or five opponents, a single man, properly trained, could win. Six experienced warriors could prevail over any one man, and more than that would overwhelm even the greatest fighter.

Cresting the top of a small rise, Eric saw the riders. They were still too distant to make out clearly, but Eric could count their number: nine; nine of Svenson's best warriors, men whom Eric had sailed and marched and ridden with most of his life. Today they'd earn a great credit, the death of Eric Bjornson, an honor they'd boast of forever. Eric wondered who they were, which men Svenson had selected to bear this honor. Eric clenched his sword-hand tightly; the Valkyrie were watching, and Eric would take out as many as he could.

Eric dismounted and left his horse on the road. He buckled his helmet on tightly and tightened the strap of his shield. Drawing his sword, Eric stretched and flexed, trying to ignore the sadly-familiar pains in his aged joints. Then he wandered down into a grassy field, surveying the terrain with experienced eyes. It was firm ground, gently sloping to a level basin; perfect for fighting.

The Viking riders rode up. Some shouted "Thorland!" angrily, while others grinned wickedly. They reined in on the road and stared down the slope at their helpless prey.

Eric's eyes widened. He recognized them all; some he knew all too well, and others were fools he purposely avoided. These weren't Svenson's best. They were all experienced fighters, some as renowned as he, but these warriors weren't chosen for their fighting skills.

Suddenly the depth of Svenson's anger, the blackness of his hate, was revealed. These men hadn't come to kill Eric; each of them was an eternal enemy.

The eldest, Thorvald the Wrecker, Eric had known for most of his life. They hated each other, and had been feuding for over thirty years, arguing over everything from battle plans to the divisions of spoils. They were political rivals; Thorvald had been a favorite nephew of Svenson's father, Eric's chief competition for the post as Svenson's champion. Thorvald was a deadly killer of anything that got in his way. Svenson couldn't have picked a meaner foe.

Morrigarr, a would-be sea pirate, was another of Eric's foes. He was savage, a ruthless dragon captain known to kill men just for questioning his orders. Eric thought he killed just to hide his bad judgment, and had many times publicly denounced him as incompetent. Eric's position as Champion protected him from reprisal, but Morrigarr's hatred for him was legendary.

Three of the rest were the same, old rivals and enemies Eric had acquired long ago, men who hated Eric with every ounce of their being. The other four were youths; Eric recognized their faces but he'd never known their names; they were Thorland's cronies, the bullying friends of the prince he'd killed in Gunthar's Alehouse. They weren't as experienced as the older warriors, but they were young and fast, with an endurance elders could only remember.

A shudder ran up Eric's spine; Svenson had chosen Eric's worst enemies to hunt him down. At nine to one, Eric had no chance; Svenson wanted his vengeance to be so horrible men quailed at the thought of it.

These men hated Eric too much to reward him with eternal Valhalla. They hadn't come to kill Eric, but to capture him alive, badly wounded, and carry him back to Svenson, where Eric could be slowly tortured into madness before he'd be allowed his final, ignoble death. The Valkyrie would spit upon his spirit, and Eric would be doomed forever.

Eric's end had come ... but he wouldn't die a warrior.

Eric had failed.

Chapter 14

Valkyrie

KARL

Karl struggled to focus as he rode south. He didn't like deserting Eric, but Eric wanted to die. *Who was he to tell Eric how he should end his life?*

Rafe's shout startled Karl. Roselyn had pulled free of Rafe's grip, ridden off the road, and turned her horse around. Karl sighed, exasperated.

What did Roselyn expect to accomplish?

Karl steered to intercept Roselyn; they had no time for this. Alone, even Eric couldn't withstand a dozen of his kinsmen long, and they had to escape while Eric was still alive ... or they wouldn't escape at all.

Roselyn tried to outrace him, but Karl rode right into her path and forced her to halt or collide.

"Let me go!" Roselyn cried.

"No, Roselyn," Karl said, seizing her reins. "We have to go on! Eric would ..."

"I need Eric!" Roselyn shouted.

"Eric wants us to ride on!"

"No!" Roselyn shouted. *"Eloise! Ride back! Go!"*

Karl cursed himself; he'd dropped Eloise's reins to chase down Roselyn. Eloise had pulled back her reins and could flee from him at will.

Eloise didn't flee. Softly she kicked her horse and rode toward them, as did Rafe.

"Eloise ...!" Roselyn shouted desperately.

"No, Roselyn," Eloise said. "I can't save Eric. No one of us can ... not alone. Together, I think we could save him. I vote we go back."

"You don't even have swords!" Karl shouted. "There's a dozen Vikings back there. Eric stayed to give us a chance. Don't let him die in vain!"

"We can help!" Roselyn argued. "I vote we go back. That's two votes to go back."

"We're not voting!" Karl shouted.

"Please, Karl, please?" Roselyn said, laying her soft hand on his. "I need Eric, and I need you to save him."

"Need ...?"

"I'll never get out of England without him."

"What ...?"

"My father will track us down," Roselyn said. "No matter where we go ..."

"Who's your father?"

"That's not important!" Roselyn insisted. "What matters is that we need Eric to get away. My father's smart and dangerous, but Eric's clever and crafty. Without Eric, you might as well leave me here."

"They won't let a baroness escape, either," Eloise said. "We need Eric ... and you ... and Rafe."

" *We're wasting time!"*

"Karl, please," Roselyn said, pleading with her eyes. "I'll do anything you ask: just help us. We have to go back for Eric."

She'll never understand, Karl thought darkly. *Only death existed behind them.* Roselyn had no concept of what armed warriors could do to unarmored, weaponless women.

"No," Karl said firmly. "You ... women ... are coming south with us ... *now!"*

Roselyn winced at his words.

"Karl, don't do that," Roselyn said. "Please. Yes, we're women, but you've respected us up to this point, and we've tried to earn that respect. Please, don't disrespect us."

"It's suicide."

"If we all helped, our odds would be better."

"What if you're wrong? Eric said you should always take your best bet for survival. If we ride away, we keep our lives and a fortune in gold. If we go back, we risk losing everything."

"I know the risk," Roselyn said, reaching out to him, touching his arm. "But I'm not willing to give up. Please, Karl. Name your price. I'll give you ... *anything ...!"*

Karl staggered, staring into Roselyn's desperate brown eyes. *What was she saying?*

Was Roselyn really offering ...?

No! They couldn't go back. Despite his age, Eric had been more than a match for Karl. What good would he be against a dozen of Svenson's best?

"We can't. They'll kill us. Tell them, Rafe."

A silent moment passed. Karl glanced at the hesitant horse-trainer.

"Rafe ...?"

Rafe sat still in his saddle, fingering his bag which contained Eric's treasure bag.

"When I first saw Eric," Rafe said, "I thought he was a liar, a thief, and a murderer. I was right, of course. Naturally I thought I was a better man; Eric was a heathen Viking while I'm a Christian Saxon. Now I'm not so sure. Outside the Baron's hunting lodge, Eric promised me all of his treasure when he died, if I'd forgive him for what he'd done to our lives, well, to my life, and then Eric gave me his treasure, exactly as he promised. I believe Eric is essentially a good man, a good friend, and maybe someday, a good

Christian." Rafe looked up and stared into Karl's eyes. "I vote we go back."

Karl stared incredulously; *they were all mad!* Rafe had his bent pitchfork and a small axe he'd picked up in Grusshire, and Roselyn had her bow and arrows. Eloise had a stout javelin from Grusshire, but only Karl had any armor; they needed him, his sword and his skill. If he refused then they'd have no choice: they'd have to flee.

"Please, Karl ...?" Roselyn said one final time, and she leaned her head against his shoulder and started to cry.

I am an idiot, Karl thought.

"I have a plan," Rafe said. "You women won't like it, but it might work. Karl, you must gain us a few minutes. Ride back and keep them from killing Eric before we get there. Go; we'll be right behind you."

"Can't you tell me ...?"

"There's no time!" Rafe insisted. "Hurry! We've only got one chance!"

I don't believe that I'm doing this, Karl thought.

The road back was different only in Karl's direction. He pressed for speed and galloped faster than he could've with Eloise and Roselyn beside him. Soon Karl saw Eric's stallion on the road right next to nine other horses. Karl galloped toward the crowd of horses and dismounted.

Eric was downhill, in a shallow vale, with three arrows in his shield and Vikings as young as Karl running to surround him while several older Vikings slowly advanced. As Karl dismounted, all turned to stare at him. The strange Vikings halted their attack, confused as Karl quickly strapped on his silver helmet, raised his sturdy shield, and drew his glittering sword. The elder Vikings quickly conversed, and then shouted orders; two of the elders began marching towards Karl, joined by two of the running youths. The other five turned back to face Eric.

Karl walked towards them slowly, leading away to the right, his shield raised. He was in no hurry to engage; the longer it took the more time Rafe would have to enact his plan. At least Eric had a fighting chance now; his attackers had shrunk from nine to five. Karl wished he could've done more but he'd done all he could. Eric had to look after himself now; Karl had to focus on four men anxious to kill him.

The Vikings smiled grimly, safe in their numbers, eager to plunder Karl's valuable sword and armor. Rafe's plan had better be good, and soon, or they'd find no one left to rescue.

An elder Viking with long, gray-and-black streaked hair shouted orders to the others in Norwegian, which Karl didn't speak. The other elder was bald, but both had long, dark beards, carried swords like Eric's, and had center-grip round shields with heavily-ornamented bosses. One youth held a long pike and the other had a bow nocked with an arrow.

Where was Rafe? Without rescue, Karl wouldn't survive.

As the first arrow flew low at him, Karl dropped to one knee and let his shieldpoint stab into the ground while he hid behind it. The arrow struck his shield and stuck. Karl stood back up and walked to his right, and then the lead Viking shouted and, as a wall, they charged. Karl braced, waited until he stood within range of the youth's spear-point, and then Karl threw up his shield and heard, more than felt, its deadly point crash. Suddenly Karl dashed forward, slammed into them, struck at their leader, and burst between the two elders. Instantly Karl darted towards the archer, sword raised, but he jumped behind the elders, and Karl was forced to draw back. His rapid attacks on both elders had accomplished nothing; they'd blocked his attacks with the practiced ease of experienced warriors.

Karl risked a glance at Eric, who was still alive but hard pressed. He heard Eric's sword clash but he couldn't risk another glance.

The bald elder charged Karl and swung his heavy sword at Karl's exposed legs. Karl dipped his shield to block, but the elder suddenly twisted and the arc of his swordswing abruptly turned upwards and crashed hard into the side of Karl's helm. Karl fell back, flashing stars painfully dancing in a red sky across his eyes.

Karl stumbled and struggled to keep his balance, desperately raised his shield to block any blows that might come before his eyes cleared, and rapidly backed away.

An eternal second later, Karl's sight cleared, and he was chagrined to grasp his situation. The bald elder had run clean past him, unable to turn the momentum of his charge. But he was laughing, laughing at Karl, and his fellows were equally amused; the Vikings were toying with him.

The youth with the spear circled to get behind Karl, but the bald elder shouted and waved him back.

Again the elder charged, swinging low. Karl started to block it, then remembered that he'd already failed at this once. Karl tried a trick he'd only used fighting against his brothers with sticks in the backfields of their farm; he jumped as high as he could, shield-first at his attacker, and then swung his sword downward. From high in the air, Karl crashed down upon his foe, and his sword sliced hard. The surprised Viking elder crumbled under his weight. He'd forgotten the extra poundage of his mail; Karl fell upon the aged Viking like an avalanche, and his swordblow, aimed at the elder's shoulder, caught his opponent's left ear. Blood spurted; a Viking ear fell free.

A sword-swing instantly retaliated, striking Karl's mailed ribs, but it lacked any force, a flailing blow which only managed to throw Karl off. Karl rolled away and drew back his sword only to find the elder had rolled in the opposite direction, out of his range, and called for help.

Karl turned just in time to see the archer loose his arrow. Too late to block, Karl ducked and heard the arrow 'plink' off of his helmet. Quickly he raised his shield, cursing himself. The ear had been a lucky blow; Karl couldn't let one success distract him. A lucky fighter could kill an experienced fighter, but experience stays ... while luck eventually runs out.

The wounded elder dropped his sword and used his hand to staunch the red flow, but Karl couldn't take advantage of it. The other elder was walking toward him with wide, measured steps, his shield raised, murder in his eyes, and an angry youth on each side.

Karl jumped back, warily watching as another arrow was nocked. The youth with the spear edged forward; Karl sidestepped away. Steel swords couldn't match a long spear's range, and Karl couldn't charge the spearman without giving the archer an easy target.

Karl stole a quick glance at Eric, heartened when he spotted two of Eric's foes lying on the grass, but Eric's swordarm was drenched with blood.

Suddenly the spear-wielder ran off to the side. Karl quickened his pace backwards, trying to keep from getting surrounded, keeping his shield facing the archer. Yet he couldn't watch both; the spear-wielder circled him, and Karl wondered how he was going to get out of this. The youth charged and jabbed with his spear. Karl blocked with his sword, keeping his shield protecting his vitals from the archer.

Agony exploded in Karl's thigh. Karl cried out, and the spear-wielder backed off with a wicked laugh; an arrow shaft stuck out from Karl's bleeding leg.

Karl winced, gritted his teeth, and fought to concentrate. He'd known this was going to happen; *they were going to die!* He'd told them so, but would they listen ...?

The elder advanced cautiously, shield low, sword ready. Karl struggled to stand, fell to his knees, and yet raised his shield. The elder came almost in range, and then slowly leaned forward, muscles tensed, ready to strike like a snake.

A loud whistle pierced the air. Everyone startled except Karl, who struggled just to stay upright.

"Valkyrie ...!" the bald, wounded elder cried.

The other Vikings chorused his shout. The fighting stopped, and all looked up with wonder and surprise.

Atop the far rise sat a naked, strikingly-beautiful maiden on a magnificent horse, a tall spear in her raised hand, her pale skin radiant in the clear daylight which shone like a halo around her sun-bright yellow hair. She pointed her spear across the field in mute salute. All eyes turned to the direction of her gesture. There, another Valkyrie, taller, but as naked as the first, rode over the hillcrest with an axe in one hand and a strung bow in the other.

"Valkyrie ...!" one youth cried, staring at the naked beauties.

The elders stood flabbergasted, watching the naked women with unmasked confusion.

"Those aren't Valkyrie!" the elder facing Karl shouted, but he couldn't take his eyes off of them.

Karl seized upon the moment; grimaced against his pain, and levered himself up and swung hard at the back of his foe's neck. The elder collapsed as Karl's sword bit through his spine. Viking blood sprayed Karl, but he ignored it and lunged toward the archer. Then his leg gave out and he fell forward, unable to stand. The archer drew his bow and, at close range, aimed at Karl's back.

A hurled axe flew past the archer's head as hoof-beats charged closer. The axe landed near Karl, bounced as it hit the ground, and spun away. Karl looked up to see the dark, approaching Valkyrie draw her bow and shoot the Viking archer before she reined in beside Karl. But Karl couldn't get up, not even to save his own life.

The naked Valkyrie, as Karl had suspected, was Roselyn. As she rode up, she called to him, but he couldn't move.

"Here ....!" Roselyn shouted, and she threw a short rope at Karl. Karl switched his sword to the hand behind his shield and grasped the rope. Roselyn kicked her horse and it took off running, dragging Karl behind. He slid on his shield, using it as a sled; it was agonizing, but Karl held on and even managed to look back.

The Vikings quickly realized the deceit. One sword-wielding youth charged Eloise as she rode toward Eric, yet Eloise simply lowered her javelin and speared through his chest. The impact knocked Eloise from her horse, but Eric caught the beast as it passed him, jumped into its saddle, and then rode back for her. Eloise grabbed Eric's bloody arm, pulled herself up behind him, and together they rode off as fast as they could.

Some of the Vikings chased, but most ran for their horses still by the road.

Suddenly Rafe appeared amid the horses grazing on the hilltop. With the reins of a horse in each hand, Rafe quickly mounted Eric's powerful warhorse, rode off, and pulled the other horses with him. Despite his pain, Karl actually laughed. Each horse Rafe led had the reins of another horse looped over its neck, so each horse pulled the next. Rafe rode away, stealing all nine of the Viking's horses.

Roselyn dragged Karl over the hillcrest before he dropped the rope and passed out.

Karl awoke to a rough hand slapping him.

"He's awake," Rafe said.

Stinging eyes wedged open. Light blinded and grew brighter as Roselyn pushed her face into view.

"Hold still," Roselyn said. "The arrow shaft broke off while you were being dragged. The tip's still in you."

Karl's growing awareness of the throbbing in his leg became acute as reality drug him back to consciousness. Agony flamed up his left side into his shoulder like burning-hot coals, and below his hip he felt nothing but fire. Karl writhed, and Roselyn, Eloise, and Rafe tried to hold him still.

"Get it out!" Karl hissed between clenched teeth.

"Hold on," Rafe said. "There's a farmwife here who doctors. She's treating Eric now."

Karl fought to maintain control. He was no longer wearing his mail, which was piled beside his ruined helm, which had another arrow-dent and a deep crease at the base of its crown. Slowly Karl lifted his hand to his scalp, feeling a bruise the size of a goose egg over his left ear, which explained why his head was pounding. Grimacing, Karl looked down to see torn cloths drenched with blood tied tightly around his thigh.

Just like Ferny Creek ... only now I'm the victim.

Karl shook his head slowly. He mightn't have seen as many battlefields as Eric but he'd seen enough. All the fighting he'd seen, all the death, and not one good thing had come from any of it. So many good men died fighting, and so many innocents got caught up in their squabbles; what was the point? The wives of Grusshire probably didn't even know their husbands and sons were dead yet, and that pain would last generations.

What good did fighting do anyone?

Karl lay on his back against a thick tree trunk. It was near vespers, the shadows long, but the bright sun still illuminated the newly-planted fields around them. A large farmhouse stood nearby, a crowd of horses tied to its fence, and the laughter of small children filled the air. Karl saw them out of the corner of one eye; two happy cherubs chased a baby goat while their older brother watched, fascinated, as their mother treated strangers who'd gotten wounded fighting Viking invaders.

Eric lay across from him, seeming invulnerable to his pain despite the wide-hipped woman kneeling over him, stabbing him with a needle and sewing his skin closed. Karl gritted his teeth and wished he were as strong as Eric, embarrassed that he was making such a fuss while Eric was enduring his injuries so well.

"Five Vikings stranded three miles back?" an old farmer asked Rafe. "Should I get some of the locals and go after them?"

"No," Rafe said. "Five are too few to matter, and you don't want to antagonize their whole army. Leave them to their leader; he won't be happy with them."

The farmwife slid over to Karl. She was a plump, short woman with smears of Eric's blood on her face and dress. First, she looked at the bruise on Karl's head, frowned, and slapped a wet cloth onto his lump, and had Roselyn hold it there. Then she probed his thigh-wound with her fingers, sending fiery stabs shooting up his side. Karl tried not to squirm ... but failed utterly.

"Hold him still," she said to the others. "This's going to hurt."

Everyone came over to help. Karl tried to be strong, but it felt like someone had stabbed him with huge hooks and was using wild stallions to pull his flesh apart.

"Enough," she said. "It's a hunting tip: we're going to have to push it through. This is really going to hurt. You're gonna wish you were unconscious, like your friend."

Insult to injury, Karl thought.

Bright stars danced and creaked as Karl's eyes slowly opened. Out of pain's haze, Karl realized he was on a rickety two-wheeled cart, roughly rocking back and forth as they journeyed down a dirt road. Starlit pasturelands, dotted with cows, drifted past them. Eric lay beside Karl, his swordarm bare and layered with thick cloths.

"Welcome back," Eric said weakly.

"Where are we?"

"About a day's ride from Madrone," Eric raised a brass flask. "Here, try this."

"Where'd you get that?" Karl asked as he reached for the flask.

"Rafe traded Thorvald's horses to that farmer. Got a big jug of whiskey, some dresses for the girls, medicines for us, and this cart."

"This is a dung-rig," Karl said, drinking from the flask.

"Everyone's packing to leave," Eric said. "Wagons are expensive when armies march."

"How are we?"

"Lost a lot of blood," Eric said. "My arm's cut deep, but between the big muscles; not too bad. I've a broken rib that should heal. Your head's cracked, and they pushed that arrow out of your leg."

"Are you angry with us?"

"Angry ...?"

"We robbed you of your glorious death."

"Those blackguards wouldn't have honored me," Eric said. "Hastwulf was right when he said I was making mistakes. Those villains weren't sent to kill me, only to capture and drag me back so I could be tortured for Svenson's amusement."

"I thought you were friends ..."

"I killed his son," Eric said plainly, "I escaped his vengeance, took his father's drinking horn, stole his dragonship, plundered his treasure, cost him three hundred warriors fighting farmers, and forced him to chase me across half of the Danelaw."

"That's all ...?"

Eric laughed.

"Without you, I'd be roasting over Svenson's campfire by now," Eric said.

"It was Rafe's plan."

"He's a good man."

"So are our women," Karl chuckled, and Eric laughed.

"They're like women of my homeland," Eric said. "Norse women are strong-willed, and our laws give them rights Saxon women will never know."

"Sounds frightening," Karl said.

Both men laughed again, and passed the whiskey back and forth.

"How do you do it ...?" Karl asked.

"Do what?"

"Fight wars, kill, slaughter whole towns ...?"

"Blaze the Trail of Death?" Eric asked. "Plow the Wake of the Valkyrie? We've many names for it. I've spent most of my life on the Blood Wagon, where every day is an adventure. Ask yourself this: if so many people die in wars and feuds, how is it that there're any people left?"

"Huh?"

"If war and death are so pervasive, then why isn't everyone dead?"

"I don't know ..."

"It's because those on the Death Trail see only others who are on the trail. You saw Demril and Bristlen and Grusshire because you're on the trail.

What of the dozens of villages north of here, those missed by the Death Trail? What of the big cities like York and London that the Death Trail veers away from?

"All this fighting has drawn most of the warriors from Southern Norway, and if it continues, it could attract every warrior in Northern England. What effect will that have on other areas once their warriors are gone? Peace: huge pockets of peace. It's not always a good peace; a land conquered by a tyrant may suffer horribly, but tyrants need a populace to rule, so life continues no matter where you are."

"But ... all of Bristlen," Karl argued, "all of Grusshire ...!"

"Not all," Eric said. "We escaped Bristlen, many refugees escaped Demril, and more than half of Grusshire packed and left before the battle began. Even if Svenson has only lost half of the number he's killed since invading, less than five hundred have died, and most of those were warriors."

"The men of Grusshire were farmers!"

"When they fought, they became warriors. If they'd fled with their wives they'd still be alive."

Karl frowned, drank deeply from the flask, and handed it back.

"So, what now?" Karl asked. "Are you willing to give up your deathquest?"

"Curse the thought!" Eric cried, looking up, and Karl smiled; Eric only said that in case his Valkyrie

were listening. "Actually, I'm back to my original plan, despite all our delays. If I can lead Svenson to Madrone, this might just work. Our delays may even have improved things; the Saxon nobles are certainly gathering an army by now and will be ready to challenge Svenson. I expect we'll see signs as we travel; wagons loaded with supplies, knights riding, and men marching in clans."

"You arranged a war ... to earn your honorable death ...?"

Eric grinned and took a long swig.

Chapter 15

Surrender

ROSELYN

Roselyn rode smiling under the twinkling starlight. Eric had been saved, and now they could sail to the continent. Their treasure would afford them a nice country manor and conceal their true identities. Roselyn would finally be more than her father's daughter, never again a tarnished coin for her father to invest.

Eloise rode beside her; she'd been lucky to escape Bristlen before her own life had become a nightmare. As a child, she'd been mostly ignored, free to live her own life. Now old enough to marry, Baron Vandislidge would've gladly sold her off to anyone, once he'd prevented Eloise's succession by fathering a son. Then Eloise would've been as unwanted as a sack of moldy wheat, quickly sold to the highest bidder.

Until they escaped, Eloise was probably better off not knowing; orphaned, unmarried, and the sole heir to a baronial throne, Eloise was the most valuable commodity in England. The first Saxon nobleman who could legally claim himself as her guardian would own the barony of du Harmonn, and doubtlessly every Saxon lord who suspected Eloise was still alive had men out looking for her.

Eric was their best key. With his skill at lying, Eric could purchase new lives for all of them far away from the callous greed of the Saxon nobility. As a woman, Roselyn couldn't even purchase a small house without attracting unwanted attention, and Rafe and Karl were too honest to get away with complicated lies.

Karl, Roselyn thought, rolling his name around in her head like a heated ruby, too hot to hold but too precious to let go. Karl was like a young Farmer Tiller, honest and courageous, and he respected women as few Saxon men did. His tall, muscular body and smooth, handsome face didn't detract from his inner qualities. Roselyn couldn't believe she had feelings for a peasant, but somehow, the more he treated her like an equal, the nobler he seemed. Karl was a great fighter; he'd certainly have been a knight if noble-born, yet he was also tender and a little shy, and Roselyn flushed as she thought of him.

Rafe was the foundation of their company. He probably didn't know it, but ever since he'd led them out of Bristlen, they'd been following Rafe, except for when Eloise had been kidnapped, and even then, Rafe had saved them all. The strength of his faith sustained them, and only his horse-skills had kept them ahead of the pursuing Viking army. Roselyn silently vowed she'd find a way to repay him.

"There it is," Eloise said.

"Finally," Roselyn yawned.

Roselyn had wanted to spend the night at the farmhouse where Karl and Eric had been treated, but Rafe insisted they buy the wagon and ride on. News of their company had traveled fast, including reports of their mysterious bag that clinked like gold coins. The farmer hadn't asked Rafe directly but he'd hinted that their supplies were valuable; Rafe didn't want to risk sleeping under his suspicious nose. At Rafe's request, the farmer had detailed several places where they could spend the night indoors. His first suggestion had been a recently-abandoned farmhouse, but Rafe had insisted on directions to a good quality inn with warm beds and good beer. The farmer told him of two fine inns, but Rafe only feigned interest; too many people at the inns would've heard the rumors and he'd already decided on the farmhouse.

The green horse on the white sign that the farmer had told Rafe to watch for looked black in the pale starlight. The house was set back from the road behind some muddy, reeking pigpens under a tall tree that stood like a giant under the stars. No lights or signs of life showed as they rode up. Rafe insisted on entering first, pitchfork in hand, and Roselyn and Eloise made no attempt to dissuade him.

"It's empty," Rafe said, coming out moments later. "There's some firewood out back and a pen for the horses. It should be safe enough ... if we sleep lightly."

Roselyn and Eloise started unloading. Eric and Karl had woken up when they drove off of the hard main road and both slowly limped inside. The women piled their gear by the huge fireplace and then went back for more. Eric dug through the thick piles of ash in the fireplace and sifted with his sword for any pieces of charred wood big enough to start a fire from. He found a few, and had a chunk of flint, but his wounded arm was too sore to start a fire.

Karl obliged, crawled forward and ripped a raggedy patch off his tunic to start the fire with. He tore the patch into strips, pinched a few hairs from Eric's leathers, and mixed them together on the hearth while Eric scraped thin, dry shavings from the charred wood he'd found. Then Karl scratched Eric's flint across the stone hearth until the sparks caught. Carefully they held up the shavings over the glowing patch-strips while they blew the tiny embers into a flame.

Roselyn watched intermittently as she helped Eloise unload; she'd never started a fire herself, having always had servants she could send to light her candles. After their gear was all inside, even Karl's mail, which took both women to carry, Eric hinted that they needed more firewood. Grudgingly Roselyn and Eloise went out back, where Rafe had stripped all of their gear from the horses. Rafe asked them to carry it all inside so no one could steal it in the night.

Roselyn felt guilty, thinking how the men had always done these labors without her even being aware of them. Doubtless they'd do so again, when they were healthy, without a word of complaint. Finding dirty firewood in the dark, having to carry in heavy logs, and then having to return to tote in saddles, horse blankets, and bridles, Roselyn couldn't help but wish she'd brought at least one servant along.

By the time they'd carried in last of their loads, Rafe had finished clearing hooves and brushing the horses. He came inside shortly after them, commenting that he'd hurried his work and would have to finish it in the morning. Together they stood in the warm light of the fire, Karl and Eric sitting at their feet.

On the hearth between their wounded companions lay their bag of provisions, open beside their big jug. Karl had a hunk of mutton stabbed onto the tip of his sword and Eric had a thick sausage on his, and both were holding their swords over the fire, roasting the meats. Eric passed his flask to Rafe, who took a big swig and then smiled and passed it to Roselyn.

Roselyn smiled as Rafe handed her the flask; the men were finally treating her and Eloise like equals. They weren't 'just women' anymore. Still smiling, Roselyn took a big drink.

Fire cascaded down her throat. Tears squeezed from her eyes as her face flushed scarlet. Roselyn choked, coughed, and spewed a mouthful of whiskey all over Eric and Karl.

Laughter erupted from everyone. Fighting to suppress their mirth, Rafe and Eloise supported Roselyn as she gagged. Roselyn hacked and coughed: she'd never tasted whiskey before and was instantly convinced she'd never try it again.

Karl handed her a waterskin, and Roselyn took a few sips to clear her throat before she passed the flask to Eloise. Eloise took a tiny sip, grimaced, and then handed it back to Rafe. Rafe held it while he bowed his head and recited a prayer of thanks for the meal they were anxiously awaiting.

Dinner was hot and delicious. They ate with their fingers, using daggers to cut off slices of hard cheese and hot meats, both washed down with either water or whiskey. Wastefully they piled on firewood; the small farmhouse quickly grew hot. Then they sat around and talked and laughed about small things, their backs against the wall, or stretched out before the crackling fire.

Roselyn imagined how much better it would be in France when they were resting on thick-cushioned chairs with servants to bring their food and pour their wine. Their house would be bright with gold tapestries and crystal chandeliers. Rafe could have as many horses as he wanted, and Eric would eventually thank her for not letting him foolishly throw his life away. Karl ... would be very happy; *Roselyn would see to that.*

Roselyn yawned loudly, a big, stretching yawn that worked like magic. Minutes later, everyone was yawning, and Eloise started to nod. Their conversations lessened and Karl curled up before the warm fire while Rafe started to snore.

"Oh, I'm supposed to change your bandages!" Roselyn said, still yawning.

"Worry about it tomorrow," Eric said.

"No, the farmer's wife insisted I do it tonight," Roselyn said. "She said you'd both get infected if I didn't."

Eric scowled, but Roselyn got up and fumbled open the bag with the supplies they'd bought from the farmer. Inside it were clean rags for bandages, a clear glass bottle of herbs soaked in alcohol, and a clay jar of healing salve that smelled like honey, mint, and wildflowers. Setting the medicines on the hearth, Roselyn knelt and poked Eric in the ribs until he sat up. Carefully she unwrapped his bandaged swordarm, trying not to break the long scab. Strangely, the scab was very thin, just a narrow crust along the incision. Eric's skin was pink and tender around the tiny stitches of pale woolen thread: a good sign. Roselyn was no healer but she'd been an energetic child and had learned a lot watching the healers tend her.

Roselyn uncorked the bottle and Eric gritted his teeth and winced as she liberally poured the stinging liquid over his wound, but Eric didn't cry out. Roselyn admired him; she'd screamed through the roof when even one drop of alcohol had touched her skinned knees.

Roselyn blew gently on his cut, then smeared salve over his wound. When thoroughly coated, she bound it snugly with clean bandages. Eric said nothing, just covered his bandaged wound protectively with his left hand, rolled over, and tried to sleep.

"Your turn," Roselyn whispered to Karl, trying not to disturb her sleeping friends.

Karl resisted, yet he couldn't roll onto his right side because of his wound, and Roselyn easily pinned him and unwrapped the bandage a handspan above Karl's knee. Amazingly, Karl's wound was even cleaner than Eric's, so much that she wondered if she should wake the others and show them. While it was a blessing, it was unnatural, and Roselyn felt a twinge of worry, wondering how it could be so. Yet she decided to wait: if her concerns weren't just her imagination then they'd both be fully healed tomorrow, and they could worry about it then. Besides, Roselyn had other plans.

Quickly Roselyn repeated her ministrations. Karl jerked slightly when she applied the stinging tonic, but like Eric, he said nothing, despite that she cleaned both the arrow's entrance and exit wounds. Heavily salved, Roselyn tied a new bandage over his cleaned wounds.

"Thank you," Karl whispered, looking up at her.

Roselyn smiled and wiped her hands on the old bandages before she threw them into the fire. Karl smiled back at her, his handsome face mysterious in the deep, wavering shadows.

Roselyn took Karl's hand, stood up, and pulled on his arm. Obviously puzzled, Karl let her help him to his feet, favoring his other leg. Roselyn pulled Karl toward the open door that led to the dark, empty bedroom of the farmhouse's previous owners; Roselyn helped him limp inside and closed the door behind them.

It was chill in the room, away from the warm fire. The blackness that swallowed them was broken only by thin, glowing cracks in the walls and around the flimsy door, casting thin lines of light. Roselyn could barely perceive Karl's tall outline; she reached out her hand to touch his face, and only then noticed she was trembling.

When she'd been only thirteen, a Norman duke, a friend of her fathers, had expressed an interest in her. Despite her young age, her father had decided to capitalize on that interest. That night, after the feast, Roselyn was sent to the Duke's chamber to cement the alliance her father had forged. The Duke was delighted and eagerly took the nervous, naive child to his bed.

Roselyn's terrified, youthful screams had awoken the whole castle. She'd fought back, and was finally thrown naked out of the Duke's chambers right in front of dozens of castle guards and servants, who'd come running to investigate the screams. Her father stormed up only to find his youngest daughter hysterical, sobbing as she crawled across the cold flagstones, frightened and ashamed, while the adults laughed.

Furious, the Duke had torn up the treaty in front of her father's eyes and vowed revenge.

Later, Roselyn had been savagely beaten, and then her father consulted with his top clergymen, who proposed a common solution; that afternoon, while Roselyn lay naked on her bed, gasping in pain and barely able to move, four priests came in, one of them holding a small sack of coins; a generous donation from her father to the church. Under their watchful stares, the youngest priest was ordered to disrobe, and Roselyn had no strength left to fight. He roughly kissed her several times, each time under explicit directions from his three elders, and then he climbed on top of Roselyn and forced himself inside her.

Roselyn cried as he raped her, wanting only to die. The fool priest was as inexperienced as she, and hurt her in body as much as in mind, and he whispered prayers in Latin the whole time, hardly even looking at her or noticing the tormented expression which stayed on her face for weeks afterwards. He continued until the three watchful elders instructed him to stop. Then he crawled off of her and dressed, and the senior clergy offered up a long prayer and blessed their practice while young Roselyn lay helpless before them, naked and sobbing, blood on her thighs.

Afterwards, no longer a virgin, Roselyn was considered unmarriageable by all of the royalty and most of the nobility. Her father continued to use her, whenever he had guests, as a pawn in his games, a twist in his political maneuverings. Roselyn could do nothing but comply; she'd gone from being his third daughter to his first whore, to be rented out wherever a glint of profit shone.

Remembering, Roselyn shuddered. *Was she insane?* All of those horrid nights, lying in the beds of lecherous old men; *did she want Karl to become one of them?*

Roselyn foundered, confused by emotions she couldn't name. Karl was more than handsome; he was kind and thoughtful. He treated her with respect, listened to her, and cared for her needs. She'd never known anyone like him. He wanted her; no woman could mistake that look in a man. *Why did she want him so badly?*

Roselyn trembled all over; tears came unbidden. She shouldn't be acting like this. She'd faced danger and death, and even fought a demon from Hell, without the fear she felt being alone with Karl.

"Roselyn ...?" Karl asked softly. "Are you ... crying?"

His strong arms encircled her with the warmth of a hundred summer suns. His touch dazzled her. Slowly Roselyn's arms slid around Karl's waist and up his back, and almost against her will, she clenched him tightly as if he were her only hope of salvation. Powerless, Roselyn raised her face and drew Karl close.

They kissed, and the darkness flared with flashing stars. Roselyn had no resistance or denial left. She pressed Karl back against the frail, thin wall and kissed him more desperately than any man had ever kissed her. Urges she'd never known burned; Roselyn felt alive, primal, demanding like no woman ever should. Inhibitions vanished and her mother's strict trainings faded like smoke in a breeze.

Slowly Roselyn spun in Karl's arms, sliding her back against his chest, feeling his strong arms still around her. Paradise sang and Roselyn reached up and pulled her long hair out of the way, exposing the tight row of laces down her back.

"Roselyn," Karl whispered, "I know you promised me, but ... you don't have to do this. I want you, but not because you owe me ..."

Roselyn's mind raced; *she didn't have to do this!* He was giving her a way out. She could end this, push away from Karl and walk slowly, with all the poise and dignity of her birthright, out of the door into the safety of the light and the company of the others. Despite his qualities, Karl was only a commoner ... no matter how uncommon he might be.

Yet Roselyn couldn't push away. She didn't want to. Shamelessly Roselyn lifted Karl's hands to caress her breasts.

"I owe you nothing," Roselyn breathed.

Minutes later, Karl gently opened the door, trying not to wake the others. Limping slightly, Karl tip-toed across the room, picked up two thick, rolled blankets, and quietly turned back. Eagerly Roselyn watched him through the barely-open door, standing alone in the dark, her unseen dress brazenly cast aside. She shivered slightly in the cold air, anxiously watching as Karl crept back to her. Never before had Roselyn dared hope she could sleep with a man of her own choosing.

Never before had she ever been in love.

Chapter 16

Madrone

RAFE

Rafe awoke to a nearby movement. He'd been dreaming of Valkyrie, beautiful angels with swords, naked except for their shining silver helmets, and abandoning that dream seemed extremely arduous. If something was wrong with the horses he'd have heard it, not seen it, and still he would've been tempted to stay in his warm, happy dream. Yet Rafe slowly forced one eye open.

Their abandoned farmhouse was exactly as it'd been save that their blazing fire was now a black pile of charred logs still smoking as morning light beamed through a narrow crack in the roof. Eric was still asleep, snoring loudly, rolled onto his side, his head resting on a saddle. Rafe wished he'd thought of that; his own neck felt like Beowulf's Grendel had twisted his head off.

Eloise's gasp had awoken him. Eloise was standing by one of the inner doors, her face against the wall, and it took Rafe a few seconds to realize she was peering through its cracks into the empty bedroom. As Eloise turned away, a stunned glaze on her face, Rafe noticed Karl and Roselyn were missing.

Without a word, Eloise ran outside.

Rafe smiled, ignoring a slight twinge of regret. When he'd been a young man nothing would've stopped him from chasing after women as beautiful as Eloise and Roselyn. Actually, he'd have preferred Eloise. Besides being a baroness, Eloise was energetic and delightful; just being near her made Rafe feel young again. The sheer exuberance she'd shown since Grusshire made him as glad as he could ever remember being. Satan had done his worst to her, both in sieging Bristlen and sending his foul tormentor, who'd thrown her into a darkness Rafe had from which he'd feared she'd never emerge. But Eloise was a strong girl; Rafe was amazed by her resilience, the power of her youth.

Rafe had taken a huge risk going back to save Eric; it'd been a hard decision but it had paid off a thousand-fold. Again, Rafe was exceedingly proud. He'd thought all Vikings were scoundrels, vagabonds, heartless thieves and murderers. Grusshire had only validated this opinion, and Rafe had thought he was betraying his people and his faith by helping Eric. Having heard Eric's friend, Hastwulf, explain their strange Norse religion, Rafe now understood Eric's goals: admirable, if he truly believed all that nonsense about Odin and the final battle. Eric was a good man, too religious, if that were possible, to stop and think about all the havoc he caused chasing his heathen beliefs. Yet Eric was a religious man; in time, perhaps Rafe could make him a Christian. Unlikely, but while Rafe still hated what they'd done to Grusshire, he no longer hated himself for helping them escape that damned place.

Their chase was almost over. They'd be in the city of Madrone this afternoon, and Svenson Two-Sword couldn't track them through a huge Saxon city where even his army would be outnumbered.

Yawning, Rafe felt another hot meal would start the day off right. Grimacing at his sore joints, he levered himself up, went to the fireplace, and drew his dagger to rearrange the smoking logs.

Eric sat up suddenly, snarling, pointing a steel knife at Rafe. Rafe froze, surprised, and made no sudden moves while Eric focused his eyes.

"Oh!" Eric exclaimed, sheathing his blade. "Sorry."

"You must've been hard asleep," Rafe said. "Eloise stepped right over you."

"Where'd she go?"

"Outside," Rafe said. "There's a water-closet near the back door."

"Where're Karl and Roselyn?"

Rafe pointed toward the closed door and smiled.

"About time," Eric grinned.

Both men tried not to chuckle.

By the time Eloise returned, a false smile plastered on her face, Rafe had piled two more logs in the fireplace and was down on all fours blowing last night's coals into a roaring fire. They got out some more hunks of beef, grateful Karl hadn't taken his sword into the bedroom with him, and after a small argument, Eric refusing to let Rafe use their helmets as cooking pots, they made breakfast. Eloise cut thin slices of cheese ... and then a soft, rhythmic creaking noise came from the bedroom. Karl and Roselyn were awake ... though not ready to join the company.

"I need to check my horse," Eloise said, and she hurried out.

"There's nothing wrong with her horse," Rafe said after Eloise left.

"Just hope they settle this between themselves," Eric said. "Some battles swords can't win."

"This morning I greatly envied Karl," Rafe smiled. "Tomorrow I may pity him."

"Men always lose when women fight."

"Do you always talk in proverbs?"

"Only when I want others to think I know what I'm talking about."

Karl and Roselyn finally came out, fully-dressed carrying two rolled blankets, just as Rafe finished cooking their breakfast. Both tried to look innocent, but ear-to-ear smiles belied their half-hearted pretense.

"Breakfast is ready," Rafe said warningly. "I'd best go and see if Eloise is still with us."

At his words Karl and Roselyn's smiles vanished. As Rafe went outside he guessed they were so involved they hadn't even noticed Eloise's absence. Rafe didn't want to spoil their moment but he did want them aware of Eloise when she came back.

In the morning light Rafe saw the pathetic condition of the abandoned farm, including the broken-down pen where he'd put their horses. No wonder this place was deserted; the buildings and fences were falling apart and the weeds in the gardens were taller than any crops. Eloise stood there, beside the horses, leaning against the rail, her face hidden by the fall of her yellow hair.

Slowly he leaned upon the fence beside her. Rafe frowned; *he'd been here before.*

"Are they done?" Eloise asked, her pained voice almost a whisper on the soft morning wind.

"Breakfast is ready," Rafe said slowly. "I think it'd be better if you came in rather than wait for them to come out."

Eloise bowed her head.

"Do you blame her?"

Eloise sighed.

"Do you blame him?"

"It doesn't matter who I blame!"

Rafe paused to let that one sink in.

"My first love was a kitchen maid named Rose," Rafe said. "I lost her during the snows of our first winter together. There were several others that caught my eye after her, but the son of a horse-trainer wasn't good enough for most fathers ... or most girls. I was married just before my twentieth year to Anne, daughter of Malcolm the Tinker. We were together for less than a year; she died trying to bring our daughter into the world. I buried them together."

Eloise lifted her head and looked at Rafe.

"There were others, after a while," Rafe said. "A tavern wench, a handmaid, and, well, every man in the barony was jealous of your father. Before he died, your mother was like a raging fire in an ice storm, imperious, bright as the sun. No one ever told her, of course; after your father, your real father, was killed, everyone knew she'd never love another. We became friends, and then she was taken away."

"Why are you telling me this?" Eloise asked.

"Young people think love lasts forever," Rafe sighed heavily. "It doesn't. And friendship is just as tenuous."

“They could’ve ...,” Eloise started, but then she fell silent.

“I know,” Rafe said. “But breakfast is getting cold and there’s nothing we can do about either out here.”

Little was said during breakfast. Then they packed, toting out their gear while Rafe again cleaned the rocks from their horse’s hooves. Both Karl and Eric seemed much recovered from their injuries; Rafe wondered how they could heal so quickly but didn’t think it wise to mention.

Rafe make everyone pull three or four silver coins from their treasure-stashes and he handed each a few coppers he’d bought off the farmer for a piece of hacksilver. Then they hid all their treasure packs back inside Eric’s bag.

“We can’t be seen showing off more wealth than we have to,” Rafe said. “In Madrone there’ll be thieves and spies about; best keep your wits. Stay quiet. Be cautious what you say. Don’t be overly generous; we can’t afford to attract attention.”

They mounted and rode away. They left their rickety cart behind; Eric and Karl rode mounted and nobody volunteered to pull it.

Eloise spurred to take the lead, with Rafe and Eric close behind. Roselyn and Karl rode single-file in the rear. The morning was crisp with a mild southward wind at their backs. Their road was wide and straight but deeply rutted. No one spoke.

They passed populated farms. Peasants plowed and planted as chickens were fed and wash was hung. No one was packing to flee. Yet everyone stopped to watch as the company rode past; Rafe got the uncomfortable feeling news of them had spread fast and grown in the telling. Twice farmers asked about the Viking invaders, and Rafe and Eric warned them to be ready to flee their homes at a moment's notice. The farmers listened carefully but glanced longingly at Eric's bag.

The sun rose high and Eric passed around his flask again, but it did little to lighten their mood.

A huge, thick cloud of smoke appeared in the distance straight ahead: the city of Madrone. Carts and wagons passed them constantly, some so wide they had to leave the road to let them by. All of the carts and wagons headed toward the city were full of wood, some chopped up for fireplaces, others sawn into long planks, or stacked high with baskets and barrels of flour, food, and beer. All of the carts heading away from the city looked empty.

Finally, as they crested a small rise, they spied a forest of buildings with thick lines of people pouring into it. Madrone was huge, the largest city Karl and Eloise had ever seen; both gaped in wonder at the uncountable buildings and the horde of strangers. Madrone spanned a wide river, which was crowded with boats of all shapes and sizes, and above the city hundreds of chimneys poured smoke into the sky.

Rafe looked for other ways to enter the city but all were inside fenced areas or through guarded gates. No gate blocked the main road but there'd be guards and spies who worked for the wealthy men of Madrone, who informed their masters when someone of importance entered or left. With their parade armor and weapons showing, not to mention having a Norseman, they were sure to attract attention. Rafe might've suggested they skirt around the city and buy passage on a boat, to enter at the docks, but they'd been through too much, too quickly, and nerves were on edge. Rafe decided to enter here and lose themselves in the crowd.

Noises and stinks assailed. Hammerings and the slammings of doors thundered while merchants shouted praises of their wares, children screamed, babies cried, and a loud, unintelligible roar of a hundred muted conversations echoed.

Dozens of ill-favored, squint-eyed men watched them enter Madrone from windows and doorways of outlying buildings. Excited merchants with piled carts proclaimed rare prices and unbelievable quality. Rafe kept his eyes open, his pitchfork visible, and their horses close together. He led them down the main road past several inns and smithies, past muscular men blackened with ash-smudges wielding hammers and tongs. Other buildings had painted signs picturing their purpose; a golden loom at a weavers, a pair of rearing stallions at a stables, and a severed hog's head at a butchers.

Rafe turned down several narrow side streets at a rapid pace and led them deep into the city. He checked behind them several times but saw no one obviously following. The side streets were, if anything, more crowded than the main road, and a few pedestrians cursed at them for riding dangerously fast.

After countless detours, Rafe rode right into a large stable. He called for the master and a tall, bald man in a dirty horsehide apron, looking as big and strong as his horses, came out.

"Is this place safe and clean?" Rafe challenged him. "I need stabling for five horses and storage for our gear. What're your rates?"

"If you don't like it then you can ride those plow-mules right out of here," the stable-master snarled.

"Show me where you stow your feed," Rafe said. "If I see moldy grain I will ride out of here."

Rafe followed the stable-master, examining the feed, the stalls, the other horses, and the stable-hands as they performed their duties, their stable-master occasionally shouting at them as they toured. Rafe was careful not to mention he'd been a stable-master all of his life and could tell at a glance their horses would get good care here. He easily pointed out a few bad things, like empty water buckets, and succeeded in impressing the stable-master with his mastery of horsemanship so much that the stable-master enquired if Rafe needed employment. Soon they were laughing like old friends and Rafe gave him a silver coin and four coppers. The stable-master promised Rafe their horses would get the best care possible, and his saddles and other gear would be stored and guarded day and night.

"I'll stop by every day to check on my horses, and I and my friends must have access to them at any time, day or night," Rafe said.

"That won't be a problem," the stable-master said, and he called all his hands over to look at them and memorize their faces.

"Excellent," Rafe said, who was equally impressed with the stable-master. "Now, where can I find a clean, safe inn with good food?"

"And a bath!" Roselyn interjected.

"Not in this part of town," the stable-master said. "I'd recommend the Silver Swan in the merchant's district near the river. It's too fancy for the likes of me, and expensive, but it has a high reputation."

Rafe thanked him profusely. Eric took their bag of treasure, Karl took their bag of clothes, and Rafe took their bag of provisions. They wandered out into the street, looking out of place with their armor, weapons, and big shields.

"There!" Rafe said, and he led the way to a building with a foaming beer stein painted above its door.

"Here ...?" Roselyn questioned. "I thought we were going to a respectable inn!"

"After dark," Rafe promised, "We don't want to advertise where we'll be staying, so we need a place to hide out."

"All right," Roselyn said unhappily, "but couldn't we find someplace ... cleaner?"

"We need to hide someplace where we won't be looked for."

"Well, I wouldn't ever look to be caught in a rat-hole like this," Roselyn acquiesced. "But I expect to be somewhere with a bath and clean sheets right after dark!"

The wide door creaked open to reveal an interior only slightly more decrepit than its exterior. Smoke, stale beer, and other, less desirable stenches reeked. Inside, the tavern was vast and long, extending into several smaller rooms, with a dozen sturdy tables against its walls. A large open space lay in the center, and a wide, filthy doorway led to a big, greasy kitchen. Copper candle sconces hung everywhere, but daylight was pouring in through oiled-skin windows set high in the walls. Five swarthy men sat at a table near an enormous fireplace. The men looked startled when the companions walked in, but they quickly lowered their heads and began whispering.

Rafe piled his bag on the table nearest the door and Karl and Eric did the same, adding their shields and helms to the pile. Roselyn set her bow and quivers beside them, and they all pulled out chairs and benches. Eric took a big chair against the wall and Rafe set his pitchfork behind him.

"Get out!" shouted a short, burly man in a heavily-stained white tunic, who stormed suddenly out of the kitchen. "Get out of here!"

Surprised, Rafe started to get up but Eric waved him down.

"Beer!" Eric shouted at the barkeep.

"We're closed!" he shouted back. "Get out!"

"I'd like some wine," Roselyn said.

"No wine!" he shouted. "Get out!"

"I want food," Eloise said.

"Out, child!" he shouted. "No women in my place save those that work here!"

"Just bring us all the food and beer you have," Karl chuckled.

"I'll serve your heads on a platter!" he growled, and he marched back into the kitchen only to return with a huge cleaver in his hand. He stormed towards them as Karl and Eric reached for their swords.

Suddenly Eloise jumped up and slapped Karl's hand aside. She seized Karl's sharp sword, jerked it from its scabbard in one fast pull, and then stabbed it between the angry barkeep's knees and lifted it until it struck pay-dirt.

"Hey!" the barkeep cried, rising up on his toes, unable to escape the razor's biting edge.

"My friend said beer!" Eloise shouted angrily. "My other friends said wine and food!"

"Take that away!"

"Fine!" Eloise said, pulling slightly.

"No!" he squealed.

"You want me to leave it there?" Eloise grinned.

"Please!" he whined, squirming comically. *"T-t-think of the loss!"*

"No loss that I can see," Eloise said, "except my temper, if my friends don't get their drinks right now!"

"At once, little mistress!"

Shaking with laughter, Rafe plucked the meat cleaver out of the barkeep's hand. Everyone in the tavern, even the swarthy men and the workers in the kitchen, laughed.

Eloise withdrew Karl's blade from the barkeep's crotch, receiving cheers from everyone as the barkeep fled back into his kitchen. Eric howled with laughter and Roselyn was nearly hysterical. Karl fell off of his chair, clutching his ribs, and then he got up and bowed to Eloise.

Eloise glared for a moment and then a slight smile stretched her lips. She absently waved Karl's sword triumphantly and then set it on the table as a tall, lanky young boy about Eloise's age ran out with five large mugs of beer. With noble grace, Eloise sat back down on the worn wooden bench.

"That was wonderful!" Roselyn laughed. "Why did you do that?"

Eloise stopped smiling.

"I don't like people thinking of me as a child," Eloise said testily. "I am El...."

"No!" Rafe hissed, interrupting her. "No names here! This place has ears, just like ..." Rafe lowered his voice, "... like a royal court. Tell no one who you are or where we're from, and don't believe anything anyone says. It's a common practice to lie in places like this."

Everyone agreed, not a moment too soon; one of the swarthy men had gotten up and approached their table. He didn't look like a thief; he was at least thirty, average height, and wearing a plain, clean tunic. Rafe would've guessed him for a common townsman, a simple laborer, but what would an honest laborer be doing in a seedy tavern in the middle of the day?

"Greetings!" he said as he bowed to Eloise. "I'm Charles the Tinker, and I couldn't help admiring your performance; few men are brave enough to challenge old Cedric, and I've never seen him turn tail before. Might I ask the name of a lady so bold?"

Eloise glanced at Rafe, and then she smiled wickedly.

"Impudent fool!" Eloise snarled haughtily. "Don't you recognize me? I'm the Queen of England!"

Laughter exploded from every pair of lips, including Eric, who spewed a mouthful of beer all over himself.

"Your Majesty!" the tinker cried, and he bowed again, more deeply than before and with elaborate flourish.

Their meal became a celebration. Food and wine were quickly brought, though Cedric didn't reappear. The tinker pulled out a bench and sat down at the next table, and soon his friends joined him. They asked about the approaching Viking army, but Rafe only told them he'd heard the same rumors and didn't know what to think.

"It doesn't matter," said one of the men sitting beside Charles the Tinker. "Earl Sir Guldwin is gathering men; he'll route those barbarians."

"No doubt," Rafe smiled, glancing at Eric.

Eric smiled and looked away, taking another drink from his mug.

After their closeness on the road it felt good to have others to talk to, and they all relaxed.

The swarthy men asked several leading questions but mostly they talked about Madrone, its politics and problems, as if glad to have people willing to listen. More people came in as the afternoon deepened, and the tavern became lively. Most were regulars, Rafe guessed, since the patrons inside greeted them by name. Then a dozen prostitutes arrived all at once, delighted to find a party already begun. They included women of all ages, shapes, and sizes, some fully dressed, others exposing enough flesh to shock Eloise and Roselyn.

Rafe grinned: everyone called Eloise The Queen, and the story of her attack on Cedric had already escalated, as stories tend to do when alcohol flows, to a terrible, drawn out battle which only ended when Cedric begged Eloise from his tiptoes not to make him a eunuch. The rest of them took on similar names; Eric became The Jarl, Roselyn The Princess, and Rafe took The Governor. Rafe would've preferred The Earl, but in Earl Sir Guldwin's city, Rafe shied away from any unwanted connotation. Rafe was better off than Karl; Karl wanted to be called Captain Sir, like Captain Sir Gunderson, but Eloise insisted that Karl was her Jester, and the name stuck despite his protests.

Charles the Tinker, who showed a remarkable interest in Roselyn, pulled out a flute and began to play, and three women, two bare-breasted youngsters and another old enough to be Rafe's mother, started dancing in the center of the room. Eloise looked scandalized, but she was The Queen, and all of the women bowed to her as they passed, although the young ones glared at Eloise jealously.

Rafe couldn't help but laugh. Eloise and Roselyn had been horrified when he'd insisted that they ride naked to save Eric and Karl, and would've never done it if any alternative existed. Rafe had tried not to notice; he was a mature man and the girls were embarrassed enough already, but his tired old eyes feasted that day.

"Get away from me, hag!" shouted a man sitting next to Charles.

Rafe looked up to see a beautiful woman, about his age, with long, pale gray hair, turn sadly away.

"Apologize to that woman!" Rafe bellowed, standing up.

Both the man and the prostitute stared at Rafe as if he were mad. Rafe angrily snatched up his pitchfork and those nearby scrambled to get out of his way.

Rafe started to lean a little and realized he'd drunk too much to be playing with a pitchfork. In fact, Rafe was quite drunk, and felt suddenly foolish. No one ever apologized to prostitutes, not that he'd ever heard of.

Self-conscious, with everyone watching him, Rafe set his pitchfork down, reached into his pouch, and pulled out a shiny large copper and held it out to the older prostitute. Laughing, she brushed back her long hair, plucked the coin from his hand, and then she playfully pushed Rafe back onto his chair and sat down on his lap. Everyone laughed.

"So, what your name, 'andsome?" the prostitute asked. "Me Seren, and can make this wonderful night for 'ou!"

Rafe looked carefully at her. She was a handsome woman, not quite as tall as Roselyn and a little heavier, with wrinkles just starting around her eyes and mouth. Doubtless she'd once been very beautiful.

"They call me the Governor," Rafe said, and he embraced her tightly.

Chapter 17

New Troubles

KARL

By the time they lit the candles the tavern was packed with laughing, drinking patrons. Music filled the warm, smoky air along with singing, shouting, and the playful screams of flirtatious whores being chased through the crowd. Everyone except Karl was having a great time.

Charles openly flirted with Roselyn and she seemed to enjoy it immensely. The tinker had a smooth, cultured tongue, flowing with compliments and interesting stories, and Karl hated him for it. Every word from the villain's throat stung his ears like barbed hornets and Karl took another swallow of beer.

Karl tried to force his way into the conversation, but the fool tinker kept referring to him as Jester; Karl lifted his beer to wash away the urge grab his sword and chop the miscreant in two.

Karl kept staring at the topless young prostitutes, admiring their shapes, although trying not to let Roselyn see him doing it. Roselyn and Eloise had stripped to rescue him and Eric from their losing battle, but he'd been in no condition to appreciate it at the time. Secretly Karl was delighted; he knew nothing less than his life would've prompted them to ride naked.

Eventually a bright idea pervaded Karl's drunkenness.

"Princess!" Karl interrupted. "It's after dark!"

Roselyn turned to Karl and stared uncomprehendingly, and then she glanced up at the darkened windows and her eyes widened. Standing up, Roselyn looked around.

"Where's El... I mean, the Queen?" Roselyn asked.

Karl startled. He'd seen Eloise recently, as drunk as she could get, trying to dance with a group of young prostitutes, although stumbling with every step. Now he could see Eloise nowhere, and Roselyn wouldn't leave without her.

"I'll find her," Karl scowled, and he stood up as the room started to spin. He paused, steadied himself, and staggered into the crowd.

The folk of Madrone were packed tightly yet there seemed to be a fluid stream of people sliding through the crowd. Karl half-followed, and was half-pushed, along with the flow of people, straining for a glimpse of bright yellow hair.

Traversing the length of the tavern without success, Karl pushed his way into one of the smaller rooms only to duck as a huge knife flew across the room, slapped flat against a wall, and bounced back at a crowd of men scrambling to dodge it. The men cheered and laughed, picked up the knife, and passed it back across the room to a beautiful young blonde girl, her clothes drenched with beer and a mug at her lips, sloppily pouring more beer down her throat. The men handed her the knife and she took it and steadied, aimed at the far wall, drew back to throw, started to fall backwards, and hurled the knife straight at the ceiling. It struck pommel first and the townsmen cheered and jumped to avoid getting killed.

"Your Majesty!" Karl shouted, pushing his way into the room as the men helped her to stand.

"Karl!" Eloise shouted. *"Karl, Karl, Karl ...!"*

The knife was passed back but Karl caught Eloise's hand before she could take it.

"Come on, Queen," Karl said. "Time to go."

Angry complaints made Karl a little nervous, but he was in a hurry; he'd left Roselyn with that honey-mouthed weasel and wanted to get right back. Despite their objections, Karl pulled Eloise over his shoulder and carried her out of the room to a mixed chorus of cheers and curses.

Carrying Eloise back to their table, Karl got a lot of laughs, including several loud comments about 'The Jester's Queen' and 'King Jester'. Karl eventually pushed his way through the crowd only to find Charles had pushed his chair even closer to Roselyn.

Eloise staggered as Karl set her back on her feet in front of Eric, who had a prostitute on each knee, one of the topless young ones and one older than him. Karl signaled that they were leaving, but Eric only smiled back, oblivious to his intent. Each of the women in Eric's lap held a large mug of beer and they were taking turns giving Eric drinks.

Rafe fared better than Eric; Rafe was cuddled in his chair with the prostitute with long gray hair and Karl was reluctant to interrupt what they were doing. Yet Rafe looked up after Karl yelled 'Governor' for the second time. Rafe nodded in return, then whispered in the old woman's ear. She kissed him, jumped off his lap, and started to help him gather their things. Roselyn got up, too, and Karl sheathed his sword and picked up both shields.

A big commotion arose nearby; Charles had fallen onto his knees before Roselyn.

"No!" Charles cried at the top of his lungs. "Princess, I love you! Marry me, and make me king of your heart!"

Everyone laughed at Charles, including Roselyn, who stumbled a bit as she tried to politely refuse and get past him.

"No, marry me!" another man shouted, throwing himself on his knees next to Charles, and the crowd cheered and applauded. Soon another joined them, and another, each demanding Roselyn marry him, declaring their love before all. Eight others joined in the revelry, falling to their knees and begging Roselyn to marry them.

Karl actually smiled, enjoying the sheer insanity of it, but Roselyn was forced backwards, so many men pressed her, and more pushed their way forward. Roselyn begged them to stop but none heeded her.

Suddenly the crowd surged, and several men shoved too close. Roselyn fell, knocked over by the proposing men. She rose punching and kicking. Some men were grabbed, accused of pushing Roselyn over, and fists started flying.

The bar fight exploded. Some jumped into the fray; others pushed to get away. Rafe snatched up the treasure bag, his pitchfork, and Roselyn's bow, and his gray-haired whore grabbed both helmets. As the crowd surged toward them, Karl grabbed Eloise and both shields just before they were shoved into the press of bodies. Rafe and his lady didn't even try to fight the crowd; they climbed over the table toward the door.

As Karl and Eloise pushed out the door, Karl caught one last sight of Eric, who was laughing as he watched the fight, until a thrown beer mug suddenly hit him in the face and splashed all over his beard and leathers. Eric roared up out of his big chair, dumping both prostitutes from his lap, and jumped into the thick of it, swinging his fists, near Roselyn, who had a wooden stein in one hand and was beating some poor man senseless with it. Then Karl was pushed out of the door.

Figures poured out into the dark street. Struggling with both shields in one hand and Eloise in the other, Karl pushed to a clear area only to find Rafe pushing through the crowd along the wall, followed by the gray-haired woman, who had Karl's helm in one hand and Eric's helm in the other. Pulling Eloise, Karl pushed to intercept them.

Suddenly the prostitute spun around and swung Eric's helm like a weapon. A group of dark figures jumped back and cursed, but she held her ground.

"Back, Charles, James!" she shouted.

"Stand aside, Seren!" Charles shouted, a long knife in his hand.

Karl gasped, dropped Eloise and the shields, and swept out his sword. He jumped to meet them, backing up the old whore Charles had called Seren. The men facing her stepped back before Karl's sword, and Rafe appeared beside them, his pitchfork in one hand. The men fled; they crashed into the crowd still pouring out of the tavern. Shouts and curses burst as they drove their way through the fleeing patrons, but the men quickly vanished, lost in the dark, crowded street.

"Thieves ...!" Seren cursed.

Too late Eloise stumbled to join them, a small dagger naked in her hand, confused but ready.

"We'd best get out of here," Rafe said, motioning at the crowd, many of whom were watching them.

"Can you get us to the Silver Swan?" Karl whispered to Seren.

"I know way," she said. "Follow Seren!"

Karl snatched up Eric's big shield and gave Eloise his own shield.

"What about Roselyn?" Rafe asked.

"Eric'll watch out for her," Karl said. "Let's go!"

"Follow!" Seren said, and she darted along the building toward the stable, which she dashed into. The companions followed her, glancing behind them as they ran. Stable-hands gasped as they ran past, and then Seren opened a door and ran into a pitch-black alley.

"Hey, where're we going?" Karl demanded, but Seren ignored him and started banging his helm against a door.

"Open!" she cried. *"It Seren! Hurry!"*

A door opened and Seren ran in. Rafe followed her, Eloise behind him, and Karl came last. They stepped inside a dim, candlelit brothel; a naked woman held the door open while a naked man, still lying on a bed, pulled a blanket over himself and cursed. A narrow doorway led to an equally narrow hall and Karl followed Eloise down it.

The hallway opened onto a tiny room with three benches, a table, and a keg. Seren dashed out the front door as Karl entered the room, and he only glanced at the surprised old woman sitting by the keg before he followed Eloise out of the front door.

Stars shaded behind low clouds, oiled-skin windows glowed from interior lamps and fireplaces, casting pale sheens on the streets. Seren led them on a wild route down several more narrow streets before she slowed down and let them catch their breaths. The companions were lost yet Seren seemed to know her way. Giving them little time to rest, she pressed on.

"Charles and James try again," Seren insisted. "They thieves, murderers."

They had no choice but to trust her. It wasn't a short walk, and they had to rest several times, but finally they arrived at a tall, fancy building with wide steps and graceful swans painted in silver on its doors. Met by an innkeeper, who glared at them disdainfully, Rafe asked for two rooms, and had to pay a whole uncut silver coin before the innkeeper agreed to let them spend the night. Karl couldn't blame him; fresh from a bar fight, they looked like a filthy bunch of scoundrels.

The innkeeper took several candles in brass stands and escorted them to two adjacent rooms on the second floor, one with just one bed, and a larger room with two beds, a wide table, and three chairs. Both rooms had sturdy brackets beside their doors and stout braces to bar them safely inside. Rafe set their gold-clinking bag on the table and then patted Karl on the back. Saying nothing, Rafe reached his hand out to Seren; holding hands, they left for the other room. Karl and Eloise unburdened themselves, dropping their belongings inside the door.

Karl leaned against the wall, still breathing hard. He was exhausted and still slightly drunk, but he had to go back for Roselyn. He didn't know how he'd ever find the place, yet he had to try. Yet he was taking nothing but his sword; he was too tired for additional weight.

Karl unbuckled his swordbelt, set it across a chair, and pulled up the skirt of his mail as high as he could. Then, leaning forward, he shrugged the heavy coat off onto the floor, letting its woven rings cascade off of his back with a loud ringing clatter. Karl sighed deeply; his shoulders freed as the weight rolled off.

Perhaps now he'd have the strength to go back.

A heavy garment flopped to the floor in front of Karl, somehow familiar, although he couldn't make it out. Soft, thin arms wrapped around him, and hands with grasping fingers seized him.

Karl jumped and spun, ready for anything ... except what he saw. Eloise was naked, and she didn't look like a child anymore. Eloise was golden in the candlelight, almost glowing, from blonde curls to miraculously pert breasts, tiny waist, and long legs. She looked at Karl like a hungry cat at a sugar-coated mouse. Eloise seized the front of Karl's quilted coat and pulled him into a hard, demanding kiss.

Karl's mind reeled. He'd been about to do something, but as Eloise's hands started to tear his clothes off, he could think of nothing but helping her. They fell upon the bed, and Eloise ripped the rest of his clothes off while kissing him. Then Eloise pushed him onto a bed, climbed atop him, and directed his hands to explore her whole body, her mouth never once leaving his skin.

Karl gasped and groaned, writhing as if on fire. Roselyn had been slow and graceful, every movement, every touch an eternity of ecstasy. Eloise was like a living whirlwind, insatiable and desperate, grasping, her appetites relentless. Karl couldn't speak or think, as if Eloise's hungers had become his own and nothing mattered but driving need. Theirs was pure passion, raw lust that consumed and fanned wants into actions neither had dared before. Like hungry beasts they devoured each other, again and again, deep into the night.

Much later, their door suddenly opened, and Roselyn entered, the innkeeper behind her. He gasped, shocked at the condition of his tenants, and quickly pulled the door shut.

One eye bruised, her hair frizzed and tangled, her clothes torn to tatters barely hanging upon her, Roselyn stared disbelieving at Karl and Eloise.

The bed was a shambles, their blankets on the floor, and on the fallen blankets Karl lay atop Eloise, both naked, uncomfortably frozen and staring at Roselyn.

Roselyn threw back her head and laughed.

Slowly she limped to the other bed and gracelessly collapsed upon it. Karl looked at Eloise, wondering what to do; Eloise stared back, then giggled, and Karl grinned wide. They shrugged and continued.

Karl rose before the roosters crowed, careful not to wake Eloise or Roselyn. He quietly dressed, buckled on his swordbelt, threw his mail over his shoulder, took his helm in his hand, lifted the brace on one bracket, and opened their door just enough to squeeze out, holding up the brace with one finger until their door was almost closed. When he let go and pulled their door closed, the brace fell into its bracket, sealing the women safely inside. Karl quickly scooted down the hall, descended the stairs, and ran out into the street. He didn't know what Roselyn and Eloise would say to each other when they woke up, but Karl was certain he didn't want to be nearby.

Karl checked his pouch to see how much money he had; four pieces of silver, two whole, and six coppers. Before Bristlen, Karl had never held one silver; now he wished he'd taken more, yet he wasn't going back.

Karl had never been alone in a city as large as Madrone; everywhere he looked something new caught his eye. Most of the streets wound like serpents, tall, narrow houses squeezed against each other, many with wide windows already open. Fresh, fragrant aromas of hot breads wafted from a baker's shop. Some houses had large shelves built onto their fronts, which merchants loaded with wares for sale. One house had a real glass window and a hawker called to passersby, inviting them to look through it. Karl obliged; inside was amazingly finished furniture gleaming, newly-oiled, masterfully built, and arranged just inside the window with a busy woodwright's shop behind them. The hawker tried to get Karl to go inside where he could examine them more closely, but Karl declined.

Karl came to an open air market, filled with huge carts and wagons, many of which had poles supporting cloth sunshades, selling all types of food, drink, jewelry, furs, and everything else. A few sold swords, daggers, and old pieces of armor, but Karl only briefly looked at them; none equaled the quality or artistry of his own treasured sword.

As Karl wandered through the lanes of the early-morning market, a crowd started to gather. All were peasants, mostly wives and servants, many with children in tow or babies in their arms. All seemed to be in a hurry, and Karl felt uncomfortably out of place, walking leisurely around while they pushed past him. Karl bought a tasty stick of hot lamb chunks marinated in spiced wine for one copper, and the cheerful merchant traded him twenty-two coppers for one of his half-silvers and gave him directions to the shop he required.

Soon Karl stood in front of an armorer's shop, almost deafened by the pounding of hammers upon anvils. Karl introduced himself to a young apprentice, who instantly brought him to the owner, an old, wrinkled man who walked with a cane, who seemed to give orders more than practice his craft. Karl laid his helmet and mail out on a table and the Master examined both with an expert's eye. The helm had a deep crease from a Viking sword and dents from deflected arrows. His mail had been battered by swords and torn apart by hellish Wolflord claws; several gaps showed missing rings. The Master studied both closely and finally announced he could restore them, but it would be expensive: five silver coins. Karl tried to barter but the old man refused to go lower, although he promised his work would be flawless and stronger than before. Karl finally agreed, but only if the work was done that day, in case he needed to leave town. The Master shook Karl's hand to seal the deal, and Karl departed.

The tavern where they'd gotten drunk was well-known. Karl asked directions to the bar where the big fight had occurred and quickly got directions. Yet, when he entered, Karl barely recognized it. Two of its sturdy tables were flat on the floor, lying atop broken legs. Shattered pottery and torn clothes littered its center, beer puddled beside broken pitchers, and three youths were trying to clean all of it.

"You ...!" cried a deep, angry voice.

Cedric burst out of the kitchen and attacked Karl, demanding payment for damages to his tavern. Karl felt he should refuse, but the tavern-master glowered and bristled, and finally Karl offered him one whole silver coin, but only if he could tell Karl where the old Viking called The Jarl was. Cedric took the coin, gave Karl directions, and unmistakably invited him never to return.

Following Cedric's directions, Karl made his way to another brothel. He knocked on its door and a short, round, naked woman clutching a blanket around her shoulders opened the door.

"Come in!" she smiled. "Young and handsome's always welcome!"

Karl poked his head inside, seeing only a large, dark room with stalls, like a stable, with thick straw scattered on its dirt floor. A crumbling fireplace rested against one wall with two women cooking over a small fire.

"I'm looking for a friend," Karl said. "He's a Viking named Jarl, and ..."

"You don't need him!" the short, round woman laughed, dropping her blanket and running a finger familiarly down Karl's chest. "You come in and let Martha make you happy."

Karl smiled.

"But I have no money ... and neither does the Jarl."

"What?!?" Martha shouted. "Helgaret! Shar! The old Viking lied! He's got no gold or jewels ...!"

Suddenly Eric's scream broke the quiet of the brothel. A commotion burst from one of the stalls, and Eric came running out, carrying his clothes, leathers, boots, and sword, with two angry women close behind, and more coming from other stalls. The women at the fireplace left their cooking, bringing sharp carving knives.

Suddenly Martha grabbed Karl and pulled him inside with a strength her size belied. Martha grabbed a knife from a shelf near the door and brandished it. Karl backed up until he stumbled into Eric. They stood back-to-back, encircled by twelve mostly-naked, angry prostitutes with large daggers.

"Karl, pay them!" Eric shouted.

"Me?" Karl asked. "You spent the night here!"

"I was robbed!" Eric cried. "Someone cut my pouch from my belt during the fight."

"One of you had better start coughing up coppers!" Martha shouted. "After the things that you made me ...!"

Suddenly Karl laughed, reached into his pouch, and pulled out several coins. He selected ten coppers, held them out to Martha, and then tossed them over her head. The women jumped for the coins, and Karl grabbed Eric and pulled him toward the door. They ran outside, safe at last.

A woman screamed, several men whistled, and a chorus of laughter followed; Eric was still naked, standing in the middle of the street in broad daylight, clutching his clothes. Karl smiled, and suddenly a rock-hard Viking fist knocked him to the ground.

Clothes in his hands, Eric stormed into a narrow alley beside the brothel. Karl shook his stunned head and got up slowly. Eric hadn't hit him as hard as he had in Castle Bristlen, yet Karl's head rang. He shouldn't have done that to Eric but he was feeling cocky; *he'd paid the price.*

Eventually Karl stumbled into the filthy narrow alley to apologize to Eric, but all he found were thick piles of stench in front of a tall wooden wall.

"Your Viking friend climbed over the fence," said a strange voice.

Karl spun around to find a stately young man, not much older than he, with coal-black hair and eyes.

He was of average height, lean, wearing an elaborately embroidered long wool coat, black on black, and he seemed to be wearing a black robe underneath it. Over his shoulder was a black leather strap from which hung a five-foot-long oiled leather case.

"Don't be afraid," he said.

"I'm not afraid," Karl snapped.

"I'm called the Seer," the black-robed youth said. "I have news for you about your enemies from the North."

Karl frowned, doubtful and distrustful.

"I can't tell you here," the Seer said. "Nor should I tell you alone. You and your companions are in grave danger. You must leave Madrone at once."

"Really ...?" Karl asked dubiously.

"Go back to the Silver Swan," the Seer said. "Gather your friends and stay in your room. I'll come and speak to you there."

"Why should I?"

"Otherwise many will die ... tonight ... including you."

The Seer turned his back on Karl and walked back to the street. Karl followed, intending to demand how the Seer knew where they were staying, when Karl noticed something strange; as the Seer emerged from the alley, the people of Madrone stopped and gasped, and many made the sign of the cross. Some hid their faces, and as the Seer walked off, people hurried to get out of his way.

Karl wondered what new problem had just found them.

Chapter 18

Warnings

ELOISE

Eloise looked up as Eric stomped into the Silver Swan, his hair tangled, sword naked in his hand, and a fierce snarl on his face. The fool innkeeper ran up to him, obviously distressed by his appearance, but then Rafe and Roselyn called to Eric by name. The unhappy innkeeper hung his head and slunk away. Eric joined them at the table, which was heavily laden with food, his scowl contrasting sharply with everyone else's smile. She and Roselyn both wore silk scarves from Bristlen over wet hair; after days on the road, she could've stayed in that hot bath for weeks.

"Eric," Rafe said, seeming oblivious to Eric's scowl, "this is Seren."

Rafe motioned to the gray-haired older woman sitting beside him, who looked at Eric apprehensively. Eric's scowl didn't vanish but he bowed slightly to Seren. She nodded back.

"Eric, are you all right?" Roselyn asked.

Eric growled.

"Where's Karl?" Eloise asked.

"On the street ...," Eric hissed, "... having ... *fun.*"

Eloise and Roselyn exchanged furtive glances.

"We'll fix that," Roselyn promised.

Eloise smiled wickedly. Whatever was bothering Eric would come out soon enough; subtlety wasn't Eric's forte. Karl would return; neither she nor Roselyn had been happy to discover he'd snuck out before they awoke, but Karl wouldn't leave them; of that both were certain, confirmed by their long discussion while they bathed. Their company was growing; Rafe seemed happier than he'd ever been. Seren seemed to be a nice ... whore, although Eloise never used such words. Despite her age, Seren had a youthful face, cheerful, with deep lines of experience and character, an upturned nose, high cheeks, and a still-trim figure. Eloise hoped she looked as attractive when she was old and gray.

"Where are our *things?"* Eric asked pointedly.

"Under the table," Rafe whispered, and Eric looked to see their treasure bag tucked between Rafe's feet.

"Your helm and shield are upstairs, with my bow and Rafe's fork," Roselyn said. "The other bags, our provisions and clothes, and my quivers, are gone."

"Stolen in the fight," Eloise said.

"Seren saved us," Rafe said. "Thieves followed us outside the tavern and attacked us in the street. Without Seren, we wouldn't have seen them until too late."

"They try rob everybody," Seren said sheepishly.

"Still, it was very brave ...," Rafe smiled.

Rafe and Seren kissed, and everyone pretended not to watch.

"Eloise, your word is golden," Eric said. "Despite our delays, we're in Madrone. I'm back to my original plan: Svenson can't stop now unless he wants his own army to turn against him. The local Saxon Earl is raising his army. War's coming; the Valkyrie fly, and I'm ready for them."

"Must you continue on your quest?" Eloise said.

"Eloise ...!" Eric started, but suddenly the silver swan-painted door opened again.

Karl walked in and Rafe called to him; Eric scowled and looked away. Karl walked over to the table slowly, his shoulders slumped. A huge, swelling bruise colored his cheek.

"Karl, who hit you?" Eloise demanded.

Karl said nothing but he glanced at Eric, who grunted a sarcastic chuckle and then took a deep, long drink.

"We ... may be in trouble again," Karl said. "A strange man accosted me on the street. He said we were in danger and must leave Madrone. He seemed unusually certain, and said he'd come here to tell us more. At first, I thought that he was insane, or playing some game, but the people in the street seemed ... afraid of him."

"Who was he?" Eloise asked. "Did you get a name?"

"No, but you couldn't miss this guy in a crowd," Karl said. "He was all dressed up in a fancy black robe."

"Seer!" Seren gasped, and she paled with fright.

"Who ...?" Rafe asked.

Seren glanced around before speaking as if afraid to be overheard.

"Evil man," Seren whispered. "They say he a priest of Old Faith that betray his calling, sacrifice infants, and summon demons. Seer rarely leave house and never speak to anyone. Rich, powerful men visit Seer; seldom leave happy. Call him Seer because people fear to speak his name; evil vapors enter mouth."

"Is he dangerous?" Roselyn asked.

"More than any in Madrone," Seren warned. "They say he most powerful of Old Faith for many generations, and his eyes are gates to Hell."

"A wise-one," Eric grumbled. "Why would he want to warn us, let alone talk to us?"

"He didn't look terrifying to me," Karl said.

"What should we do?" Roselyn asked. "Ride out ...?"

"Could it hurt to listen?" Karl asked. "I'm telling you: he was just a little guy."

"This is no place to discuss this," Eric warned.

They took their mugs, and Eric grabbed a pitcher of ale and a loaf of fresh bread, and they hurried upstairs and closed their door behind them.

"Now, anybody have any suggestions about what to do about this Seer?" Karl asked.

"I do," said a strange voice. "Listen to him."

Everyone jumped. Seren let out a stifled scream. Behind Karl stood the Seer, leaning casually against the wall.

Eloise's eyes opened wide; she'd been the first in the room and it had been empty. Shivers ran up her spine as it had in the Wolflord's cave. Magic had caused her more misery than everything else in her life; to see it standing in her own room made Eloise's skin crawl.

Yet the Seer didn't look frightening. He was a small man, thin, shorter than Roselyn, with delicate features, immaculately clean, and dressed in austere black as if attending a royal mass. Even his hair and eyes were coal-black. He had an amused smirk on his face but there wasn't anything funny about him.

"How did you ...?" Karl demanded.

"I'll gladly to teach you," the Seer abruptly interrupted. "It only takes ten years of study. After seven years I could explain it in words you could understand. Are you willing to dedicate yourself to me for a decade just to learn a simple trick?"

Karl glared but said nothing.

"Oh, well," the Seer smiled, turning to face everyone. "I'm sorry to force myself upon you, but I've come to give you a warning. The sign of two swords is tired of chasing you. He's called upon his magician to kill you; I suspect you're all going to die tonight."

"Capsizes!" Eric cursed.

"What can we do?" Roselyn asked.

"Seer can save," Seren said. "Why else he warn? He want something."

Everyone looked suspiciously glaring at the figure in black.

"You're smarter than you sound," the Seer sneered at Seren. "Yes, I can save you tonight, but what about tomorrow night ... or the next? How long will you need my protection?"

"You want our treasure," Karl guessed.

"Try thinking next time," the Seer snapped. "If I can enter your room at will, then I could just wait for you all to die and help myself. Your wealth is of no concern; my goal is more important."

"So tell us already," Karl said huffily, "or do you just like hearing yourself talk?"

"My price is simple," the Seer said. "You will accept me as the new leader of your little group, go where I go, and do as I say."

The companions gasped.

"How about we just kill you instead?" Karl threatened.

"You should stay silent while those with brains speak," the Seer said to Karl. "That's my price: serve me ... or die tonight."

"For how long?" Eric asked.

"I can't say," the Seer said. "I have a great task to perform, and I need your help to achieve it. When I'm done, I'll have no need of you."

"What task?" Rafe asked.

"This bag," the Seer said, pulling the long, hard black leather case from his shoulder. "Do any of you know what this is, or recognize what it's for?"

Eloise looked closely at it. She'd seen lots of good leatherwork and this was certainly excellent. The case was a long tube, dyed pure black and soaked in clear bee's wax. It was at least five feet long and probably waterproof. One end was a handspan in diameter with a leather cap sealing it shut, laced together with black leather thongs. The case smoothly tapered to the other end, which was only a thumb's length in diameter, and permanently sealed with a leather cap. The bulk of it was made of one hide of good, quality cow's skin, and it had a strong shoulder strap. But Eloise couldn't imagine what would go in it. No one ventured a guess.

"I don't know either," the Seer said, frowning. "But the Lady commanded me to make it, and She said that, when the time came, I'd understand its purpose."

"The Lady ...?" Seren asked accusingly. "They say you betray Lady."

"They ...?" the Seer snarled. "Fools say much, although they know little. I've heard the stories they tell to frighten children. They insult me as they'd never do to others of the Old Faith. If you're a fool then believe what you want. Service to the Lady is my life."

"What Lady?" Karl asked. "The Queen ...?"

"The Goddess," Rafe said. "The Lady of the Druids."

"Druids ...?" Roselyn asked. "I thought they were dead."

"Not all," Rafe said. "They're few and they don't go about openly, but they're around. I've only seen them a few times, long ago, when they led the Lantern Dances on Midsummer's Eve."

"Christian priests hate them," Eric said.

"They're pagans!" Rafe protested.

"We are," the Seer said. "But I didn't come here to debate religion. I require your services, and in exchange, I'll keep you alive. When I no longer need your help, you're free."

"What do we have to do?" Rafe asked.

"Stay in this room tonight, inside a circle I'll draw," the Seer said. "That'll protect you from evil demons. But tomorrow will be far more dangerous and my magic alone may not protect us. We'll have to leave Madrone and go out where our conflict won't endanger my city."

"How do you know this?" Eric asked. "If Svenson's wise one is sending assassins to us tonight, why's he planning something even worse for tomorrow?"

"The Lady knows all," the Seer said. "She's sent me messages, and Her predictions always come true. But She doesn't tell me everything; I'm only Her servant."

"Why should we believe you?" Karl asked.

"Fine," the Seer said, and he pulled his long, empty leather case back over his shoulder and turned toward the door. "Come see me tomorrow, if you can. However, if you're still here, I'll be back at sunset. You can spend the afternoon shopping for supplies ... or shrouds to be buried in."

The Seer opened the door and walked out into the hallway. He closed the door behind him and his footfalls tramped down the hall.

"I don't like him," Karl muttered.

"What can we do?" Eloise asked.

"Nothing," Eric said.

"There has to be something ...," Karl said.

"We can run and spend the rest of our lives hoping another Wolflord isn't chasing us," Eric said. "That assumes we live to see the dawn."

Rafe made the sign of the cross and Seren clutched his arm.

"What is Wolflord?" Seren asked.

"The devil," Rafe said. "Maybe we could hide in a church ..."

"Risky," Eric said. "We don't know we'd be protected there and we have a promise of protection here. It's dangerous to deal with wise ones, but sometimes we must."

"I don't trust that Seer," Rafe said. "Why would he want to travel with us?"

"Why should we swear to take orders from him?" Roselyn agreed.

"Wizards have strange purposes," Eric said. "I don't like wizards, but what choice do we have? I've watched wizards kill. Besides, we only need to worry about the Seer while Svenson's army stands; wizards are powerful, but swords kill them just like anybody else. If Svenson loses the war, then his wise one's only interest will be to flee before he's caught. Since the war's only a few days off, I think we should accept the

Seer's protection, but keep our daggers handy, just in case."

"I'll have no part of murder," Rafe said.

"Nor will I," Eric said flatly. "I don't kill for sport or game. Defending oneself isn't murder."

"Well, I'll be here at sunset," Roselyn said. "Until then, I'm going shopping. Who's with me?"

In the end, they all went. Eric got out plenty of coins, mostly hacksilver, and then divided their treasure-rolls back into their three packs. Eric, Karl, and Rafe each wore one, and Eric looped his bag over his shoulder. Eloise noticed Seren didn't even blink while their treasure jingled inside their rolls or while they were fishing out silver coins and tossing back gold. As they filled their pouches with wealth, Eloise wondered how much Seren knew and how far she could be trusted.

They left their shields with Roselyn's bow, but Rafe took his long fork and Eric took his helm, insisting that Karl show them the armorer that could pound out his dents.

Down the street Karl led, Eloise clenched tight onto his left arm while Roselyn clung to his right. Eric and Rafe followed with Seren in-between. They attracted quite a few stares but felt like they were on a holiday. Eloise pointed out curiosities she'd never seen and was delighted by every sight and sound. Inside the bustling city Eloise felt at home.

When they reached the armorers, Karl found them hard at work on both his helm and mail. They'd silvered a length of steel wire, coiled it, and cut out individual rings to replace the broken links in his mail. Karl's helm was blackened where a band of steel plate had been welded inside of it, around its crown, and they were planishing it smooth before the polishing began. All of the men examined the work, approved it, and Eric commissioned them to repair his helm as well, and to straighten the bent prongs on Rafe's pitchfork. They promised to return for their things before sunset, and the master armorer swore they'd be ready.

After they left the armorers, Eloise and Roselyn insisted on shopping for new clothes. Rafe and Eric argued that they should gather supplies for the road but the women wouldn't be gainsaid. They found several tailors in the marketplace, stalls filled with used garments of all sorts. In Heaven, Roselyn and Eloise dove into stacks of carefully-folded clothes, laughing like children. Their first purchases were fancy, formal dresses, but Rafe reminded them that they were going back to the road and should consider more practical garments. Then Rafe purchased an expensive bright blue silk waistcoat with big silver buttons brought all the way from Persia. Yet the women did listen, next purchasing warm cloaks and sturdy shoes.

Their new clothes were all second-hand but clean and showed little wear. Each seemed to have a delightful little story about who and where they came from; stories the merchants loved to tell but no one believed. Many tailors displayed heavy bolts of new, bright cloths, offering to make custom-fitted dresses. Both women wanted new gowns but had to refuse.

Eloise loved shopping. She bought at least one item from each merchant, and word quickly spread. Soon merchants crowded around them, several outfits on each arm. Roselyn and Eloise found a long, red velvet tunic for Karl, which he thought made him look like a gypsy, but Roselyn loved it so he bought it anyway. Seren helped them barter and usually got everything at a much lower price. Then Roselyn and Eloise turned on Eric, picking out a clean, well-mended gray-and-black striped tunic for him, and Rafe bought several dresses for Seren.

Eventually the swarming merchants became annoying. Hemmed in, their path blocked, the merchants pressed them to buy everything.

"Time to chase off these fleas," Eric growled to Karl.

Together they drew their swords and raised them threateningly, but the merchants refused to leave, offering to trade their wares for Karl and Eric's swords.

"Me do it," Seren said, she pointed at a black shawl, raising her voice. "Me bet the Seer like that! We get gift for our friend, Seer!"

At the mention of the Seer, a hush fell over the merchants. Some looked frightened, others indignant, but soon all quietly fled back into the maze of shops and booths, leaving the companions alone.

"Why do they fear him so much ...?" Karl asked.

As sunset approached, Seren led a more somber party back to the Silver Swan than the one that had left it. Eloise had spent a fortune. They walked burdened with new bags and stuffed saddlepacks, for Eric had suggested they purchase the means to carry their new belongings. They each had, at least, two spare outfits, and they also had their helms, mail, and pitchfork, now in excellent condition, and Roselyn had bought three new quivers stuffed with steel-tipped arrows.

The Seer was in their room when they arrived. He'd moved all of their furniture; the beds, table, and chairs lay pressed together in the center of the room. The sight of the table pleased everyone, for it was covered with brimming pitchers and wide platters of food. Yet not all of the odors in the room were pleasing; sulfur-scented smoke seeped from a brass incense burner in the center of the table, surrounded by a stand of lit white candles. A wide circle was painted around the furniture looking red and wet.

"It's lamb's blood," the Seer said. "Please don't step on it or track it around the room. Everything's ready so we can pass the night undisturbed. If you need to visit the shed out back, do so now. The sun will set in less than an hour, and once it does, no one can step outside of this circle until dawn. Not for any reason; is that clear?"

"What made you so sure we'd come back?" Karl asked.

"My visions from the Lady," the Seer said. "She's never wrong; we're all going on a journey together, although I don't yet know where."

When the sun set, the Seer barred their door, entered the blood-circle, lifted up a tall rowan staff, and began to chant. He spoke softly, loud enough for them to realize he wasn't speaking a language any of them recognized, but not loud enough to be heard from the hall. His chant droned on and on, some phrases repeating, others wholly unique, for over an hour, and then he suddenly stopped. He sighed, set his staff aside, sat down, and took a drink of ale.

"That's it?" Karl asked.

"What did you expect?" the Seer asked. "Lights flashing, monsters appearing, the dead rising ...?"

"Well, something," Karl said.

"You're better off not seeing such things," the Seer said. "If they're illusions then they might be safe, but illusions can kill. If you ever see visible magic and it's not illusions, enjoy it, because you probably won't live to see anything else. Visible displays are called Divine Magic because they're beyond mortal ability, requiring more knowledge than one can learn in a single lifespan and more power than a mortal body can channel."

"So you say," Karl sneered, still doubtful.

"It doesn't matter what you think," the Seer said. "Until you understand magic, pray you never see it. Most people want to see Divine Magic although it'd kill them. People don't care about True Magic because it doesn't have instantaneous, visible results. So all they get is False Magic, illusions and deceptions, and then they claim magic isn't real."

"Is that what rich men pay for?" Karl asked. "Illusions and deceptions ...?"

"Oh, no," the Seer smiled. "They want knowledge of the future."

"You can tell the future?" Eric asked.

"No," the Seer laughed. "I can divine a little of what's happening elsewhere, but tell the future? Even the most powerful Divine Magic can see little of that. I tell rich fools what they want to hear, and after a few illusions, they believe anything."

Rafe laughed, but no one else did.

"What's True Magic?" Eric asked.

"Magic that works," the Seer said. "Magic most people scoff at because it doesn't come with lightning bolts and thunderclaps."

"Like what?" Karl asked.

"Like Rafe," the Seer said. "Christian, right? Christian priests specialize in blessings: very powerful magic."

"Blessings ...?" Karl asked.

"Sure," the Seer said. "Powerful magic, if you understand it."

"How so?"

"Hard to explain," the Seer said.

"Seven years of study?" Karl asked sarcastically.

"Think of it like this," the Seer said. "Imagine your spirit is a dark, empty void. Even the richest, most powerful men on Earth lead miserable lives if their spirits are dark and empty. Every blessing is like a lit candle in your spirit; it lifts you up and brightens everything in your life. A light spirit can make your life better, your problems smaller. Some people, like children, have spirits like roaring bonfires; light spirits make children glad."

"That's not what people want," Karl said.

"People want to be rich, dangerous, or somebody else," the Seer said. "I hear it every day. But magic requires years of training and practice; people who want wealth could earn it sooner without magic, and magic has costs gold can't cover. Magic can be fatal to the magician, if spells aren't cast correctly."

Eloise glanced nervously at her companions, wondering if the Seer's spells would protect or kill them. Little else was said; the thick, perfumed air seemed oppressive, and their few attempts at conversation softly dwindled away. She and Roselyn finally crawled under the covers of one bed and Rafe and Seren snuggled quietly in the other. Eric and Karl stayed awake with the Seer.

Roselyn fell asleep quickly, but Eloise lay still and silent, awake, but giving no sign. She rolled to face away from them, but listened to the men converse long into the night.

"Do you really think it's dangerous to step outside this circle?" Karl asked Eric around midnight, after Rafe, Seren, and Roselyn were asleep.

"Don't," the Seer said. "Upset my circle and we all die."

"I don't know," Eric answered Karl. "But I know it's safe here, and I've nothing to gain by moving."

"Do you really want to see what's out there?" the Seer asked in a whisper. "I must admit: I'm curious, but we mustn't wake the others, so don't move or speak, no matter what you see."

Quietly, Eloise rolled back to watch although she kept her eyes narrow so no one could tell she was awake.

Seeing no objection, the Seer untied a dark wool pouch.

"This is a blessed moonstone, my most-treasured relic," the Seer said. "It illuminates many things that can't be seen by normal eyes. It doesn't show everything, but I'd like to see if it can make something visible."

"I'm willing," Eric said.

"I'll bet we see nothing," Karl snickered.

The Seer unlaced his pouch and pulled out a round, white rock, a spherical gemstone almost too big to hide in one hand. It was misty white, like a thick fog, hazy, as if you could see deep inside of it, but the round stone seemed to glow, radiant in the Seer's hand.

Suddenly a thin purple mist appeared, filling their room everywhere except inside their circle of lamb's blood. Menacingly silent, it was faint, visible only as it swirled around their protective circle in strange, random gusts. Then the Seer slid his moonstone back inside his pouch, and the purple mists vanished.

"Interesting," the Seer said.

"What was that?" Eric asked.

"I don't know," the Seer said, "but I wouldn't want to breathe that mist. It seemed ... alive."

"I'm impressed," Eric said.

"You should be," the Seer said. "It would cost you most of your treasure to see that, if I were charging you for my protection. Unfortunately, I need you as badly as you need me."

"What do you really want?" Eric asked.

"To bless your boots," the Seer said.

"My boots ...?"

"In my vision from the Lady, I saw tracks made by a Viking bound for Valhalla," the Seer said. "I could bless your boots and they'll help you toward that goal."

"I guess it can't hurt me ...," Eric mused, reaching down.

"No, you have to be wearing them," the Seer said.

"You're serious?" Eric asked.

"Afraid so," the Seer said.

As Eloise watched, Eric lifted up his boots, one at a time. The Seer reached into his robe, which was lined with many pockets, and took out a small copper vial of yellow salve. He also took out a small silver knife, scooped out some of the salve onto it, and marked the soles of Eric's boots with it, smearing each with two wide yellow lines, joined at the toes. Then he spoke a short, mumbled incantation, as if he were blessing Eric's boots, and the yellow salve melted into the worn leather soles and disappeared. Finally, the Seer pulled out his moonstone. The eerie purple mists again appeared outside their circle, but Eloise noticed only Eric's boots. Where the Seer had marked them, Eric's boots glowed with yellow lights, looking like bright yellow 'V's beneath his toes.

"The 'V's are for Valhalla," the Seer said. "May these guide your way there."

"You'll regret this day if these marks ever betray me," Eric warned the Seer. "I don't like magic; it always works out in favor of the magician."

The Seer grinned at Eric as if he were an impudent child. Eloise closed her eyes, nervous. She pulled her blanket up over her face and breathed through it for fear of inhaling the purple vapors. She wondered if she'd sleep at all; once they'd entered Madrone Eloise had felt safe for the first time since leaving Bristlen. Now another terror had found them.

Chapter 19

Revenge

KARL

Regretfully Karl steered his horse behind the Seer as he led them out of the crowded city of Madrone in the early hours of the morning. The Seer rode a magnificent black stallion, so impressive Rafe had whistled when he saw it. Eloise and Roselyn each had two large bags of clothes strung by short ropes across their horse's shoulders, in front of their saddles, and they were all wearing newly-bought clothes.

Seren rode with them. No one had said a word when Rafe bought a gentle mare for her. Seren had never ridden a horse before and had to be assisted onto her saddle, but Rafe rode next to her and gave riding lessons as they went. The others looked at her dubiously, but Rafe seemed as happy as a child in a sugar bag, and Seren couldn't have asked for a better instructor.

Their journey wasn't long. The Seer led them north, back the way they'd come. They rode away from Madrone for two miles, then took a smaller road west toward some low forested hills.

"Where are we going?" Karl asked the Seer.

"A special place," the Seer said. "A hilltop crossed by Britain's strongest lines of power, a focal point of magical essence. We won't need a circle there; it's been a Druid sacred place for centuries. Whatever's sent against us, I should be able to battle it there, but it'll take me all day to prepare. You may rest and eat the food you brought."

"Food ...?" Karl asked, suddenly feeling foolish.

The Seer reined in short.

"Supplies for the road ...?" the Seer asked. "Isn't that why you went to the marketplace?"

Karl hung his head.

"We bought clothes."

The Seer closed his eyes, sighed heavily, and shook his head.

"How did you survive making brilliant decisions like that?"

The Seer altered their course and headed for a distant cluster of farmhouses. Karl fell back to report their side-trip, and his feeling of foolishness became shared. The Seer led them within half a mile of the first house and then he called on Karl and Seren to go ahead and purchase supplies.

"Remember to ask for breads, cheese, and fruits; things that don't have to be cooked," the Seer said.

"We know what we need!" Karl snapped.

"Then why didn't you get it yesterday?"

Karl pulled on his reins and rode away, furious; he didn't know how long he'd be able to tolerate the mouthy Seer.

"Karl ...!" Rafe shouted. "Wait for Seren!"

Rafe spurred gently, holding on to Seren's bridle, and pulled her horse towards Karl. Seren clung tightly to the crest of her saddle more than to her reins. Riding the well-trodden road had been difficult for Seren on her first day on a horse; riding across the rougher, pathless grazelands, her horse bounced harder, yet she didn't fall off.

"Karl," Rafe said seriously, "take care of Seren. Protect her as if she were Roselyn or Eloise."

"Any friend of yours I'd die for," Karl smiled.

The stable-master grinned at him, then turned and rode back toward the others.

"Whoa!" Karl shouted as Seren's horse turned to follow Rafe. Karl took hold of its bridle and pulled it after him toward the farmhouse. Soon Karl released it; the docile mare followed his horse as readily as she'd followed Rafe's.

"You no like Seren ...?" Seren asked him suddenly.

"W-what?" Karl stammered. "No, I-I mean, we really don't know ..."

"You no want Seren with Rafe?" she cocked her head questioningly.

"No!" Karl said. "I mean, yes, I want you with Rafe ... in the city. Out here, our travels are ... dangerous. This one could be fatal."

"Seren no mind danger," Seren said. "Madrone not safe, if not careful. Seren know to be careful."

"Why Rafe?" Karl asked bluntly. "You meet new men every night."

"Rafe good, and rich," Seren said. "Seren not young; new men wanted Seren once, but no more. Seren never hungry, but see many sisters starve. Rafe kind to Seren, generous, and Seren be good to Rafe."

"What if Rafe lost his wealth?" Karl asked.

"No leave," Seren smiled. "Rafe a loyal man. Sisters say loyal man greater treasure than gold. Seren no afraid of Rafe; more afraid if no Rafe."

"Rafe's a loyal man," Karl agreed. "He deserves a loyal woman."

Seren looked squarely at Karl.

"Seren be loyal. Seren earn Karl's trust."

Karl nodded silently; he'd give her a chance, but she understood that he was Rafe's friend first.

"Now, tell me about that smug-mouthed Seer," Karl said. "Tell me everything; the worse, the better."

"Many rumors, much nonsense," Seren sighed. "Seer's servants say little; Seer pay them well. But

Seren see Seer's home; big house, private stable, guard at door. Men with crowns visit often, pay much gold. Seer rich man."

"Why do people fear him?" Karl asked.

"Seer wields Druid magic," Seren said. "Britons rule England before Saxons come. Druids rule Britons; very wise, very powerful."

"They can't have been that powerful," Karl said. "If they were so powerful then how were they overthrown?"

"Seren not know. Some say the Lady weaken, that time comes when Mother Goddess must fade. Seer like no Druid before; keeps neither to forest nor temple, and casts forbidden magics. Seren never see, but know other Druids shun him."

"How do you know that?"

"Seren know Druids; good people, host moon-dances and sacrifice to Lady. Druids friendly to Seren, even when little girl."

"Rafe's a Christian," Karl warned.

"Seren like Christians; more good people."

A tall man with a hoe came around the corner of the house. Karl broke off his conversation and raised his open right hand in a gesture of peace. The farmer welcomed them, after they explained their need, and offered them a huge sack of food for only fifteen coppers. Karl offered him no more than six and didn't pay him until after Seren had examined its salted meats, dried vegetables, cheeses and fresh breads.

They rode back quickly, Karl carrying the sack, Seren desperately clinging to her saddle.

Hours later, they emerged from a thin stand of dogwoods to see a gentle rise ringed with tall, sturdy oaks and tenuous willows swaying in the gentle breeze. The Seer led them up the slope and inside the circle of trees, where the hilltop was crowned with a lawn of thick, knee-high grass surrounding a stack of sawn logs piled atop the ruins of a large fire.

"Tie the horses to an oak," the Seer said. "Stay within the trees and light the fire an hour before sunset. It'll take me all afternoon to gather the forces of the mystic lines; please let me work in peace. Wander about as you wish, just be quiet and leave me alone."

The Seer dismounted and wandered off across the hilltop, silent, his head bowed.

Eric snapped his fingers softly and nodded to his left, to the far side of the clearing. The stern expression on his face warned them something was up, so they all dismounted and led their horses to the side. Rafe caught the reins of the Seer's horse and pulled it along.

As they reached the trees, Eric waved them closer.

"This ends tonight," Eric whispered to them all. "I've been thinking; Svenson's magician must know we survived his attack last night or he wouldn't be threatening us tonight. He may or may not know who helped us survive his first assault, but he'll be watching. Once he recognizes the Seer, then we'll no longer be important to him. He and the Seer will battle each other, and we'll be free to flee. We need the Seer tonight, but tomorrow we can abandon the Seer to fight this wizard alone."

"What if the Seer won't let us leave?" Eloise asked.

"By dawn, the Seer will have finished dueling Svenson's magician, so he'll be tired," Eric smiled. "I'll knock him out, and we'll be gone before he wakes up."

"What should we do now?" Karl asked.

"Rest," Eric said. "We'll be awake all night and riding fast tomorrow, so we'd best sleep while we can."

In hushed voices everyone agreed. They unsaddled and brushed their horses, and Rafe checked their shoes for rocks and staked them out so they could graze. Then they spread out their horse blankets to dry and ate some food, speaking very little. The Seer came by while they ate, mumbling a chant in words no one could understand, and he continued walking around the perimeter of the hilltop. Then the Seer walked to the fire logs stacked in the very center of the ring, waved his arms, and shouted more arcane words.

Eric shrugged and stretched out on the grass, leaning against a saddle. The others did the same, spreading out their sleeping blankets on the soft green cushion. Soon Eric started to snore. Karl kept looking over at Eloise and Roselyn, who were sharing one blanket, wishing he could join them.

Rafe and Seren began giggling, and suddenly they got up. Rafe rolled their blanket and picked it up, and hand-in-hand Rafe and Seren walked toward a thick willow, vanishing inside its curtain of fresh green leaves. Karl smiled and glanced at Eloise and Roselyn, who'd stretched out side-by-side on a blanket not far away. Surprisingly, he discovered both girls were staring at him ... and broke out laughing when he looked.

Karl stood up, but both women quickly rolled over and faced away from him. Karl walked towards them only to find them curled up together, eyes closed, pretending to sleep. Karl wondered why they were ignoring him, yet he could think of nothing to say. He glanced at the Seer, who stood before a mighty oak on the north side of the clearing, both arms raised, as if he'd catch the towering tree should it suddenly decide to fall.

He's crazy, Karl thought. Then he glanced at the willow tree Rafe and Seren were under; both were clearly visible, although mostly obscured by the leaves. Karl turned away, giving them a semblance of privacy. Karl looked back at Eloise and Roselyn, still pretending to sleep, and wondered what they'd do if he laid down between them. Yet Karl wasn't that brave, and after a minute he dropped back onto his own blanket.

Karl tried to sleep but found it impossible. The sun was shining high and he wasn't tired at all. Time crept by and Karl shaded his eyes with his arm, frustrated.

Suddenly Karl felt a presence. Eloise's shadow covered him. She smiled sweetly down at him, her thin blonde hair blowing in the breeze. Roselyn was softly snoring on her blanket. Eloise licked her soft lips and tilted her head; Eloise gestured for Karl to follow her, and then walked towards a different willow tree. Karl eagerly got up, snagged his blanket, and followed as Eloise darted lightly inside its leafy curtain.

As Karl pushed between the long hanging branches, Eloise stood by the trunk wreathed in fresh leaves. Eloise smiled and held out her arms, and Karl threw his blanket down so it fell spread out, and he rushed to embrace her. Their hungry mouths merged, and Karl had never been happier or more willing. He kissed her hard and Eloise pressed for more. Her hands reached for his swordbelt, loosened its buckle, and let it fall. Then she began pulling up the skirt of his mail as if she could tear the metal tunic off him.

Karl stepped back to take off his mail without hitting her. Quickly, although it seemed an eternity, he pulled up the linked metal rings, bent over, and let his armor slide off. He should've thought to have taken it off before; it couldn't have been comfortable for Eloise with only a thin layer of cloth between her beautiful, luscious breasts and his hard, cold rings of armor. As soon as its weight left him, Eloise rushed into his arms. Her hands grabbed his padded coat and new red tunic and pulled both up and over his head. Karl let her undress him, eager for her to finish.

After stripping him to the waist, Eloise threw herself down on his blanket and drew Karl down upon her. They kissed long, passionately, and deeper than Karl had dreamed possible, oblivious to the living leaves hanging over them.

A strange noise distracted him. Karl glanced over, shocked to see Roselyn walking past the willow.

"Karl ...? Where are you, Karl?"

Karl froze, nervous.

Suddenly Roselyn pushed through the hanging branches, lightly blossomed new spring leaves in her hair. Roselyn turned to Karl and held out her arms.

"Lover," Roselyn breathed heavily. "Come to me, my love."

Karl gasped, confused, uncertain. Eloise seemed as unaware of Roselyn as Roselyn did of her. Karl didn't want to leave Eloise's hungry embrace; he loved her fiery passion, her youthful, shameless need. Eloise was raw pleasure, insatiable, satisfying. Yet Roselyn was deep, like a dark steaming pool, or the warm shade of a summer night. Roselyn's beauty was mysterious, enticing, and her slow, sensual passion seared his lusts like a hot brand he couldn't refuse, whose pain carried gratification and desires that never died.

Karl lay confused. He wanted to rush to Roselyn, to fall into her embrace and bury his lusts in the one fountain he could drink from forever.

Panicked, Karl glanced back at Eloise.

"Take me, Karl," Eloise whispered softly.

Karl looked back at Roselyn; her hands slid up her thin dress, her waist, her large, round breasts.

Torn, Karl fought to quell his rising fear and confusion. Back and forth he glanced, golden sunshine to dark temptation.

"Go to her," Eloise whispered, so softly Karl barely heard, and then he looked to find her smiling, and Eloise nodded toward Roselyn. "Go."

Karl smiled, grateful, certain he could've never decided on his own. Thinking only that he owed Eloise a debt he'd gladly repay, Karl pushed off of Eloise and stood, aiming all of his desires at Roselyn. Roselyn was the beauty he loved, the woman he truly wanted.

Suddenly Roselyn stepped back, away from Karl. Roselyn's arms drew in, from open and reaching to tightly folded across her chest. A tight-lipped frown replaced Roselyn's smile, and her sly, tempting eyes suddenly glared angrily.

"What were you doing with Eloise ...?"

Karl gasped, horrified and confused.

"How dare you leave me ...!" a younger voice screeched, and Karl spun around to find Eloise standing right behind him, furious, her right hand a blur as it arced toward him. Eloise slapped Karl hard, leaving a hand-shaped welt on his cheek, and then Eloise stormed away, tearing through the branches.

Exasperated, Karl heard someone huff behind him, and he turned, almost surprised to find Roselyn still standing there. Roselyn's hand swung furiously, making a second welt atop Eloise's. Then Roselyn pushed her way out from under the willow branches and stormed off.

Panting like a dog, frightened and confused, Karl wavered, and then collapsed to his knees onto the dried, fallen branches. He was trembling like a child, not knowing what had happened or what he'd done to deserve it. Karl didn't follow Eloise or Roselyn, but stayed frozen where he was, hidden inside the hanging branches, grateful for their concealment and certain of only one fact: *he was very afraid.*

Chapter 20

Svenson's Evil

SEREN

Impressed, Seren watched as thin, gray wisps of smoke appeared beneath Rafe's experienced hands.

"See ...?" Rafe said, motioning to the tiny flames. "Flint and steel: that's how you start fires out here."

Seren smiled, amused and a little proud. She liked that Rafe knew so much; most of the men of Madrone understood as little as she did about life outside their city. She'd never seen someone start a fire from scratch before. In Madrone, there was always someone nearby who'd light a candle for her.

The Seer came by eating a dried pear. Seren steeled herself, determined not to flinch, and even tried to smile at him, but it was difficult; shivers danced up her spine whenever he came near. She didn't know what to make of him, walking around in his fancy black robes as if he were the King of England. The stories she'd heard about him horrified her, yet in the daylight he seemed just like any other man, austere, too stern and serious for his youthful face. The Seer carried his wealth and power as obviously as possible, with the snooty airs of a nobleman in the stilted way he moved and how he stood, his back perfectly straight, as if trying to be taller, probably so he could justify looking down upon everybody.

Seren didn't fear magic; once she'd known a very powerful Druid priest, when she was a little girl, who could blow the fluff off a dandelion and make the flying seeds dance in circles around her. He was a kindly old man, beloved by farmers, who asked him for good weather to make their crops grow. He lived in the forests outside of Madrone where Seren had played while her mother worked the brothels. From him Seren learned of the Lady, whom he called the Great Mother, who cared for all of the children of the world, and of her wild lord, the Horned Hunter, so terrifying even the bravest quailed before him. But Seren didn't fear the Horned Hunter; he roamed the deeps of the darkest forests where she'd never go. Seren loved the Lady, who bloomed the flowers and set laughter in her heart.

The Seer was an abomination. Seren understood Christian priests; their murdered God taught of love and justice, and they were loyal to him as the Druids were to the Lady, but the Seer had taken the Lady's gifts and rejected her. Despite his protests that he still served the Lady, Seren didn't trust him.

The Seer sat down beside them on the stacked wood, nodded to her, and watched Rafe stack dry willow branches onto the tiny flame he'd started in the shelter of a large log, which he was using as a windbreak.

"Thanks for starting the fire on time," the Seer said.

"That's what you commanded, isn't it?" Rafe snapped. "Obey ... or die?"

Seren stiffened at the hatred in Rafe's voice; she hadn't guessed he felt so strongly.

"If I could be relaxing in my Roman bath tonight, I would," the Seer said. "Don't forget that I have orders to follow, or that my commands come from She I serve."

"So Seer say," Seren muttered, trying to show support for Rafe.

"Believe what you will: fools always do," the Seer said as if they were both unimportant. "I hope our business is quickly resolved; then neither of us will have to associate with people we don't like."

"Speaking of that," Rafe said, "what's this journey that you spoke of? It'd better not take long ..."

"The Lady sent me a vision of us, all of us, riding through dark woods at night," the Seer said. "We were following a trail Eric left us; that's all I know."

"When did you see that?"

"A few days ago," the Seer said. "I didn't even know any of you existed until then. When I first searched, I found you exactly where my vision had said you'd be, riding down the North Road with nine Vikings chasing you."

"You saw that?"

"And your clever solution," the Seer smiled, and he looked over at Eloise and Roselyn. "Didn't you guess? I cast healing spells on Karl and Eric after they were wounded."

"I knew something was wrong; wounds like theirs usually take a month to heal," Rafe said.

"It was no small effort on my part," the Seer said. "I was so weak afterwards that for more than a day I couldn't even stand, which is why I didn't meet you on the road before you entered Madrone."

"Thanks for your help," Rafe huffed reluctantly.

"I've no use for thanks," the Seer said. "I've rested long enough and must continue my preparations."

"Can Seren help?" she offered hesitantly. Seren didn't really want to help or even be near him, but she did want to learn as much as she could.

"No," the Seer said. "Only I can do this."

"What you do?"

"I'm awakening the lines," the Seer said. "Magical lines connect to all the Sacred Sites of Britain. Using them, I've drawn powers from all over England, which I can use when the Viking mystic attacks. When the sun sets, then our battle will begin, and I'll need all the power I can get. Once it starts, stay inside the crown of trees or I won't be able to protect you. No evil can enter uninvited, so you'll be safe."

The Seer took a deep, sighing breath, began mumbling prayers, and walked off across the grassy hilltop, resuming his preparations. Puzzled, Seren watched him walk away. The Seer didn't seem like the horrible devil the stories about him described; he was an angry young man, frustrated, and certainly obnoxious, but not evil. Yet she still didn't trust him, and wondered if Rafe was worth involving herself which such a man.

Rafe carefully stacked more wood around his tiny fire, like a child building a wooden castle out of sticks. Soon his fire burned brightly, and its flames grew higher as the sun sank lower.

Eric, Roselyn, and Eloise wandered up. Karl walked up shortly after they did, a blanket under his arm, frowning deeply. He dropped his blanket atop their pile beside Rafe's pitchfork, quietly sat and stared into the flames; Seren wondered what had happened to him but decided not to ask.

The Seer was wandering around the circle again, occasionally waving his arms over his head, his lips always moving, muttering chants they were too distant to hear.

Slowly the sun set, streaming orange-red streaks across the cloud-filled sky as it slid like a ball of fire toward the horizon. It was a beautiful sunset, if joyless.

Darkness swallowed the world outside of their circle save for the few stars peeking through the thick clouds. Rafe stacked several logs onto his fire, and their tall flames illuminated the whole crown of oaks and willows, which were swaying in a crisp, chill breeze that grew steadily stronger. Rafe and Eric hurriedly moved some of their woodpile away from the fire, which the wind blew their flames against, or they'd have ignited the whole cord. Against the chill wind, Rafe asked Karl to hand him two blankets, giving one to Eloise and Roselyn, and keeping one to wrap around himself and Seren. They sat together on the grass before the hot blaze, their backs to the wind, and passed around their brass flask.

Seren drank deeply. She smiled when Roselyn and Eloise only sipped.

An hour after sunset, Eric suddenly laughed. Everyone startled; no one had spoken since sunset, all waiting in dread anticipation.

"Ha!" Eric said. "Either the Seer's mumblings are working or Svenson's wizard is sleeping tonight. Either way, we're still alive."

"Shush!" Eloise said. "I hear something."

They all fell silent, listened carefully, and looked about the hilltop. The rushing wind rustled through the trees and whistled in their ears, and the constant crackling of the bonfire drowned out all but the loudest noises. The Seer was on the west side of the crown of trees, but any hope of hearing what he was mumbling was lost in the breeze.

"There ...!" Karl shouted, and he pointed east.

Faint red lights flickered through the trees. Torches, many of them, approached. A procession came around a small willow near the base of a tall, thick oak, and suddenly walked into view.

A company of priests with flaming torches appeared. Three of them carried tall staffs with large painted crosses on their tops. All wore robes, and the man in the lead boasted a tall, pointed bishop's hat, white with a golden cross. The bishop was shouting something yet they couldn't make out his words over the loud, blowing wind.

"It's a priest!" Karl said.

"No, it's a bishop," Roselyn said.

"Why are they here?" Eric asked.

"No know them," Seren said. "They not from Madrone."

"I'll check it out," Rafe said, and he hurried down the slope towards them. Seren questioningly glanced at the others, and then followed Rafe.

"Father ...!" Rafe shouted as he approached them, coming inside the light of their torches. Seren ran up behind him, staying close, looking gravely at the robed strangers.

The bishop was a tall, heavy-set brute of a man, crowned with a high, pointed white hat, wielding his thick staff topped with a white crucifix. Behind him stood two other priests in robes almost as decorated as his, and behind them marched a dozen monks in plain brown sackcloth robes, each carrying a large wooden torch blowing in the wind, illuminating their meeting.

"What blasphemy is this?" the bishop cried over the rush of the wind. "Heathen fires in my barony? What pagan devils are you conjuring?"

"None, your Grace!" Rafe shouted.

"I'll be the judge of that, if I may enter inside this cursed pagan ring?" the bishop asked.

"Of course!" Rafe said. "Please, come inside, good Father."

Rafe stepped back as the bishop entered, his followers trailing close behind him.

"Are you Eric?" the bishop asked.

"No, he's with my friends, by the fire," Rafe said.

"Take me to Eric," the bishop commanded.

Rafe bowed slightly and dodged aside as the bishop marched forward, not waiting to be escorted. Seren also jumped back, trying to stay away from the large bishop as he plowed past her. Somehow she felt afraid to touch him, as if his holy robes contained great evil.

As the priests approached the blazing fire, the Seer ran up shouting.

"What goes on here?" he cried. "Who are these people?"

"This is a bishop ...!" Rafe insisted.

"The bishop of St. Bunstable is Father Steffanard, a close friend of mine!" the Seer argued.

"Blasphemy!" the bishop cried. "You're a pagan and the tongue of Satan!"

"How did they enter my circle?" the Seer demanded.

"I-I in-invited them ...," Rafe stammered.

"You what ...?!?" the Seer cried. "I spend all day fortifying this place, and you ...?"

"Are you Eric?" the bishop interrupted.

"What ...?" the Seer asked.

Seren stepped back, confused and afraid. Something wasn't right, the gray hairs on her neck were standing straight as arrow shafts, and the presence of the priests was like a vaporous plague in her throat. She'd known many priests, and none of them had ever repulsed her like this foul, giant bishop. She was afraid to speak ill of any man of God, yet how did he know Eric's name? Seren lowered her head; she glanced at their shadows on the grass. Something seemed very odd: the lights of their many torches were casting a dozen shadows around the feet of the priests, but around the feet of Rafe and the Seer only their bright bonfire cast any shadows.

Seren screamed so loudly even the bishop was startled.

"Lies!" Seren shouted. *"Stay back! Him false!"*

"Where's Eric?" the bishop bellowed.

"The evil!" the Seer cried. "Two sword's evil!"

Suddenly the Seer waved his hands and vanished; one moment he was there and then he was gone.

"Warlock!" the bishop cried, and then he turned toward Rafe and angrily swung his thick arm. The bishop struck Rafe hard; Rafe bounced from the bishop's forearm as if a tree trunk had swatted him. He flew backwards and rolled across the grass.

Seren screamed and ran to help as Rafe tumbled to a stop halfway down the slope. She fell on him, frantically searching for signs of life. Rafe laid unconscious, limp beneath her hands, but he was breathing. Seren gasped, surprised by her own desperation.

Suddenly a blinding white light burned into her eyes, abruptly flashing from nowhere, glaring even after Seren squeezed her eyes shut. The light flared painfully, brilliant, shining blood-red through her hands as she covered her face, futilely attempting to block it out. Seren winced as if she'd stared directly into the sun.

The blinding light vanished unexpectedly, as suddenly as it had come. Seren blinked away the stinging, flashing spots that haunted her vision. Then she lifted her eyes to a sight more horrible than she'd ever imagined.

No monks, no priests, and no bishop stood beside their fire. Where they'd been, a huge monstrosity stood; a towering goliath, a tall, thickly-muscled man, a giant so terrifying Seren's scream choked and failed. The giant was tremendous, the largest living thing she'd ever seen, naked save for a few shaven animal skins laced onto a thick rope about his waist. He was still covering his eyes as Seren had, rubbing them as she was wiping away her tears, and blinking in the firelight.

The giant was more than oversized; he was malformed, misshapen. His head was lopsided, his arms oddly twisted, of uneven lengths, yet he moved his massive limbs quickly and dexterously.

Seren shook her head, wincing the delusion away; giants existed only in fables, and she hadn't drunk enough to even feel giddy. Yet the giant was still there when she looked again, and Seren gasped in horror at her own madness.

Karl and Eric stood nearby it, on the other side of their fire, their swords useless as both furiously blinked away their blindness. The Seer alone seemed unaffected; he was hurriedly pulling Eloise and

Roselyn away, both of whom were blindly stumbling as the Seer forced them down the slope.

"Eric! Karl! Run away!" the Seer shouted. *"He's a magician, an illusionist!"*

The Seer pushed the women onward, and then turned and faced the giant. The giant roared like a beast, cursing in some strange, barbaric tongue.

"Stay, giant!" the Seer shouted. "We've no quarrel with you!"

"How did you do that?" the giant's booming, angry voice grated like an iron plowblade scraping through gravel.

"I, too, am a sorcerer, a master of illusions," the Seer shouted to the giant. "Who are you ... and why do you threaten us?"

"I'll kill you all!" roared the giant, and he raised a huge fist and stepped toward Karl.

"Then you'll feel my wrath!" the Seer cried, and he gestured toward the giant, shouting arcane words.

The giant suddenly cried out, clutched his chest, and staggered. Slowly the giant crashed to his heavy knees, grimacing in twisted pain.

"Who are you?" the Seer demanded.

"Skaldi ...!" the giant cried. "I'm Skaldi from Utgard, a servant of Utgard-Loki!"

The giant fell forward, bracing himself with his arms, squirming in agony, twisting with torment.

"Why are you attacking us?" the Seer asked.

"I have to kill Eric!" Skaldi the giant cried. "I have to kill him before dawn ... or I'll go back to Utgard."

"How ...?" the Seer asked. "How did you get here?"

"A wise one!" Skaldi gasped. "Please, stop ... the pain!" He gritted his huge teeth, squeezing his eyes shut. "An opening appeared before me, out of nowhere, and a human conjurer offered me the chance to reenter the world of men, where I could kill and terrorize like we did in the old days."

"How could a human magician perform such magic?" the Seer shouted.

"I don't know!" Skaldi screamed. "He had to get me to agree, and joined his life with mine to bring me through."

"What a fool!" the Seer gasped. "He could die ...!"

Skaldi the giant staggered, winced, and then looked up, his eyes clear.

"I'm in no pain!" Skaldi shouted. "It's an illusion!"

"Like the blinding light," the Seer said. "It's not real, only deceived perceptions, but some perceptions are the same whether they're real or not. I'm telling you this because I'd rather not fight; if we could reach some amicable agreement, then perhaps we could ..."

"Silence!" Skaldi cried. *"I needn't answer you!"*

Skaldi pushed himself up and stood, rising to his ten-foot height. Angrily he turned towards Eric.

"You must be him I seek, Viking!"

"I am," Eric said, raising his sword, letting the red firelight glint down its surface. "Be warned, monster! Unless your flesh is immune to steel, my life is not for you!"

Karl stepped beside Eric, shoulder-to-shoulder, and raised his sword.

Skaldi stepped warily to the side, edging his way around the big fire. Eric and Karl moved back, keeping the fire between them and the giant; they had sharp steel, but the towering Skaldi looked monstrously strong.

"Leave them alone!" the Seer cried. "I'm your enemy, Skaldi!"

The giant turned to face the Seer, angrily glaring at him. Suddenly another giant appeared right in front of the Seer. The new giant raised massive fists and hammered down upon the Seer's head; Eloise and Roselyn screamed.

The Seer walked right through the new giant.

"Do you think I cower before attacks I know are illusions?" the Seer cried. "Stop this and return to Utgard before death claims you!"

"No human threatens Skaldi!" the giant roared. "I'll kill you first, wizard, and I need no illusions to that!"

The snarling giant dashed forward and hurled himself at the Seer. Seren gasped; the Seer was powerful, but no illusions could stop a giant's boulder-hard fists, and one punch could kill any human.

"Run ...!" the Seer shouted to Eloise and Roselyn, and they instantly obeyed, fleeing toward the trees.

Suddenly every light vanished, both the roaring fire and the stars overhead, plunging them in total darkness. Seren screamed, terrified, feeling unsafe, blind, although she and Rafe were the farthest from the giant.

Sunlight blasted out, clear as a midsummer's day, brightly lighting the circular hilltop and the hills beyond them under a clear, blue cloudless sky.

"Incredible!" the Seer gasped. "I've never seen such fantastic, detailed illusions!"

"I'm Skaldi of Utgard," the giant shouted. "Illusions are the heritage of my people, an art we've practiced for a thousand years, and I'm better than any human wizard."

"You're better indeed," the Seer said. "I've never seen illusions make a sun illuminate the night or create dozens of images at once. But mastery of illusions isn't the same as using illusions effectively."

"You think you're smarter than Skaldi?" the giant snarled. "I can kill Eric any time. You're the only threat to me, wizard: yours will be the first blood that wets my hands."

The giant stepped toward the Seer again, but suddenly the Seer vanished. Seren blinked, wondering if she could even help when she didn't know what her eyes were seeing. The giant stared about, and not seeing the Seer, again he approached Eric.

"Here ...!" the Seer cried, suddenly reappearing upon the sunlit grass.

Skaldi turned angrily and instantly attacked; the giant jumped at the Seer and swung his massive fists.

The Seer's image faded and the giant overbalanced, fell over, and terrible howls erupted from his lips. Skaldi screamed, flailed wildly, and finally scrambled away, his chest and legs white and red with fresh, swelling burns. The illusion of low, green grass faded away to reveal Rafe's bonfire. Hidden under an illusion of plain grass, the giant had stumbled onto, and fallen on top of, its roaring flames.

Eric and Karl charged in, swords swinging, as Skaldi fell back, charred and blistered, madly brushing away the hot coals still clinging to his flesh. Karl struck first, slicing a deep rent into one giant leg while Eric stabbed his sword deep into Skaldi's boney ribs so hard his sword stuck. The giant roared and swatted at Eric; Eric barely dodged his massive flailing hand and ran back, forced to abandon his sword.

Skaldi kicked at Karl, who was caught flat-footed as he swung his sword again. Karl sliced deep into the huge foot, then it kicked him into the air, wheeling Karl head over heels before he crashed to the ground;

Karl's bloody sword fell to the ground beside the real fire.

Lying in a heap, Karl slowly raised one arm, as if trying to stand, but then he collapsed. Karl groaned and lay like a dead thing.

Seren glanced at the trees, torn and confused. She should run, abandon these fools to their mystical insanities; *no man, however kind, was worth dying for.* Yet, was her life in Madrone worth running back to? Seren only had a few loyal customers left; the new men only looked at the young girls. Seren was tired of being called hag and crone; every copper she earned went to brothel-fees. Soon no one would want her and she'd be reduced to begging. Was that the life Seren wished to return to?

The giant jerked Eric's sword from his side with a painful howl; Eric had stabbed him deeply, and a gallon of blood poured from his wounded ribs. Gritting his teeth, Skaldi raised Eric's long, thick sword like a dagger.

"Enough!" the Seer cried. "You're hurt, and that wound could be fatal, if not treated. Stop this, and agree to return to your world, and I'll do what I can to spare your life."

"Never!" Skaldi gasped. "I could never return to Utgard defeated by humans! You're small, weak ...!"

"Why were giants banished from Midgard?" the Seer asked. "Think, Skaldi! Use brain, not brawn! Once giants ruled Earth because strength ruled; our legends speak of days when your kind roamed like Gods. But then steel was discovered, and our numbers grew, until there were so many humans, armed with steel, that numbers, not strength, carried the day. You can't bring back the days when strength ruled any more than you can unteach the making of steel. End this now! I don't want to kill you!"

"Silence, human!" Skaldi shouted. "Speak no more lies! I'll kill you all!"

Skaldi suddenly jumped over the fire at the Seer, but the Seer dodged into nothingness, vanished under his cloak of illusion. Eric stood there, weaponless, and the giant punched with his mighty fist, driving massive knuckles right into Eric's chest. Eric was only slightly knocked back, yet he collapsed at the giant's feet and crumpled onto the grass. The giant raised his heavy foot to stomp the life from him.

Suddenly Eric was gone, replaced by a roaring bonfire, pouring smoke, wafting waves of heat into the air. Skaldi jumped back; even if he knew it was an illusion, the fresh, searing blisters in his skin still burned; he couldn't bring himself to stomp on a bonfire.

The Seer reappeared and snatched up Karl's sword off the grass. The Seer faced the giant, protecting Eric, but his grip on Karl's sword was awkward; it shook in his inexperienced hands.

As Seren watched, Eloise and Roselyn ran for their pile of belongings; Roselyn grabbed her bow while Eloise snatched up Rafe's deadly pitchfork. Seren stood, decided at last, and pulled the wide knife from Rafe's belt. The giant was winning. Rafe, Karl, and Eric were down, and the Seer seemed to be weakening. Seren couldn't stand by and watch two young noblewomen fight alone; she hefted Rafe's dagger and ran to help.

The giant turned to face the Seer, warily watching the sword in his hand. Suddenly a bolt of lightning burst from the sky, striking Skaldi right across his eyes, but no thunder echoed, and the giant didn't even wince.

"Your powers are fading," Skaldi grinned at the Seer. "Where are your deals now?"

The Seer held his ground, awkwardly waving Karl's sword over his head, standing so close to Eric that his feet were straddling Eric's right arm. The giant towered over him, feinting, but he was obviously straining, his right hand pressed against Eric's swordcut in his side, which was still pouring blood. His left leg where Karl had sliced him wasn't as deep, but it was also bleeding badly, coloring his leg in crimson, and Skaldi was limping, unable to put his full weight on the foot that had kicked Karl. The giant swayed but didn't relent. Skaldi swung Eric's sword with his left hand, striking Karl's defending blade so hard it almost flew from the Seer's grip.

The giant screamed suddenly, an arrow sticking out of his back; Roselyn had shot him at close range.

Skaldi turned to face her, howling in outrage. The Seer seized the moment and attacked, slashing Karl's sword across the giant's right arm. Skaldi swung backhanded, almost absently, and struck the Seer's head, knocking him to his knees.

The giant quickly limped around the fire, almost hopping. Roselyn aimed another arrow, but held her shot trained on his massive chest. Skaldi hesitated, gauging Roselyn and her weapon, gasping for breath. Their eyes met; Roselyn said nothing, and Eloise edged forward, Rafe's pitchfork tight in her hands, a look of pure determination tightening her face.

Skaldi charged. Roselyn released, and her arrow shot deep into Skaldi's chest. Eloise dodged Skaldi's reaching arms, slipped underneath as Roselyn's arrow staggered him, and she drove Rafe's sharp prongs deep into his giant stomach. Skaldi screamed, yet he grabbed them both by their throats and lifted them high, one girl in each massive hand.

Both women cried out.

Seren dropped Rafe's dagger, stole Karl's sword from the Seer's stunned grip, and ran around the fire. She leapt, her first leap in years, and drove the swordpoint with all of her weight into the giant's back. Skaldi roared like a wounded bear, shuddered, and finally fell. Hurled to the ground, Roselyn and Eloise landed hard and rolled, badly battered.

Seren pulled out the bloody blade, aching as only an aged body could. Skaldi was prone, unmoving beneath her, but she wasn't satisfied. Seren lifted Karl's sword as if it were an axe and swung it as if chopping wood; Karl's sword struck Skaldi across the back of his head and split his skull. Blood spewed; Skaldi flinched, and then he shuddered and moved no more.

Beneath Seren, the giant lay dead.

Chapter 21

Capture

THE SEER

The Seer groaned as the morning sun, the real sun, rose dazzlingly bright, shining above their circle of trees. Despite its warmth, the Seer felt more chilled than he could remember; not since his youthful training days on the Magical Isle had he awakened so miserably. His eyes burned and his brain melted and squeezed out his ears ... if he perceived correctly through avalanches of pain.

Slowly the Seer opened his eyes, despite their intense stinging, and peered out at a world as beaten as he.

Groans of discomfort, not of his own making, stabbed his ears; the Seer wasn't alone in his world of hurt.

Eric lay beside him unconscious. The old Viking looked worse than ever, if such were possible; as pale as death, Eric coughed and hacked in his sleep, and his agonized expression, even while unconscious, looked little better than the Seer felt.

The Seer tried to sit up but an entirely new throbbing flooded his being. He foundered back onto one elbow, but managed to lift his head. He recognized the primary cause; he'd pushed beyond his magical limits and drained himself nearly to death. Yet an unfamiliar pain tortured him; his head hurt ... where the giant had struck him.

The giant! Quickly, the Seer turned his head too fast, reeled for a moment, and then he scanned the hilltop. Skaldi's body was gone, as he'd expected, vanished in the sunlight. The Seer frowned: he'd have liked to have carted it home for dissection.

Dimly the Seer recalled watching the women finish off the wounded giant before he'd passed out. Skaldi would've certainly killed him if the women hadn't challenged him; the Seer felt ashamed that he couldn't defeat Skaldi with the powers he'd drawn from the sacred Druid lines. Now he owed his life to these wretched peasants, and that debt doubled his aches.

"Lie back down," Roselyn's voice thundered inside his ears, ricocheting around the inside of his skull.

The Seer collapsed back onto the damp grass. Roselyn's face loomed into vision, her expression as tired as the Seer felt. She silhouetted the sun.

He hadn't before noticed before how lovely she was!

The Seer tried to chastise himself yet felt subdued; he'd given up trivial distractions like beautiful women long ago: all that mattered was his Art. Yet the Seer noticed Roselyn's beauty more than he liked to admit.

He hadn't chosen to be alone; his Masters had cast him out, sent him away from the Magical Isle without a thought or care. Freezing and starving, his one winter in the wild had taught him the depth of their hatred, although he'd never fathomed its source. Either they were jealous or terrified, but they didn't matter anymore. They'd abandoned him, yet he didn't die for their amusement. He'd crawled into Madrone, blinded by snow and mostly-frozen, and made a prosperous life for himself among the commoners. Neither friendship nor help was offered; the peasants feared him. Forced to accept rejection by his own kind, he filled his life with study, and alleviated his suffering with all the luxuries wealth and power could grant.

Gently but firmly Roselyn helped him to sit up. Karl and Rafe stared back at him as his eyes focused on them, but both looked even worse than Eric.

"How are we?" the Seer asked.

"Not well," Roselyn said. "Karl can't lift his left arm and his ribs are numb, probably broken. Eric's having trouble breathing and we can't wake him. Rafe keeps fading in and out, yet he insists that he's fine."

"How am I?"

"You've a huge lump on your forehead, swollen and very colorful, but otherwise you seem all right."

"The rest of you ...?"

"We're okay. Seren's limping a bit; she shouldn't be jumping on top of giants at her age. Eloise has bruises around her neck, but otherwise we're fine."

The Seer reached into his robe, sifted through his many pockets, and pulled out a scrap of paper folded around an aromatic mixture of herbs.

"Special tea," the Seer said, and he handed the packet to Roselyn. "Boil this in ... enough water ... for everyone."

"Are these magic?" Roselyn asked, opening the paper and looking at the herbs.

"Yes," the Seer lied.

"Eloise ...!" Roselyn shouted, and her volume struck the Seer like a thousand cathedral bells clanging in his ears.

Three hours later the women finished saddling the horses. It took Eloise and Roselyn more than an hour to round up their horses, which had bolted in the night, probably terrified by the giant. Rafe had to give instructions; none of the women had saddled a horse before, and none of the men could. Soon after Eric had awoken, and drunk as much tea as the women could make him, the women assisted them all into their saddles.

Thick, gray smoke blew from two huge piles of coals; embers blown by the wind had engulfed the whole cord, which was now so hot they kept their distance. The smoke worried the Seer; everyone within miles would know they were there, but he had no cure for that.

His herbal tea was weak and bitter, yet it was hot and nicely chased away his chill. The herbs in it would help his aching head ... if he lived that long.

"At least we don't have to worry about the sign of two swords anymore," the Seer groaned, gritting his teeth so he hissed his words. "The spell used to bring Skaldi to our world required several life-forces to cast. He must've sacrificed children on top of his own life's energy to bring Skaldi all the way from Utgard. He probably assumed that any giant could kill us; that was his fatal mistake. There's no need to fear him anymore; when Skaldi fell, the Viking mystic died."

His companions said nothing; the Seer wondered if they'd heard him or if they were just too stupid to understand.

"No!" Seren shouted suddenly. "Seer save you, Eric, after Skaldi hit."

The Seer startled and turned in his saddle, but the movement was too much and he almost collapsed, clutching his saddle crest to keep from falling off his horse, his hands squeezing his throbbing head. Behind him, Eric held a dagger naked in his hand. The Seer silently cursed; *if they wanted to kill him then this was their chance.*

"Traitor ...," the Seer groaned. "Betrayer ...!"

"He saved your life, Eric," Eloise said. "He stood over you with Karl's sword even after his magic was gone."

"It's true," Roselyn said. "He defended you. Please, Eric; let him live."

"Don't ... worry," the Seer gasped to Roselyn. "I can't die; even if Eric tries, something'll stop him. In the Lady's vision, I saw myself riding with you through a forest at night. That vision will come to pass: She's never wrong."

"I should kill you ... just to prove you wrong," Eric said.

"I marked your boots to get you into Valhalla," the Seer said. "Is this how Vikings repay their debts?"

Eric glared, but the Seer ignored him ... as he ignored all idiots. Soldiers like Eric hated wise ones.

Yet the Seer felt secure; he'd read the Norse myths several times: Eric couldn't kill someone who'd saved his life; the Valkyrie didn't favor traitors.

With a snarl of disgust, Eric sheathed his dagger.

"Where to ...?" Roselyn asked.

"My house," the Seer said slowly. "My servants will cook us everything in the kitchen and we can drown our pains in aged wine and hot baths."

Roselyn smiled, and even Eric didn't object.

With their fire still smoking, they rode out of the circle of trees and headed back towards Madrone. Roselyn led them back the way they'd come. They rode for about a mile in silence, and then they were forced to rein in.

A line of mounted warriors, Saxon knights on horses with long spears, silently blocked their road. The Seer's heart sank; something told him they weren't headed toward wine and hot baths.

"By order of Sir Guldwin, Earl of Northumbria, you're under arrest," shouted one of the knights. "Any attempt to resist will cost your lives."

The companions groaned; none of them had enough strength to resist a savage kitten.

The knights led them eastward, away from Madrone. Eloise introduced herself to the knights as Baroness of du Harmonn, and afterwards rode beside their leader, who had his knights pass fresh waterskins to the companions at Eloise's request, but he ignored her complaints and arguments; the companions were going to see Earl Sir Guldwin whether Eloise liked it or not. Roselyn said nothing to the knights, just covered her head with a scarf and pulled it low over her face.

Their journey took forever. Eloise improved quickly as they rode, and Seren reported that her hip felt better. Karl managed some movement in his arm, but his ribs were the opposite of numb. Eric didn't improve, and Rafe looked even worse; he swayed in his saddle as if about to fall off. The Seer wavered between agony and discomfort and hoped he didn't look as badly as he felt.

The Saxon knights led them to a wide army camp filled with thousands of men, horses, and tents arranged haphazardly on a wide, uneven pasture. Clashes of steel rang from laboring smiths and from groups of men practicing swordfighting. Shouts came from all over. In the distance, aligned in square formations, troops marched back and forth, and farther off, hundreds of archers plied their trade against dozens of thick hay bales. The scents of roasting meats filled the air and black, oily smoke rose from a huge cooking area where three full sized cows were being turned on massive spits over vast beds of red-hot coals.

The knights ushered them into the army camp, past dozens of spearmen standing guard around its outskirts. They attracted a lot of attention as they were paraded into the ocean of men. A chorus of whistles blew at Eloise, but an equal number of curses shouted when men spied Eric. A few charged forward and threatened to kill the Viking, but the tough Saxon knights warned them back with hard spear-butts. Roselyn kept quiet, hidden beneath her scarf, and rode quietly beside Karl.

Just inside the camp proper they were forced to dismount and stand on the grass, surrounded by dozens of Saxon warriors, while the knights rode off. Their new guards refused to give them food or drink despite Eloise's promises to deal with them when she was confirmed as Baroness of du Harmonn.

Finally a large gathering of armored, grim-faced men came forward, led by a tall, older knight wearing gleaming armor, all elaborately decorated, made more of solid steel plates than mail, all silvered with etchings on the plates, and riveted mail of the smallest links the Seer had ever seen. The Seer recognized Earl Sir Guldwin from the seeings he'd done for payment; Earl Sir Guldwin had a thick beard, cropped short, and a bristling mustache hiding his angry frown. Steely brown eyes glared at them menacingly; Earl Sir Guldwin walked straight up to Eloise as if he were going to hit her.

"You must be Eloise Elizabeth du Harmonn," he snapped out each word like a threat.

"Baroness du Harmonn," Eloise snapped back.

"Watch your tongue!" he shouted. "I'm Earl Sir Guldwin and I've no time to waste. Where's the treasure?"

Eloise said nothing.

"Search them!" Sir Guldwin barked at his men.

Instantly three guards obeyed. They came forward and grabbed Eric first but, despite his wounds, Eric shouldered one hard, knocked him backwards, and then reached for his sword, yet Eric failed to draw it in time. Six speartips suddenly surrounded him, each pressed close to his unhelmeted head and forcefully held by a tough Saxon guard.

"Why aren't they disarmed?" the Earl demanded.

"Take their weapons!" shouted a man beside the Earl, and more guards came forward. Every dagger and sword was quickly stripped from them, along with Roselyn's bow and quivers, and Rafe's fork, although he was so weak he almost fell over without it. The long, black, empty case of the Seer seemed to interest them; they took it with the rest. Their belongings were set under a nearby tree.

"Search them and their horses," Sir Guldwin ordered. "I want every piece of treasure."

"Earl Sir Guldwin!" the Seer spoke up. "Please! I'm the High Seer of Madrone! If I might speak ..."

"Silence!" Earl Sir Guldwin commanded. "I know who you are, and reminding me of it won't help you live! I've more important things to do than to bandy words with a Druid trickster! Now give me that treasure!"

"It's in the bags tied to our saddles," the Seer said.

The others all turned to glare at him.

"Do you think they won't find it?" the Seer protested.

"Silence!" Sir Guldwin shouted, and he turned to his men. "Show me the treasure!"

Seconds later, men held open the packs and Eric's bag before him. Sir Guldwin examined each briefly, and then turned to a man on his left.

"Carry these to my pavilion. Stay with them. No one touches them."

"Yes, Your Excellency."

The man pointed at two guards, took all three packs and Eric's bag, and departed with his guards in tow. The treasure of Bristlen and Svenson's golden horn went with them; Eric bowed his head.

"What of the prisoners?" another man asked the Earl.

"Take Baroness Eloise away and keep her under guard until I decide what use she has," Sir Guldwin said, and he turned away.

"And the others?" the man asked.

The Earl paused.

"Kill them."

"No!" Roselyn screamed, and she pulled off her scarf and stepped forward, toward Earl Sir Guldwin. *"Father, no!"*

Earl Sir Guldwin spun to face her, his expression aghast.

"Roselyn!" he gasped. "How did ...?"

"You can't kill them, father!" Roselyn screamed. "Not unless you kill me!"

Earl Sir Guldwin froze, and a sheen of anger masked his face. He stomped forward, drew back his hand, and slapped Roselyn so hard she fell to the ground. Karl jumped forward with a cry of outrage, but the Seer and Eric grabbed Karl and held him back.

"You ... the handmaid ... *my own daughter ...?"* Sir Guldwin shouted. "My scouts said you were in a bar fight, whoring! *How dare you disgrace me?"*

"Father ...!" Roselyn pleaded from her knees as she sobbed and clutched her bruised jaw.

"Drag this shameless hussy to my tent," Earl Sir Guldwin said coldly, lowering his cruel voice. "Save her 'friends'; their death's need to be ... *special."*

The Earl stormed off.

"Put them in chains," one knight ordered. "Post four guards to watch them. And bring them something to eat. Don't let them die ... yet."

While one man ran off, another, whom the guards addressed as Captain Dareth, selected four guards to watch Rafe, Seren, Eric, Karl, and the Seer. Then Captain Dareth personally helped Roselyn up and gently drew her and Eloise in the direction Roselyn's father had disappeared in.

"Wait ...!" Rafe cried, and so much pain filled his voice that everyone who heard him stopped. "Please, take Seren; she's ... Eloise's handmaid, not Roselyn. She doesn't deserve to die ... like us."

"Seren stay with Rafe ...!" Seren protested, and she wrapped her arms around Rafe, but Rafe pushed her away, although he almost collapsed from the strain.

"Eloise is your Baroness," Rafe said to Seren. "Obey her ... and remember me."

Seren burst into tears, but Rafe kissed her and then pushed her away.

"This way, Seren," Eloise commanded, her voice cracking as she fought for control.

The Seer bowed his head; Rafe and Seren would probably never be together again.

Sir Dareth said nothing, so the Saxon guards let Seren pass. Seren looked back at Rafe pleadingly, but he only stared at her, his red eyes full of sorrow. Slowly Seren turned, sobbing, and followed as Sir Dareth led Eloise and Roselyn away.

"See that they're unharmed," Karl shouted at Captain Dareth, but the knight ignored him.

The Seer shook his head. They couldn't die; his vision of the Lady had to come true. *Or ... had he failed Her?* That would be the worst death of all.

Rafe slowly lowered himself to sit on the grass. His face was swollen bright red, and carefully he stretched out to sleep. The Seer looked at him, worried.

"They told you to feed us," the Seer said to the guard. "I'm a Druid priest and I eat only garlic, dried dandelion leaves, coriander, and fresh sage. The cooks should have it: get it. Oh, yes: I drink only red wine."

"After you're chained," the guard said.

"As you wish," the Seer said, and he sat down beside Rafe. "Might as well make ourselves comfortable."

Rafe was sound asleep when a smith arrived with shackles and tools. Rafe didn't awaken when they tried to rouse him, so Karl and Eric held up Rafe's ankles while the smith riveted shackles onto him. Then they each held still while shackles were hammered onto their own legs. There was no point in resisting; they were in the middle of an army camp surrounded by thousands of Saxon warriors, each of whom would be glad to kill them, and their weapons were out of reach.

Three bowls of thin soup and several loaves of bread were soon brought, along with the herbs the Seer had requested, and a large flask of red wine.

"Use your magic to get us out of here!" Karl whispered to the Seer.

"Are you mad?" the Seer asked. "In my condition? There're no lines of Britain here. Finish your soup and give me your bowl. Mixing these herbs in the wine, I can make a potion to help Rafe, and Eric looks like he needs some as well."

Karl sighed and obediently drank half of his soup, then poured what was left into Eric's bowl. The Seer washed Karl's bowl out with a little wine, then put measured amounts of the herbs in it. Upon request, Karl unfastened his belt and gave it to the Seer, who used its metal buckle to grind up the herbs in the bottom of the bowl, and then he emptied into it a few folded pouches from inside his robe.

"Foxglove, chamomile, and willow-bark," the Seer said. "This should bring the swelling down and prevent infectious vapors from taking root. Now pour that wine in here," he held the bowl out to Karl, "and we should probably all have some."

Karl poured half of the flask into the bowl and the Seer stirred it with a finger, mumbled a prayer to his Lady, and then they pulled Rafe up and made him drink as much as he could. Then the Seer drank deeply and handed what was left to Karl and Eric.

"Best let Rafe sleep," the Seer said. "Save the rest of the wine; it may be a while before we get more."

The Seer took the loaf of bread, tore off a huge chunk, picked up Rafe's bowl of soup and dipped his bread. Karl laid back to rest. Eric cursed softly.

"Not what you planned?" Karl asked.

"Not a good way to die," Eric growled. "Prisoners have no life. If I could get my hands on a weapon, any weapon, then I'd start killing these guards, and they'd have to send me to Valhalla."

"Be ready," Karl said to Eric. "If I get my hands on a weapon I'll throw it to you."

"I'm sorry I dragged you into this," Eric said. "I could've stayed at Bristlen and manned the walls disguised as a Saxon, and earned my paradise there ..."

"I could've shouted for help in the Baron's bedroom," Karl said. "Roselyn could've, too. Rafe and Eloise could've called for help in the Bristlen's stable, but they didn't. You may have started this, but we're all to blame."

Eric shrugged, a faint, half-smile momentarily marring his deep-set frown.

"We will finish this together," Eric promised.

Chapter 22

Daughter

ROSELYN

Roselyn pushed through the heavily-brocaded flap into her father's pavilion. Inside his ornate tent, Earl Sir Guldwin and three other knights ignored Roselyn and greedily sorted through the treasure-packs. Each clink of the precious metals stabbed; all of her dreams of escaping to France were ruined. All Roselyn could hope for now was to spare her companion's lives, but anything she said might doom them. She sat down on the foot of her father's great bed and said nothing.

Svenson's golden horn delighted all of the men, but they griped over prized pieces they'd expected to find.

"Where's the rest of it?" Sir Guldwin demanded.

"We took all we could carry," Roselyn said. "We spent a few silver coins for food and clothes, but nothing else."

Her father sneered, then ordered his knights out. He unlocked a huge, heavy trunk with a key on a silver chain around his neck, put all the treasure inside, and locked his trunk.

"Why didn't you come straight to me after Bristlen?" he asked softly.

Roselyn sat there, her face downcast.

"Answer your father!"

"I ... was afraid," Roselyn said.

"Afraid of your father ...?"

"Afraid of which bedroom you'd send me to next."

"Vandislidge du Harmonn would've made you a baroness! Who do you think you should marry, the King of England?"

"Perhaps I don't want to marry ..."

"Do you think your sisters wanted to get married? Do you think your brother wanted to be a knight? They did what the family needed, what I need, and so will you. You could've born my grandson to be Baron of du Harmonn and given me control of half the Danelaw. Now that brat Eloise is baroness, and your brother is still with Duke Graymark in Italy. I suppose I can keep her locked up in one of the small castles, and marry them when he returns. Foreign lands would've been more useful, but I can't let the king auction off the barony again or I'll have to fight for it."

"I don't want to ...!"

Her father's backhand across her face caught her off-guard.

"Nobody cares what you want! You're my daughter and I'll do with you as I please! How you dare disgrace our family riding around with peasants ... like some filthy slut ... and then make demands ...?"

"I'll do as you say," Roselyn gasped slowly. "Anything, I swear ... and I ask only one thing in return."

"Wretched child!" Sir Guldwin cried and he balled up his fist and beat her again. "Willful .., insolent .., wicked child! You dare bargain with your father? I'll stake you out for my troops!"

Roselyn collapsed, sobbing, and fell off of the bed onto thick carpet covering the ground. She lay there stunned, bruised, and helpless; she wished she were dead.

"Clean yourself up," her father ordered. "You'll be married as soon as I've dealt with these invaders. Stay here in my tent and be silent. Disobey me again and I'll have your 'friends' tortured to death."

Earl Sir Guldwin stormed out of his tent, leaving Roselyn more alone than she'd ever been. Roselyn cried for herself, for her friends, and for the cruel fates that had born her to such a monster.

Chapter 23

The Awakening

RAFE

Rafe jolted awake to a blare of horns trumpeting before dawn.

"War ...!" someone shouted loudly. *"War! War! War!"*

Some soldiers picked up the chant while others groaned, crawled out of tents, or looked out from inside their damp cloaks. Soon the whole Saxon army chanted.

"War! War! War!"

"War!" shouted an armored man stomping across the camp. "Get up, you louts! Time to march!"

"What's happening?" Karl asked.

"Have you no ears?" Eric said. "Earl Sir Guldwin is marching his army against Svenson Two-Sword. Today is the day I've planned for since I sailed out of Oslo Bay; today battle rages!" Eric lowered his voice to a whisper. "I must go to the war!"

"Are you crazy?" Karl asked.

"I'm the reason these armies are here," Eric said. "I plowed the Blood Path. The Valkyrie followed me; to lead them here and then miss the battle would be a great disgrace."

"You want to break out of these shackles and escape from the Saxon army just so you can join them on the war field and help fight the Viking army?" Rafe asked. "I agree with Karl: you're insane."

"This is why I came to England," Eric said. "The Valkyrie fly today. I must heed their summons."

"Eric ...," Karl began softly.

"No," Eric interrupted. "You're true friends; don't change that in my last few hours. Today Eric Bjornson dies ... I'll fight whoever resists me."

"You're not going to die," the Seer said confidently. "The Lady's vision showed us following your trail through a dark forest. You'll live to make that trail."

"Believe as you wish," Eric said. "Today I ride with the Valkyrie, and no mortal shall stop me while a sword swings in my hand."

"You don't have a sword," Rafe reminded him, "and these chains aren't going to fall off by themselves."

"There has to be a way ..."

Groaning almost as loudly as his still-sore joints, Rafe rolled over and pushed himself up. He raised his eyes and tried to focus, although he wobbled, still weaker than he wanted to admit. Under the lightened sky before daybreak, while the last stars faded, Rafe witnessed a host of movement, like a gray cloud of Saxon hoods, woolen caps, and steel helmets, polished or painted, weaving between countless tall spears that waved as they were carried. Many banners displayed. Rafe spied horse corrals; hastily erected fences, probably stolen piecemeal from local farmers. The pens packed four hundred horses, and a line of youths carried hay bales and water toward them in a steady stream. Several times Rafe had commanded such a war-stable, although not this large, when he'd worked for Eloise's real father. Rafe looked down at the heavy iron shackles cutting into his ankles, wishing he were again in charge, or that he'd ridden off with his share of the treasure after Grusshire. Now he had nothing but his life ... and he doubted if he'd have that for long.

Karl and Eric stood beside him while four guards surrounded them, alert and wary. Rafe noticed they were small men, young and unarmored, but each bore a short spear, a steel sword, and a long dagger. Even if they could overcome these guards, while unarmed and chained, the vastness of the army around them promised no hope of escape.

"Svenson's doomed," Karl said, looking over the host of men.

"Don't underestimate Svenson," Eric said. "Earl Sir Guldwin has close to five-thousand troops, yet they'll be hard pressed against Svenson Two-Sword; Svenson has more men, but they're dispirited, with virtually no horses, supplies, or hope of reward. Yet Svenson's men are Vikings; most of Sir Guldwin's men are farmers and townsmen hoping for a share of the spoils, to sell daggers and jewelry pocketed from the slain. They'll be lucky to make it back to their homes; as hired mercenaries, Sir Guldwin will send them into battle as arrow-fodder. But tactics alone won't win this war; morale rolls a heavy die. The odds are too close to call, but the fate of the Danelaw will be decided today. If Sir Guldwin fails, then Svenson Two-Sword will stand as the sole military power in this locale, effectively King of Northern England."

"What a horrible idea!" the Seer said.

Another blare of horns blasted out over the hills.

"To your companies!" someone shouted. "Form up on the archery field!"

The first sliver of sun beamed upon the Saxon army as it jostled together. Even the wide archery field was too small to contain it, and tempers were lost as men pushed to get underneath their household banners. Angry shouts abounded, but no fights;

violent actions weren't tolerated the morning of a battle. Feuds reduced morale, and many had been slain for not saving their fighting until their enemy was in range.

Rafe was always impressed by the organization of men: what seemed a chaotic, haphazard confusion was actually a highly efficient system. Each man who'd never fought before was paired with an experienced campaigner, and a common banner stood under which anyone could fight, for those who didn't belong to any household. Earl Sir Guldwin ran a disciplined camp; riders raced around the camp and shouted at those who moved too slowly. Surprisingly quickly, the camp emptied onto the archery field and the hills around it.

A few horns sounded and the movement on the archery field lessened. The soldiers fell silent. From atop his horse, surrounded by his knights, Earl Sir Guldwin raised a hand. Rafe was too far away to make out his words, but a moment later the whole host shouted:

"Defend our families, our churches, England!"

Horns blared over riotous cheers and the march began. Earl Sir Guldwin led, followed by mounted knights. Scouts had already ridden off, keeping the army's path clear. It took almost an hour for the bulk of the army to clear the archery field and finally march over the low hills, yet eventually the last man vanished on his way to victory or death.

Rafe glanced at Eric, Karl, and the Seer's grave expressions. No words were spoken; they had to escape before the army returned. He glanced at their four nervous guards, who were standing in pairs on both sides, watching them suspiciously. These guards obviously knew they'd be executed if their prisoners escaped.

"I'm tired," Rafe yawned.

"You look it," Karl said.

"I do ...?" Rafe asked.

Karl laughed. "My ribs are black and blue from where Skaldi kicked me, but your whole face is scarlet, darkening to purple."

"Good thing the women aren't here," Rafe said. "They'd make a fuss."

"I wish the women were here," Eric suddenly shouted, grinning widely. "I could use a royal wench underneath me again!"

Rafe, Karl, and the Seer turned to stare at him.

"Almost as much fun as watching them ride naked," Eric laughed. "Remember that, Karl? I loved that, but the best thing was ..."

Eric lowered his voice, discreetly motioning toward their guards, who listened intently.

"How could I forget that?" Rafe laughed. "Countess Roselyn and Baroness Eloise: who'd have thought it? I've been in every whorehouse in Madrone and I've never seen two women do that!"

Karl looked confused but Rafe grinned widely as Eric laughed. If they could get their guards to relax then perhaps they could catch them off-guard.

Chapter 24

Transformation

ROSELYN

Roselyn spat bloodily onto her father's carpet; he'd held nothing back this time. When he got back, if Roselyn crept close enough, she'd kill him, no matter what price she paid. One blade was all she needed. He'd have to kill her to stop her.

Slowly Roselyn pushed up, off the carpet, and leaned against his bed, grateful for the concealing canvas walls. Disheveled and bruised, her whole body ached, yet she couldn't sleep while her friends were in danger. Stiff and sore, Roselyn rose and peeked out of her father's tent. His troops were marching away. She couldn't see her father but she knew he was there, ruling his army directly, as he did with everything. He wouldn't allow another to assume authority in public; Earl Sir Guldwin wanted every ounce of glory acclaimed as his own.

Yet, he'd be her master no more.

She'd do worse than kill him; Roselyn would defy him.

Roselyn stumbled to his sturdy chest and tried to pull it open, but it was locked tight. All their precious treasure was locked in that chest, her dreams of living free trapped with it. She looked around for an axe to try to cut it open, but no weapons had been left, just a table covered with maps and scrolls, a small chest of clothes, and a suit of parade armor doubtlessly packed so he could look his best as he rode back home through Madrone with Saxons cheering his victory. Her father was a proud man who won at everything, but no more. Today, no matter what it took, Roselyn would be victorious.

Roselyn closed her eyes, steeling herself. If one dream was gone then she'd find another. She reached into her father's small clothes chest, pulled out his fancy, ornamented garb in handfuls, and threw them on the rug. Quickly she found his thicker garb, some trousers and a coat, and tossed them onto the bed. Then she unlaced her new dress, the fanciest she'd bought in Madrone, and carefully draped it over his large chest as a clear message. She pulled on her father's thickest, quilted clothes and then turned to the wooden stand where her father's parade armor rested.

She lifted his helmet off of its wooden stand and set it on the bed, then started unbuckling the straps holding his armor onto the frame. Underneath its thick steel plates was a long, sleeveless shirt of mail, but unlike Karl's, the links were so small and fine it flowed through her fingers like silk, and each link was silvered and polished so it shined. It was still heavy, but Roselyn clenched her teeth, driven by raging anger, and despite her various aches and pains, she pulled the mail coat off of the stand and threw it on. Its weight almost toppled her. Then she pushed her feet into his sabatons, shoes and all, although she had to force her thin shoes to squeeze inside the large boots her father wore, which had decorated steel sabatons riveted over their thick leather. She strapped his engraved greaves over her shins, but she left the heavy cuisses; his mail covered her thighs and she needed to be able to walk.

Roselyn tried on his breastplate but to no avail; her father was a large man, but mostly round in the stomach, and her ample bosom would only flatten so far. She buckled a white knight's belt around her waist to support the weight of the silvered mail and then fastened his wide gorget around her neck, over the mail. Holding onto the cuffs of the quilted coat, she slipped her slender arms through its articulated shoulders and metal arms strapped to the gorget, buckling all the tiny straps. Then she put on his helm and lowered its brass-encrusted visor over her face, trying to breathe through its holes but tasting only her own hot breath as she stared out through the narrow eyeslots. She buckled his helm-strap under her chin, slid on his articulated gauntlets, and then turned toward the canvas flap of her father's pavilion.

Her friends needed her. Roselyn took a deep breath and pushed out of her father's pavilion into the sunlight.

The camp wasn't empty. Knights, squires, archers, and footsoldiers had left, but cooks, older blacksmiths, many youths too young to fight, and several stablehands and retainers lounged about. Many glanced Roselyn emerged, curious, amazed that a knight would've stayed behind when the army had marched to war, especially one so impressively accoutremented.

Roselyn ignored them, as her father ignored all peasants, and strode ahead. Inside his heavy armor, Roselyn was less-obviously a woman, and the closed faceplate concealed her smooth, beardless chin. With long steps she walked imperiously past her father's surprised servants, ignoring their feeble attempts to address her.

Roselyn quickly strode between the thickly-pressed tents of the other knights, losing herself from any who might be trying to follow her, only to realize she had little sense of where she was going. Yet, she kept marching, as fast as she dared, and soon she emerged uphill of a familiar group of men surrounded by four guards.

Two young boys sat in front of the pavilion closest to her, tending a small, smoky fire. They were chopping thin branches in half with a hand-axe; they looked up at her and gasped. Roselyn reached down and plucked the little axe from the hands of the oldest boy. She would've preferred a sword yet she had no time to be choosey. With a glare she silenced their youthful protests, and then she marched straight toward the guards holding her friends.

The guards turned to face Roselyn as she paced off the distance between them. One youth took off his cap and bowed as she approached.

"Greetings, Sir Knight," he said. "How may we serve you?"

Nervous, gasping, and hoping they didn't notice her trembling, Roselyn fought back her fear as she had in the cave of the Wolflord. Then, Eloise had been the only part of her old life she'd had left, the only thing saving her from being trapped alone with strange peasants in the woods. Now Eloise and those peasants were her life, and Roselyn couldn't let them die.

Roselyn stepped close, reached out and grabbed the guard's spear. Then, after a moment of indecision, she swung her hand-axe at the guard closest to him.

To Roselyn's surprise, the axe struck him hard, unprepared, across his face. The thin iron wedge cut deep into the guard's jaw, driving through bone, and then she turned back to the first guard as he tried to pull his spear out of her grip.

"Help me!" Roselyn cried, her clear voice only slightly muffled by her helmet.

"Roselyn ...?" Karl gasped.

Eric hammered his shoulder into the back of the guard Roselyn was wrestling with. Eric's bulk knocked him off his feet; the unarmored youth bounced onto the grass and Eric fell on top of him, driving hard knees into the boy's unarmored ribs. As Eric rolled off of him, he pulled the youth's sword free and jumped to his feet, still chained but smiling, a sword in his hand, ready to fight.

The other two guards, seeing their comrades downed, charged the mysterious knight with their spears; Roselyn had tripped and fallen when Eric had struck the guard from behind, but Karl and Rafe countered their attacks. Karl lunged at one youth, but had to quickly dodge away as his speartip swung toward him. His attacker chased and jabbed, and Karl was forced back, jumping in huge leaps because of his chained feet, barely escaping the deadly point.

Rafe grabbed the spearhaft of the last guard as he charged Eric from behind. They wrested for control of the weapon, the older, heavier man and the younger, more-agile youth. Rafe tried to shove him off balance but the youth was tall, thickly muscled, and pushed back with unexpected fury.

Suddenly the Seer appeared behind the guard, a small silver dagger in his hand. He clung to the youth's back, his tiny blade against his throat.

"Stop or die!" the Seer cried.

The tall youth desisted and Rafe took his spear from him as Roselyn climbed back to her feet, another fallen spear in her hands. Both turned to face the last guard, who was jabbing dangerously at Karl.

"Stop!" Karl shouted at his attacker. "It's over! You can't win!"

Eric, Rafe, and Roselyn ran to defend of Karl, brandishing weapons.

"Your fellows have fallen and you're outnumbered," Karl said to the youthful guard. "Give up ... and live."

The youthful guard glanced at his fallen comrades, yet only tightened his grip on his haft.

"I'm no traitor!" the youthful guard sneered, and he lowered his speartip and charged.

Rafe and Roselyn's stabbed their spears deep into the boy's chest; the youth choked, tottered, and fell dead onto the grass.

Roselyn staggered; *it had worked!* She'd saved her companions, but she was trembling, shaking with fear. She turned to Karl and held out her arms to him; all she wanted was to hold him once again.

Yet Karl wasn't even looking at her.

Chapter 25

Escape

KARL

Karl looked down at the lifeless body of the young guard, collapsed on the bloodstained grass; this boy was little different from the boy he'd been only a few short weeks ago when a lone Viking had sailed into Demril and changed his life. This guard had simply chosen differently. *Why did Karl feel guilty for the boy's death?*

Karl noticed Roselyn was reaching for him and jumped to hold her. Karl dodged her helmet's raised visor as she plowed into his embrace; Roselyn was unused to wearing armor, ignorant of armor's ability to inflict unintended damage. She sobbed as he held her tightly. He tried to comfort her, yet they weren't out of danger yet.

Shouts from the two boys alerted the whole camp; dozens grabbed weapons and shouted for help. Still holding Roselyn, Karl glanced around to see the whole camp raised against them. All of the warriors had gone to war, but over a hundred camp-followers remained, a handful of guards, blacksmiths, and dozens of eager youths with spears and axes.

"Over here!" Eric said. "Hurry!"

Eric had dropped to the ground, grabbed Roselyn's small axe, and was prying at the shackles around his ankles.

"Hold your legs apart as far as you can!" Rafe shouted at Eric, and he raised the guard's steel sword. Rafe swung down with all of his might and severed the iron chain.

"Perfect!" Eric cried even as the Seer sat down and stretched out his legs, carefully pulling up his black robe. Rafe swung hard again and easily split the chain. Then Eric made Karl and Rafe sit down and severed their chains.

The angry murmurs of the camp-followers grew into a steady roar. They gathered into a crowd of over fifty and slowly approached.

"We've got to get out of here!" Eric cried.

"No!" Rafe shouted. "Seren and Eloise ...!"

"We're no use to them if we die," Eric said. "We'll have to come back. Follow me!"

Belting the axe, Eric turned and ran to the tree where their belongings had been stacked, his chains flailing around his ankles. Eric dropped the guard's thin blade and grabbed his own thick broadsword, helm, and shield, but Rafe looked back at the camp as if he hoped to spy Seren and Eloise among the hundreds of tents. The Seer snatched up his long, empty black leather case, and then ran back to grab Rafe's arm.

"They'll be safe here," the Seer promised. "Come! We'll rescue them later!"

"Hurry!" Karl hissed to Roselyn, and all of them ran after Eric.

Running was awkward; their chains flapped and flailed against their legs, but they had no choice. Karl stopped at the tree to get his own helm, sword, and shield. Rafe grabbed his beloved pitchfork, although he kept a guard's sword, and Roselyn snatched up her bow and arrows, but kept a guard's spear. The rest they left behind.

A horde of youths ran towards them, outdistancing the elders. The energetic boys ran across the rutted fields, quickly getting closer. They passed several scattered stands of small trees and saw only wide fields and a few farms in the distance: no place of safety, no wall to put their backs to.

"Stop ... here!" Eric gasped, bending over to catch his breath. "We have to make a stand ... or we'll be too tired to fight."

Rafe was puffing like a bellows and Roselyn was limping, unaccustomed to running in armor. Karl was still sore, but probably in the best condition. Perhaps the Seer's healing spell was still working, but Karl didn't bother to ask; the Seer was holding one hand to his bruised forehead and looked as if he'd pass out.

Roselyn dropped her new spear, keeping her bow and quivers, but Rafe dropped his pitchfork beside Roselyn's spear, choosing to wield his new, unfamiliar sword. The Seer muttered softly through gritted teeth and frantically dug through the pockets inside his robe. Karl glanced nervously at Eric, who frowned back at him, and both raised their shields. Together they stood ready.

Around the trees their enemy charged, stopping short when they saw the companions arrayed against them. Roselyn awkwardly drew her bow, which was difficult to do in a suit of armor, but she didn't shoot.

Their attackers were children, camp boys too young to be allowed into battle, but anxious to become warriors like their fathers and uncles. Too many arrived, at least twenty, with more coming, all armed with knives, wooden clubs, axes, and a few fire-hardened spears.

Karl had no doubt they could survive the boys' attack, but the thought of hacking apart children turned his stomach. Mostly they couldn't afford the time; the guards and smiths would arrive before they killed the last boy. Karl glanced at Rafe and Roselyn, seeing his distaste mirrored in their faces.

"Roselyn, kill one!" Eric shouted.

"They're children!" Roselyn protested.

"Until they swarm over us, after which they'll be warriors," Eric said. "Look at their faces! They'll charge, when there are enough of them, and then even more kids will die. Kill one, now, and we'll have stopped them long enough to get away. One ... or we kill them all!"

Karl looked at Roselyn, who held an arrow nocked, ready. Roselyn glanced back at Karl.

"Do you want me to ...?" Karl offered.

Roselyn shook her head, pale white with fear, yet she made no move to hand over her bow. She seemed lost, as if somewhere else, and tears started to leak from her eyes. She silently raised her bow. Gasping her breaths, oblivious to the world around her, Roselyn stood, all too aware of her situation.

"Hurry!" Eric cried. "I was one of those boys once: they will attack us!"

Roselyn drew her fletchings to her ear and swung her aim across the lead line of children. Grimly she set her jaw and steadied her aim.

"At least I can save one from becoming like my father."

Roselyn loosed. The arrow shot forward. One of the tallest boys collapsed back against his friends in a tumult of youthful screams. The boy cried out and fell, the arrow shaft sticking out of his chest low on the shoulder. It wasn't a fatal wound but it had the desired effect: screaming at the top of their lungs, half of the boys turned and ran back towards the camp. A handful of boys dropped beside their friend, not knowing what to do, mostly trying to see the painful wound. The rest tried to hide behind them.

"Run!" Eric whispered urgently.

Rafe quickly gathered the weapons they'd dropped. Karl pulled Roselyn, who stood aghast at her own actions. He was stunned that she'd shot the boy; this moment would haunt Roselyn forever, but she was stronger than he'd guessed.

Eric ran ahead, leading their way. They didn't run fast, nothing like when the wolf pack had chased them, but at a steady drumming pace that lessened the painful slaps of their chains against their calves. A few older boys followed them, but at a safe distance, and the rest stayed behind.

Huffing and puffing, Rafe called for a halt. Four boys still trailed them, at a considerable distance, but no other pursuit showed.

"Under those trees, my friend," Eric said, and he took Rafe by the arm and assisted him into the shade, and then helped him sit down, his back against the trunk. Karl assisted Roselyn, who stumbled in her father's armor, and helped her sit beside Rafe.

"Feet hurt," she said, gasping.

Karl looked at her; she was wearing too much armor for her size, but he didn't want to reduce her defense. He pulled off her father's clunky boots, which were far too large for her. Her tightly-laced shoes were unarmored but better for footing, and Roselyn's best defense was running. He cast aside her father's heavy boots; they were too small for him.

Eric picked up a big rock and carried it over to Rafe. He set the rock between Rafe's feet and then went back for another. When he had two, Eric made Rafe hold his foot still and turned his shackles so one rested atop one rock, and Eric pulled out the small axe Roselyn had dropped; Eric wedged its blade into Rafe's shackle and let the Seer hold it in place. Then Eric used the other rock as a hammer and pounded it against the butt of the axe; the small hand-axe split its rivet like a chisel, and the shackle fell off of Rafe's ankle.

It ruined the axe, but soon the last of their shackles fell away.

"We should keep going," Karl said, watching the four youths, who were poorly hidden behind a thick shrub.

"No," Eric said. "Time for you four to escape; I have a war to get to."

"Not this again!" Rafe groaned.

"Eric ...," Roselyn began.

"You knew this was coming, my only reason for sailing to England," Eric silenced her. "Rescue Eloise and Seren, then hide in that big swamp until the armies leave. I'm going to war ... and I'm not coming back."

"Yes, you are," the Seer said. "The Lady said you would, and She's never wrong."

"Then, what are we waiting for?" Karl asked. "Let's go to war!"

"What ...?" Roselyn gasped.

"Karl, no!" Eric said.

"The Seer's Lady said we'd survive, and She's been right so far," Karl said, placing a hand on Eric's shoulder. "Besides, I said we'd finish this together."

Eric looked back at him.

"You're a true friend, Karl."

"Well, I'm not going to fight in a war!" the Seer said.

"Nor I," Roselyn said.

"I'll go," Rafe said. "You two will just get into trouble without me."

Karl and Eric laughed, and Rafe smiled with them. They'd fight together ... and only the Lady knew if any of them would survive.

Chapter 26

The Parley

RAFE

Rafe gritted his teeth and tried to keep up. A blind man could've followed the path Sir Guldwin's army had taken; wheels, hooves, and thousands of booted feet had trampled flat the grasses and weeds. They followed at a moderate pace; Eric's eagerness pushed them on, yet Roselyn stumbled, exhausted. Rafe also ached, although he didn't want the others to know how badly.

Karl and Roselyn fussed over each other like a pair of wet hens. Karl insisted that Roselyn should leave her heavy armor behind before she got herself mistaken for a real knight. Roselyn promised she would if Karl would stay with her, not to risk his life fighting in the war.

"There's no need to worry," Karl reassured her. "The Seer says we'll be fine, and after the things we've seen I can't help but believe him. But, if he's wrong and Eric falls, then Rafe and I'll have no more reason to be there, and we'll come right back."

"If something should happen to you ...!"

"Enough of that!" Eric snapped at Roselyn. "As a wench in Castle Bristlen, or a lady in the Baron's hunting lodge, you had the right to speak so. No more! Since then you've helped us battle Wolflords, Vikings, and a giant. Today, Roselyn, daughter of Guldwin, you joined us. You marched out on your own, armed for battle, and attacked our guards as bravely as any man. Like the farmers of Grusshire when they decided to stand against their foes, today you became a warrior."

Roselyn turned to say something nasty to Eric, yet no words came. Rafe wondered if she was stunned by his compliment or torn between her pride and desire to keep Karl safe.

"This is insane!" the Seer snapped. "None of you have any business fighting in this battle!"

"Why not?" Roselyn asked sweetly, glad to let the Seer continue her arguments.

"You two," the Seer said, looking at Karl and Rafe, "are only going to war because Eric's going. Eric's only going because he wants to die gloriously, fighting, and be carried to Valhalla by a beautiful Valkyrie. But the Lady's vision showed all of us following Eric's trail. Since he obviously won't die, he has no business going!"

"Can't argue with that!" Roselyn beamed.

The Seer reached inside his robe and pulled out his precious spherical moonstone. Suddenly, down the hill behind them, everywhere Eric had stepped, appeared a faint, glowing 'V' pointing in the direction Eric was walking, barely visible in the sunlight.

"Those are the marks you made on Eric's boots!" Karl said.

"I'm ... leaving a trail?" Eric gasped.

"Everywhere that you go," the Seer nodded. "I marked your boots because I saw this trail in the vision She sent me."

"You're making Her vision come true!" Karl accused.

"Why else would I be here?" the Seer said. "Since we know none of us are going to die, we should forget the war, go back to the camp, and rescue Eloise and Seren!"

Rafe winced; Eloise and Seren were safest where they were, under guard in the Saxon camp, yet he felt uneasy about leaving them behind. He wanted Seren to be free, although if she were here she'd be as worried about him fighting as Roselyn was about Karl. Yet the war wouldn't wait, and Rafe couldn't ask Eric to postpone his goal until the next Viking invasion.

"You're a good man, Druid," Eric said. "I've never said this to a wise-one before ... but I like you. I won't disrespect your Lady ..."

"I appreciate that," the Seer said.

"... but I must be true to my own Gods. Odin needs warriors, and my duty is to serve Him, and to do that I must die with a sword in my hand, with a bond of flesh between my weapon and my heart. Perhaps I won't die today; my skills have betrayed me before. But I can't turn from my duty to Odin because of your duty to your Lady."

The Seer nodded grimly. Rafe frowned; their devotion to their pagan deities disquieted him. *What great Christians both could be!*

They reached the top of the hill and paused to behold the grand spectacle. Below them lay two armies divided by a wide field with a few mounted horsemen in the center. Both sides were strangely silent yet the air was thick with apprehension.

"Parley," Eric said. "The war hasn't begun yet. There, in the middle, ambassadors are politely insulting each other, offering to accept the other's surrender in exchange for gold. It's pointless; Svenson can't give gold he doesn't have and Sir Guldwin can't surrender control of the Danelaw. Both know it's useless; they're only observing formalities for the sake of their men. We'd best not be seen until the battle begins."

They skirted the hilltop, circled around to a stand of trees, and slid behind concealment. Rafe peered through tall growths of weeds, Karl, Roselyn, and Eric crowded close behind him. Amused, Rafe glanced at them; Karl and Roselyn were gaping at the sight of two great armies facing each other; never had their young eyes swept over so many as they did now. Rafe had seen two wars this big in his lifetime; over ten thousand had died in each, and hundreds of good horses. Rafe had never fought in a real battle; his duties kept him from the field. Today he'd change that; that thought turned his stomach, but he'd be ashamed to stay behind while his friends rushed into danger.

Chapter 27

War

ERIC

Eric surveyed the battlefield with experienced eyes. Sir Guldwin's troops were arranged in ordered sections; four shieldwalls of footmen, in long rectangular formations, with a troop of archers behind each. Reserves with twelve foot spears stood behind them, and on each side rode hundreds of mounted knights. Eric estimated four hundred horse, five hundred archers, and a total of four thousand footmen. Half of the footmen were farmers and townsmen yet it was an awesome force, disciplined and ordered. Those troops were well fed and eager with high morale, willing to die to save their homes and families.

Sir Guldwin's army was poised to win.

Svenson's troops were the exact opposite. They had no order to their line. Their archers were intermixed with their footmen, and they had no horses, save for a few in their rear and the ones their ambassadors rode. They had no visible supply wagons, no reserve troops, little leadership, and were doubtlessly tired from days of dreary marches without rest or reward. They were far from home with little to fight for. They were losing troops, but they outnumbered Sir Guldwin's force by more than a thousand. Svenson's men were also mostly experienced campaigners, hardened warriors from fighting clans; they wouldn't fall easily.

Eric frowned; no clear victor showed. The fates of war were fickle, and it was possible both sides would be decimated by the end of this day. Yet Eric wasn't concerned with who'd win this war; with luck, he'd be beyond all Earthly concerns by then.

The mounted ambassadors separated, each side slowly riding back to their leaders. Eric guessed they'd report the same message to Earl Sir Guldwin and King Svenson; negotiations were fruitless. Both leaders would've expected it and been prepared; Eric wondered what plans they'd made. The two armies were a long arrow-shot apart, but one side would have to begin. Sir Guldwin had the advantage; his mounted knights, with their long lances, could charge at any place on Svenson's flank, and only a stout spear-defense could stop them. Svenson couldn't attack until he abated the threat of those knights, but with no Viking mounted troops, there was little he could do.

Nothing happened. Eric wasn't surprised; the worst part of any battle was always the endless waiting, the standing around, not knowing when your orders would come or what they'd be, and whether or not they'd get you killed. Experienced warriors understood that some men were always chosen to die as sacrifice troops, to bait the enemy commander into committing himself early. No man, knight or peasant, knew if he'd be chosen, but it wasn't a secret often shared with novices; the less each novice knew the more likely they'd be chosen to be sacrificed, so the older soldiers kept their mouths shut.

Trumpets sang and flags were raised; Sir Guldwin was starting early. Smart of him, Eric mused, to attack right away. Old soldiers were in no hurry, but his part-time soldiers would grow increasingly nervous as the constant waiting wore on them.

Hundreds of bows twanged and a volley of arrows shot into the sky, arced high, and fell upon the Vikings. Shields were raised to meet them, an uneven roof of wood and hides. Arrows stabbed down upon shields; some slipping through gaps, instantly followed by cries and curses. A dozen Vikings fell, dead or wounded, but they were barely noticed among the thousands.

A warhorn blasted a familiar note. Viking arrows flew skyward, arcing back a rain of death, yet Eric barely noticed. The note of the blowing horn captured Eric's attention; it was his old warhorn, his favorite, which he'd traded for Svenson's golden drinking horn on his dragonship in Oslo Bay.

Eric tried to spot Svenson, to see if he was blowing the horn, but the Viking king was either wearing someone else's helm or not mounted on a horse. Then the flying arrows caught Eric's attention; the Saxon shafts had flown at the center of the tightly-pressed Viking horde, but Svenson's archers sent their death towards a more precise target: the deadly hail rained behind the front formations, behind the stretched lines of archers, straight down upon the mounted knights.

Arrow-pierced horses reared and hurled their armored riders while others bolted forward and plowed through archers and footmen with steel-shod hooves sharpened for battle.

Eric laughed; Svenson was a crafty war-leader. Earl Sir Guldwin had struck first, but Svenson had struck harder, right where he most-needed to strike.

Eric's horn sounded again and another volley shot from the Viking ranks aimed at the same target. Yet the knights were already scattering, shields raised, and only a handful fell to the second volley. Eric smiled; Svenson had struck his primary target: Earl Sir

Guldwin's pride. If Svenson could make Sir Guldwin angry then perhaps he'd grow reckless.

Trumpets blared and the Saxon archers loosed arrows high. Viking archers loosed a second later, and the sky over the battlefield darkened with feathered shafts. The front lines seemed to be the target of both sides, and dozens fell from both shieldwalls, yet the wounded weren't allowed to crawl back; if they had enough life to crawl then they were expected to hold their positions.

Men behind replaced the dead, and not a single gap appeared in either line. Eric grinned knowingly; both sides were bleeding yet the battle had only begun.

Riding out of arrow-range, the knights suddenly turned and rode away from their flanks. Swiftly they galloped around the outskirts of battle, riding around to flank Svenson's army.

Chaos engulfed Svenson's knot of warriors as hundreds of men ran out from the front lines, each carrying a spear or pike twice their height, and scurried around the outside of their own Viking army, trying to stay even with the knights, to keep an impenetrable wall of steel spear-points between the mounted knights and the foot-bound Vikings.

Suddenly hundreds of arrows flew from the Saxons; no horns had warned. Although the Vikings who saw them shouted, arrows fell across a Viking front line only half-defended. A hundred screams echoed from the Viking shieldwall and huge gaps appeared.

Eric heard his horn blowing and thought he caught a note of desperation in it. The knights quickly circled to Svenson's flank and the Saxon archers took a heavy toll. Eric wondered what Svenson would do.

Suddenly Svenson's whole horde charged the Saxons. As one, the Viking army surged forward, away from the circling knights, turning their formation from a wide oval into a sharp wedge. Arrows from both sides filled the sky, and the lead edge of the Vikings charged at a dead run. Straight at the center of the Saxon formations, they charged like a huge, hurled spearhead.

The Saxon shieldwall closed ranks and raised spears against them, but the Vikings seemed fearless, shouting shrilly as their forces met.

The Viking spearhead slammed into the Saxon shieldwall like a fist breaking teeth. Spear-points were shoved aside or driven onto, impaled, Valhalla-bound Vikings running up bloody shafts, still swinging their swords. The dead entangled the Saxon weapons, and more Vikings charged in, using the fallen as springboards to launch themselves over the Saxon front line, crashing down upon those behind the shieldwall. The Saxon ranks split as if severed by a knife. Vikings poured into their midst.

"Odin!" Eric cheered, and he jumped from the bushes and waved his sword. Concealment no longer mattered; Sir Guldwin couldn't afford to be distracted.

The berserk point of the Viking wedge drove deep, pushed into the Saxon lines ever farther, and split their formation. Vikings poured into the gap. Shield walls collapsed as close-in fighting broke out, crazed warriors hacked and thrust to kill as many enemies as they could before they themselves fell.

Sir Guldwin's reserves charged in as his archers fled for safety. The reserves met the Viking wedge-point hard and hammered it back. Yet the Vikings kept pushing and drove into the Saxon midst as if trying to force a road through the heart of their enemies.

The Saxon knights charged, lances lowered, but had to rein in; Svenson's fierce marauders had pushed clear through the front lines of the Saxon footmen, which had closed in around them, completely encircling their foes. The knights were trapped on the outside of their own circle, hemmed out, unable to reach their enemies without riding down their own countrymen.

Svenson had tricked them, securing his troops in the one place where mounted knights couldn't reach: in the center of the Saxon infantry.

Vikings decimated Saxon footmen, experienced soldiers against farmers and peasants. Screams of the dying echoed as one vast wailing screech across the field of slaughter. Spears jabbed, swords swung, axes hacked, and daggers stabbed. Blood rained and the Valkyrie feasted.

Sir Guldwin's trumpets sounded and his archers rallied. Upon the hills, behind the packed reserves, the fleeing archers turned back toward their foes. Arrows rained, not in volleys but in a steady downpour at close range. Vikings fell by the hundreds, shouting curses and epitaphs and calling upon Odin's maids in their last moments of life.

Dust rose in a great cloud above the battlefield, masking everything into an indistinct frenzy, yet Eric knew Svenson's mind and the strategies of war. Twice he spied groups of Vikings break off, push uphill through the reserves, the bulk of Sir Guldwin's regular infantry, his real soldiers, professional fighting men who weren't wealthy enough to become knights or squires. Svenson hoped to break through to the archers, whom his swordsmen could easily scatter and distract. Yet the tough Saxon reserves held firm, and both times the Viking assassins were overwhelmed. Svenson's troops had slain almost a thousand Saxons, but they were too quickly losing to the archers.

"Are we going to stay here?" Karl asked.

Eric grinned. A hopeful tone rang in Karl's voice; he'd be glad not to go. Eric turned to face Karl and Rafe.

"You two stay," Eric said. "This isn't your fight. Guard Roselyn, and save Eloise and Seren. I'll go alone, but not yet. Svenson's chosen a fast battle to protect himself from the mounted knights, but thousands of men don't die instantly. I'll wait until the moment's right."

"I gave you my word," Karl said firmly. "I won't have falseness be your last memory of me. If the Seer is right, you may need me to get away."

"Speak for yourself," Rafe grinned. "I intend to win this war!"

They laughed.

The fighting went on. Svenson's fewer Vikings used the shields of the fallen, so fewer fell to arrows. Also, the Viking archers rallied, shot back, and disrupted the Saxon archer's relentless assault. Solid shieldwalls sprung up between the front lines, defended by long, deadly spears. The wails of the wounded continued, but firm formations forced an impasse. Behind rigid shieldwalls, neither side killed more than the occasional lucky spear-thrust.

Svenson's maneuver had slain a thousand Saxons, but only the chaff; most of the real Saxon warriors still stood, and Svenson had lost hundreds to the Saxon archers. Svenson needed to drive his whole force to the archers, to kill as many as he could and scatter the rest, so his own archers could concentrate on the knights. Once enough Saxon footmen had fallen, Svenson's troops would be exposed to the knight's deadly lances, so the archers had to be scattered first.

Already it was too late: the Saxon circle surrounding the press of Vikings was thin except on the side of the reserves, which protected their archers. Eric had the advantage of perspective; from inside the press of warriors, Svenson could rely on nothing but his eyes, which were often obscured by the dust of battle.

Suddenly the knights charged. They'd regrouped a distance from the battle and lined their horses in four rows, each row fifty knights wide. Then, with their squires blowing trumpets, the knights charged the trapped Vikings. The Vikings paled, and the few Saxons between them ran away, clearing a path for the deadly warhorses. The Saxon knights spurred hard and lowered keen lance-points; those Saxons who couldn't get out of their way would suffer.

The Viking shieldwall braced. Thirty spears pointed stoutly at their charging foes, but they were too short and too few. Most of the long spears meant to hold the knights at bay were held by other men, who couldn't get through the press of warriors to the shieldwall in time.

"Valkyrie!" many voices cried.

Saxon knights slammed into Vikings like a boulder rolling across a wheat field. Long lances drove through shields and armor. A few leapt upon the knights, when the press of bodies finally halted them, trying to drag the knights down off their horses, but the heavy chain and plates of the knights defied sword-thrusts better than the simple mail and leathers of the Vikings. The knights behind defended their brothers, and Vikings fell beneath them.

"Time to go," Eric said, and he turned to face Roselyn, ducked under her raised visor, and kissed her on each cheek. "Give one of these to Eloise when you see her," he said. "Tell her truly that my last thoughts were of her."

Roselyn nodded slightly, anguish in her eyes. She didn't ask Eric to give up his madness, barter herself, or reason away his arguments. Eric noted her pride and nobility; this was their last moment together, and Roselyn faced it bravely.

"This is from both of us," Roselyn said, and she pulled Eric close and kissed him hard on the lips. She trembled slightly in his embrace, then pulled back and looked her old friend straight in the eyes.

"The V-Valkyrie await," Roselyn stammered.

Eric felt sorry for her, but he was also proud. In Karl, Eric had seen great potential; Roselyn reminded him of Norse shieldmaids; she could become a great warrior, if she tried.

Eric turned to the Seer.

"I've never done this to a magician before," Eric said, and then he held out his open hand to the Seer. The Seer smirked yet shook hands with him.

"This is pointless," the Seer said. "Let me place a blessing on you to ward off stray arrows."

"Your magic might prevent me from my glory," Eric refused, "but place your spells over Karl and Rafe, if you can do it quickly."

"Please ...!" Rafe agreed.

Reaching into his robe, the Seer pulled out a small, thick glass vial, pulled out its cork, and smeared some oil onto his index finger. Karl lifted his helm; onto both men's foreheads the Seer traced a mystic rune as he whispered a prayer to his Lady.

"This isn't a shield or a helmet," the Seer warned. "Stay low and watch everywhere. I don't want to waste any more time casting healing spells."

"We'll be careful," Rafe promised. "Take care of Roselyn until we get back, and see that she, Eloise, and Seren live free and happy if we don't make it."

"I promise," the Seer said.

"Let's go," Eric said, and he walked downhill towards the war. Rafe smiled reassuringly and followed.

Chapter 28

Into the Fray

KARL

Karl watched Eric and Rafe walk away. He wanted to follow, but turned to Roselyn, who was wiping away tears as if ashamed to let them show. Karl grasped her gauntleted hands and drew her into his arms.

"I have to do this," Karl whispered.

"I know," Roselyn sobbed.

"I'll be back," Karl promised. "I love you, and not even death shall keep me from loving you."

Roselyn burst into blubbering tears, unfit for a warrior, but Karl only held her tightly. Slowly he pulled back, then placed her hand in the Seer's grip. He gave the Seer a stern glance, and the Seer nodded grimly; no words needed to be said. Karl started down the hill after Eric and Rafe.

"I love you ...!" Roselyn shouted at Karl, her musical voice strained with misery.

Karl couldn't turn around; if he did, he'd run back and never leave her again. Tears welled but Karl pretended not to notice. Quickly he hurried down to catch up with Eric and Rafe.

As they approached the rear lines, many of the Saxons turned and looked at them suspiciously.

"Let us through!" Eric shouted, and he walked past them, shouldering into the press of men. The Saxons glanced questioningly at them, especially Karl, but Karl silently shrugged and pushed after Eric. Easily they made their way through the thin ranks to the front line, pushing to join the shieldwall.

Men on both sides were pushing and jostling, ducking to avoid sudden spear-thrusts, and being pushed from behind when one of their own leaned forward to stab at an enemy. No orders or formations existed here, only allies behind and enemies in front. They halted in the shieldwall, and Karl pushed up beside Eric, raising his shield high, as Eric had, just peeking over its top edge, his sword hand behind his protective shield, his blade pointing up, ready to strike or defend. Rafe, who had no shield, helm, or armor stayed low behind them, his sword in his belt, his pitchfork raised to strike any who threatened his friends.

"What now?" Karl shouted to be heard over the tumult.

"Stay alive!" Eric shouted back. *"Watch everything! Be careful!"*

"Spear!" shouted the Saxon beside Karl, and both dodged as a thrust jabbed toward them. It bounced up, off of the Saxon's large rectangular shield, clattered against the side of Karl's helm, and then drew back toward the Viking wielding it. Someone from behind tried to catch the spearhead with the hook of an axe, but failed.

Long moments passed. Karl recognized a stand-off. If anyone jumped forward, spears would pierce them, so both sides stood their ground, watching carefully as speartips unexpectedly thrust back and forth. Occasionally one spear stabbed its target and someone fell ... only to be replaced by one of his kin.

It was Ferny Creek all over again, only a thousand times worse.

The Saxon knights, who'd backed off, suddenly charged again, and screams of the dying filled the air. Their second charge drove even deeper, and whole companies of foot-bound Vikings were sent to their Valkyrie. Many Vikings turned and fled at the last minute only to see lance-points burst out of their chests. Thousands lay dead on both sides, and for what? Would Svenson's death end Viking invasions? Had Svenson won, would the Danelaw accept a Viking king? Neither side could succeed. Nothing of this war would last except the misery of the mourners and the afterlives of the fallen.

Even in the midst of combat, Karl shook his head.

A Viking spear shot past him, aimed at Rafe's face. Eric caught it with the corner of his shield. Karl gasped; the spear had been closest to him. His quiet reverie had almost cost Rafe's life. Quickly he focused on the spears of the enemy, ignoring his inner turmoil; the front line of a pitched battle was no place for debates of conscience.

Another horn sounded over the battle.

"Svenson ...!" Eric cried. *"That's my horn! Look! There he is, in the golden helm!"*

Karl easily spied the tall, old king, his bright helm decorated in polished brass with a tall crown riveted to it, blowing a horn and shouting to his men. He was a huge man, the first king Karl had ever seen, and he somewhat resembled Eric, but Karl turned back to watching the spears he was in range of; Karl didn't want to end up like his fellow conscripts at Ferny Creek.

Eric leaned close, almost touching helms.

"Get ready to charge!" Eric said to Karl and Rafe.

"Are you crazy ...?" Karl shouted, and he glanced at his friend, but Eric only smiled back.

Karl remembered; Eric wasn't here to live, but to earn his glorious death, so Eric could take chances sane men wouldn't.

Suddenly Eric drew his sword-arm across his body, and then swung his sword. Pommel first, Eric smashed his sword into the face of the Saxon on the other side of him, flipped his heavy blade over the man's head, and pushed him out in front. Every spear in range centered on the stunned, wounded Saxon, and forcefully drove through him. He died instantly, but he couldn't fall; his body was impaled on all sides by Viking spears.

"Charge ....!" Eric cried, and he rushed forward.

Low behind his shield, Eric slammed into the Viking shieldwall, knocked two men over, and pushed into his countrymen's midst. The surprised Viking spearmen turned to face Eric, but their spears were stuck through the body of the unfortunate Saxon and couldn't be brought to bear. Eric swung his sword again and again; his thick wedge of steel sprayed blood and harvested heads.

Four Viking shieldmen instantly fell beneath four quick swings, yet Eric didn't stop to revel in his success, only turned and hacked at more. Karl and Rafe jumped to join him; the confused Vikings turned to see a berserk elder Viking attack their own ranks, not watching the rest. Karl swung his sword and caved in the iron caps of two shieldmen before they were even aware of him, and Rafe's deadly prongs punctured every Viking face around them save Eric.

The Saxon warriors charged in behind them.

The Viking shieldwall crumbled.

"Svenson ...!" Eric shouted, his booming voice rising above the clamor. *"Svenson Two-Sword, face me! Eric Bjornson comes for you!"*

Vikings nearby paused and stared incredulously as Eric raised his sword and pointed at their king. They'd chased Eric across the North Sea and England. His sudden appearance stunned them.

Svenson's helm turned and as his eyes fell upon his hated friend. Svenson Two-Sword glared like explosions of blood-red suns.

"Bjornson ...!" Svenson cried.

Svenson raised Eric's horn high, then threw it down, and from the scabbards on his back Svenson drew two long, bright swords. With a guttural animal's scream, knocking aside his own guards, King Svenson Two-Sword charged.

Eric screamed deafeningly and ran to face him.

Viking warriors parted to make way for Eric; none dared deny their king his prey. Karl moved forward to chase after Eric but Rafe's arm enveloped him.

"Let me go ...!" Karl cried. *"Eric ...!"*

"No!" Rafe shouted. "Karl, stop! We've come this far, but here we hold. This war is their fight! Eric wouldn't want us to interfere!"

Karl heard Rafe's words but didn't want to listen. *Eric was his friend, his brother! Karl couldn't let him fight alone!* But Rafe held him tightly, and Karl would've done anything to save Eric ... except kill Rafe.

Svenson and Eric met with a blinding clash of expert swordplay, so fast Karl could barely see it through battle's dust. Eric hammered his heavy sword in, but Svenson always managed to barely cross one of his lighter swords against Eric's in time. Svenson swung fast and hard with both swords, but Eric managed to duck each, or caught the blows off the corners of his shield or against his thick blade.

The two turned and pivoted, charged in and fell back, and wove in and out in a ferocity of certain death, the fates of the slayer and the slain tilting. Svenson slashed and stabbed and Eric chopped and shield-slammed until they seemed to be the only two fighting on the whole field, soldiers of both armies frozen side-by-side, slack-jawed in fear and amazement at the spectacle the Vikings had been awaiting since Svenson first hit the cold black waters of Oslo Bay, the conclusion the Saxons, after fighting a costly war, never expected to see: two Vikings, perhaps the oldest, fiercest fighters on the battlefield, locked in mortal combat, a Viking duel to turn nations upon, which even Gods paused to watch.

Eric slashed a power-shot, knocked Svenson's swords aside, and rushed in, swinging wide around to the back of Svenson's golden helm. Svenson ducked it, slashed at Eric's helm and stabbed inside his shield, yet Eric suddenly jumped back, and even the extension of Svenson's long-muscled arm fell short. Snakelike, cracking his sword as if it were a whip, Eric snapped forward, cracking his sword into Svenson's helm like lightning blasting apart a tree. Svenson fell back, merely startled; his golden helm was the best Norwegian steel underneath its decorative brass, and long years had inured Svenson to all but the heaviest stuns. Yet the crease denting his helm was long and deep; another strike there would kill him.

Svenson and Eric paused, facing each other in silent deference. No words could avail them. Neither had anything left to lose, and both knew the other as well as they knew themselves. They paced off their range in inches, gliding slowly, almost imperceptibly, swords coldly swaying from stance to stance, Svenson's long and bright, shimmering of silver and polish, Eric's thick and heavy, dripping with Viking blood.

Eric slammed his sword straight down Svenson's nasal, but Svenson crossed his swords before him and caught Eric's blow, then swung wide with both weapons. Eric jumped back and caught both on his shield before leaping forward again to crush Svenson's mailed ribs. Svenson blocked with his left and, twisting his right, stabbed just over Eric's shield-rim and into Eric's face. Eric snapped his head back and the thrust, glancing off of his nasal, slammed swordflat against his brow, up inside his helm's padding, busted his chinstrap, and sent Eric's steel helm, stolen from Castle Bristlen's treasury, flying off of Eric's head over lines of astonished onlookers.

Eric fell back, unhelmeted. Svenson came at him, wolfish teeth grinning in morbid delight. Karl couldn't watch or turn away, his terrified eyes transfixed. Karl shrugged off Rafe's hold but couldn't rush forward, as if a silent stillness had fallen upon all the Earth, only Eric and Svenson immune to its stifle, until one killed the other ... or the world ended.

Karl knew this fight wouldn't last forever; already it had lasted too long. Svenson had been bearing the strain of his now-decimated army, and Eric had to impress his Valkyrie and earn his ride across the Rainbow Bridge, or both their lives would be wasted. Both were dangerous fighters with reputations on the line. Neither could endure the strain eternally.

Svenson attacked, whirling his blades in a blaze of flashing steel. Eric held out his weapon, letting Svenson's swords clash against his in a failing motion, and then Eric slid almost to one knee under his shield and slashed at Svenson's ankle. Svenson leaped the blow, slammed both of his swords against Eric's shield, and jumped forward to kick Eric down beneath his shield. Yet Eric rose suddenly and shield-slammed Svenson. The King toppled backwards, then kicked with both legs, catching Eric's stomach and knocking him back.

Instantly Svenson rolled to his feet while Eric paused to recover his breath.

Both charged; Svenson stabbed inside and struck, but only hard enough to scar Eric's thick leathers. Eric swung at Svenson's face, then backswung across his gut. Svenson blocked both and kicked his foot against Eric's shield, drawing back to swing with both swords, when Eric's blade suddenly came flashing out from inside his shield, thrusting forward with all of the old Viking's weight.

Eric's sword caught Svenson's chest unprotected, snapped and spread his rings of mail, stabbed under his breastbone, up through Svenson's vitals, glanced off of his spine, and burst out between his ribs into the mail covering his back. It pushed the mail out and held it like a centerpole upholding a tent of steel.

Svenson cried out, a deep, echoing shout resounding across the countryside, a death-knell tolling the fall a Viking king. Savagely Svenson glared at Eric, who grinned back; *the old king had breathed his last!*

Yet Svenson didn't die, his vengeance unfulfilled. Seconds before death, Svenson threw all his weight onto his left hip, whipped his right sword up, and slashed close and hard. Svenson's blade caught Eric's right arm at the elbow and severed Eric's forearm off in a spray of blood and vengeance.

Eric screamed.

Karl screamed.

Rafe screamed.

Svenson smiled evilly, and then fell lifeless to the ground.

Karl threw his weapon aside and rushed forward in a blaze of madness and tears. He had to save Eric, stop his flow of blood, and get him back to the Seer. *Eric couldn't die here, not now, not after Svenson had finally fallen!* Yet as Karl ran forward, Eric fell onto his back, blood shooting from the stump of his arm in a gushing stream of failing life. Eric was fighting to sit up, shaking his left arm free from shield-bindings meant to be unbuckled by his sword-hand.

Karl reached Eric and pressed red-soaked furs to his pulsing stump, spraying his mail with Eric's blood.

"Hold on!" Karl shouted to Eric. *"Rafe ...! Get the Seer ...!"*

"S-S-Sword!" Eric hissed, trembling mortally.

Captain Gunderson's shield finally flew from his other hand and Eric reached toward Svenson, laying dead across his legs. *"S-Sword ...!"*

Karl tried to reach a sword without releasing the pressure on Eric's wound, but it was too awkward. He looked at Eric and Eric looked back: *Eric was dying.*

Dropping his wounded stump, Karl grabbed Svenson's corpse, flipped it over, and grabbed one of Svenson's swords, but it was held fast in Svenson's death-grip. Karl pulled but couldn't pry it out.

Karl grabbed Eric's sword by its crossguard and wrenched it out of Svenson's chest. He turned its grip to Eric, when Karl froze; Eric's beefy hand and forearm still clung to the swordgrip between its blood-bathed hilt and pommel.

Karl shoved the bloody sword at Eric, arm and all, when Eric's reaching left hand faltered. A shudder went through Eric's stocky frame. Eyes rolled ... and Eric fell back.

Eric was dead.

"Nooooo!!!" Karl cried.

A light burst from the sky. Numbly Karl looked up and saw a winged horse streak down from the clouds. Upon the winged steed sat a huge woman, fierce and dark, muscled more than most men, wearing golden armor and wielding a silver spear. Onto the ground beside Karl the muscled woman landed her horse in a graceful slide, and she bent to touch Svenson with the point of her outreached spear. Svenson arose, although his body never moved, and, seemingly gliding, the Viking king mounted behind her. Then she spurred hard; her horse rose with a mighty flapping of formidable wings.

Svenson was on his way to Valhalla!

Karl stared upwards, watching them rise, as another winged horse descended. Upon this winged horse rode a stern woman, armored like the first, but smaller, almost frail, a wisp of a woman. Her sword was sheathed, yet a white cloud enshrouded her, moving as she did. She landed and held out her hand to Eric. Her white mist flowed from her fingers toward Eric's corpse, but her fog didn't touch him. The small, beautiful Valkyrie paused, looked sad in her radiant silver helm and breastplate, and then she silently turned away.

"Wait!" Karl cried to her. *"Eric ...! You must take Eric ...!"*

"Beware the Valkyrie, mortal," she said in a cold voice that cut through him like a frosty chill. The mists about her turned ice blue.

"But Eric ...!" Karl pleaded.

"Bound to the weapon by a bond of flesh," the Valkyrie said slowly. "So it is written."

"But he is ...!" Karl cried, and he displayed Eric's sword, still clenched by his severed hand. *"You must take him!"*

"The bond is broken," the Valkyrie said. "Only Hel, should the arm and sword be brought to her before the Gates of Valhalla, could admit him now."

"Take it, please!" Karl shouted, holding the grisly weapon out to her.

"That is your burden," the Valkyrie said. "You must take it to Hel."

"But ... I ... I ...!" Karl stammered, uncomprehending.

"Beware the Valkyrie!"

As her bright eyes flashed, she tugged on her golden reins. Her powerful steed leaped into the air with mighty beats of white wings. She spiraled upwards into the dust-hidden sky.

Karl watched her go, tears raining from his eyes, unable to move or speak, feeling as dead as Eric.

Gone ... Forever ...
Eric ...!

The remaining Vikings surrendered, but Karl didn't move save to wipe tears from his eyes. Eric had lost; his chance to enter Valhalla was gone, and there wasn't anything either of them could do about it.

Eric had failed.

Chapter 29

Epilogue

THE SEER

"Insane fools!" the Seer grumbled as he walked across the battlefield, carefully avoiding the wasteful piles of gory corpses, fallen weapons, and countess trampled arrows. Although wrapped in illusion, the best he could summon, which simply made him look like he was wearing peasant garb, the Seer stepped over the dead bodies and made his way toward Eric's corpse.

Karl and Rafe were long gone, arrested by the knights of Sir Guldwin.

The battle had ended when Svenson Two-Sword had died, after which the remaining Vikings had yielded their swords. Sir Guldwin had ordered all of the Vikings to be searched, stripped of weapons, armor, and any coins or jewelry, and then marched towards his camp in small groups, led by knights and surrounded by reserves. Archers were sent back onto the battlefield to scavenge among the dead for every weapon, piece of armor, and trinket they could find, all of which belonged to Sir Guldwin.

Walking among the fallen, the Seer made his way between puddles of fresh blood, dismayed and angry. Eric was dead: *the Lady's vision could never come true!*

Spellclad, the Seer reached Eric's remains. Eric's skin was ghostly white, his severed arm dropped to the ground, still grasping his heavy broadsword.

"Forgive me, my Lady!" the Seer sighed; *he should've used his magic and stopped Eric from fighting.*

Suddenly his vision blurred and darkened.

The world of daylight vanished.

The Seer stood alone upon an empty field under bright, twinkling stars. He recognized these stars; they were the same ones he'd seen in his dream-vision from the Lady.

Karl stood before a winged horse on which rode a frail, silver-armored woman wrapped in a flowing white mist.

"The bond is broken," the woman said to Karl. *"Only Hel, should the arm and sword be brought to*

her before the Gates of Valhalla, could admit him now!"

Mists wrapped the frail armored woman and her winged horse suddenly vanished.

Eric appeared, standing white and translucent, a pale ghost wandering the battlefield. Never before had the Seer imagined a face as forlorn.

Karl knelt umoving; apparently he couldn't see Eric's spirit, but Eric could see his young friend. Yet, after only a moment, Eric turned and walked off, leaving a yellow trail of magical, glowing 'V's.

As his vision faded, the Seer gasped: *Eric's ghost had left tracks ... in death ... just as his feet had in life!*

The Lady's vision could still come true ...!

Quickly the Seer pulled out his blessed moonstone and held it high over Eric's corpse.

Away from him led a broken trail of glowing yellow 'V's, barely visible in the bright sunlight.

They could still follow Eric's trail, even though he was dead ...!

This news wouldn't comfort Roselyn, but it might spare her mind from grieving. Perhaps this was a gift to Eric from the Lady; obviously She'd known this would happen, that Eric would die, and no Valkyrie would carry his spirit.

"Alas, Sweet Lady!" the Seer whispered. "Cruel are the needs that serve you! At least now I understand Your purpose. Alas that such a burden be mine!"

Slowly the Seer unshouldered his long leather case, the skinny black oiled pouch. None could guess what it could hold, yet he unlaced its wide end. Bending reverently, the Seer lifted Eric's severed arm and his heavy, still-grasped sword, and gently slid both, swordpoint first, inside the pouch.

They fit perfectly.

The Seer knelt, re-laced the strings, and sealed the grisly contents inside.

"Thy will be done," the Seer said aloud, looking up to the sky. "Why You care for the spirit of this one Viking I can't imagine, but I'll follow him, if this be Your will, even to the Gates of Valhalla."

End of Book 1

See Book 2 - "The Mourning Trail"

All Books by Jay Palmer

The VIKINGS! Trilogy:
- DeathQuest
- The Mourning Trail
- Quest for Valhalla

The EGYPTIANS! Trilogy:
- SoulQuest
- Song of the Sphinx
- Quest for Osiris

The Magic of Play

The Heart of Play

The Grotesquerie Games

The Grotesquerie Gambit

Souls of Steam

The Seneschal

Jeremy Wrecker - Pirate of Land and Sea

Viking Son

Viking Daughter

Dracula - Deathless Desire

ABOUT THE AUTHOR

Born in Tripler Army Medical Center, Honolulu, Hawaii,
Jay Palmer works as a technical writer in the software industry in Seattle, Washington. Jay enjoys parties, reading everything in sight, woodworking, obscure board games, and riding his Kawasaki Vulcan. Jay is a knight in the SCA, frequently attends writer conferences, SciFi Conventions, and he and Karen are both avid ballroom dancers. But most of all, Jay enjoys writing.

JayPalmerBooks.com

Made in the USA
Middletown, DE
25 June 2021

42631563R00243